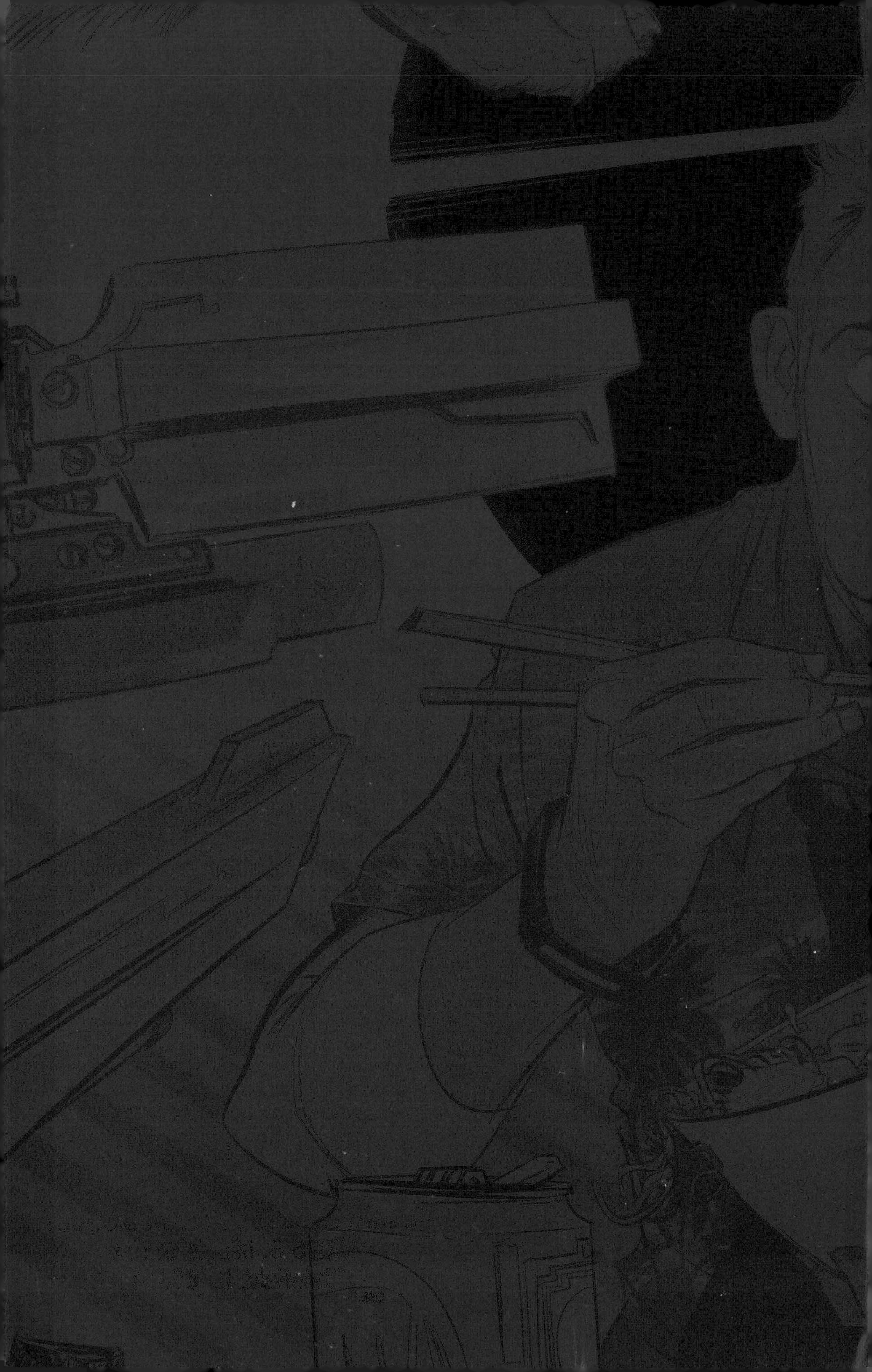

The Weather man.

Vol. 1

CREATORS:	JODY LEHEUP AND NATHAN FOX
WRITER:	JODY LEHEUP
ARTIST:	NATHAN FOX
COLORIST:	DAVE STEWART
LETTERER:	STEVE WANDS
DESIGNER:	TOM MULLER
EDITOR:	SEBASTIAN GIRNER
COVER:	NATHAN FOX
"THE WEATHERMAN" DIGITAL CONTENT MANAGER:	JOSH JOHNS
PRODUCTION ARTIST:	DEANNA PHELPS
NATHAN FOX HAND LETTERED FONT DESIGN:	JOHN GREEN

Originally published as THE WEATHERMAN #1–6

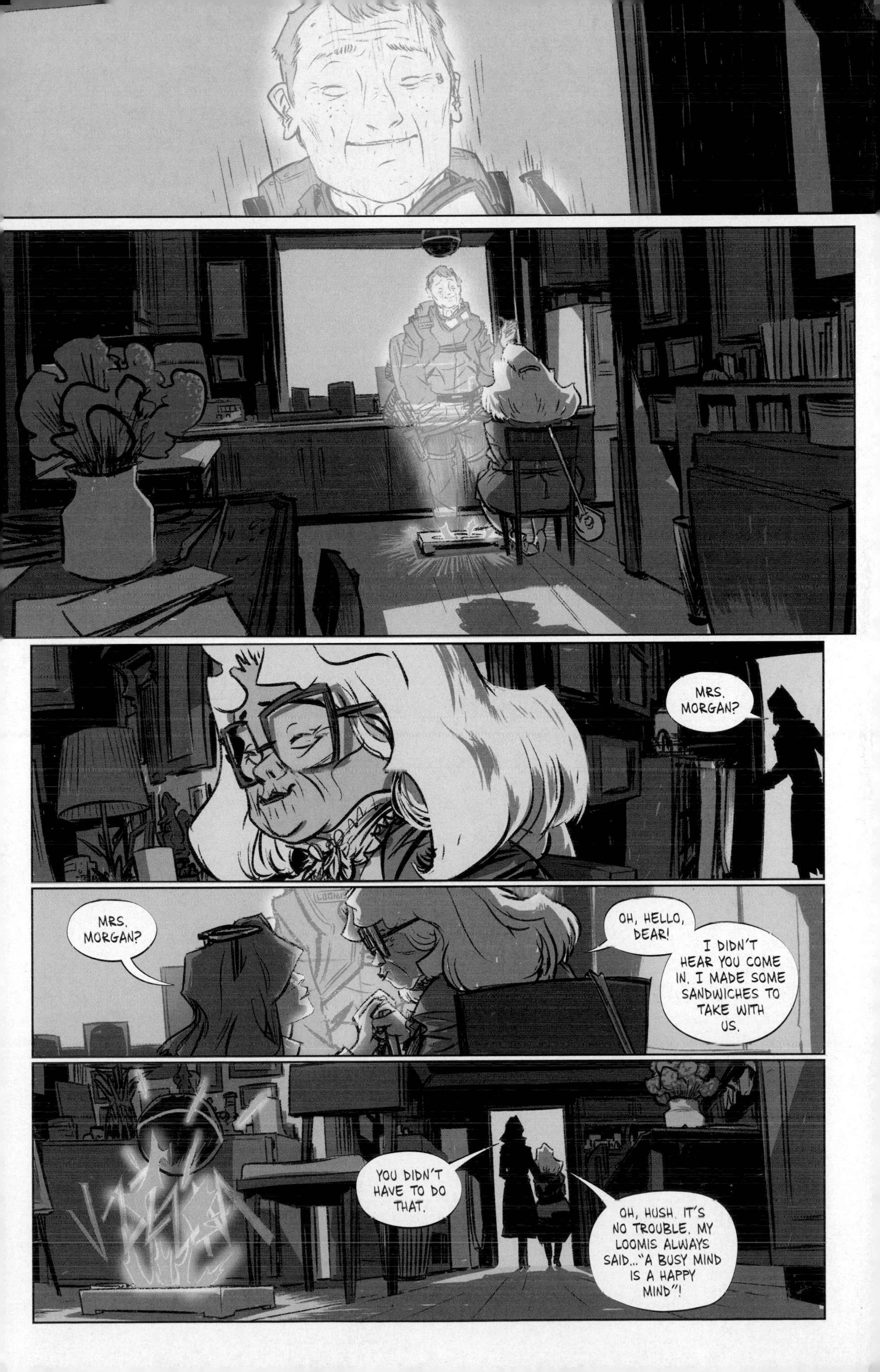
MRS. MORGAN?
MRS. MORGAN?
OH, HELLO, DEAR!
I DIDN'T HEAR YOU COME IN. I MADE SOME SANDWICHES TO TAKE WITH US.
YOU DIDN'T HAVE TO DO THAT.
OH, HUSH. IT'S NO TROUBLE. MY LOOMIS ALWAYS SAID..."A BUSY MIND IS A HAPPY MIND"!

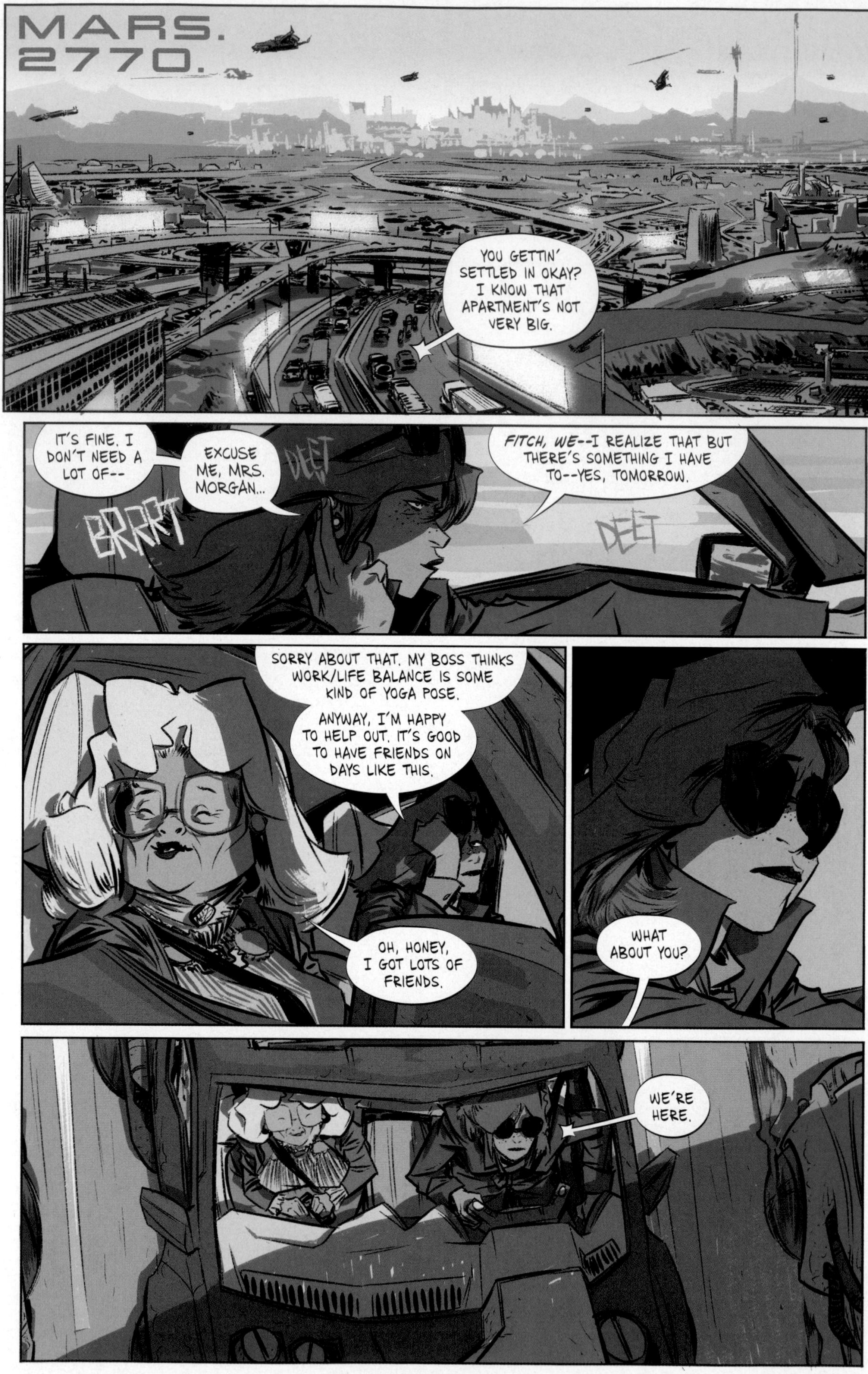
MARS. 2770.
YOU GETTIN' SETTLED IN OKAY? I KNOW THAT APARTMENT'S NOT VERY BIG.
IT'S FINE. I DON'T NEED A LOT OF--
BRRRT
EXCUSE ME, MRS. MORGAN...
DEET
FITCH, WE--I REALIZE THAT BUT THERE'S SOMETHING I HAVE TO--YES, TOMORROW.
DEET
SORRY ABOUT THAT. MY BOSS THINKS WORK/LIFE BALANCE IS SOME KIND OF YOGA POSE.
ANYWAY, I'M HAPPY TO HELP OUT. IT'S GOOD TO HAVE FRIENDS ON DAYS LIKE THIS.
OH, HONEY, I GOT LOTS OF FRIENDS.
WHAT ABOUT YOU?
WE'RE HERE.

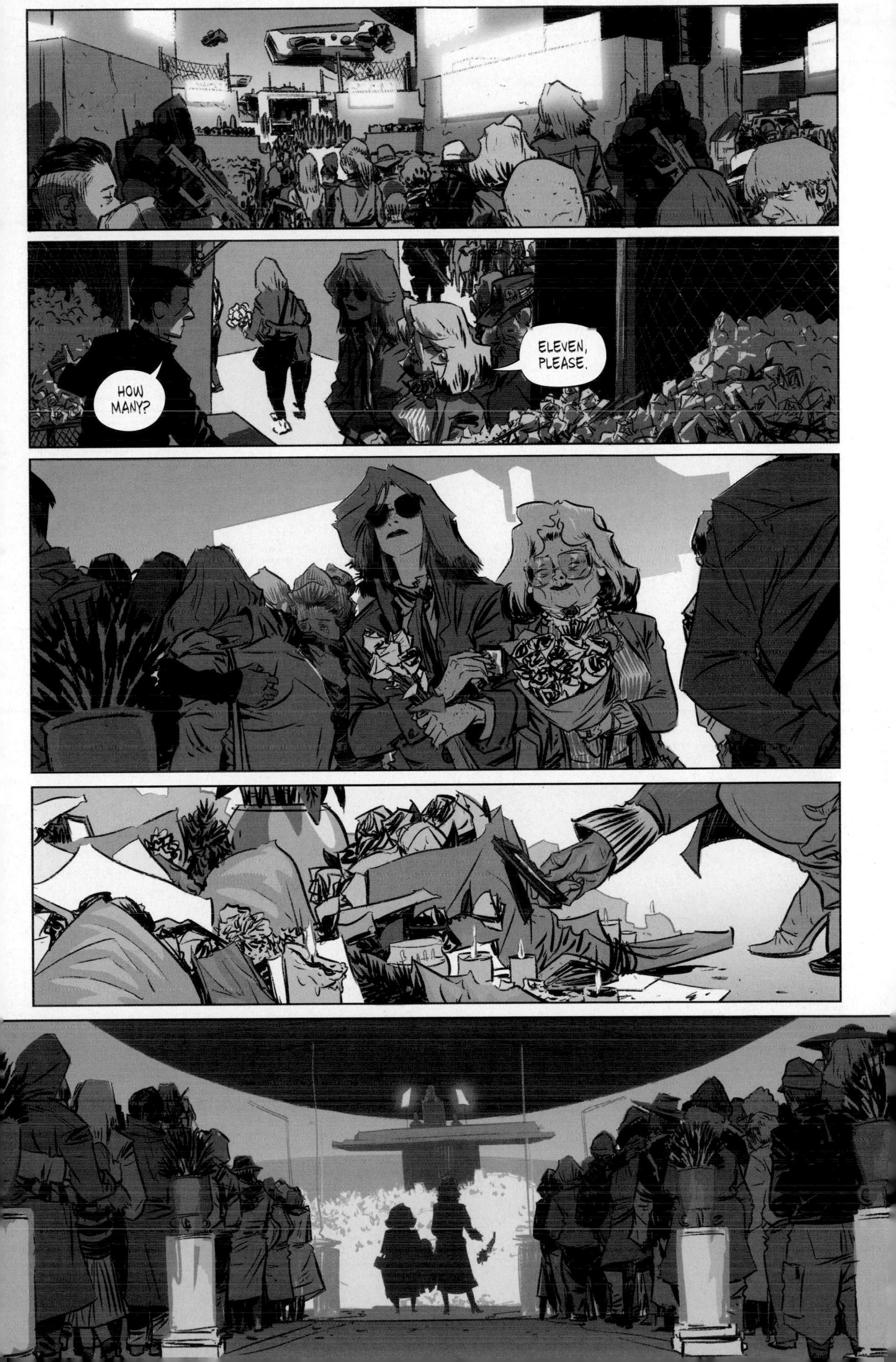
HOW MANY?
ELEVEN, PLEASE.

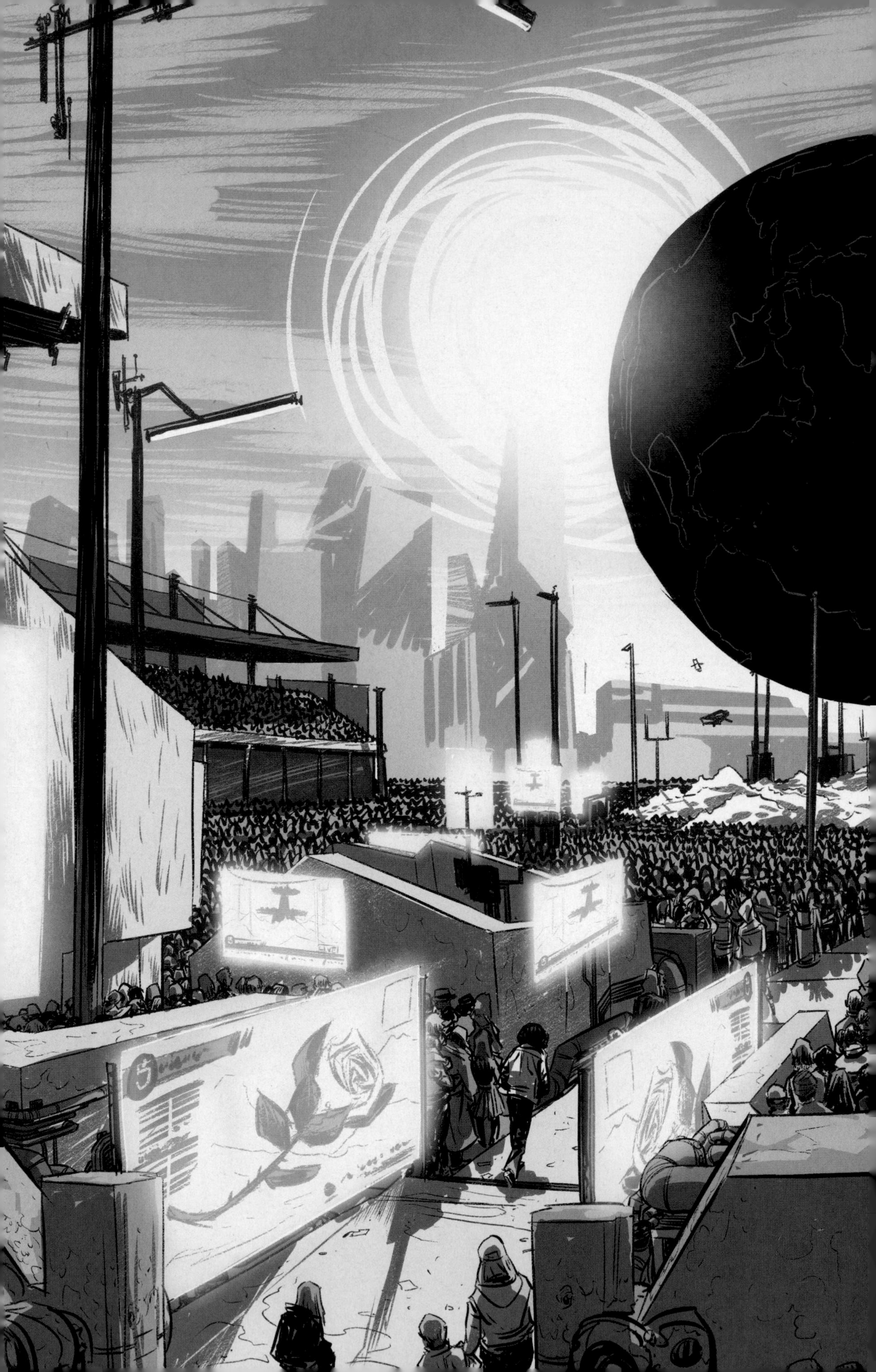

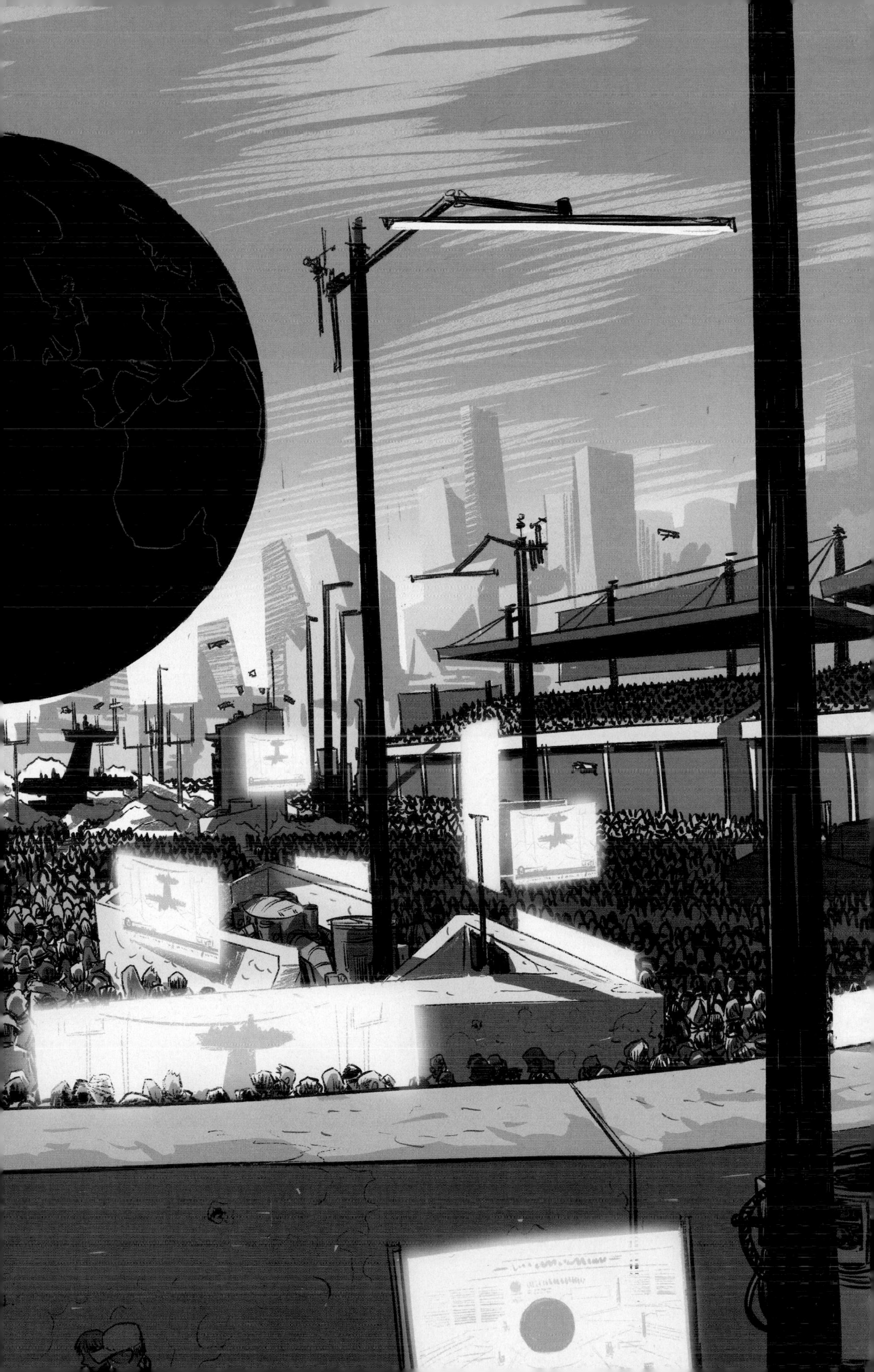

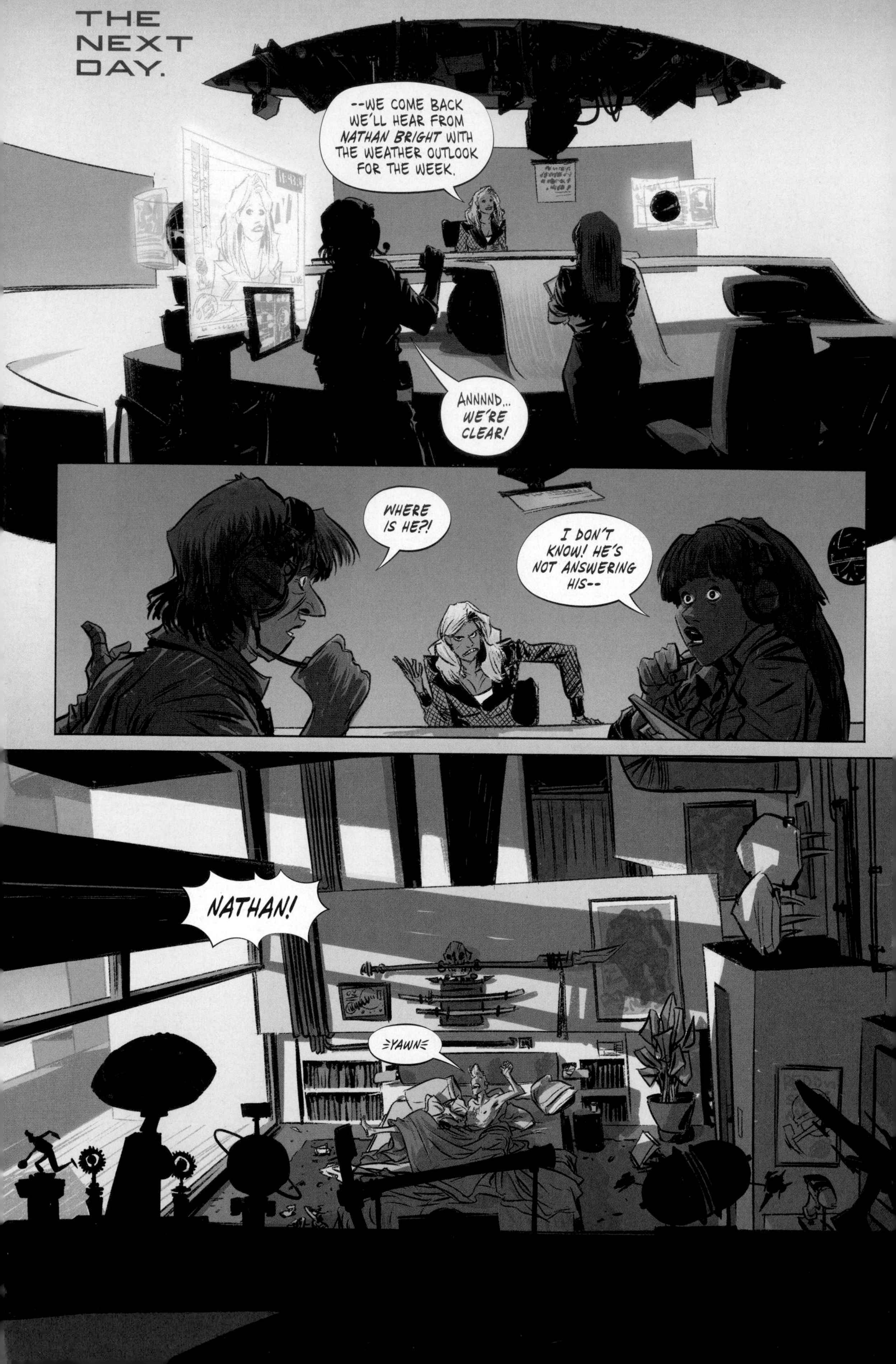
THE NEXT DAY.
--WE COME BACK WE'LL HEAR FROM NATHAN BRIGHT WITH THE WEATHER OUTLOOK FOR THE WEEK.
ANNNND... WE'RE CLEAR!
WHERE IS HE?!
I DON'T KNOW! HE'S NOT ANSWERING HIS--
NATHAN!
=YAWN=

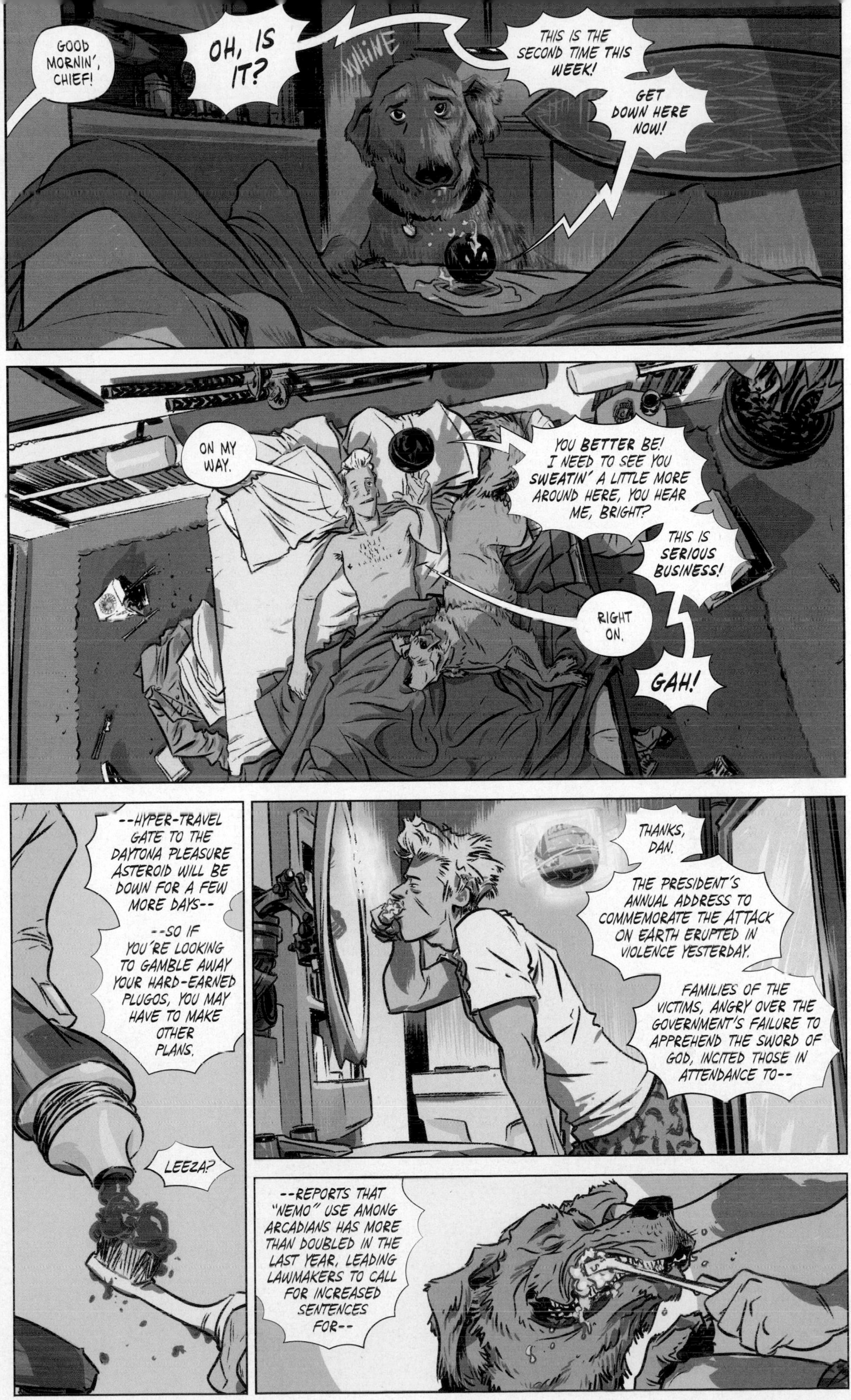
GOOD MORNIN', CHIEF!
OH, IS IT?
WHINE
THIS IS THE SECOND TIME THIS WEEK!
GET DOWN HERE NOW!
ON MY WAY.
YOU BETTER BE! I NEED TO SEE YOU SWEATIN' A LITTLE MORE AROUND HERE, YOU HEAR ME, BRIGHT?
THIS IS SERIOUS BUSINESS!
RIGHT ON.
GAH!
--HYPER-TRAVEL GATE TO THE DAYTONA PLEASURE ASTEROID WILL BE DOWN FOR A FEW MORE DAYS--
--SO IF YOU'RE LOOKING TO GAMBLE AWAY YOUR HARD-EARNED PLUGOS, YOU MAY HAVE TO MAKE OTHER PLANS.
THANKS, DAN.
THE PRESIDENT'S ANNUAL ADDRESS TO COMMEMORATE THE ATTACK ON EARTH ERUPTED IN VIOLENCE YESTERDAY.
FAMILIES OF THE VICTIMS, ANGRY OVER THE GOVERNMENT'S FAILURE TO APPREHEND THE SWORD OF GOD, INCITED THOSE IN ATTENDANCE TO--
LEEZA?
--REPORTS THAT "NEMO" USE AMONG ARCADIANS HAS MORE THAN DOUBLED IN THE LAST YEAR, LEADING LAWMAKERS TO CALL FOR INCREASED SENTENCES FOR--

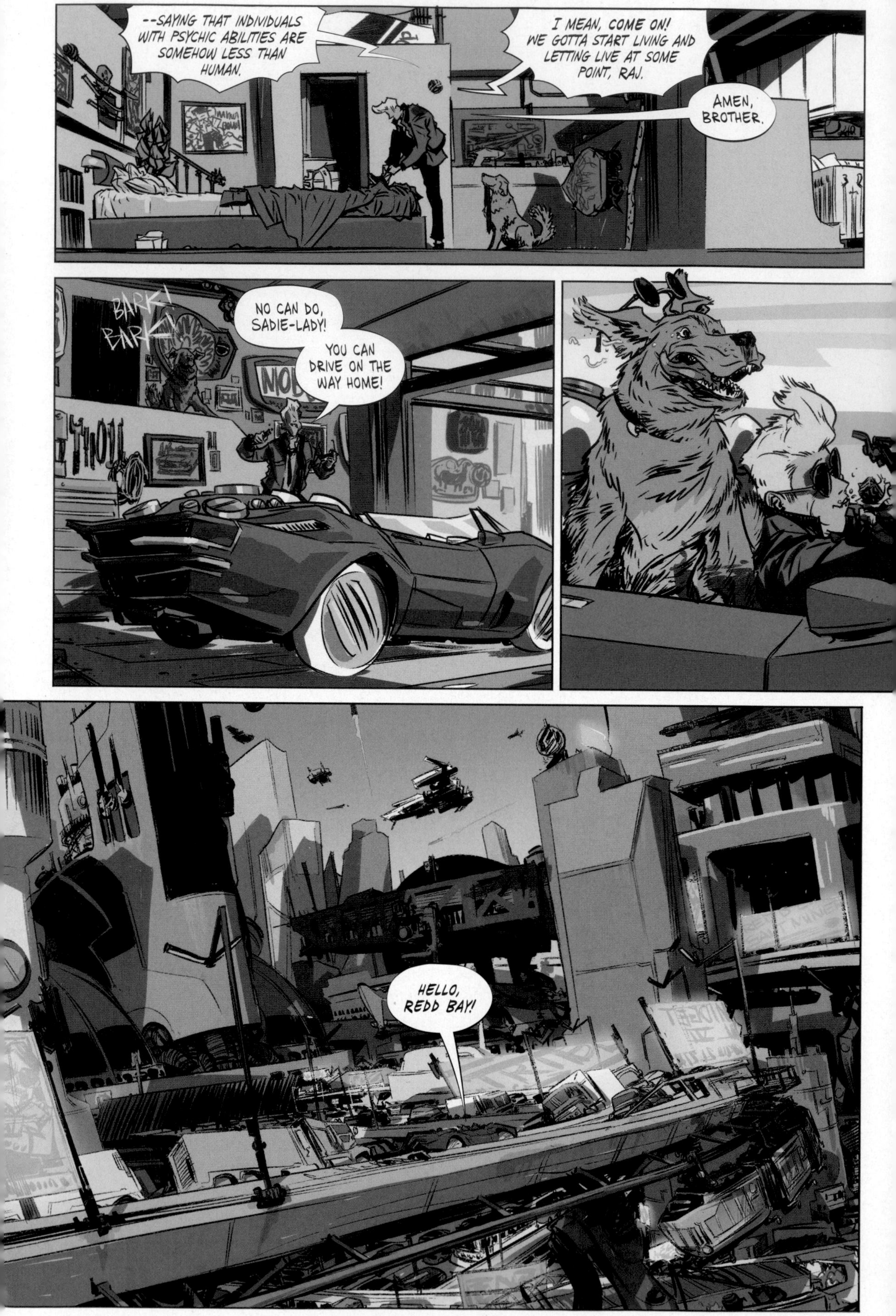
--SAYING THAT INDIVIDUALS WITH PSYCHIC ABILITIES ARE SOMEHOW LESS THAN HUMAN.
I MEAN, COME ON! WE GOTTA START LIVING AND LETTING LIVE AT SOME POINT, RAJ.
AMEN, BROTHER.
BARK! BARK!
NO CAN DO, SADIE-LADY!
YOU CAN DRIVE ON THE WAY HOME!
HELLO, REDD BAY!

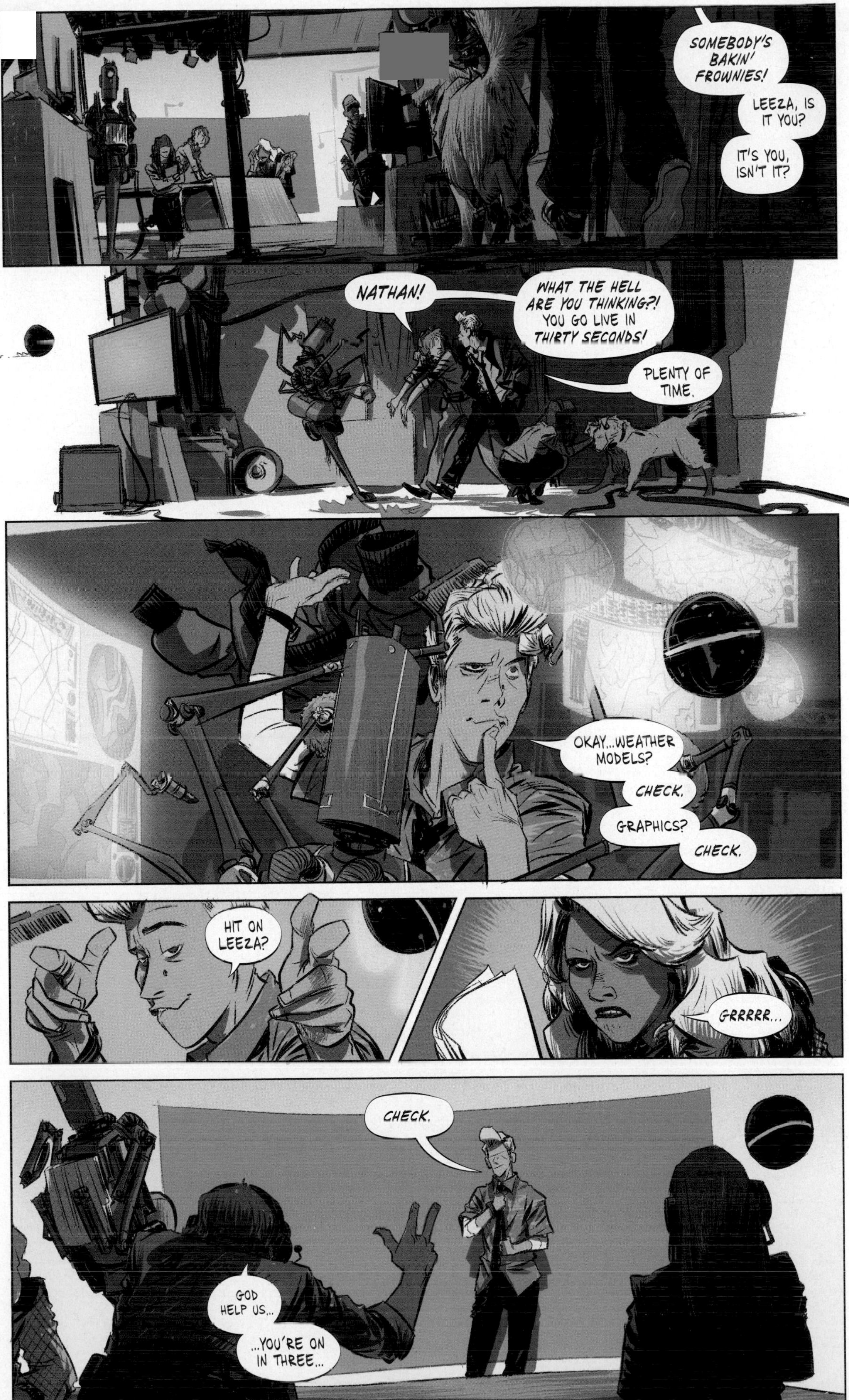
SOMEBODY'S BAKIN' FROWNIES!
LEEZA, IS IT YOU?
IT'S YOU, ISN'T IT?
NATHAN!
WHAT THE HELL ARE YOU THINKING?! YOU GO LIVE IN THIRTY SECONDS!
PLENTY OF TIME.
OKAY...WEATHER MODELS?
CHECK.
GRAPHICS?
CHECK.
HIT ON LEEZA?
GRRRRR...
CHECK.
GOD HELP US...
...YOU'RE ON IN THREE...

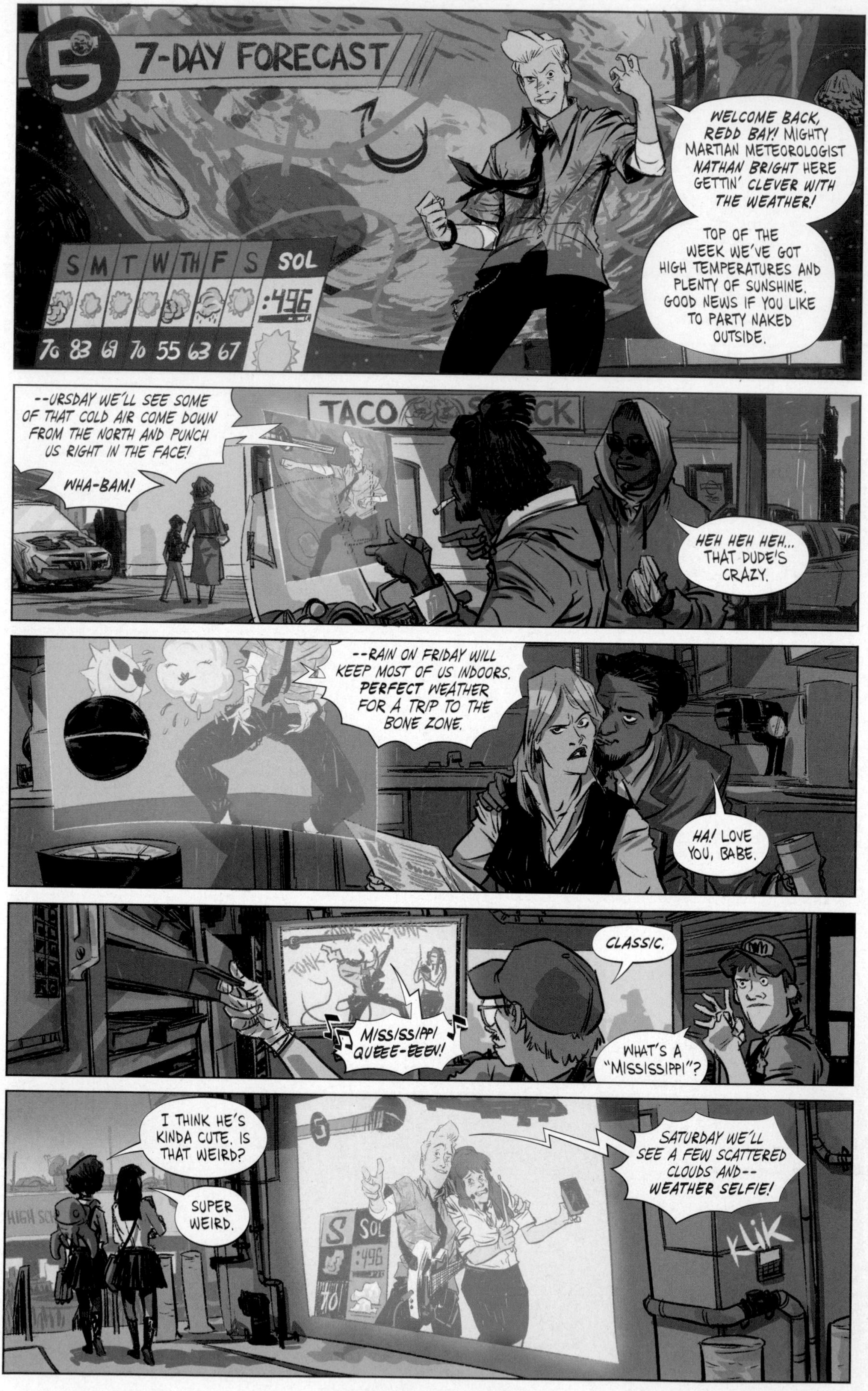
7-DAY FORECAST
S M T W TH F S SOL
:496
70 83 69 70 55 63 67
WELCOME BACK, REDD BAY! MIGHTY MARTIAN METEOROLOGIST NATHAN BRIGHT HERE GETTIN' CLEVER WITH THE WEATHER!
TOP OF THE WEEK WE'VE GOT HIGH TEMPERATURES AND PLENTY OF SUNSHINE. GOOD NEWS IF YOU LIKE TO PARTY NAKED OUTSIDE.
--URSDAY WE'LL SEE SOME OF THAT COLD AIR COME DOWN FROM THE NORTH AND PUNCH US RIGHT IN THE FACE!
WHA-BAM!
HEH HEH HEH... THAT DUDE'S CRAZY.
--RAIN ON FRIDAY WILL KEEP MOST OF US INDOORS. PERFECT WEATHER FOR A TRIP TO THE BONE ZONE.
HA! LOVE YOU, BABE.
TONK TONK TONK
CLASSIC.
MISSISSIPPI QUEEE-EEEN!
WHAT'S A "MISSISSIPPI"?
I THINK HE'S KINDA CUTE. IS THAT WEIRD?
SUPER WEIRD.
SATURDAY WE'LL SEE A FEW SCATTERED CLOUDS AND-- WEATHER SELFIE!
KLIK

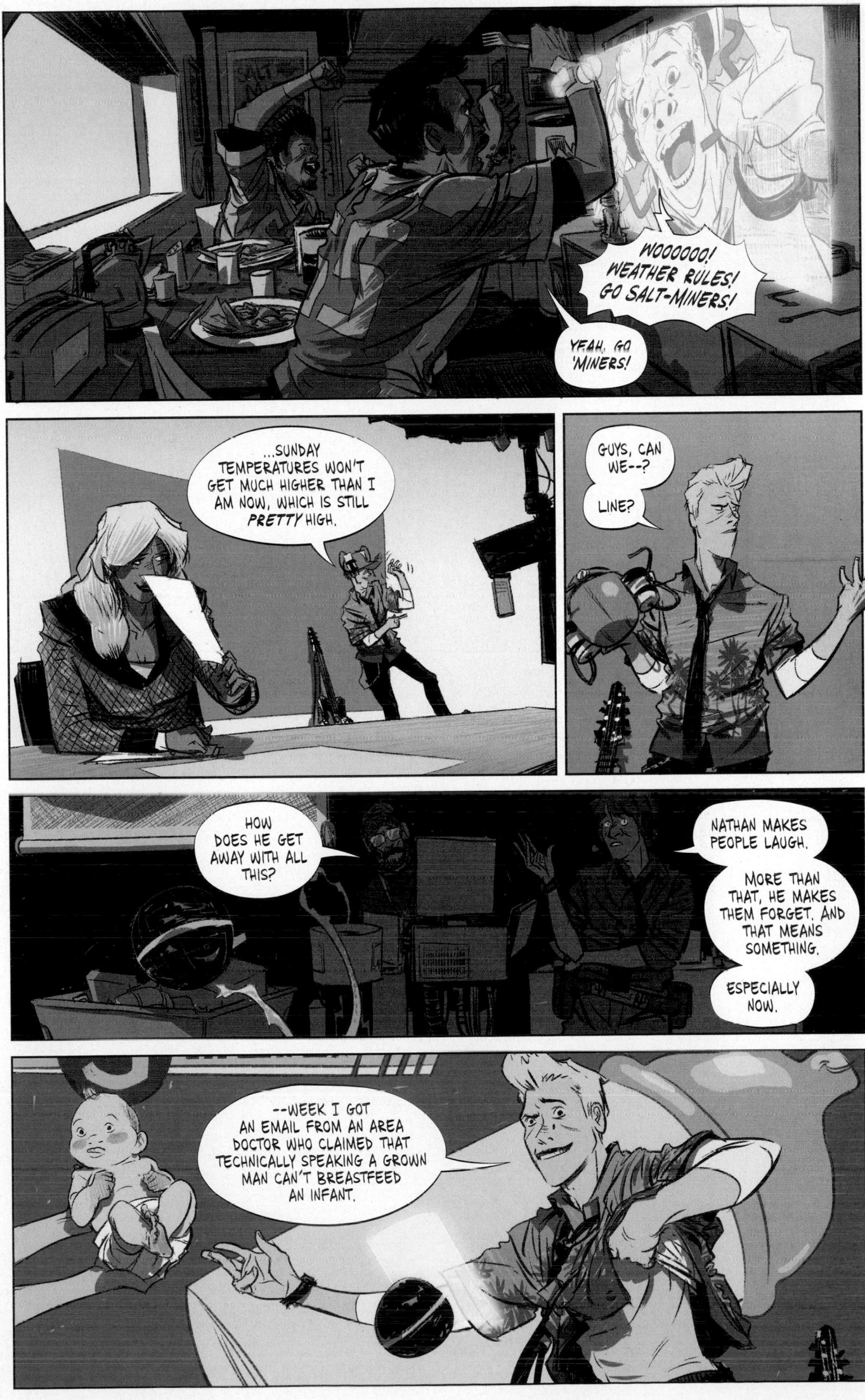
WOOOOOO! WEATHER RULES! GO SALT-MINERS!
YEAH, GO 'MINERS!
...SUNDAY TEMPERATURES WON'T GET MUCH HIGHER THAN I AM NOW, WHICH IS STILL *PRETTY* HIGH.
GUYS, CAN WE--?
LINE?
HOW DOES HE GET AWAY WITH ALL THIS?
NATHAN MAKES PEOPLE LAUGH.
MORE THAN THAT, HE MAKES THEM FORGET. AND THAT MEANS SOMETHING.
ESPECIALLY NOW.
--WEEK I GOT AN EMAIL FROM AN AREA DOCTOR WHO CLAIMED THAT TECHNICALLY SPEAKING A GROWN MAN CAN'T BREASTFEED AN INFANT.

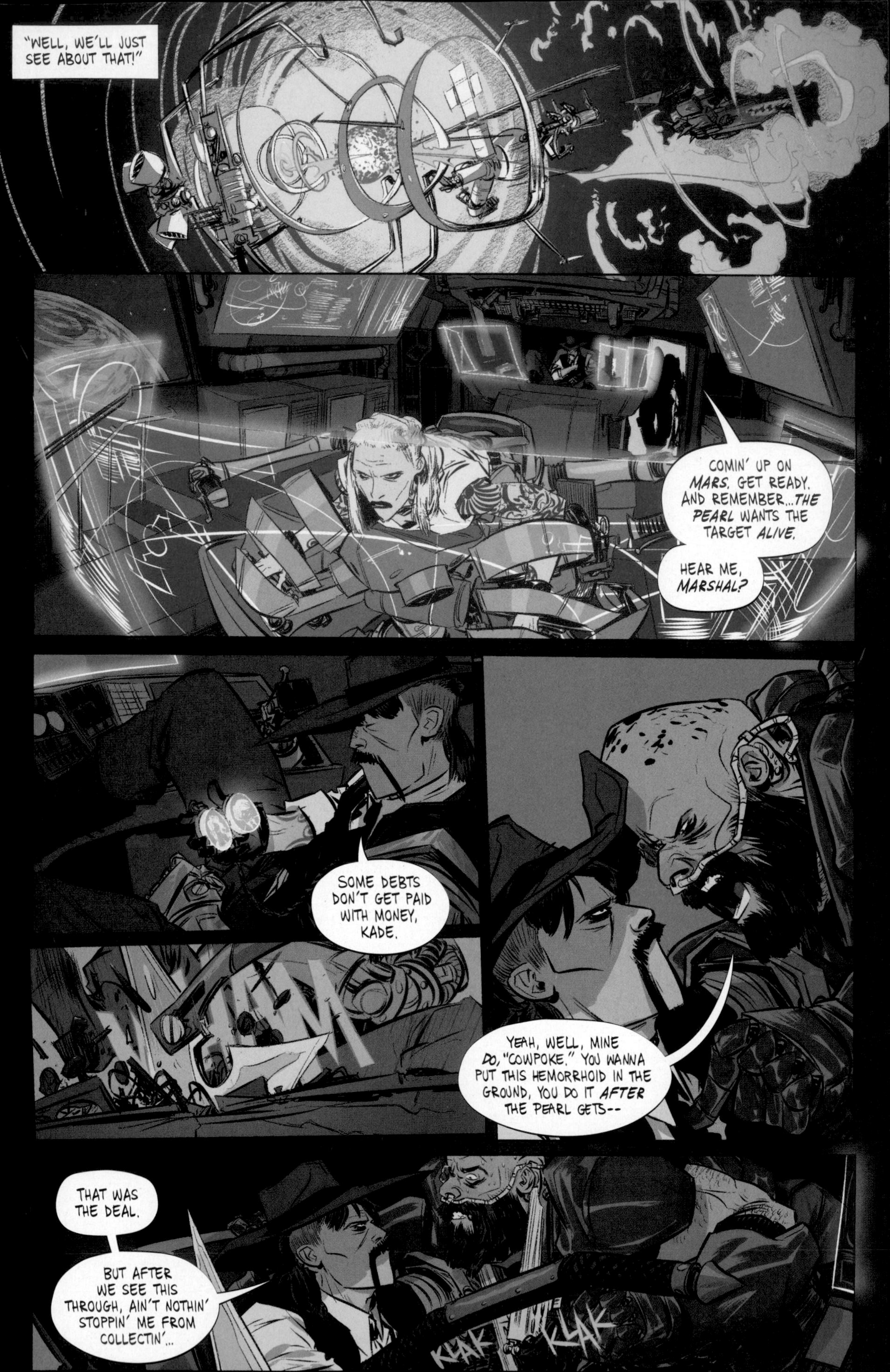
"WELL, WE'LL JUST SEE ABOUT THAT!"
COMIN' UP ON *MARS*. GET READY. AND REMEMBER...*THE PEARL* WANTS THE TARGET *ALIVE*.
HEAR ME, *MARSHAL?*
SOME DEBTS DON'T GET PAID WITH MONEY, KADE.
YEAH, WELL, MINE *DO*, "COWPOKE." YOU WANNA PUT THIS HEMORRHOID IN THE GROUND, YOU DO IT *AFTER* THE PEARL GETS--
THAT WAS THE DEAL.
BUT AFTER WE SEE THIS THROUGH, AIN'T NOTHIN' STOPPIN' ME FROM COLLECTIN'...
KLAK
KLAK

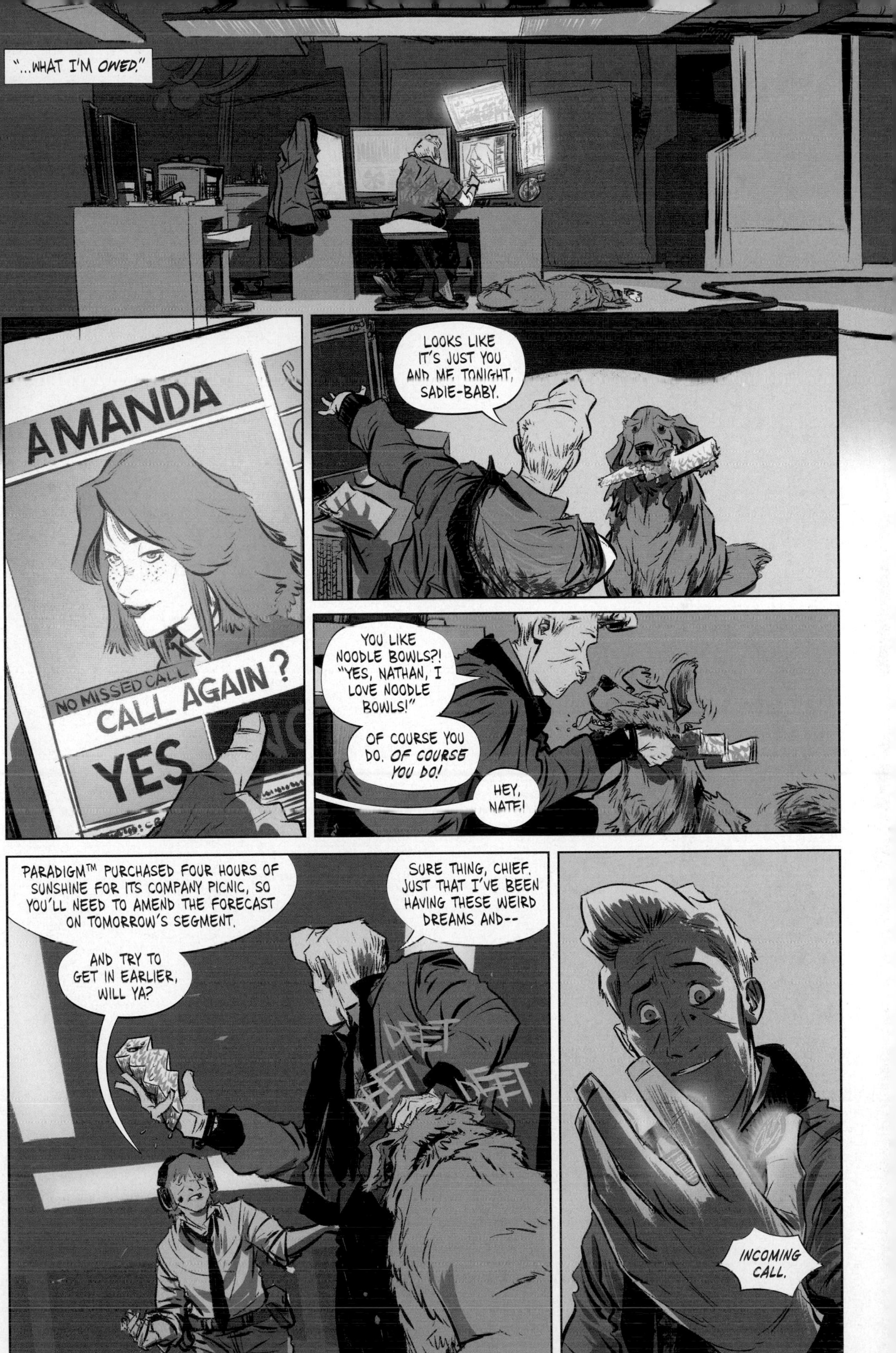
"...WHAT I'M *OWED.*"
AMANDA
NO MISSED CALL
CALL AGAIN?
YES
LOOKS LIKE IT'S JUST YOU AND ME TONIGHT, SADIE-BABY.
YOU LIKE NOODLE BOWLS?! "YES, NATHAN, I LOVE NOODLE BOWLS!"
OF COURSE YOU DO. *OF COURSE YOU DO!*
HEY, NATE!
PARADIGM™ PURCHASED FOUR HOURS OF SUNSHINE FOR ITS COMPANY PICNIC, SO YOU'LL NEED TO AMEND THE FORECAST ON TOMORROW'S SEGMENT.
AND TRY TO GET IN EARLIER, WILL YA?
SURE THING, CHIEF. JUST THAT I'VE BEEN HAVING THESE WEIRD DREAMS AND--
DEET DEET DEET DEET
INCOMING CALL.

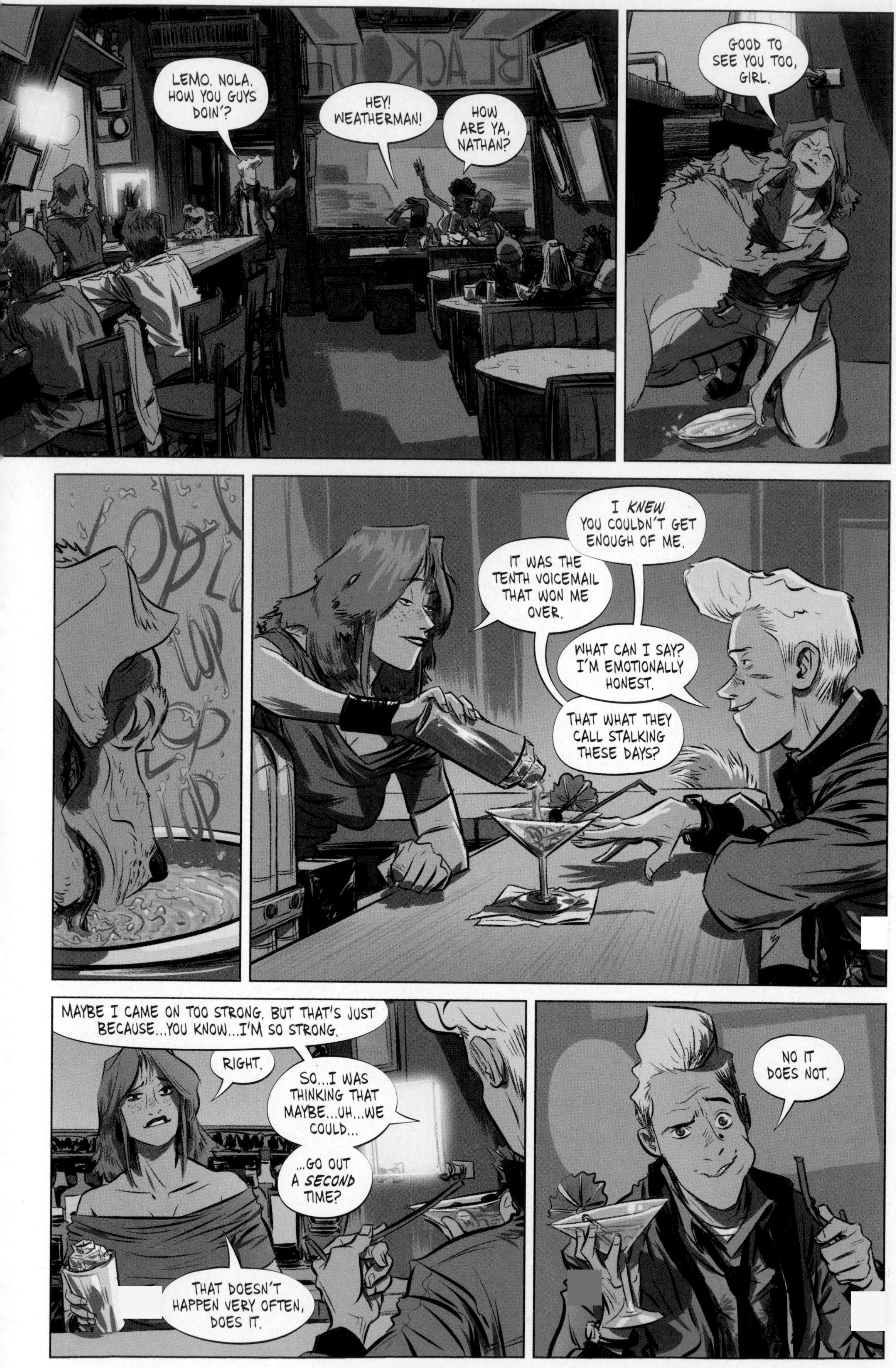
LEMO. NOLA. HOW YOU GUYS DOIN'?
HEY! WEATHERMAN!
HOW ARE YA, NATHAN?
GOOD TO SEE YOU TOO, GIRL.
I *KNEW* YOU COULDN'T GET ENOUGH OF ME.
IT WAS THE TENTH VOICEMAIL THAT WON ME OVER.
WHAT CAN I SAY? I'M EMOTIONALLY HONEST.
THAT WHAT THEY CALL STALKING THESE DAYS?
MAYBE I CAME ON TOO STRONG. BUT THAT'S JUST BECAUSE...YOU KNOW...I'M SO STRONG.
RIGHT.
SO...I WAS THINKING THAT MAYBE...UH...WE COULD...
...GO OUT A *SECOND* TIME?
THAT DOESN'T HAPPEN VERY OFTEN, DOES IT.
NO IT DOES NOT.

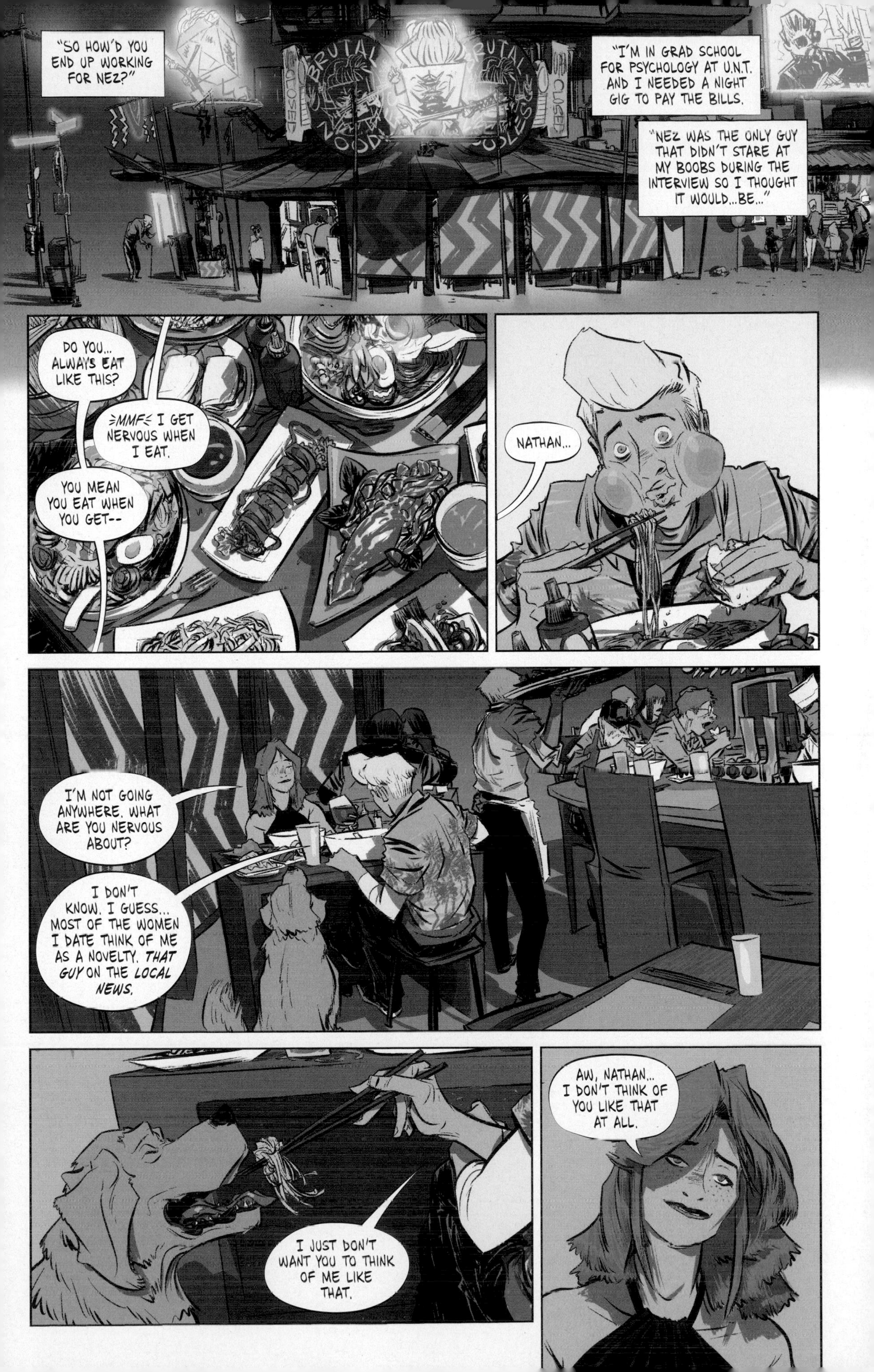
"SO HOW'D YOU END UP WORKING FOR NEZ?"
"I'M IN GRAD SCHOOL FOR PSYCHOLOGY AT U.N.T. AND I NEEDED A NIGHT GIG TO PAY THE BILLS.
"NEZ WAS THE ONLY GUY THAT DIDN'T STARE AT MY BOOBS DURING THE INTERVIEW SO I THOUGHT IT WOULD...BE..."
BRUTAL
CLOSED
DO YOU... ALWAYS EAT LIKE THIS?
MMF I GET NERVOUS WHEN I EAT.
YOU MEAN YOU EAT WHEN YOU GET--
NATHAN...
I'M NOT GOING ANYWHERE. WHAT ARE YOU NERVOUS ABOUT?
I DON'T KNOW. I GUESS... MOST OF THE WOMEN I DATE THINK OF ME AS A NOVELTY. THAT GUY ON THE LOCAL NEWS.
I JUST DON'T WANT YOU TO THINK OF ME LIKE THAT.
AW, NATHAN... I DON'T THINK OF YOU LIKE THAT AT ALL.

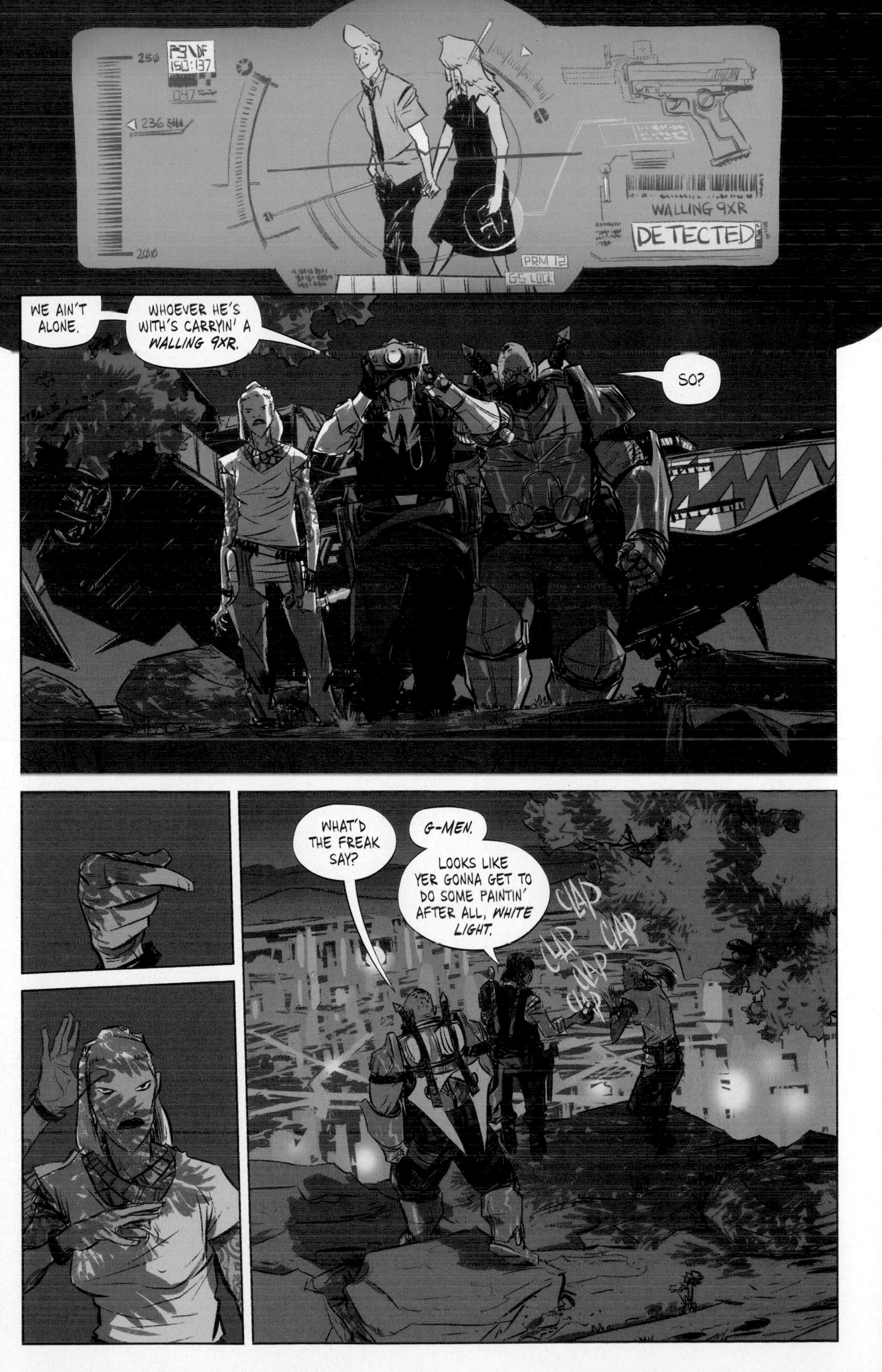
250
P3 VDF
150:137
047
236
200
WALLING 9XR
DETECTED
PRM 12
GS LOCK
WE AIN'T ALONE.
WHOEVER HE'S WITH'S CARRYIN' A *WALLING 9XR*.
SO?
WHAT'D THE FREAK SAY?
G-MEN.
LOOKS LIKE YER GONNA GET TO DO SOME PAINTIN' AFTER ALL, *WHITE LIGHT*.
CLAP CLAP CLAP CLAP CLAP

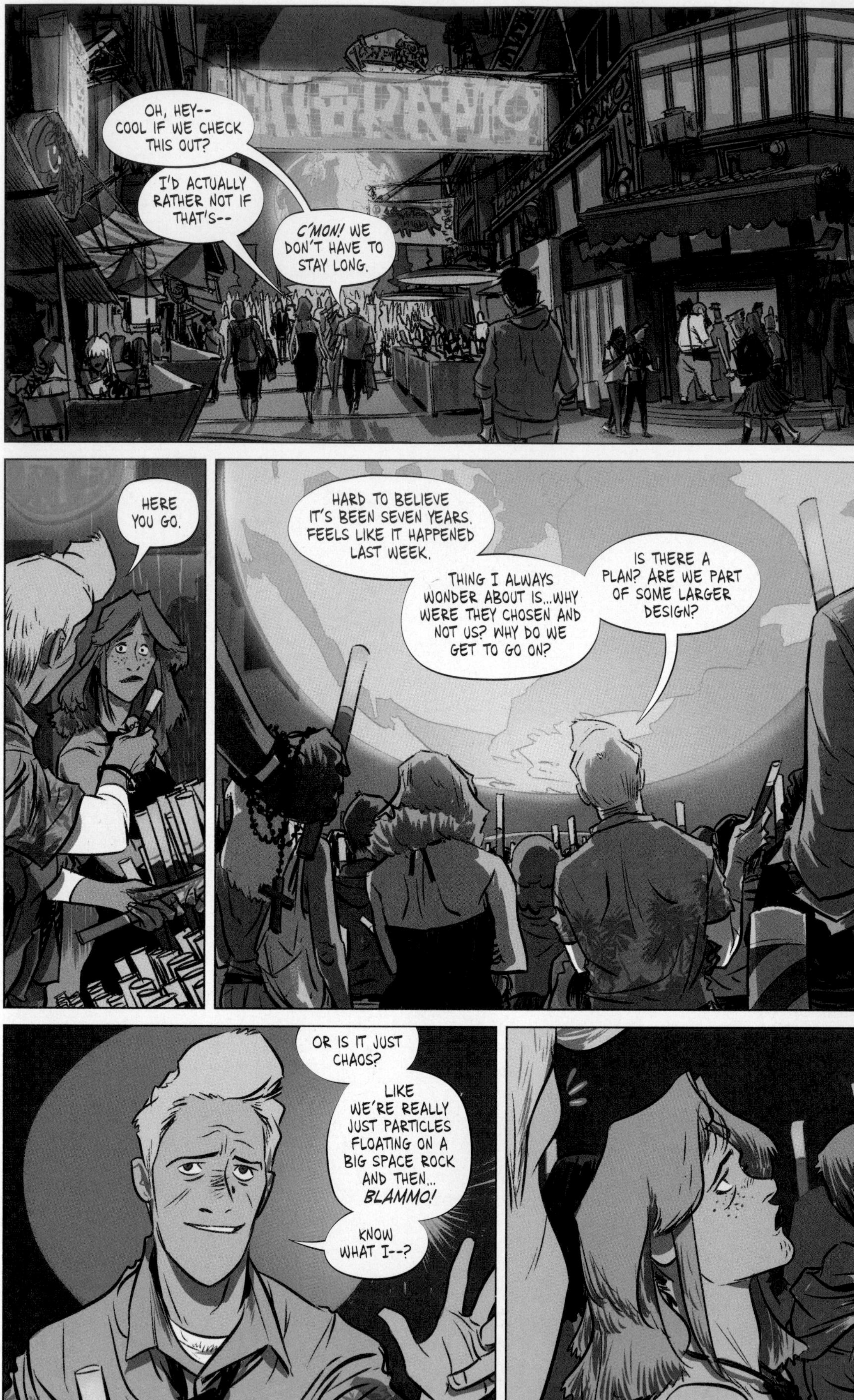
OH, HEY-- COOL IF WE CHECK THIS OUT?
I'D ACTUALLY RATHER NOT IF THAT'S--
C'MON! WE DON'T HAVE TO STAY LONG.
HERE YOU GO.
HARD TO BELIEVE IT'S BEEN SEVEN YEARS. FEELS LIKE IT HAPPENED LAST WEEK.
THING I ALWAYS WONDER ABOUT IS...WHY WERE THEY CHOSEN AND NOT US? WHY DO WE GET TO GO ON?
IS THERE A PLAN? ARE WE PART OF SOME LARGER DESIGN?
OR IS IT JUST CHAOS?
LIKE WE'RE REALLY JUST PARTICLES FLOATING ON A BIG SPACE ROCK AND THEN... BLAMMO!
KNOW WHAT I--?

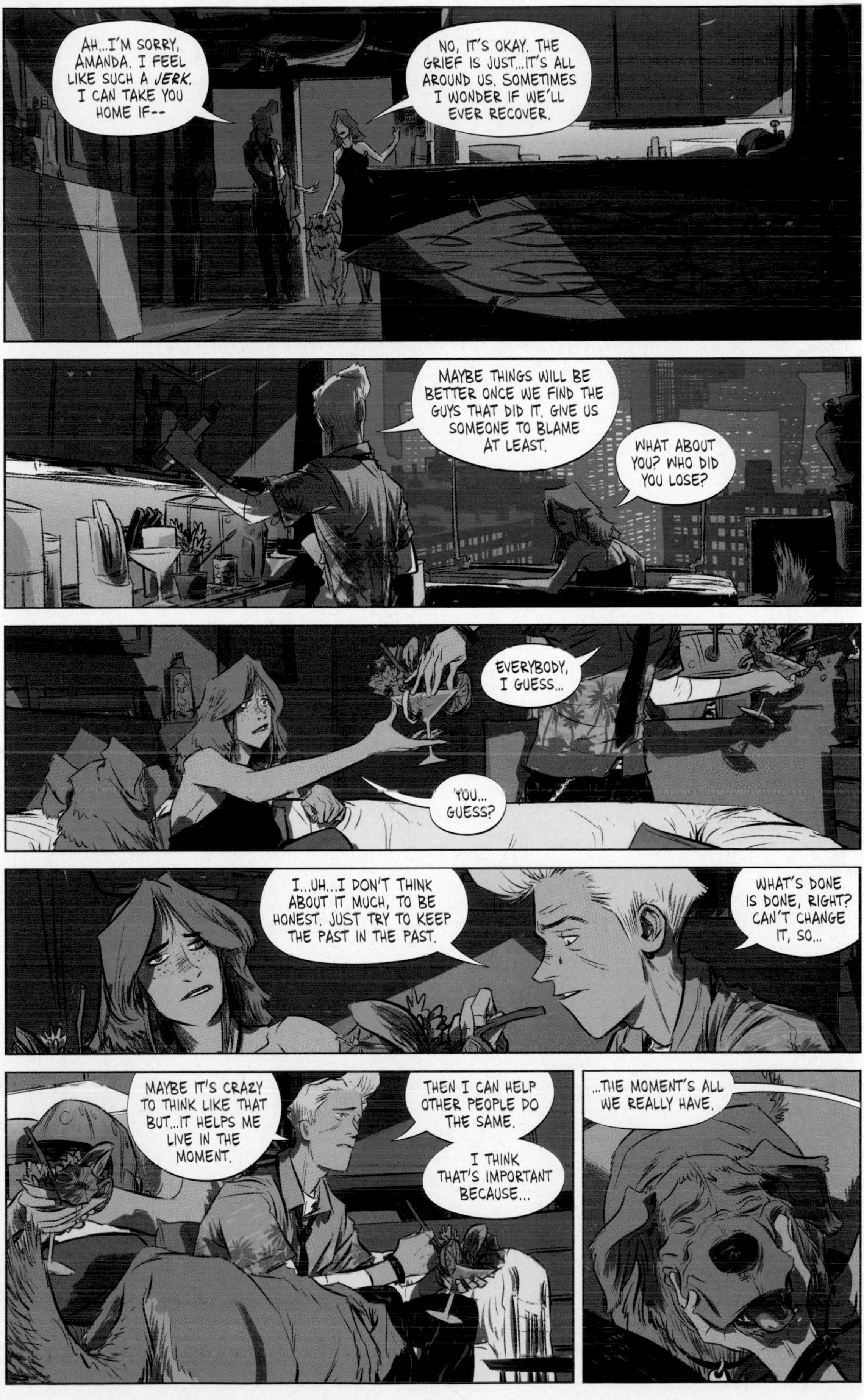
AH...I'M SORRY, AMANDA. I FEEL LIKE SUCH A *JERK*. I CAN TAKE YOU HOME IF--
NO, IT'S OKAY. THE GRIEF IS JUST...IT'S ALL AROUND US. SOMETIMES I WONDER IF WE'LL EVER RECOVER.
MAYBE THINGS WILL BE BETTER ONCE WE FIND THE GUYS THAT DID IT. GIVE US SOMEONE TO BLAME AT LEAST.
WHAT ABOUT YOU? WHO DID YOU LOSE?
EVERYBODY, I GUESS...
YOU... GUESS?
I...UH...I DON'T THINK ABOUT IT MUCH, TO BE HONEST. JUST TRY TO KEEP THE PAST IN THE PAST.
WHAT'S DONE IS DONE, RIGHT? CAN'T CHANGE IT, SO...
MAYBE IT'S CRAZY TO THINK LIKE THAT BUT...IT HELPS ME LIVE IN THE MOMENT.
THEN I CAN HELP OTHER PEOPLE DO THE SAME.
I THINK THAT'S IMPORTANT BECAUSE...
...THE MOMENT'S ALL WE REALLY HAVE.

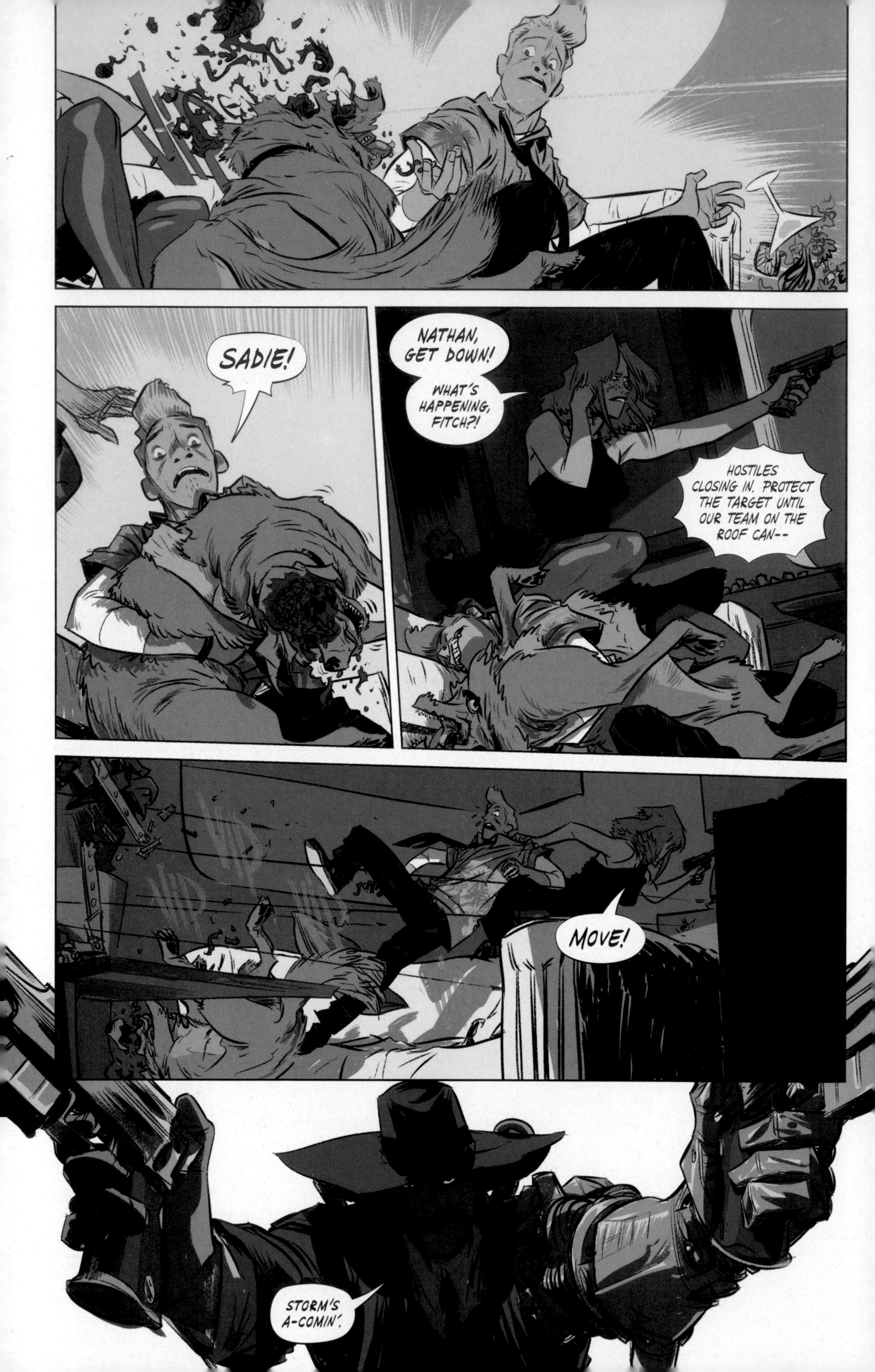
SADIE!
NATHAN, GET DOWN!
WHAT'S HAPPENING, FITCH?!
HOSTILES CLOSING IN. PROTECT THE TARGET UNTIL OUR TEAM ON THE ROOF CAN--
MOVE!
STORM'S A-COMIN'.

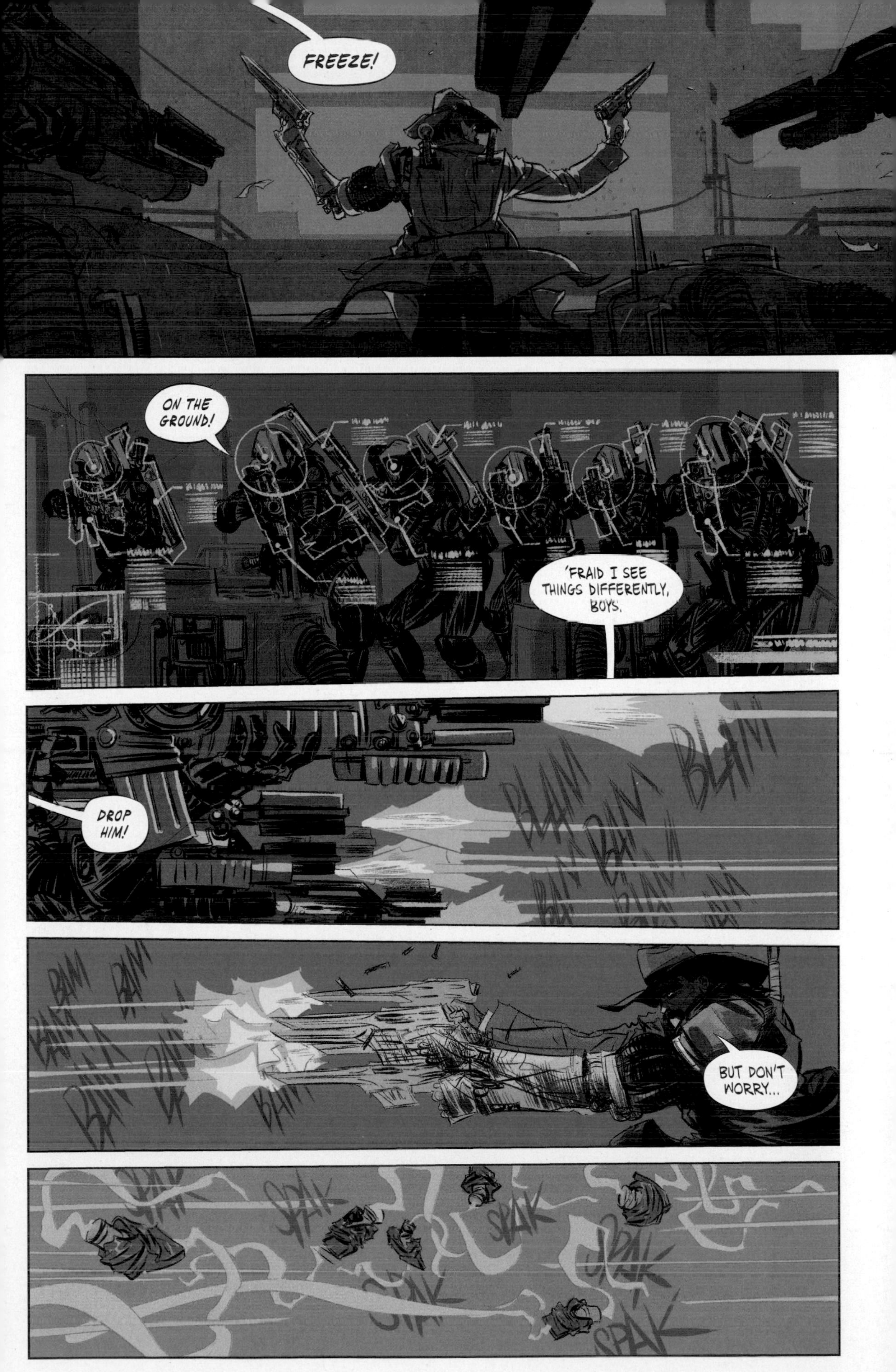
FREEZE!
ON THE GROUND!
'FRAID I SEE THINGS DIFFERENTLY, BOYS.
DROP HIM!
BLAM
BLAM
BUT DON'T WORRY...
SPAK

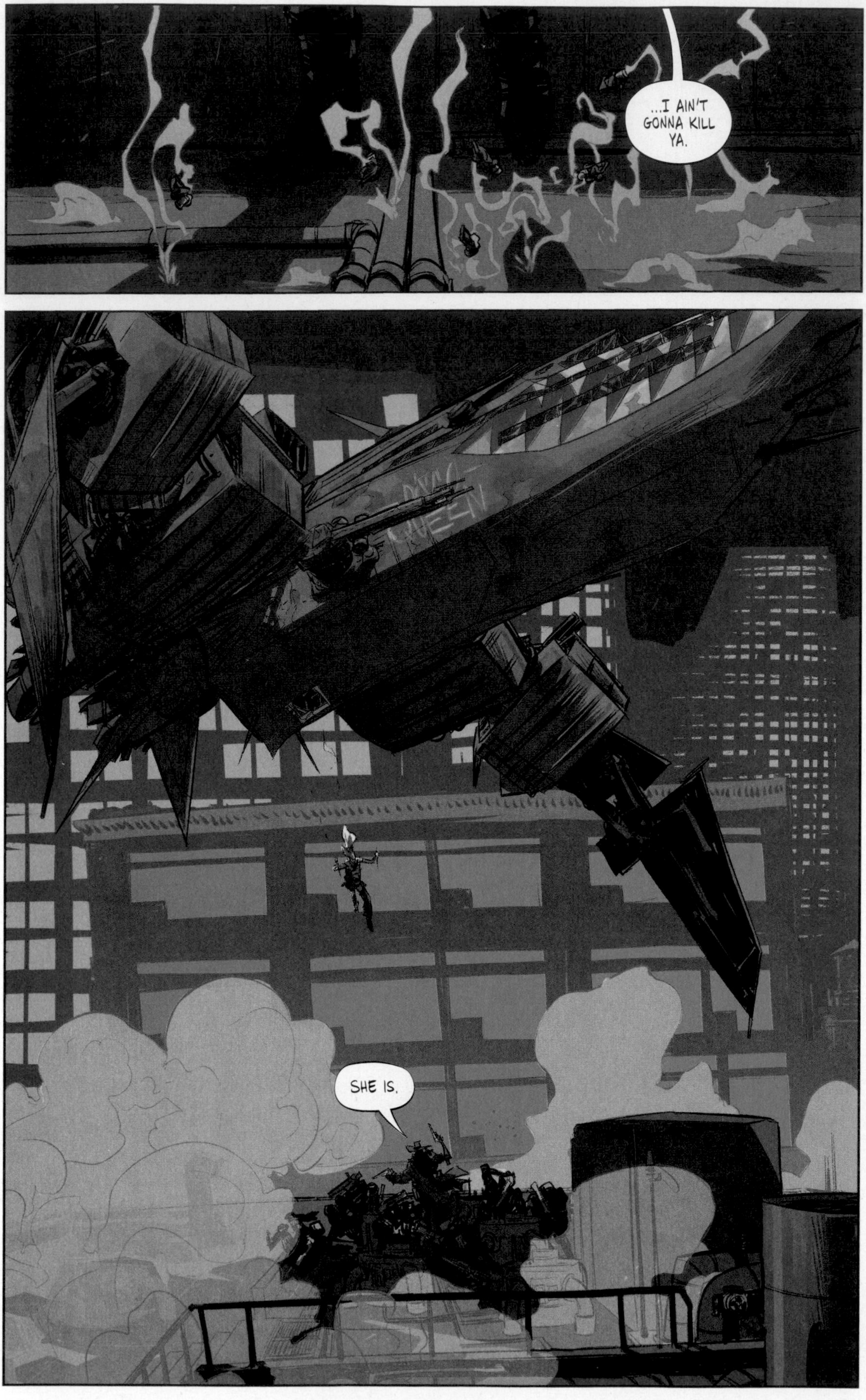
...I AIN'T GONNA KILL YA.
SHE IS.

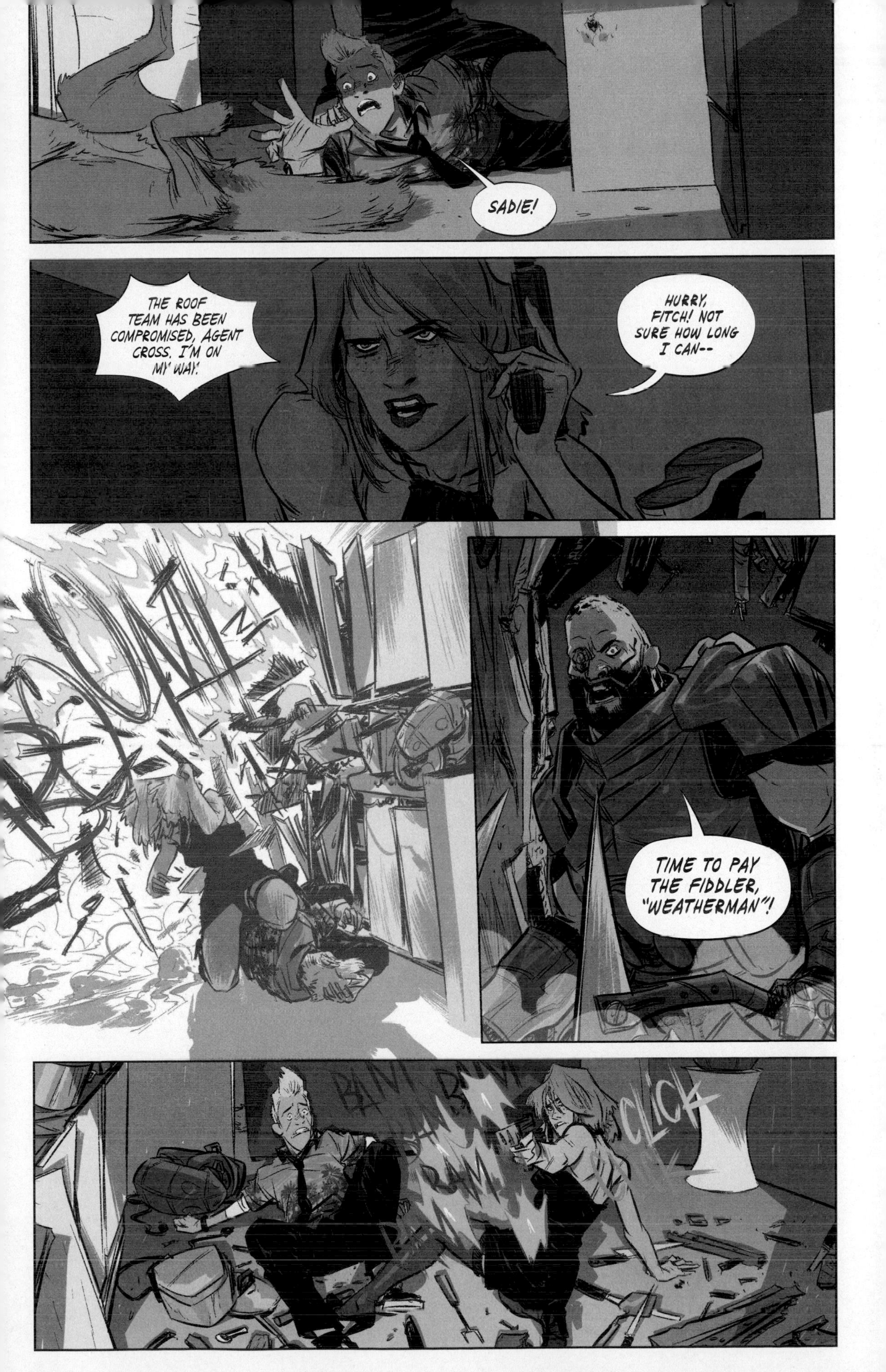
SADIE!
THE ROOF TEAM HAS BEEN COMPROMISED, AGENT CROSS. I'M ON MY WAY.
HURRY, FITCH! NOT SURE HOW LONG I CAN--
TIME TO PAY THE FIDDLER, "WEATHERMAN"!
CLICK

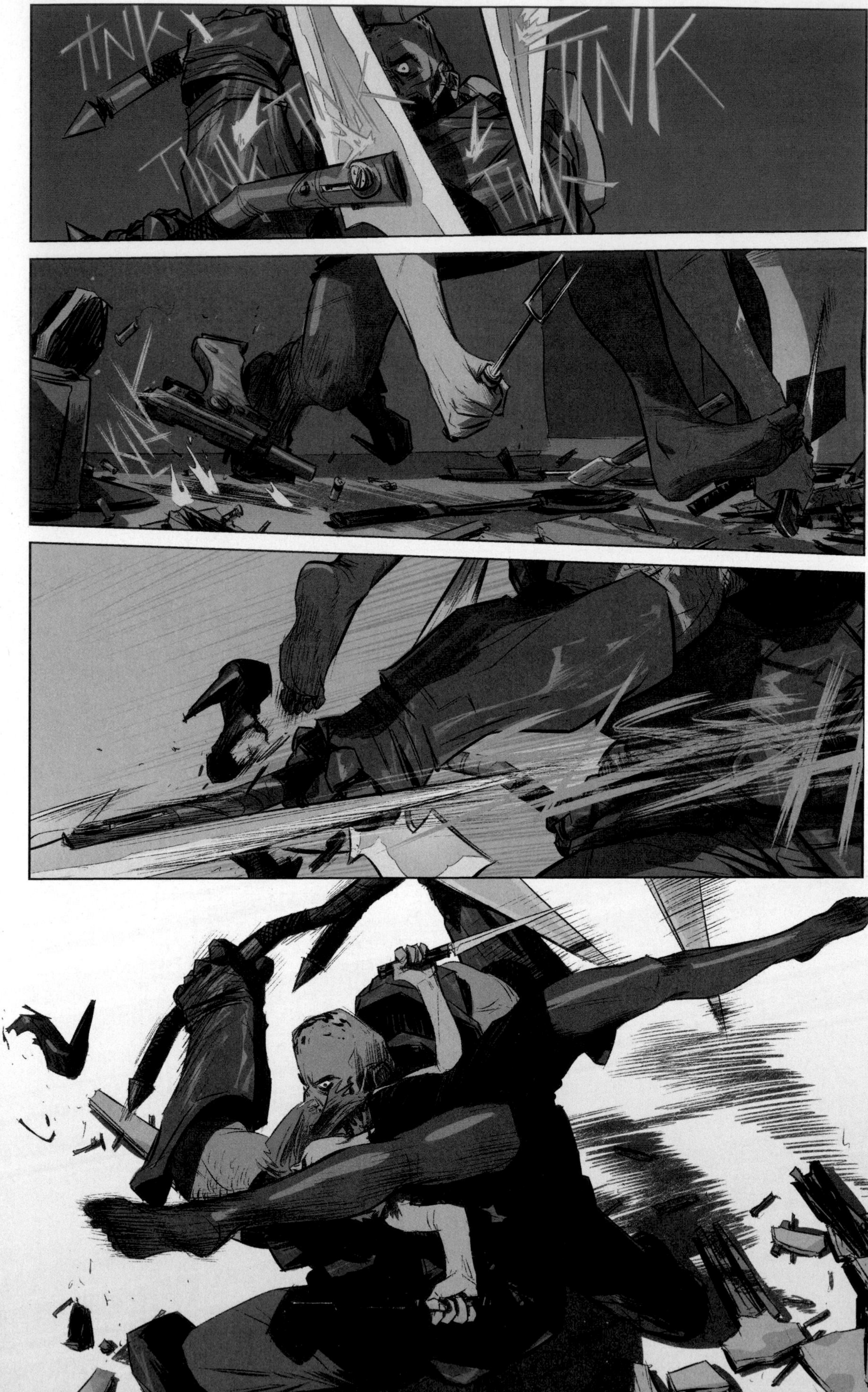
TINK
TINK
TINK
TINK
TINK

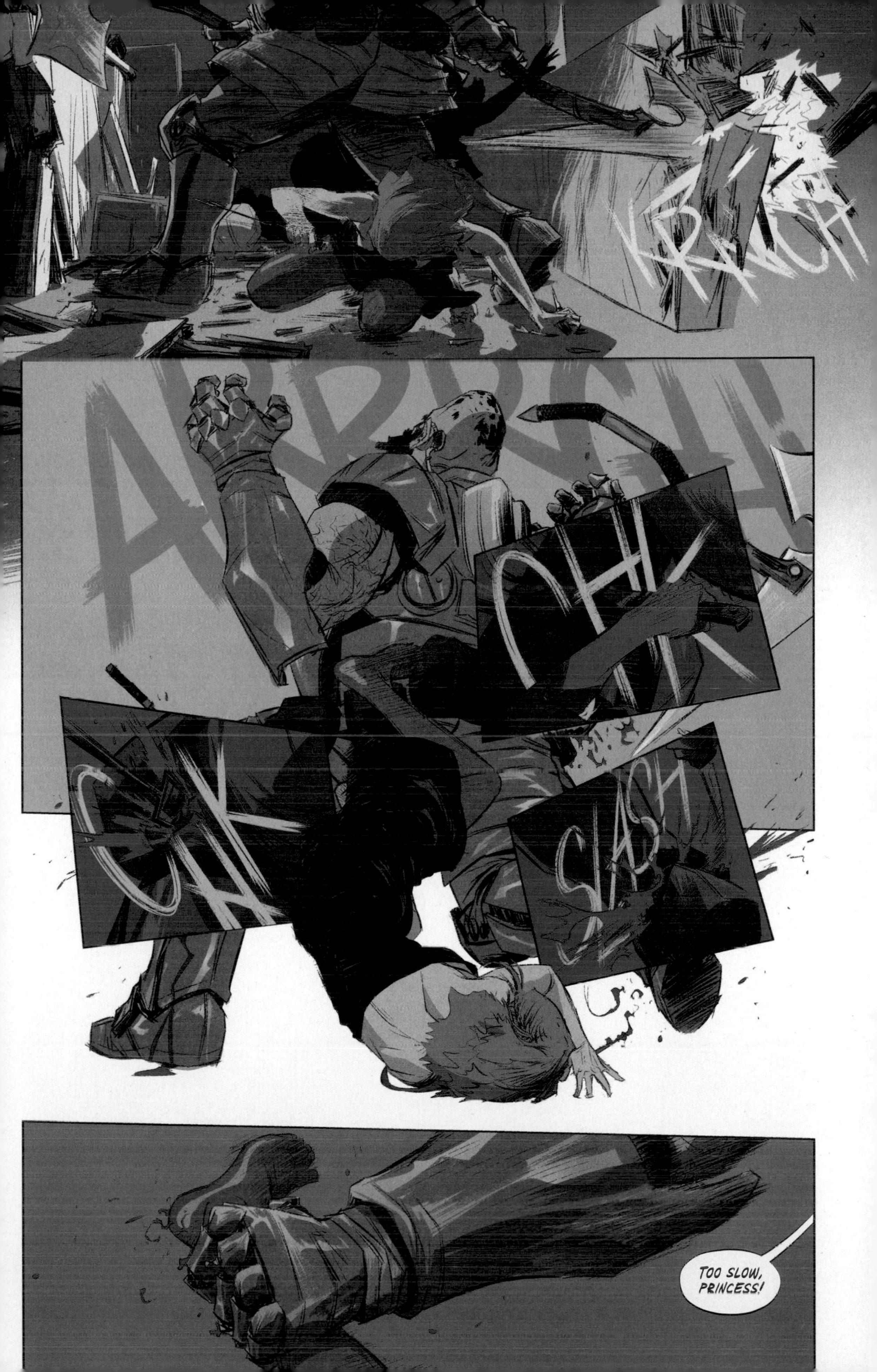
KRANCH
ARRGH
CHK
CHK
SLASH
TOO SLOW, PRINCESS!

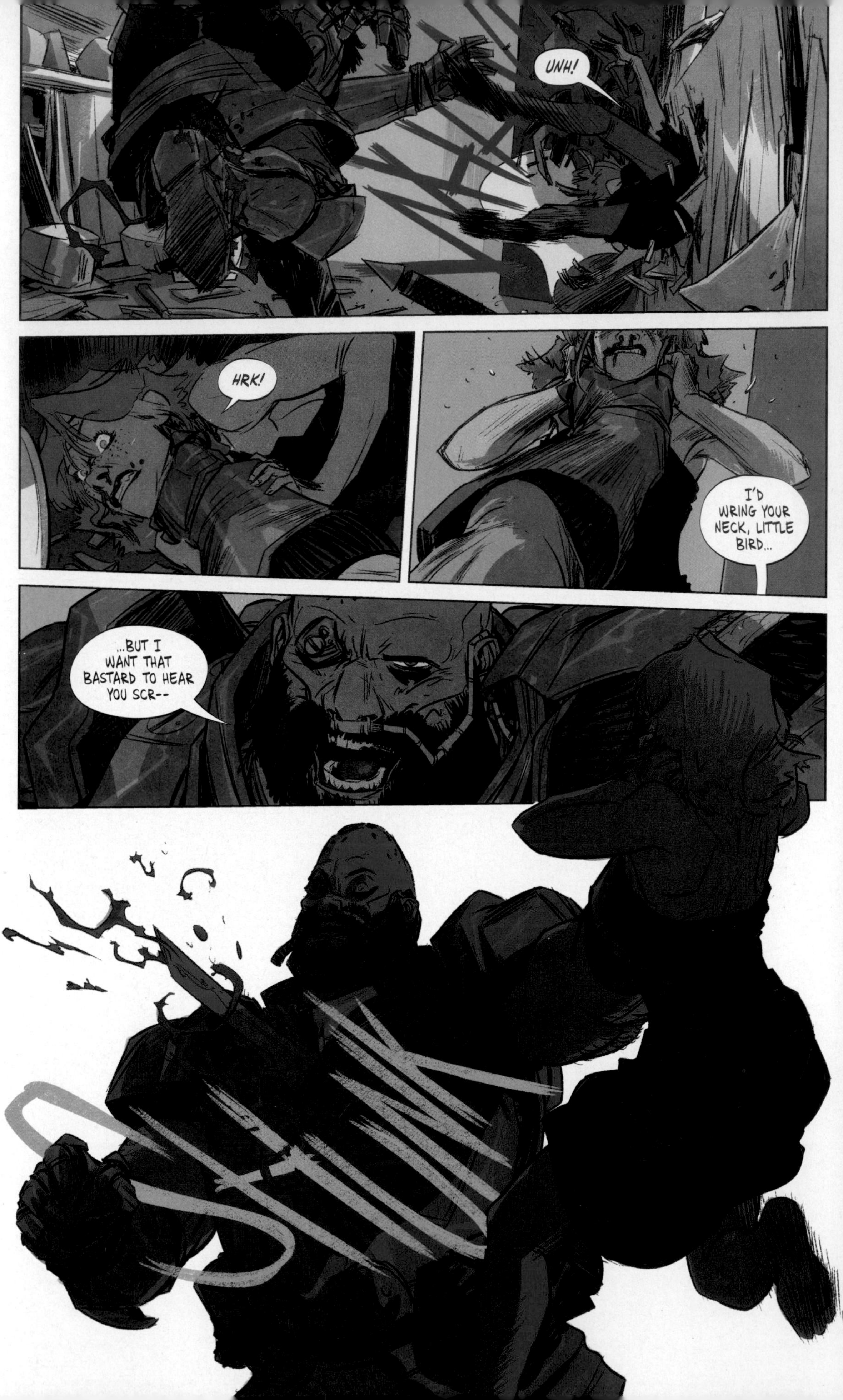
UNH!
HRK!
I'D WRING YOUR NECK, LITTLE BIRD...
...BUT I WANT THAT BASTARD TO HEAR YOU SCR--

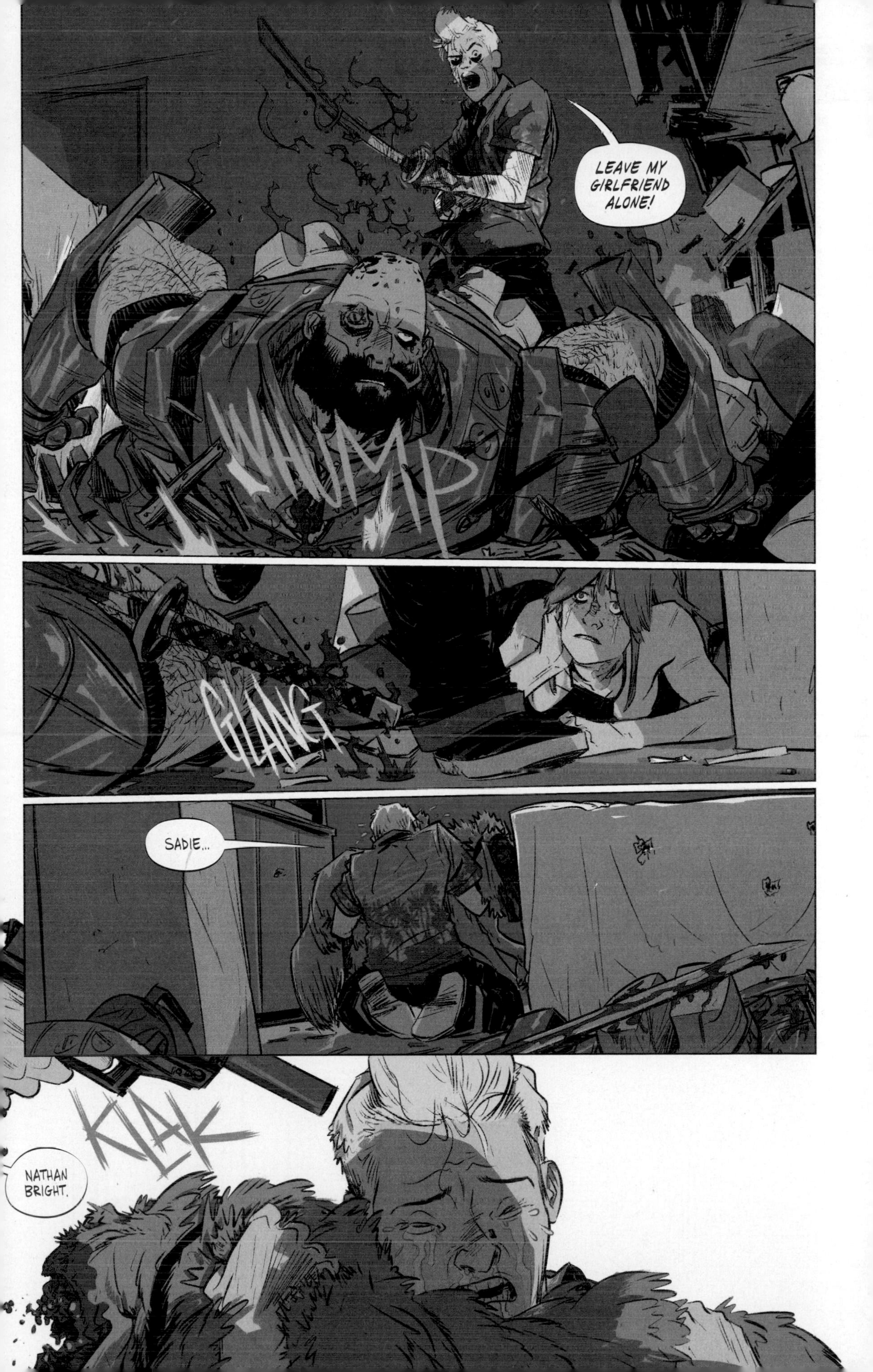
LEAVE MY GIRLFRIEND ALONE!
WHUMP
CLANG
SADIE...
KLAK
NATHAN BRIGHT.

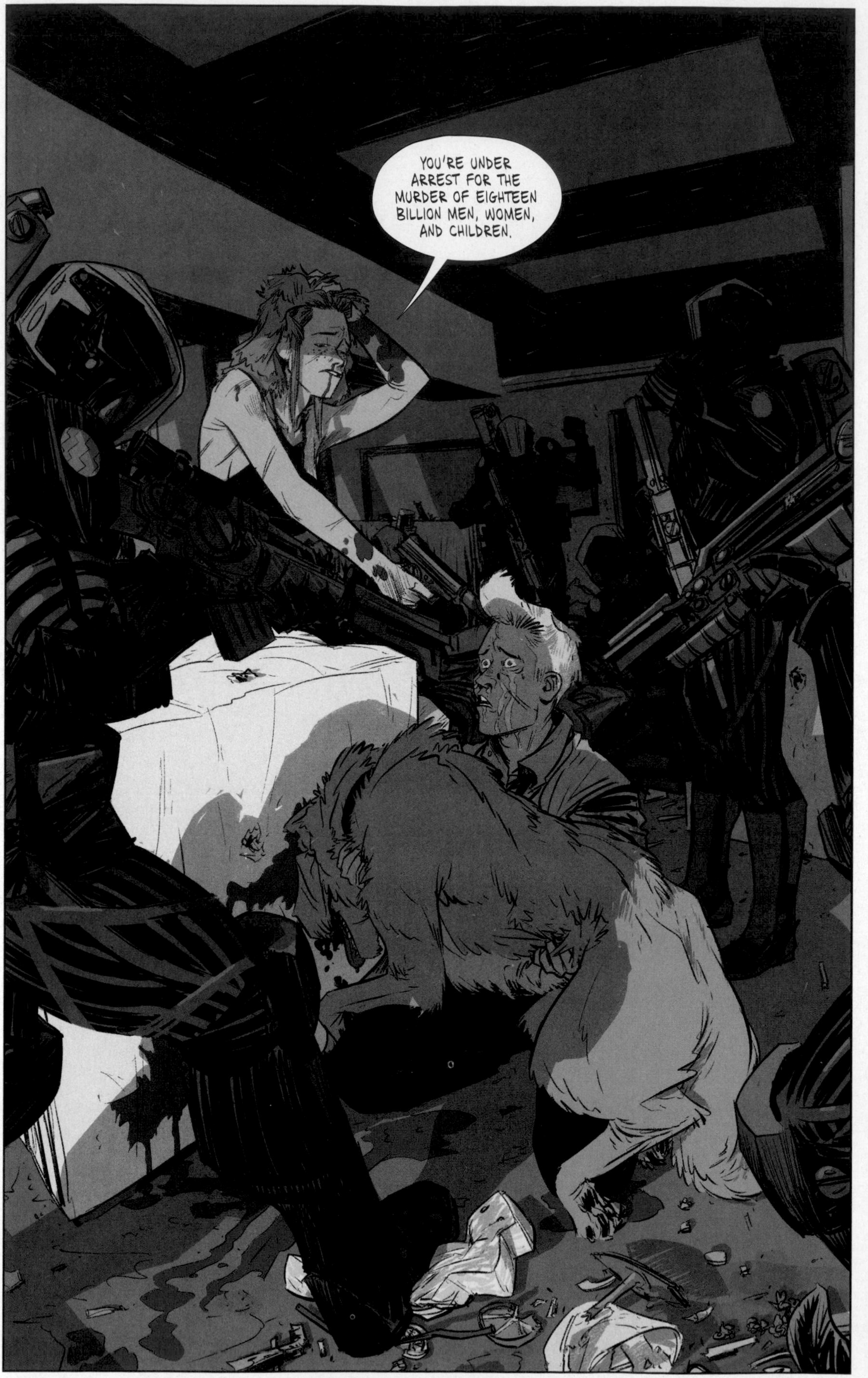
YOU'RE UNDER ARREST FOR THE MURDER OF EIGHTEEN BILLION MEN, WOMEN, AND CHILDREN.

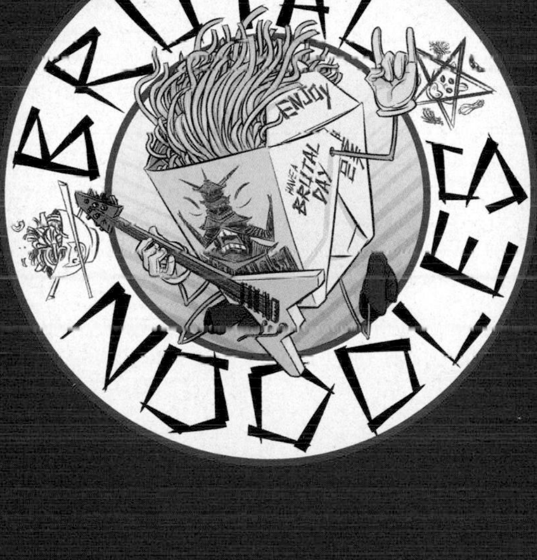
BRUTAL NOODLES
ENJOY
HAVE A BRUTAL DAY

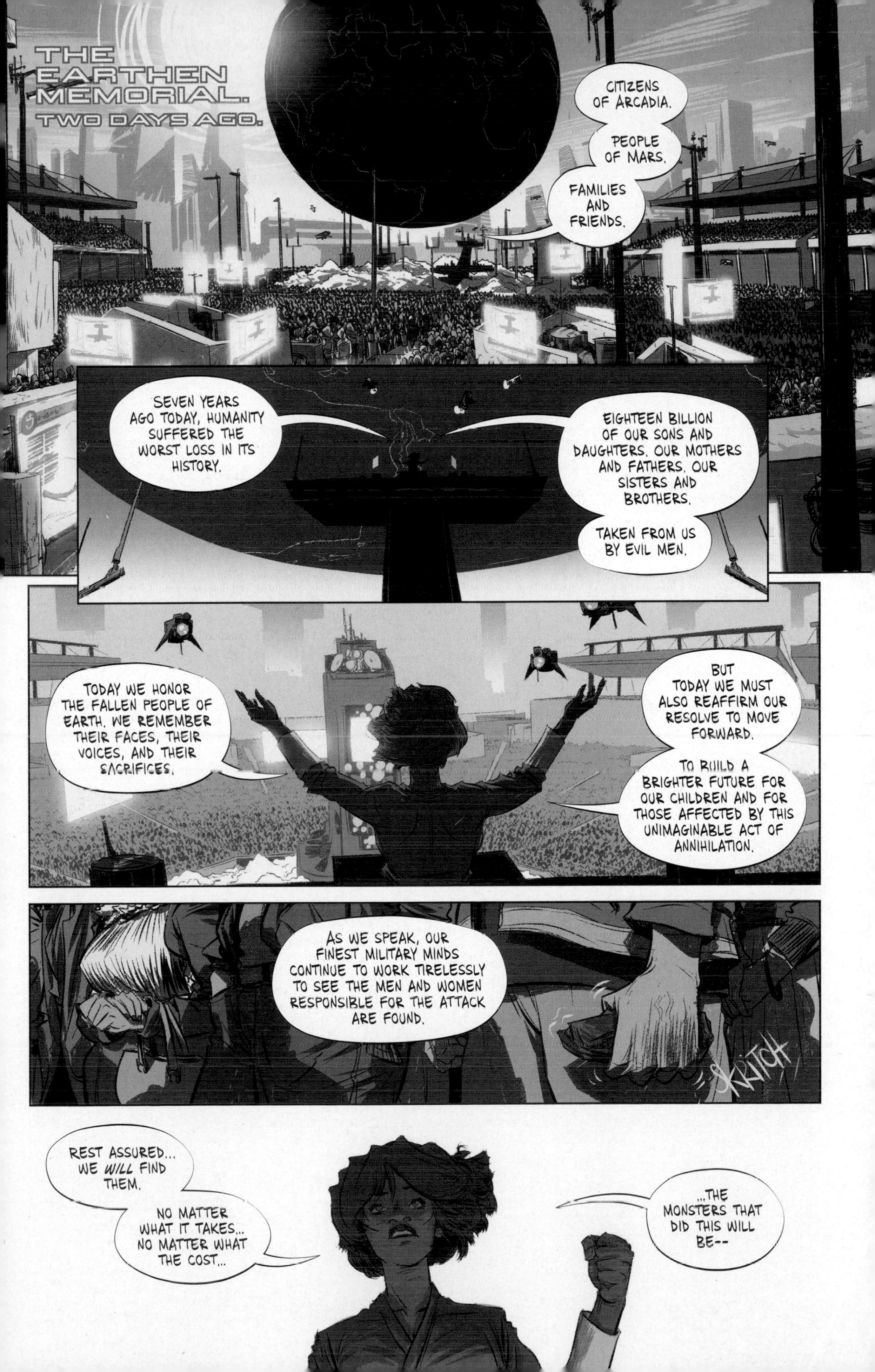
THE EARTHEN MEMORIAL.
TWO DAYS AGO.
CITIZENS OF ARCADIA.
PEOPLE OF MARS.
FAMILIES AND FRIENDS.
SEVEN YEARS AGO TODAY, HUMANITY SUFFERED THE WORST LOSS IN ITS HISTORY.
EIGHTEEN BILLION OF OUR SONS AND DAUGHTERS. OUR MOTHERS AND FATHERS. OUR SISTERS AND BROTHERS.
TAKEN FROM US BY EVIL MEN.
TODAY WE HONOR THE FALLEN PEOPLE OF EARTH. WE REMEMBER THEIR FACES, THEIR VOICES, AND THEIR SACRIFICES.
BUT TODAY WE MUST ALSO REAFFIRM OUR RESOLVE TO MOVE FORWARD.
TO BUILD A BRIGHTER FUTURE FOR OUR CHILDREN AND FOR THOSE AFFECTED BY THIS UNIMAGINABLE ACT OF ANNIHILATION.
AS WE SPEAK, OUR FINEST MILITARY MINDS CONTINUE TO WORK TIRELESSLY TO SEE THE MEN AND WOMEN RESPONSIBLE FOR THE ATTACK ARE FOUND.
SKRITCH
REST ASSURED... WE *WILL* FIND THEM.
NO MATTER WHAT IT TAKES... NO MATTER WHAT THE COST...
...THE MONSTERS THAT DID THIS WILL BE--

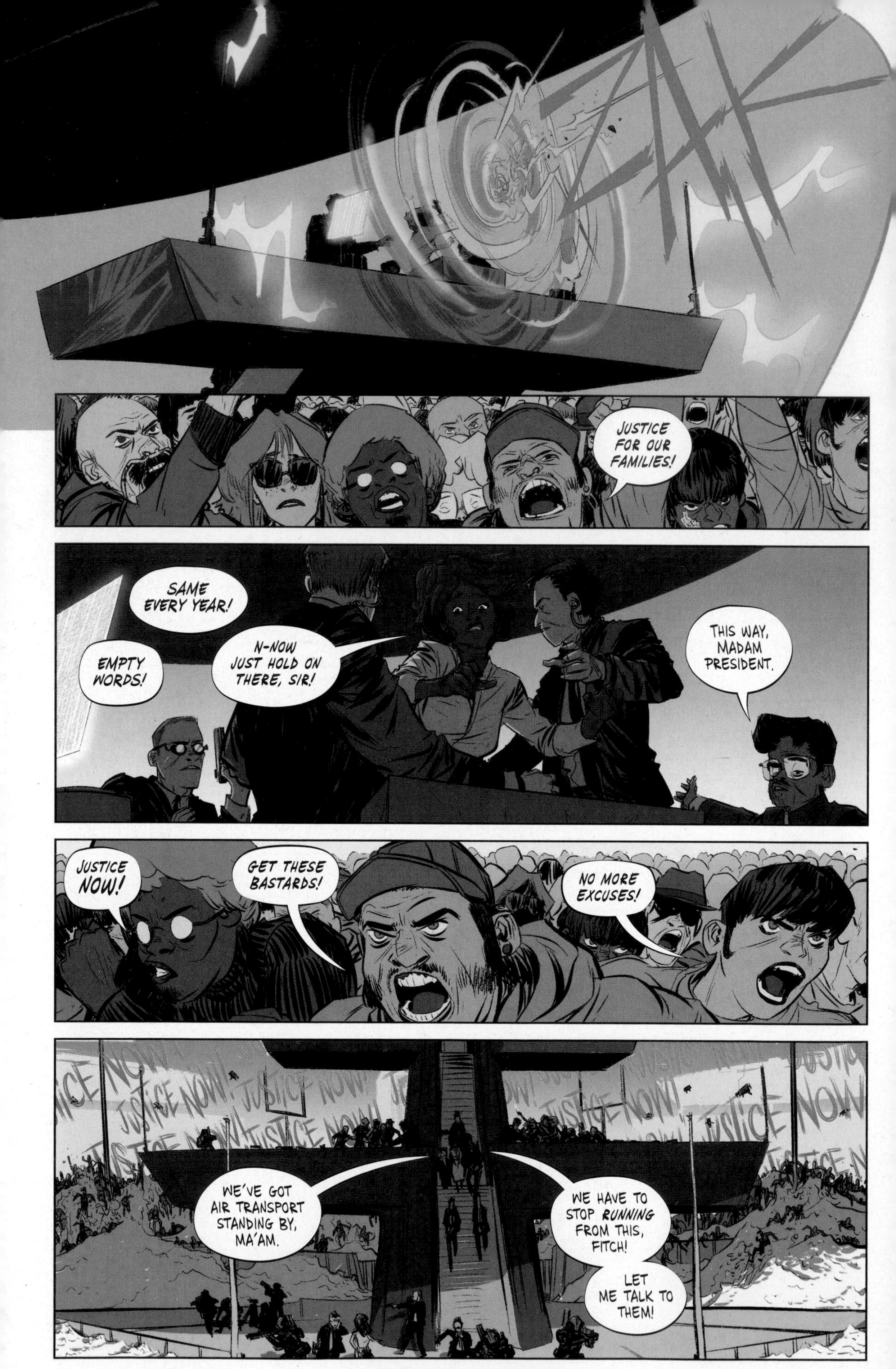
ZAK
JUSTICE FOR OUR FAMILIES!
SAME EVERY YEAR!
EMPTY WORDS!
N-NOW JUST HOLD ON THERE, SIR!
THIS WAY, MADAM PRESIDENT.
JUSTICE NOW!
GET THESE BASTARDS!
NO MORE EXCUSES!
JUSTICE NOW! JUSTICE NOW! JUSTICE NOW! JUSTICE NOW!
WE'VE GOT AIR TRANSPORT STANDING BY, MA'AM.
WE HAVE TO STOP *RUNNING* FROM THIS, FITCH!
LET ME TALK TO THEM!

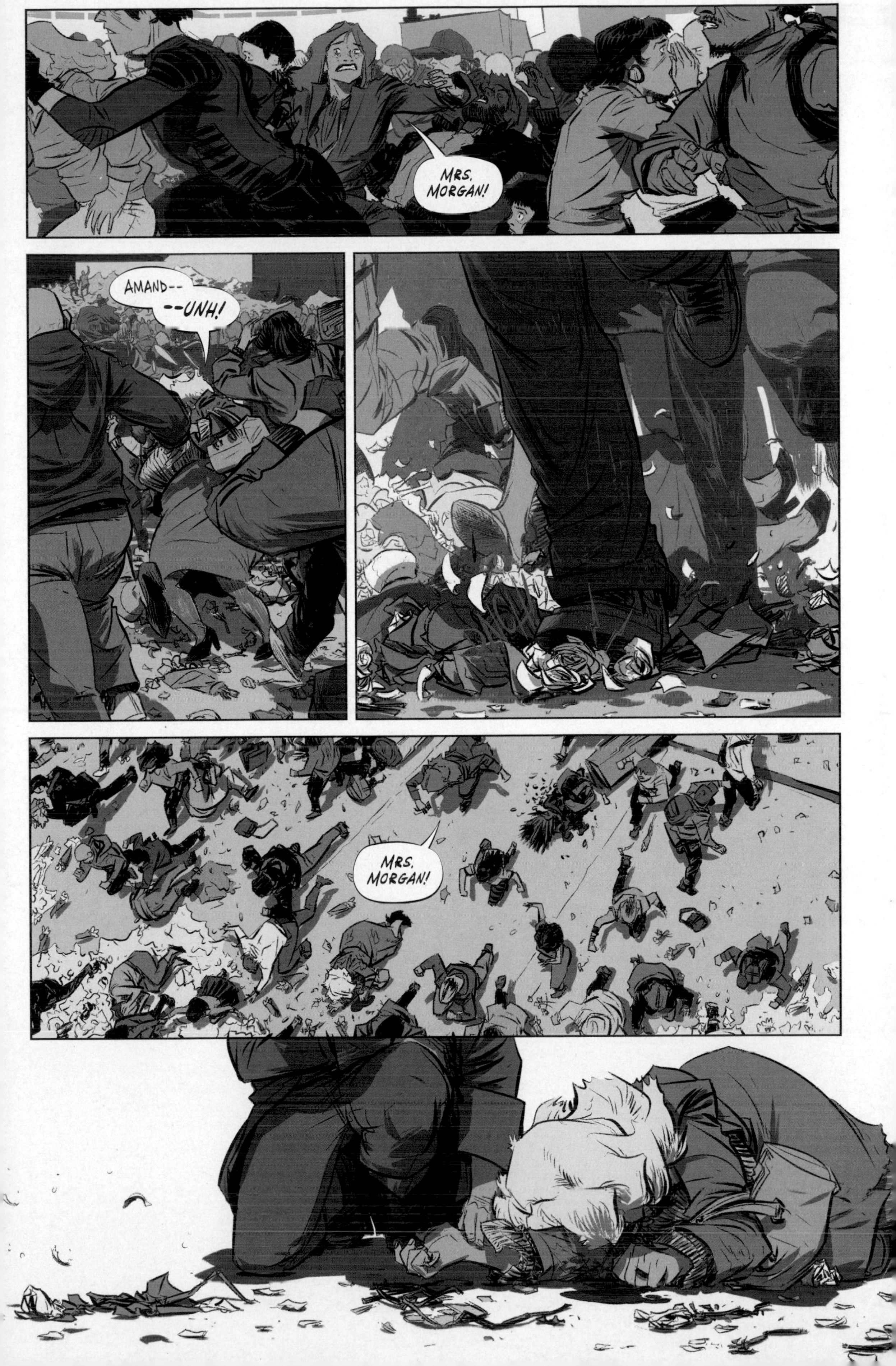
MRS. MORGAN!
AMAND--
--UNH!
MRS. MORGAN!

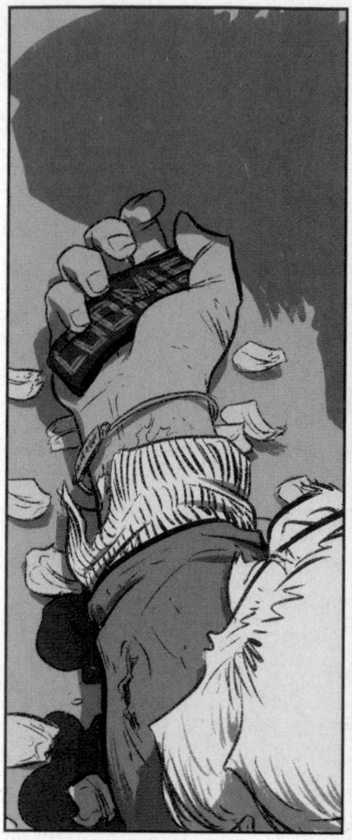

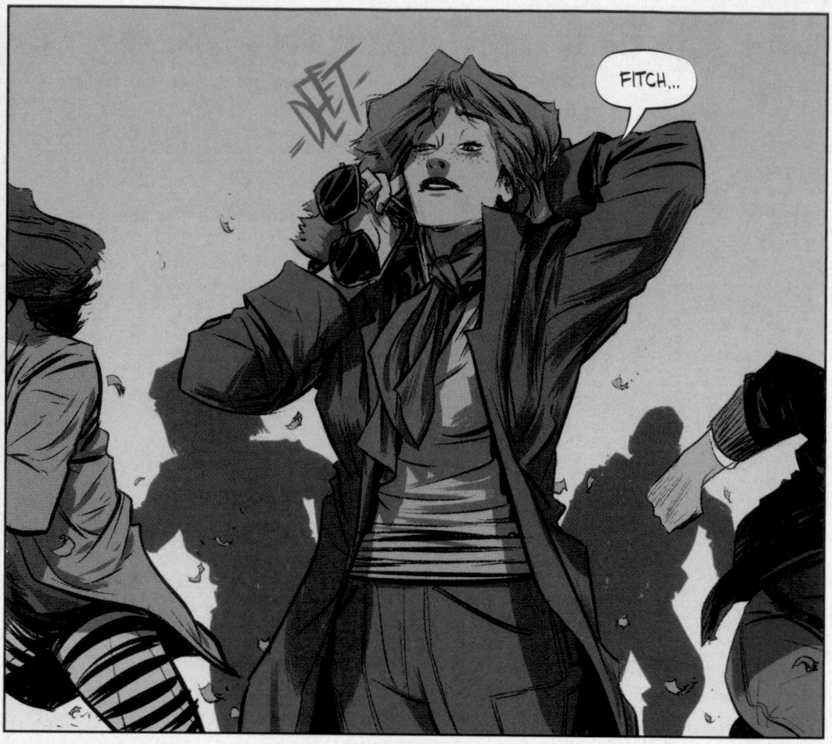
DEET
FITCH...

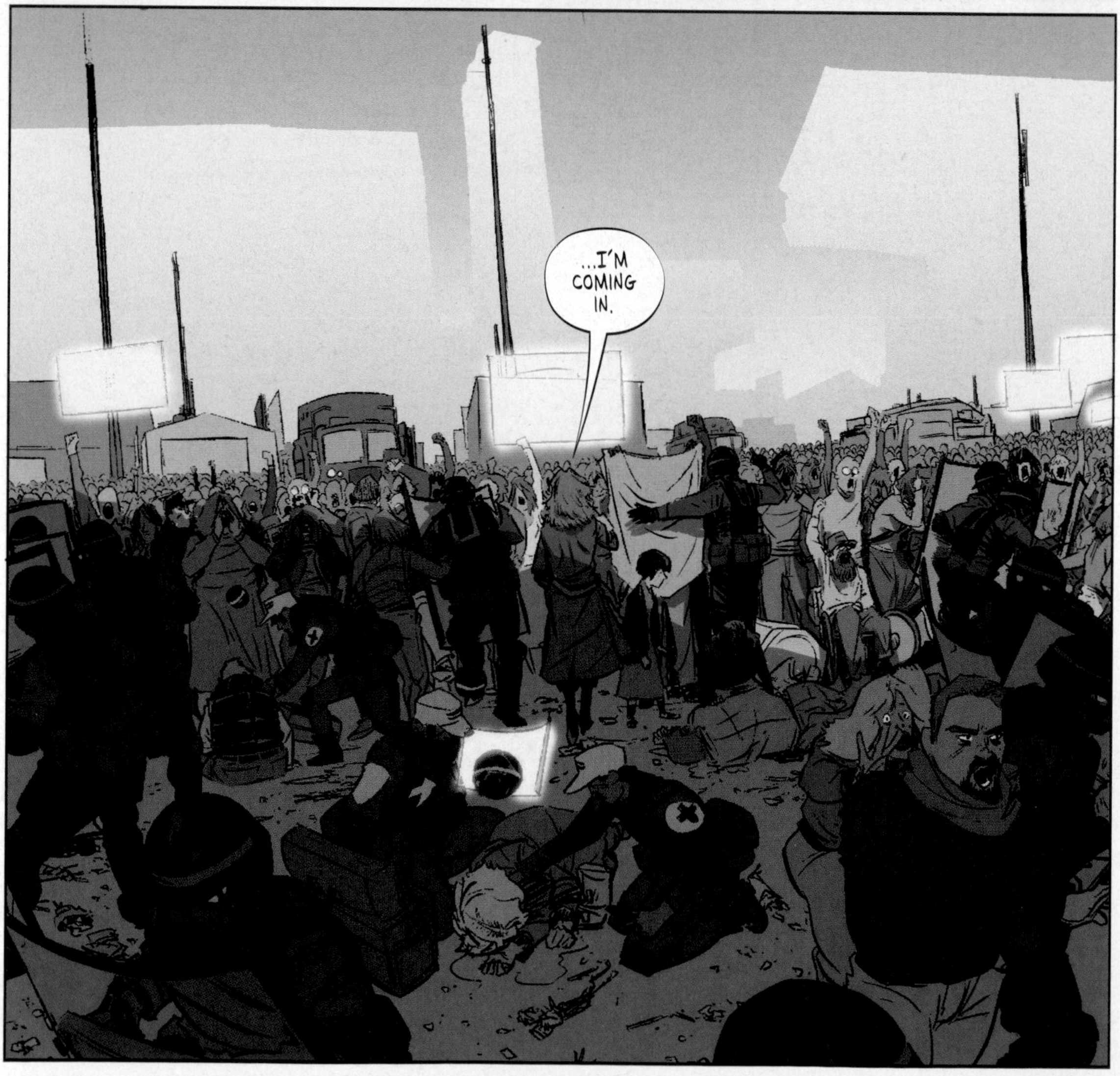
...I'M COMING IN.

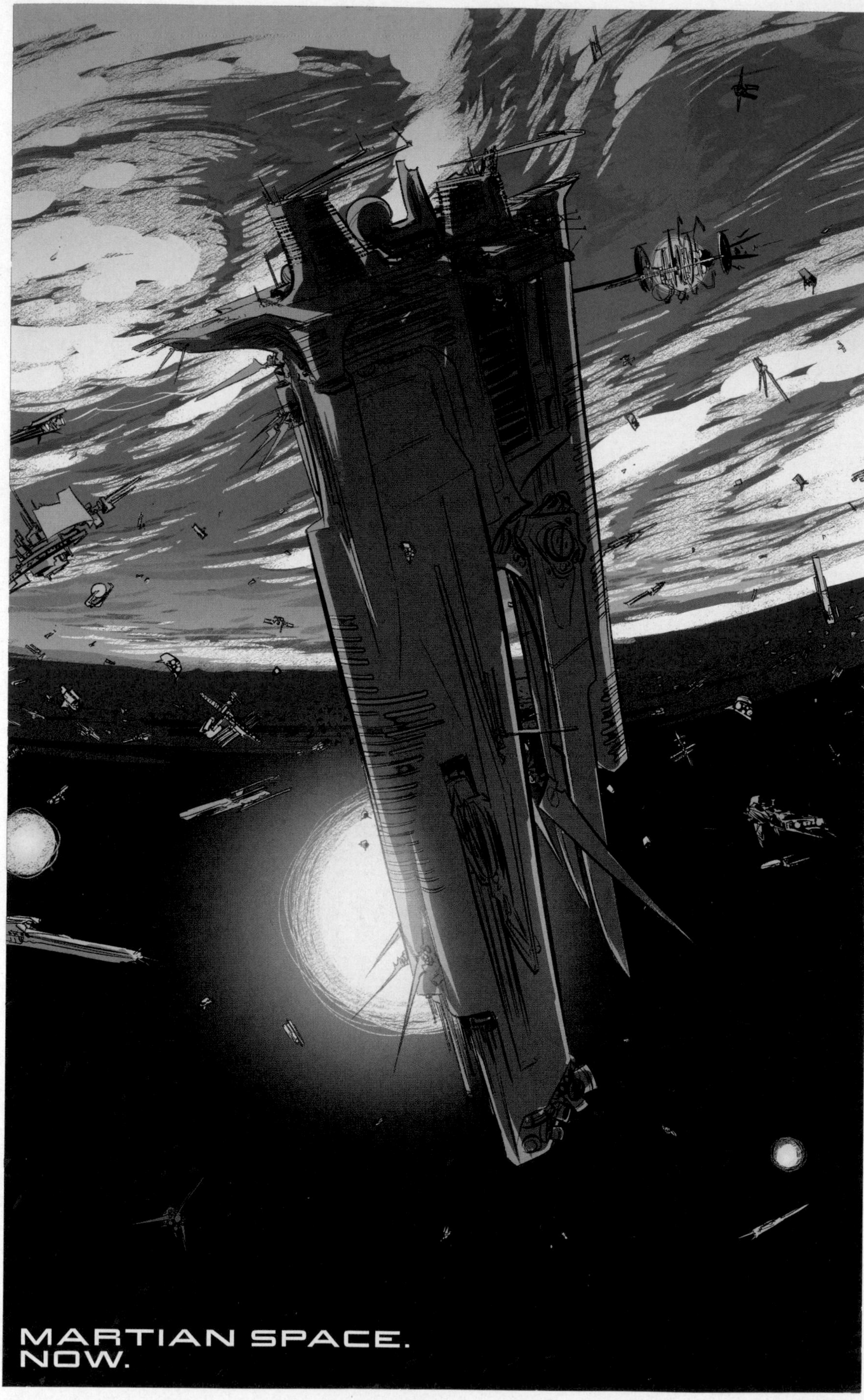
MARTIAN SPACE.
NOW.

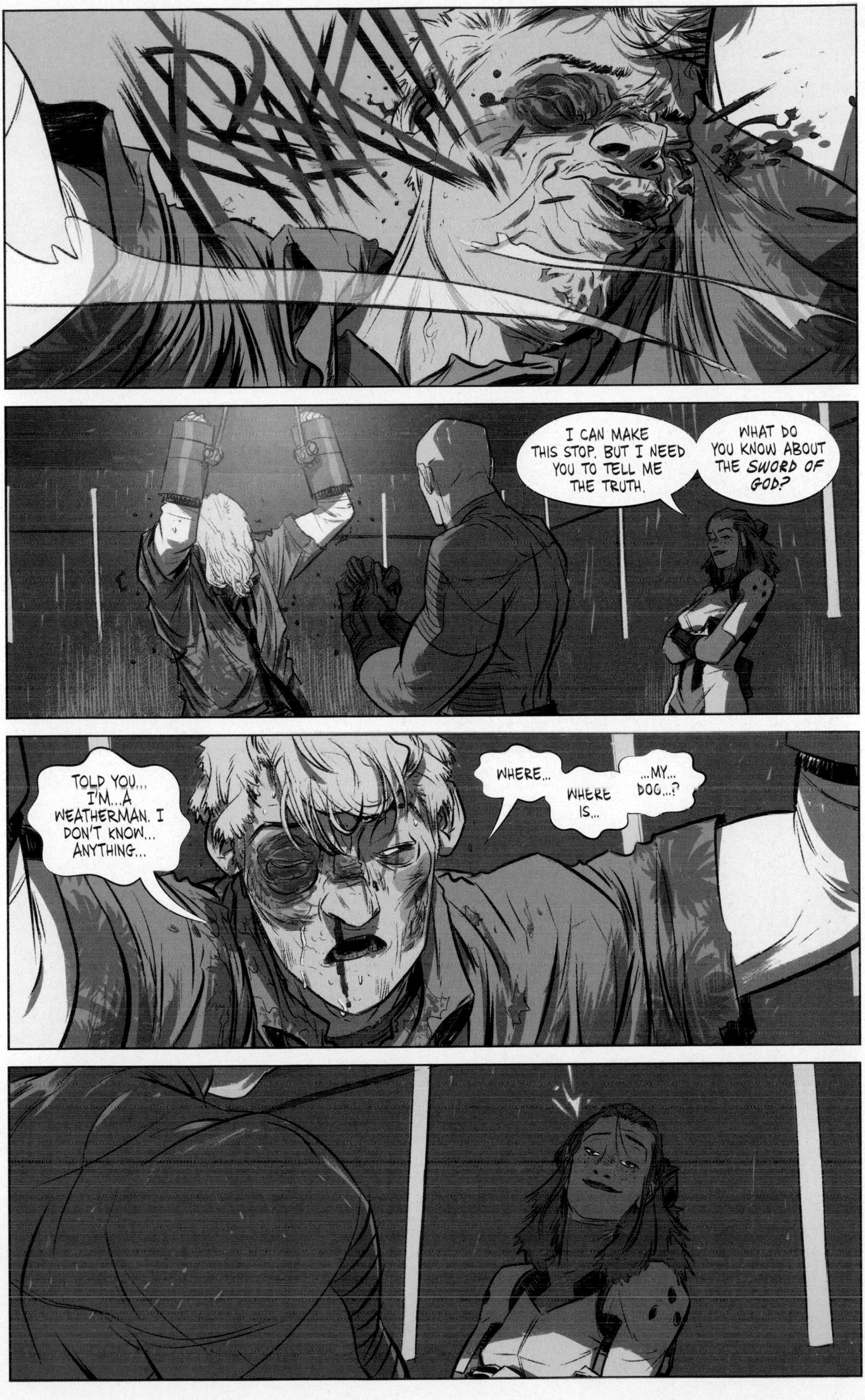
I CAN MAKE THIS STOP. BUT I NEED YOU TO TELL ME THE TRUTH.
WHAT DO YOU KNOW ABOUT THE *SWORD OF GOD?*
TOLD YOU... I'M...A WEATHERMAN. I DON'T KNOW... ANYTHING...
WHERE...
WHERE IS...
...MY... DOG...?

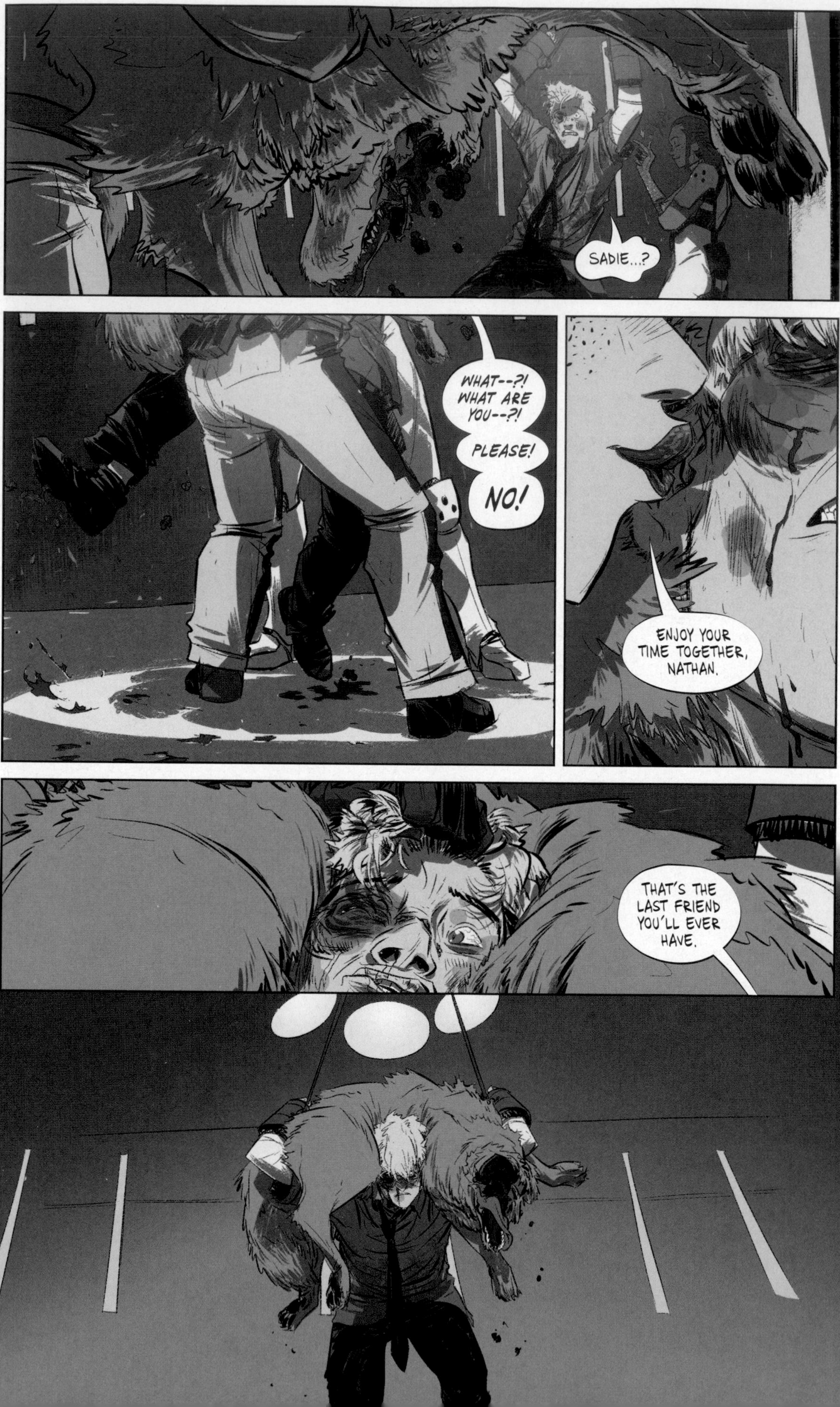
SADIE...?
WHAT--?! WHAT ARE YOU--?!
PLEASE!
NO!
ENJOY YOUR TIME TOGETHER, NATHAN.
THAT'S THE LAST FRIEND YOU'LL EVER HAVE.

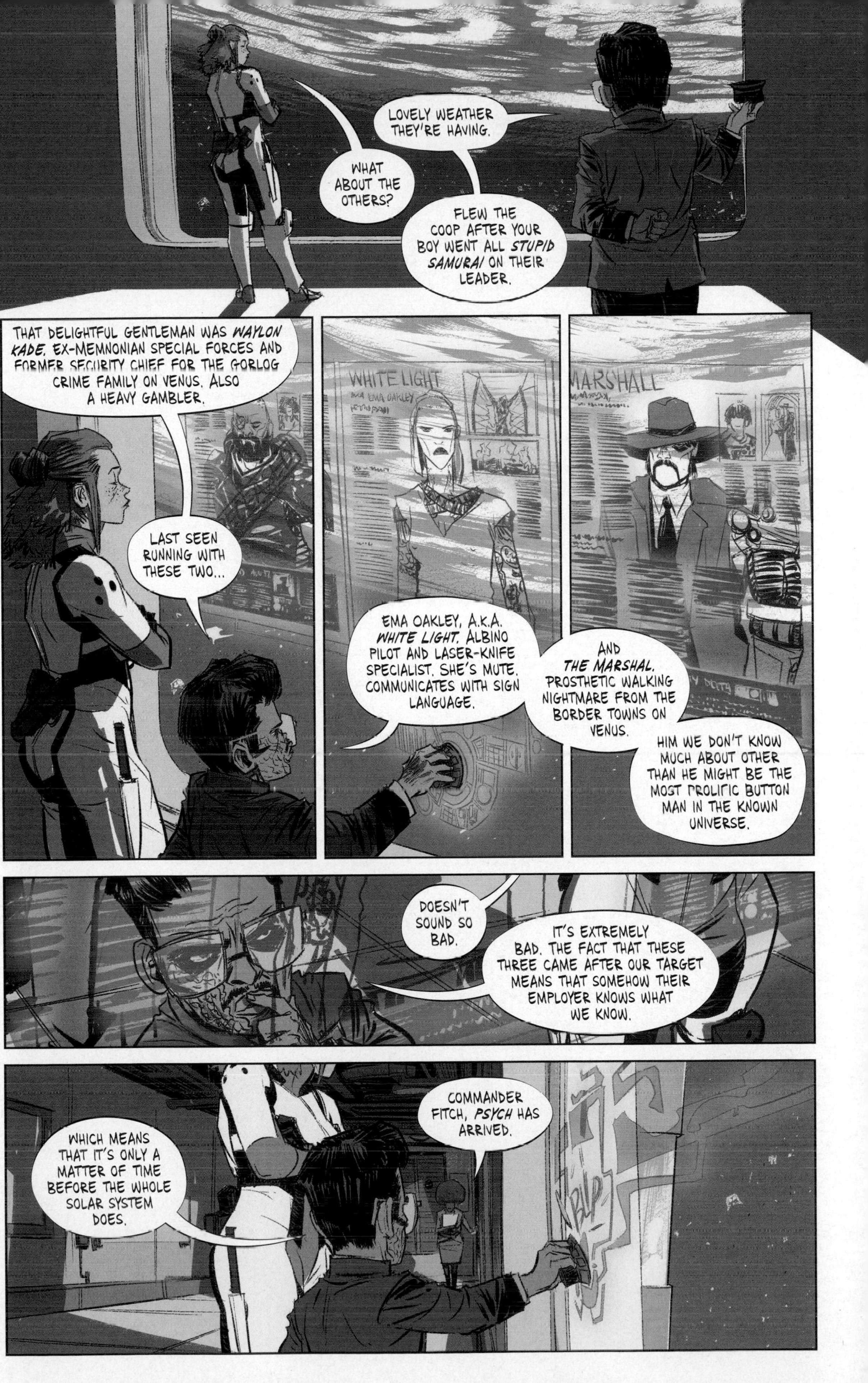

LOVELY WEATHER THEY'RE HAVING.
WHAT ABOUT THE OTHERS?
FLEW THE COOP AFTER YOUR BOY WENT ALL *STUPID SAMURAI* ON THEIR LEADER.
THAT DELIGHTFUL GENTLEMAN WAS *WAYLON KADE*, EX-MEMNONIAN SPECIAL FORCES AND FORMER SECURITY CHIEF FOR THE GORLOG CRIME FAMILY ON VENUS. ALSO A HEAVY GAMBLER.
LAST SEEN RUNNING WITH THESE TWO...
WHITE LIGHT
EMA OAKLEY, A.K.A. *WHITE LIGHT*, ALBINO PILOT AND LASER-KNIFE SPECIALIST. SHE'S MUTE. COMMUNICATES WITH SIGN LANGUAGE.
MARSHALL
AND *THE MARSHAL*, PROSTHETIC WALKING NIGHTMARE FROM THE BORDER TOWNS ON VENUS.
HIM WE DON'T KNOW MUCH ABOUT OTHER THAN HE MIGHT BE THE MOST PROLIFIC BUTTON MAN IN THE KNOWN UNIVERSE.
DOESN'T SOUND SO BAD.
IT'S EXTREMELY BAD. THE FACT THAT THESE THREE CAME AFTER OUR TARGET MEANS THAT SOMEHOW THEIR EMPLOYER KNOWS WHAT WE KNOW.
WHICH MEANS THAT IT'S ONLY A MATTER OF TIME BEFORE THE WHOLE SOLAR SYSTEM DOES.
COMMANDER FITCH, *PSYCH* HAS ARRIVED.
BLIP

SEE ME AFTER.

ON THE STOOL IS FINE.

EASY, PAL.

THIS WON'T HURT A BIT.

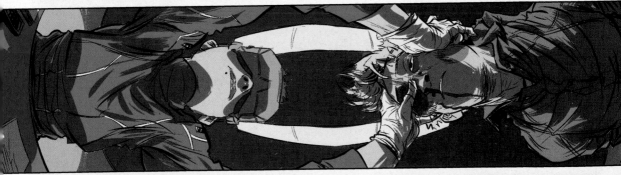

WELL?

HE'S TELLING THE TRUTH.

HIS MEMORIES GO BACK TO THE DAY AFTER THE ATTACK AND THEN...THERE'S NOTHING. IT'S LIKE HIS MIND HAS BEEN WIPED CLEAN.

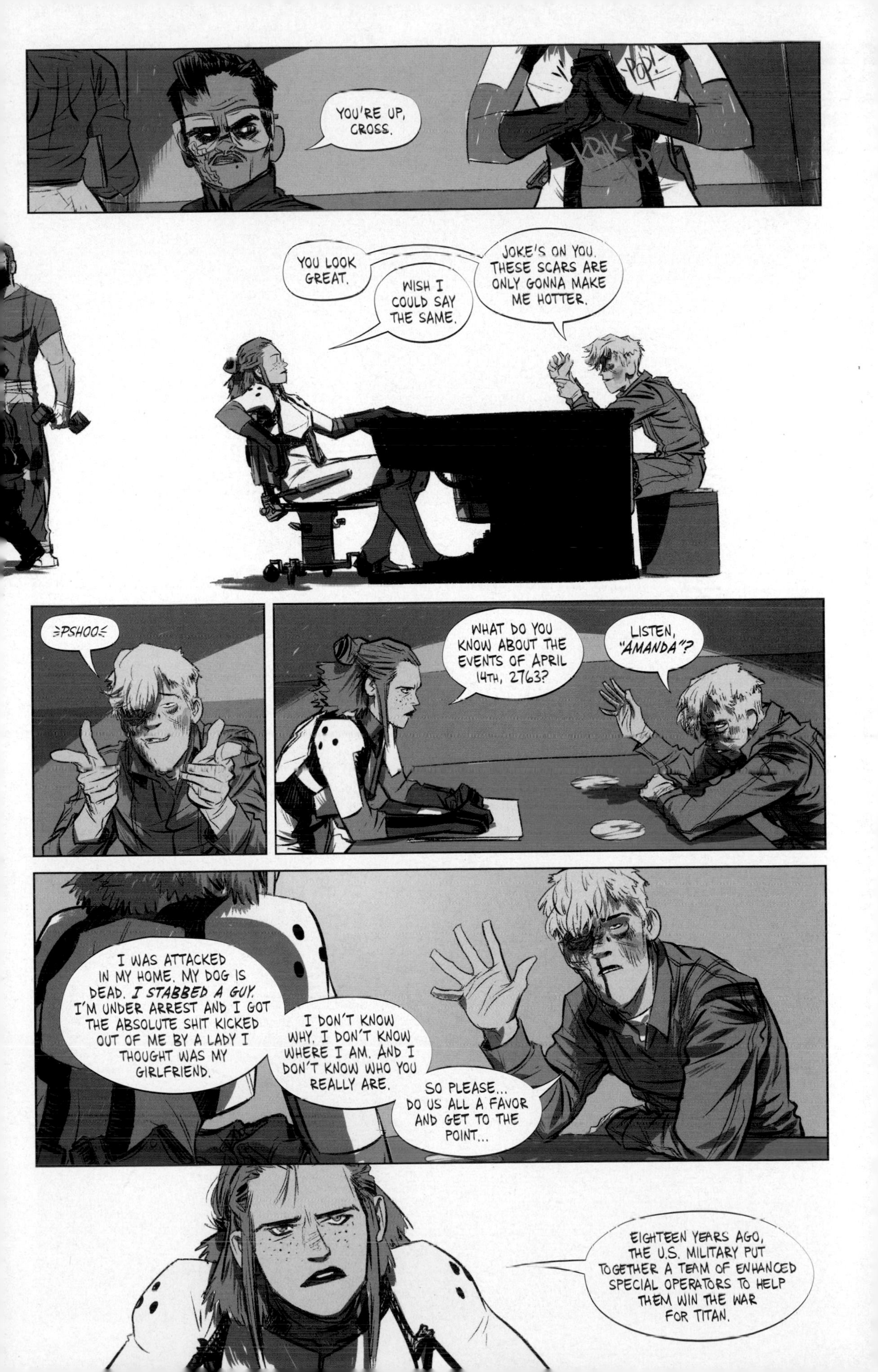

POP!
YOU'RE UP, CROSS.
KRAK
YOU LOOK GREAT.
WISH I COULD SAY THE SAME.
JOKE'S ON YOU. THESE SCARS ARE ONLY GONNA MAKE ME HOTTER.
PSHOO
WHAT DO YOU KNOW ABOUT THE EVENTS OF APRIL 14TH, 2763?
LISTEN, "AMANDA"?
I WAS ATTACKED IN MY HOME. MY DOG IS DEAD. I STABBED A GUY. I'M UNDER ARREST AND I GOT THE ABSOLUTE SHIT KICKED OUT OF ME BY A LADY I THOUGHT WAS MY GIRLFRIEND.
I DON'T KNOW WHY, I DON'T KNOW WHERE I AM. AND I DON'T KNOW WHO YOU REALLY ARE.
SO PLEASE... DO US ALL A FAVOR AND GET TO THE POINT...
EIGHTEEN YEARS AGO, THE U.S. MILITARY PUT TOGETHER A TEAM OF ENHANCED SPECIAL OPERATORS TO HELP THEM WIN THE WAR FOR TITAN.

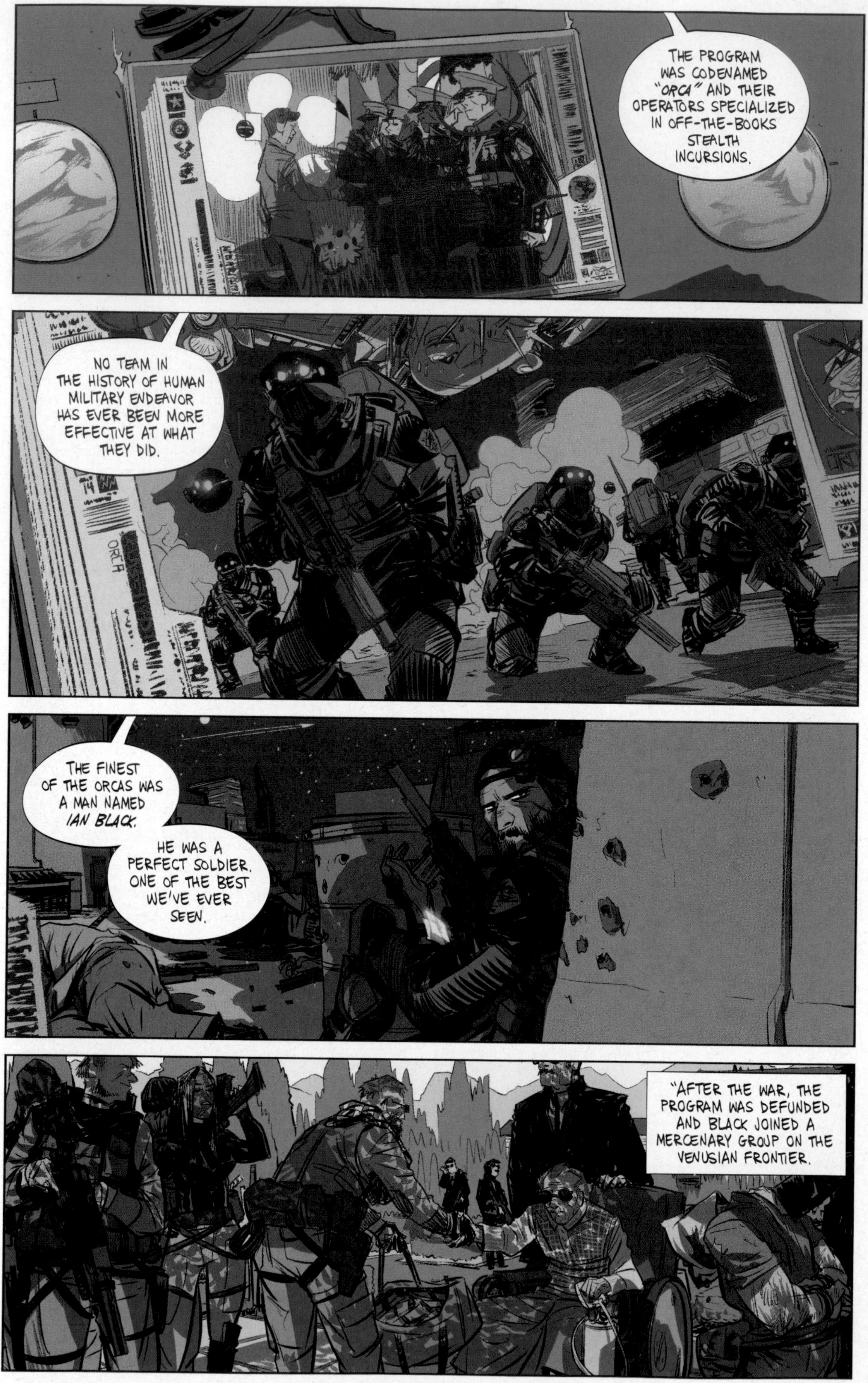
THE PROGRAM WAS CODENAMED "ORCA" AND THEIR OPERATORS SPECIALIZED IN OFF-THE-BOOKS STEALTH INCURSIONS.
NO TEAM IN THE HISTORY OF HUMAN MILITARY ENDEAVOR HAS EVER BEEN MORE EFFECTIVE AT WHAT THEY DID.
THE FINEST OF THE ORCAS WAS A MAN NAMED *IAN BLACK*.
HE WAS A PERFECT SOLDIER. ONE OF THE BEST WE'VE EVER SEEN.
"AFTER THE WAR, THE PROGRAM WAS DEFUNDED AND BLACK JOINED A MERCENARY GROUP ON THE VENUSIAN FRONTIER.

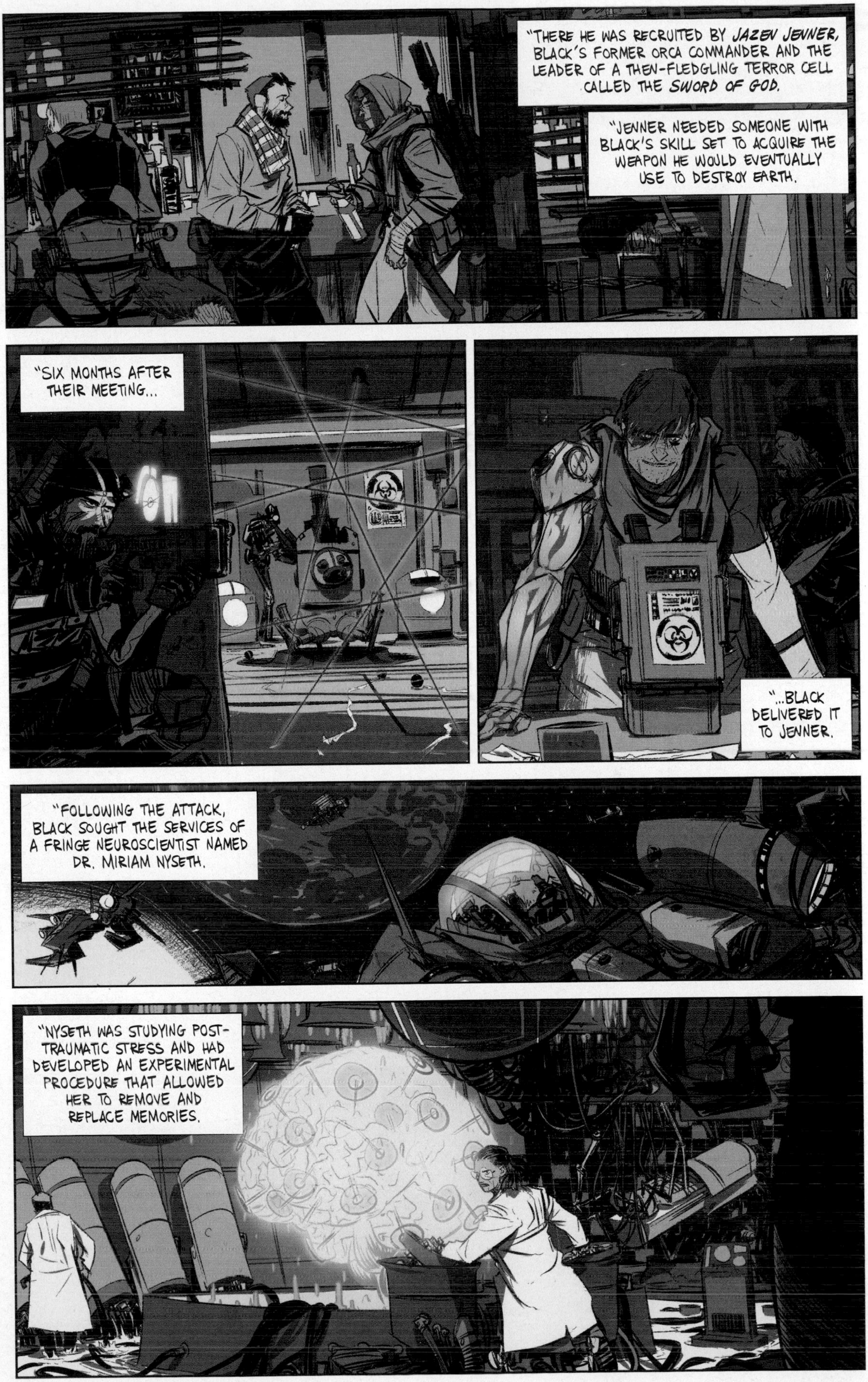
"THERE HE WAS RECRUITED BY JAZEN JENNER, BLACK'S FORMER ORCA COMMANDER AND THE LEADER OF A THEN-FLEDGLING TERROR CELL CALLED THE SWORD OF GOD.
"JENNER NEEDED SOMEONE WITH BLACK'S SKILL SET TO ACQUIRE THE WEAPON HE WOULD EVENTUALLY USE TO DESTROY EARTH.
"SIX MONTHS AFTER THEIR MEETING...
"...BLACK DELIVERED IT TO JENNER.
"FOLLOWING THE ATTACK, BLACK SOUGHT THE SERVICES OF A FRINGE NEUROSCIENTIST NAMED DR. MIRIAM NYSETH.
"NYSETH WAS STUDYING POST-TRAUMATIC STRESS AND HAD DEVELOPED AN EXPERIMENTAL PROCEDURE THAT ALLOWED HER TO REMOVE AND REPLACE MEMORIES.

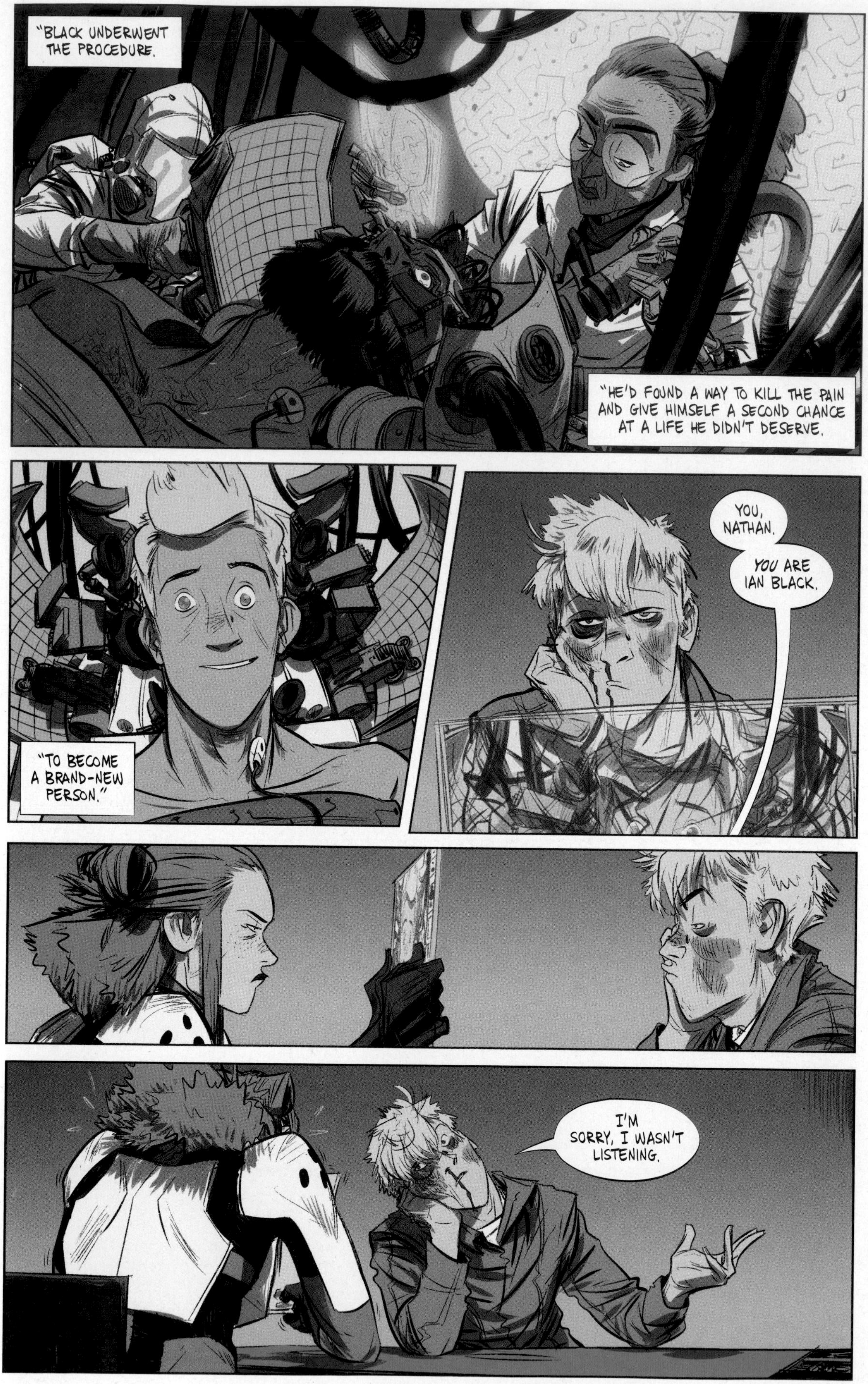
"BLACK UNDERWENT THE PROCEDURE.
"HE'D FOUND A WAY TO KILL THE PAIN AND GIVE HIMSELF A SECOND CHANCE AT A LIFE HE DIDN'T DESERVE.
"TO BECOME A BRAND-NEW PERSON."
YOU, NATHAN.
YOU ARE IAN BLACK.
I'M SORRY, I WASN'T LISTENING.

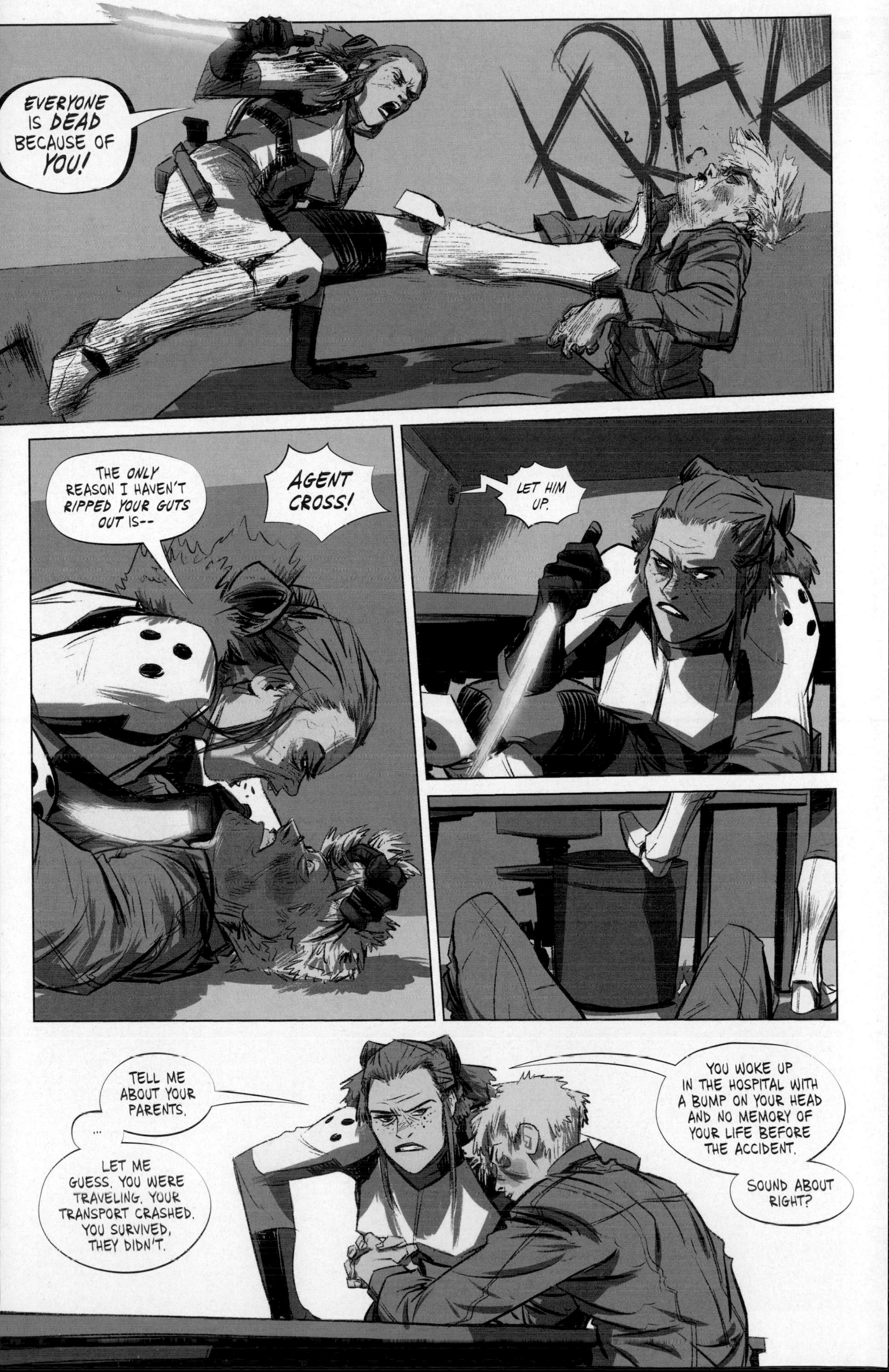
EVERYONE IS DEAD BECAUSE OF YOU!
KRAK
THE ONLY REASON I HAVEN'T RIPPED YOUR GUTS OUT IS--
AGENT CROSS!
LET HIM UP.
TELL ME ABOUT YOUR PARENTS.
...
LET ME GUESS. YOU WERE TRAVELING. YOUR TRANSPORT CRASHED. YOU SURVIVED, THEY DIDN'T.
YOU WOKE UP IN THE HOSPITAL WITH A BUMP ON YOUR HEAD AND NO MEMORY OF YOUR LIFE BEFORE THE ACCIDENT.
SOUND ABOUT RIGHT?

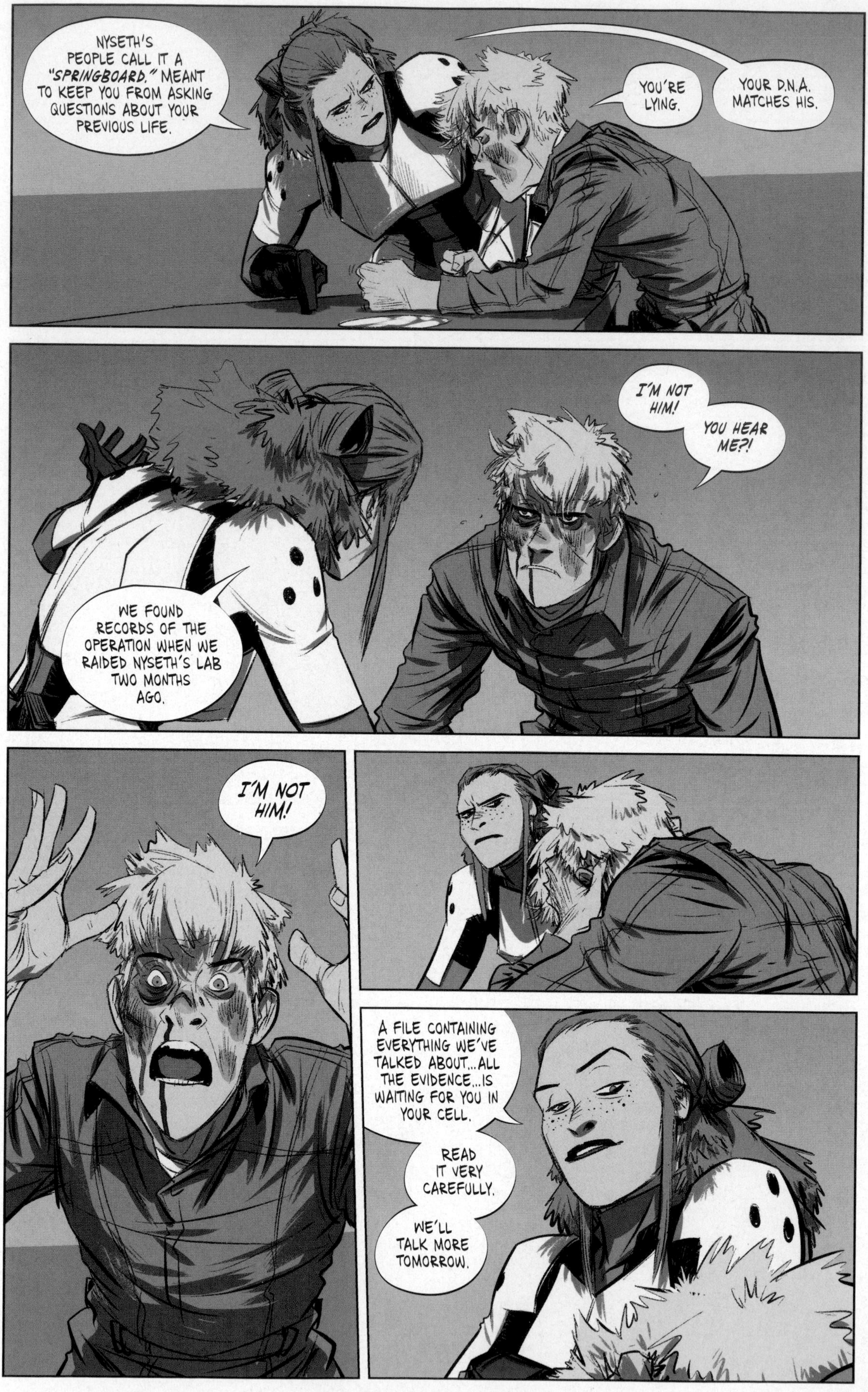
NYSETH'S PEOPLE CALL IT A "SPRINGBOARD." MEANT TO KEEP YOU FROM ASKING QUESTIONS ABOUT YOUR PREVIOUS LIFE.
YOU'RE LYING.
YOUR D.N.A. MATCHES HIS.
I'M NOT HIM!
YOU HEAR ME?!
WE FOUND RECORDS OF THE OPERATION WHEN WE RAIDED NYSETH'S LAB TWO MONTHS AGO.
I'M NOT HIM!
A FILE CONTAINING EVERYTHING WE'VE TALKED ABOUT...ALL THE EVIDENCE...IS WAITING FOR YOU IN YOUR CELL.
READ IT VERY CAREFULLY.
WE'LL TALK MORE TOMORROW.

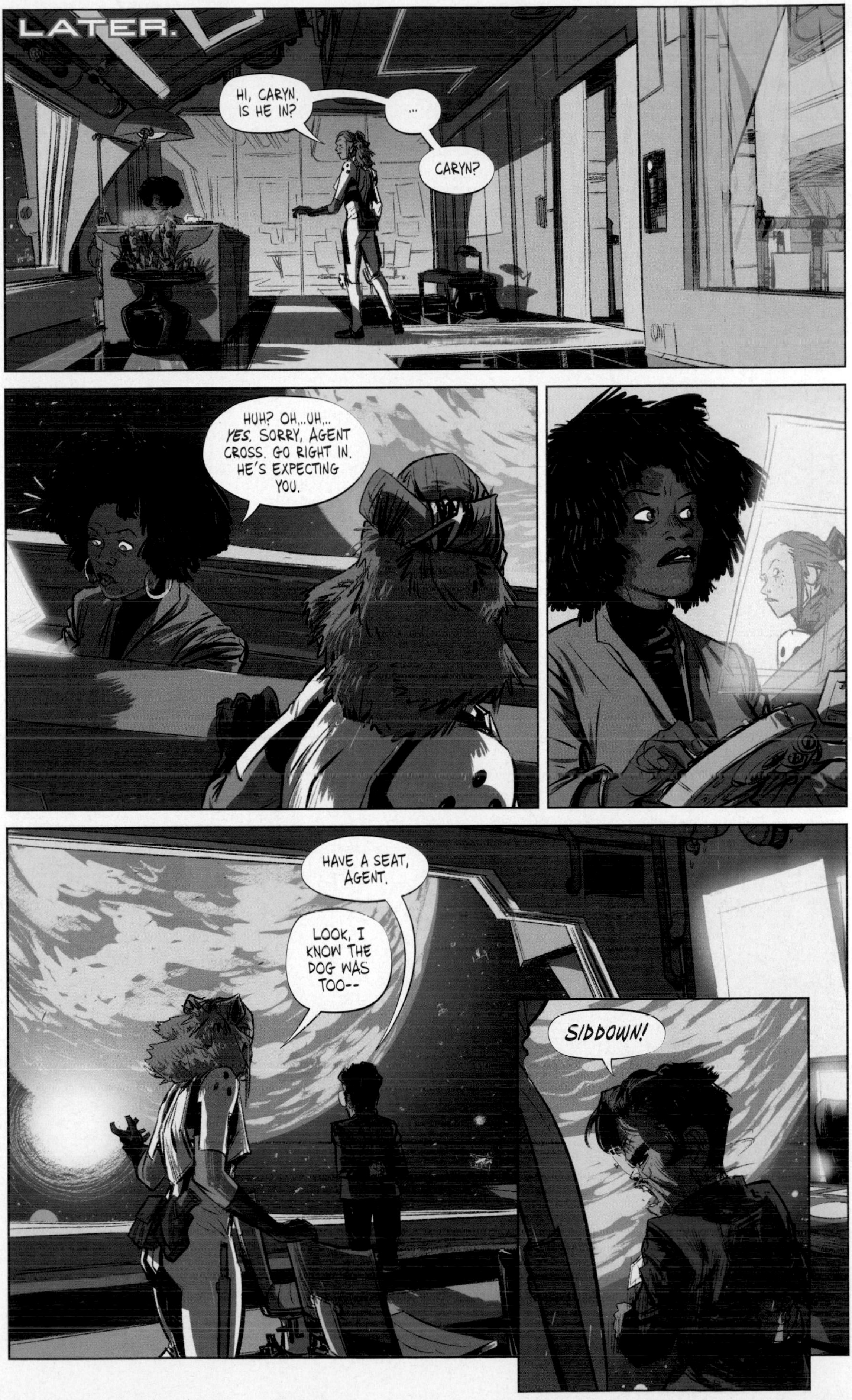
LATER.
HI, CARYN. IS HE IN?
...
CARYN?
HUH? OH...UH... YES. SORRY, AGENT CROSS. GO RIGHT IN. HE'S EXPECTING YOU.
HAVE A SEAT, AGENT.
LOOK, I KNOW THE DOG WAS TOO--
SIDDOWN!

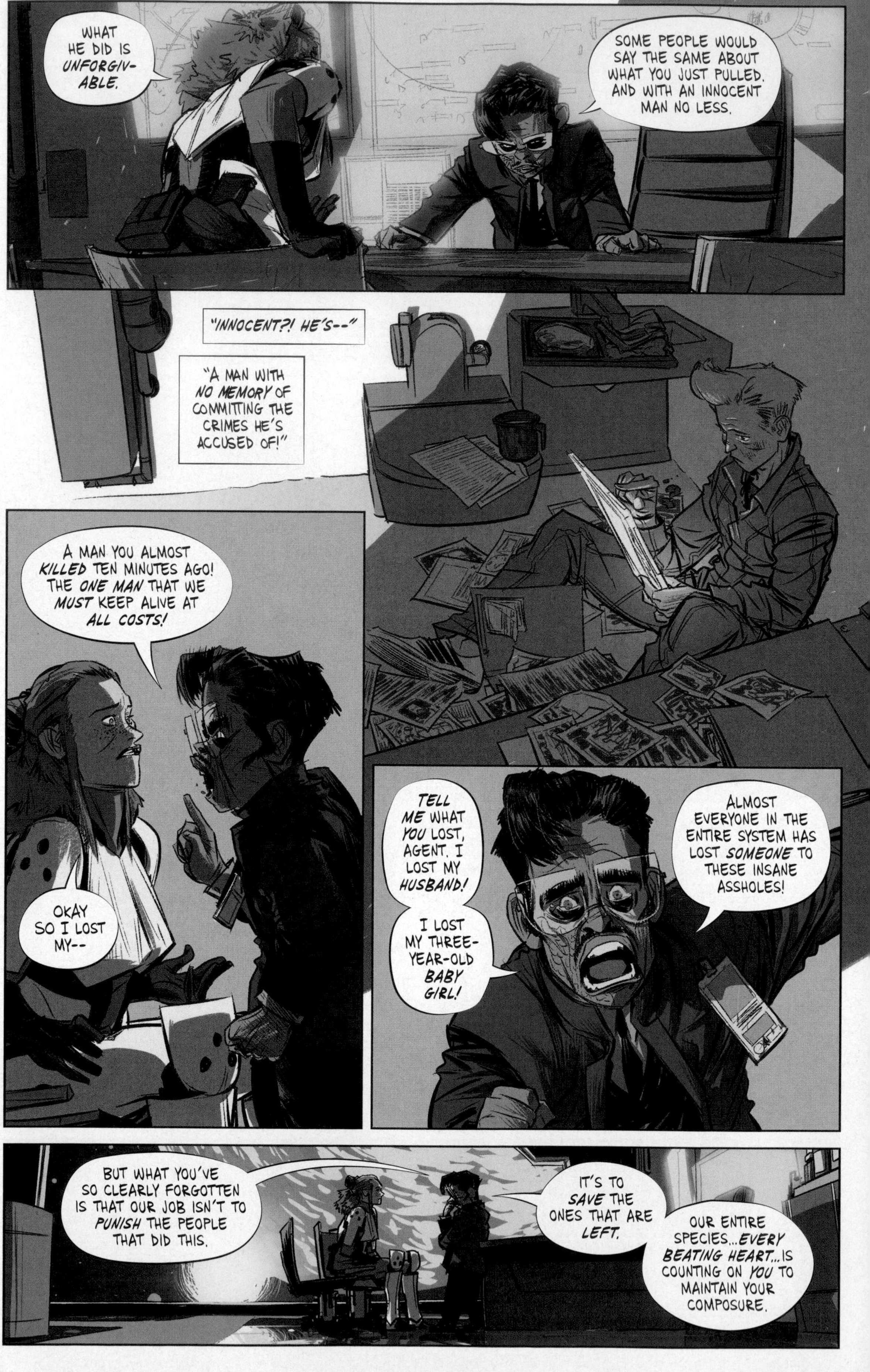
WHAT HE DID IS UNFORGIVABLE.
SOME PEOPLE WOULD SAY THE SAME ABOUT WHAT YOU JUST PULLED. AND WITH AN INNOCENT MAN NO LESS.
"INNOCENT?! HE'S--"
"A MAN WITH NO MEMORY OF COMMITTING THE CRIMES HE'S ACCUSED OF!"
A MAN YOU ALMOST KILLED TEN MINUTES AGO! THE ONE MAN THAT WE MUST KEEP ALIVE AT ALL COSTS!
OKAY SO I LOST MY--
TELL ME WHAT YOU LOST, AGENT. I LOST MY HUSBAND!
I LOST MY THREE-YEAR-OLD BABY GIRL!
ALMOST EVERYONE IN THE ENTIRE SYSTEM HAS LOST SOMEONE TO THESE INSANE ASSHOLES!
BUT WHAT YOU'VE SO CLEARLY FORGOTTEN IS THAT OUR JOB ISN'T TO PUNISH THE PEOPLE THAT DID THIS.
IT'S TO SAVE THE ONES THAT ARE LEFT.
OUR ENTIRE SPECIES...EVERY BEATING HEART...IS COUNTING ON YOU TO MAINTAIN YOUR COMPOSURE.

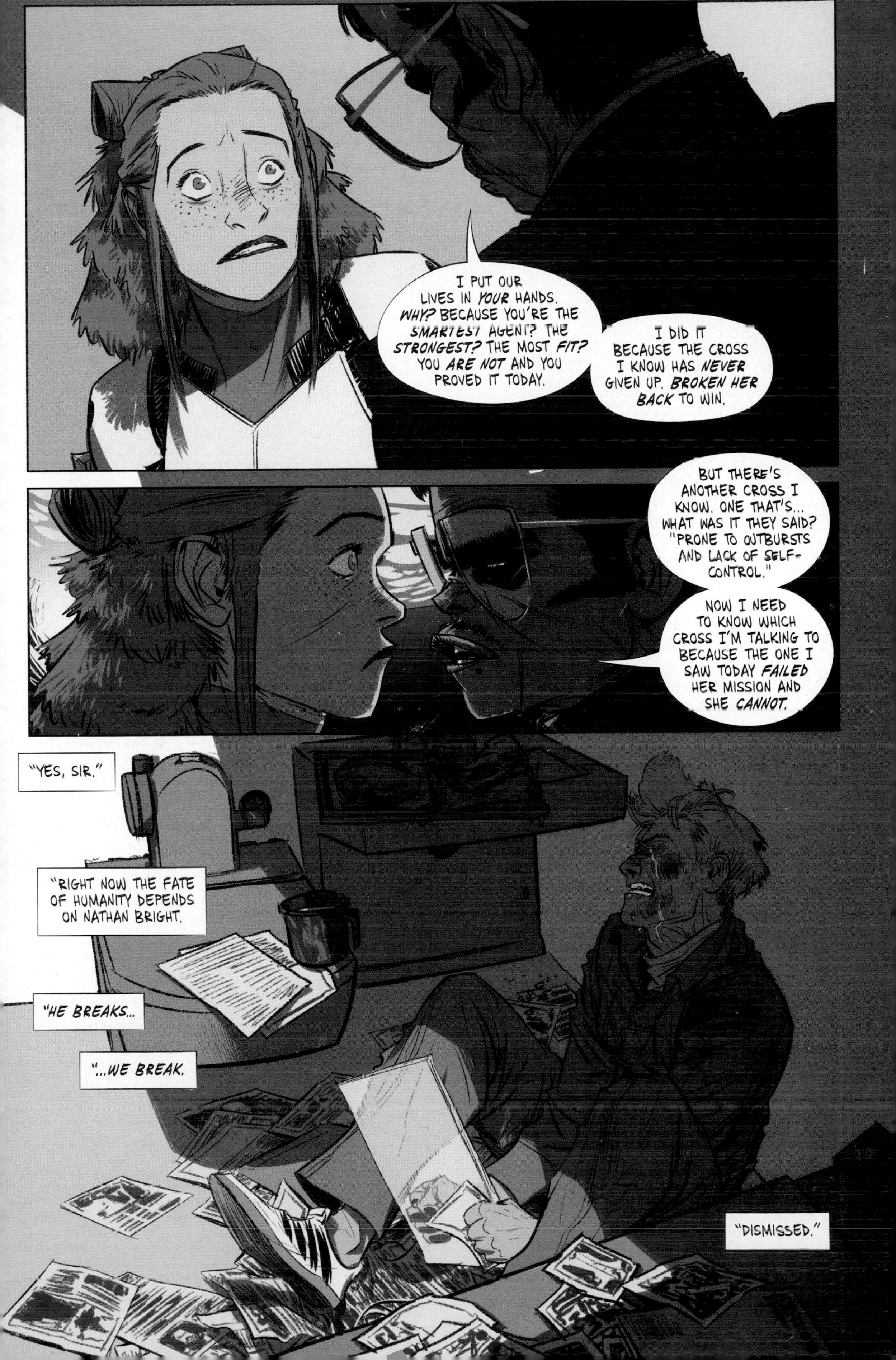
I PUT OUR LIVES IN YOUR HANDS. WHY? BECAUSE YOU'RE THE SMARTEST AGENT? THE STRONGEST? THE MOST FIT? YOU ARE NOT AND YOU PROVED IT TODAY.
I DID IT BECAUSE THE CROSS I KNOW HAS NEVER GIVEN UP. BROKEN HER BACK TO WIN.
BUT THERE'S ANOTHER CROSS I KNOW, ONE THAT'S... WHAT WAS IT THEY SAID? "PRONE TO OUTBURSTS AND LACK OF SELF-CONTROL."
NOW I NEED TO KNOW WHICH CROSS I'M TALKING TO BECAUSE THE ONE I SAW TODAY FAILED HER MISSION AND SHE CANNOT.
"YES, SIR."
"RIGHT NOW THE FATE OF HUMANITY DEPENDS ON NATHAN BRIGHT.
"HE BREAKS...
"...WE BREAK.
"DISMISSED."

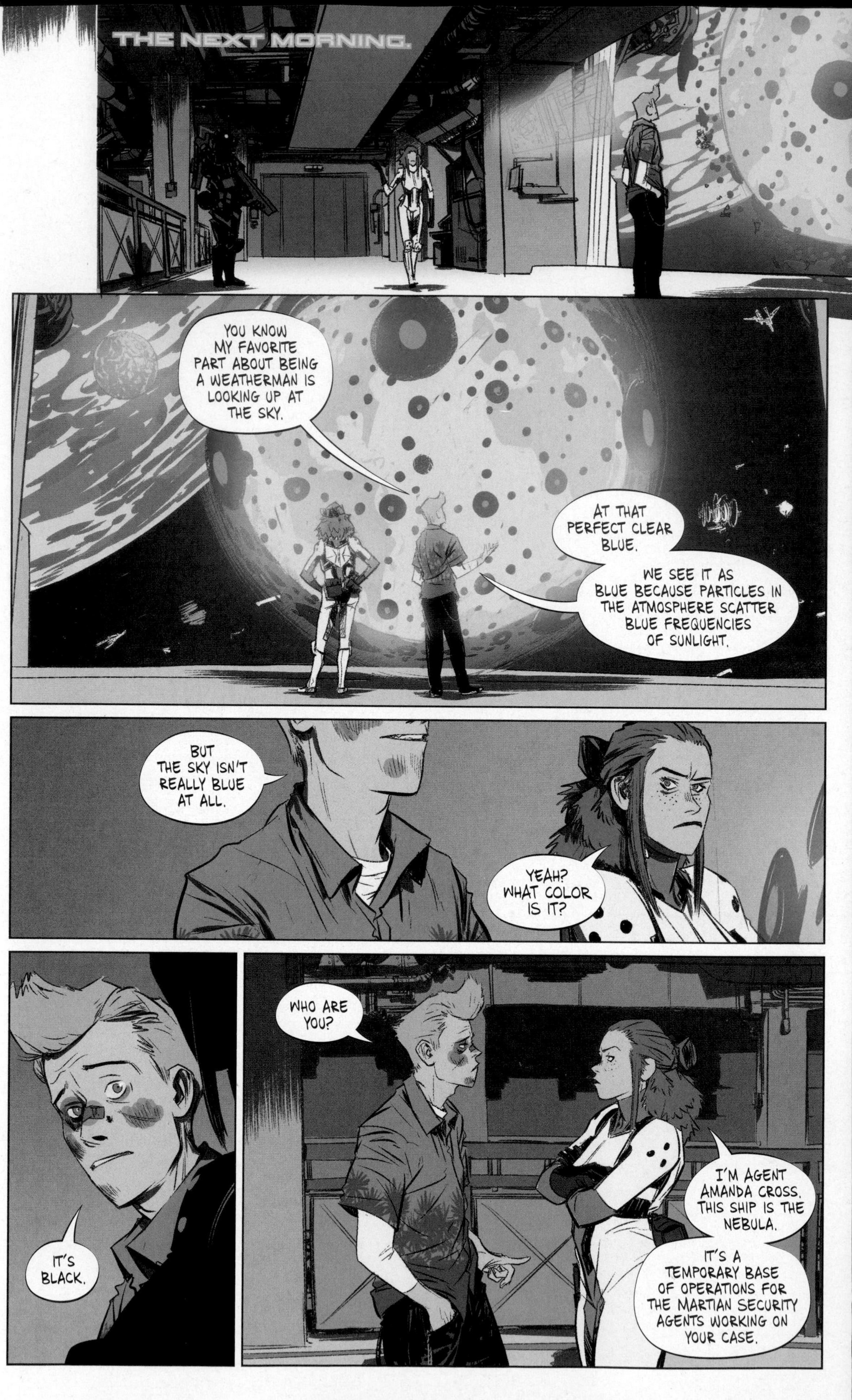
THE NEXT MORNING.
YOU KNOW MY FAVORITE PART ABOUT BEING A WEATHERMAN IS LOOKING UP AT THE SKY.
AT THAT PERFECT CLEAR BLUE.
WE SEE IT AS BLUE BECAUSE PARTICLES IN THE ATMOSPHERE SCATTER BLUE FREQUENCIES OF SUNLIGHT.
BUT THE SKY ISN'T REALLY BLUE AT ALL.
YEAH? WHAT COLOR IS IT?
IT'S BLACK.
WHO ARE YOU?
I'M AGENT AMANDA CROSS. THIS SHIP IS THE NEBULA.
IT'S A TEMPORARY BASE OF OPERATIONS FOR THE MARTIAN SECURITY AGENTS WORKING ON YOUR CASE.

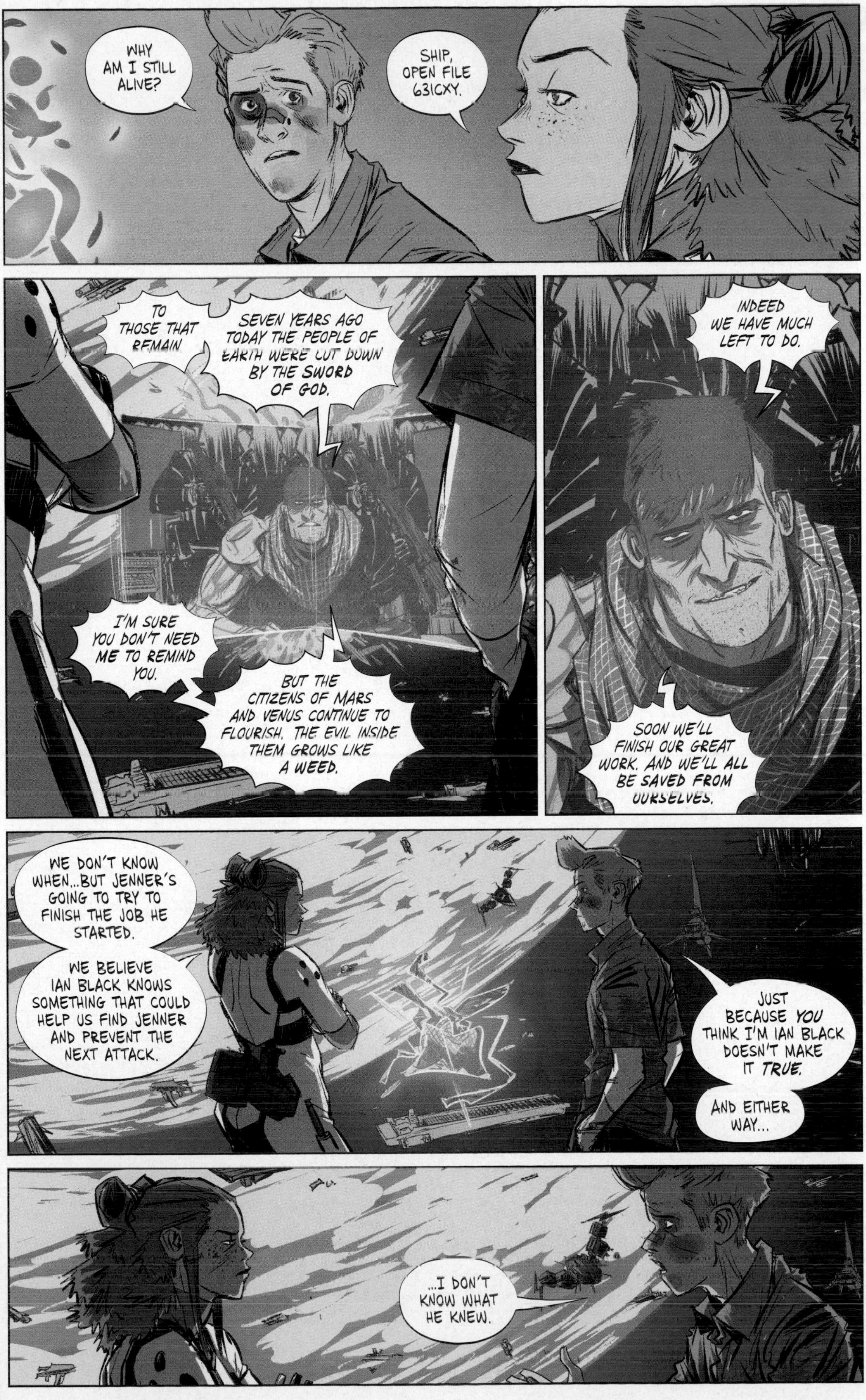
WHY AM I STILL ALIVE?
SHIP, OPEN FILE 631CXY.
TO THOSE THAT REMAIN.
SEVEN YEARS AGO TODAY THE PEOPLE OF EARTH WERE CUT DOWN BY THE SWORD OF GOD.
I'M SURE YOU DON'T NEED ME TO REMIND YOU.
BUT THE CITIZENS OF MARS AND VENUS CONTINUE TO FLOURISH. THE EVIL INSIDE THEM GROWS LIKE A WEED.
INDEED WE HAVE MUCH LEFT TO DO.
SOON WE'LL FINISH OUR GREAT WORK. AND WE'LL ALL BE SAVED FROM OURSELVES.
WE DON'T KNOW WHEN...BUT JENNER'S GOING TO TRY TO FINISH THE JOB HE STARTED.
WE BELIEVE IAN BLACK KNOWS SOMETHING THAT COULD HELP US FIND JENNER AND PREVENT THE NEXT ATTACK.
JUST BECAUSE YOU THINK I'M IAN BLACK DOESN'T MAKE IT TRUE.
AND EITHER WAY...
...I DON'T KNOW WHAT HE KNEW.

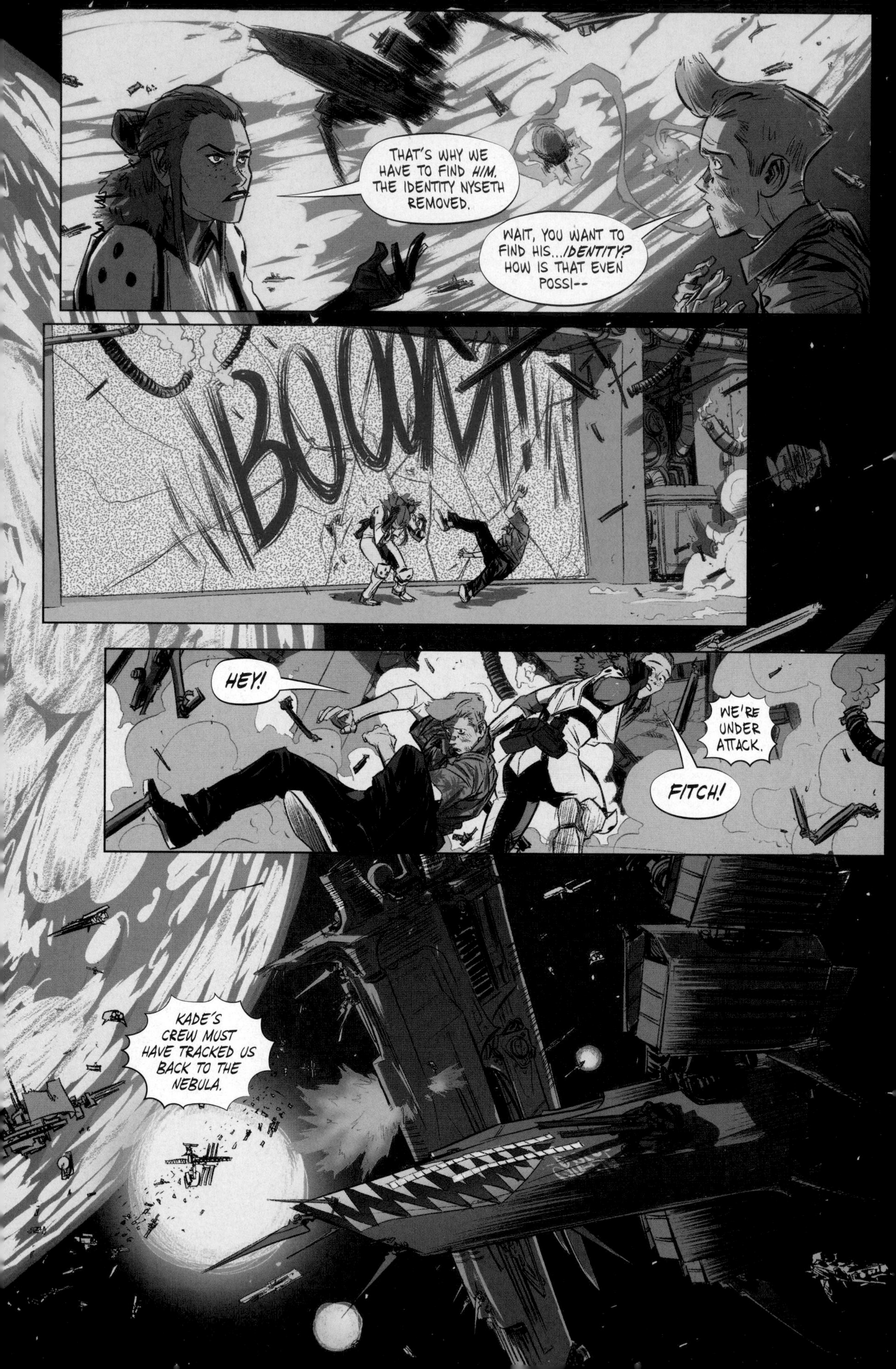
THAT'S WHY WE HAVE TO FIND *HIM*. THE IDENTITY NYSETH REMOVED.
WAIT, YOU WANT TO FIND HIS...*IDENTITY?* HOW IS THAT EVEN POSSI--
BOOOM!!
HEY!
WE'RE UNDER ATTACK.
FITCH!
KADE'S CREW MUST HAVE TRACKED US BACK TO THE NEBULA.

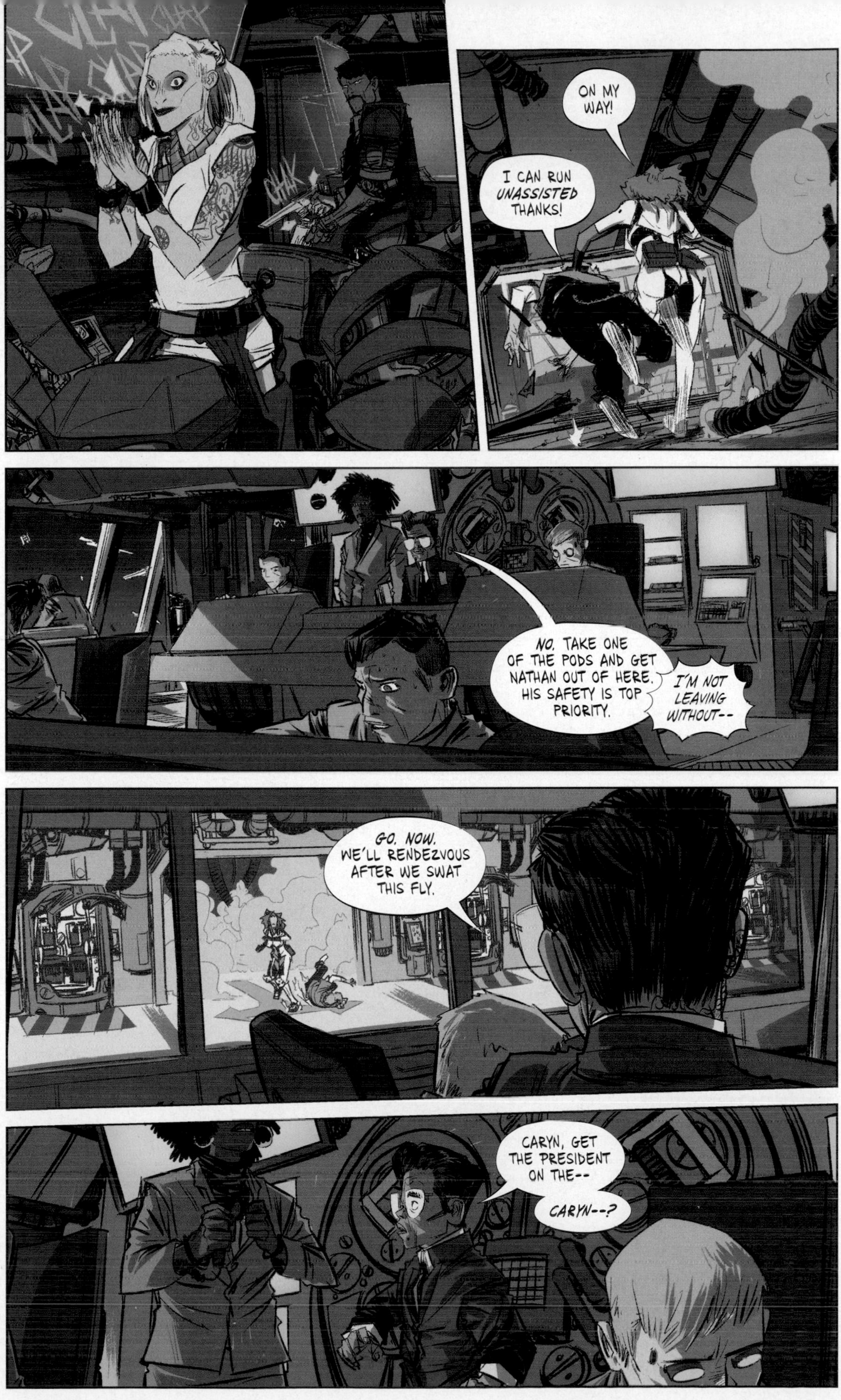
CHAK
ON MY WAY!
I CAN RUN UNASSISTED THANKS!
NO. TAKE ONE OF THE PODS AND GET NATHAN OUT OF HERE. HIS SAFETY IS TOP PRIORITY.
I'M NOT LEAVING WITHOUT--
GO. NOW. WE'LL RENDEZVOUS AFTER WE SWAT THIS FLY.
CARYN, GET THE PRESIDENT ON THE--
CARYN--?

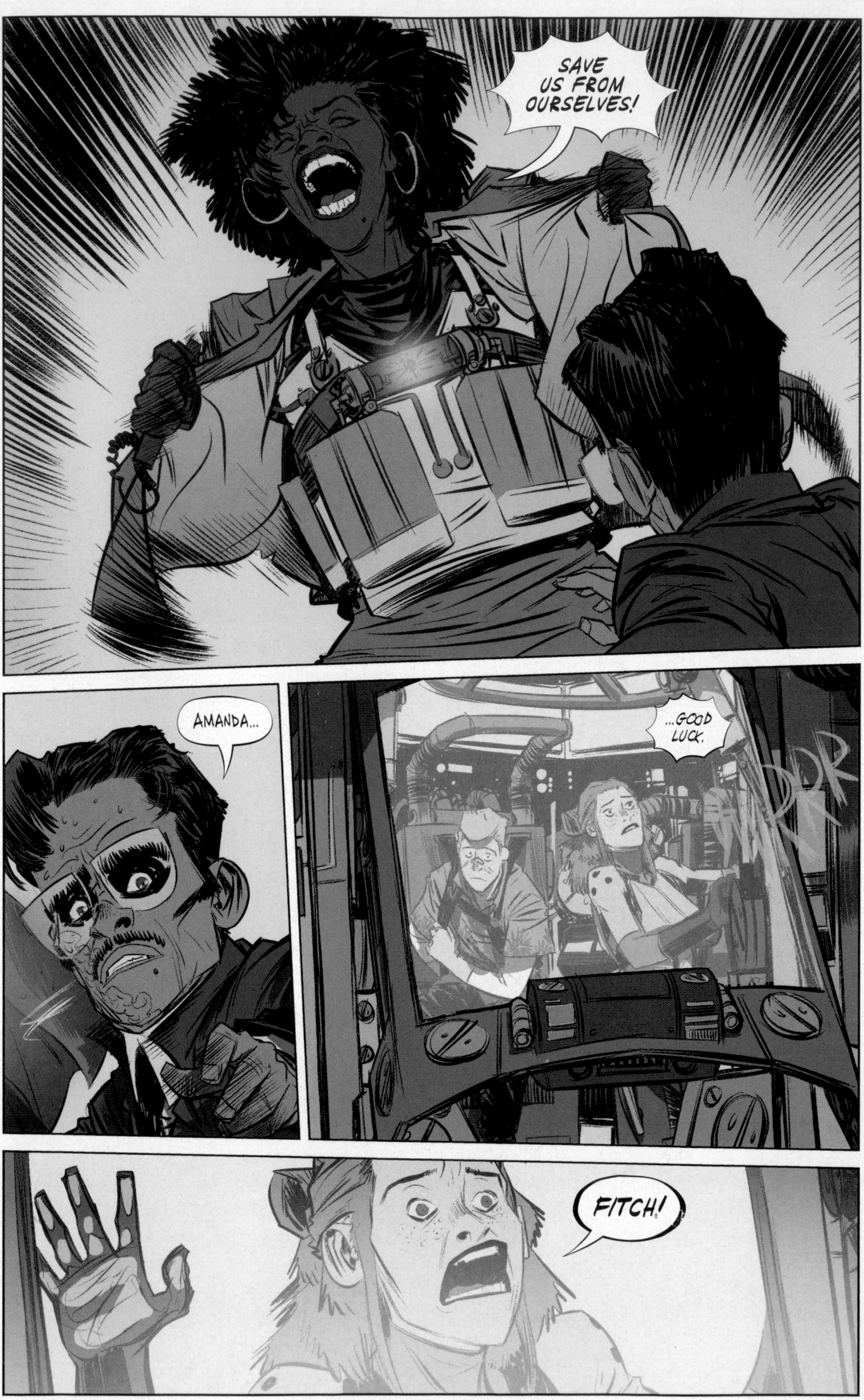
SAVE US FROM OURSELVES!
AMANDA...
...GOOD LUCK.
FITCH!

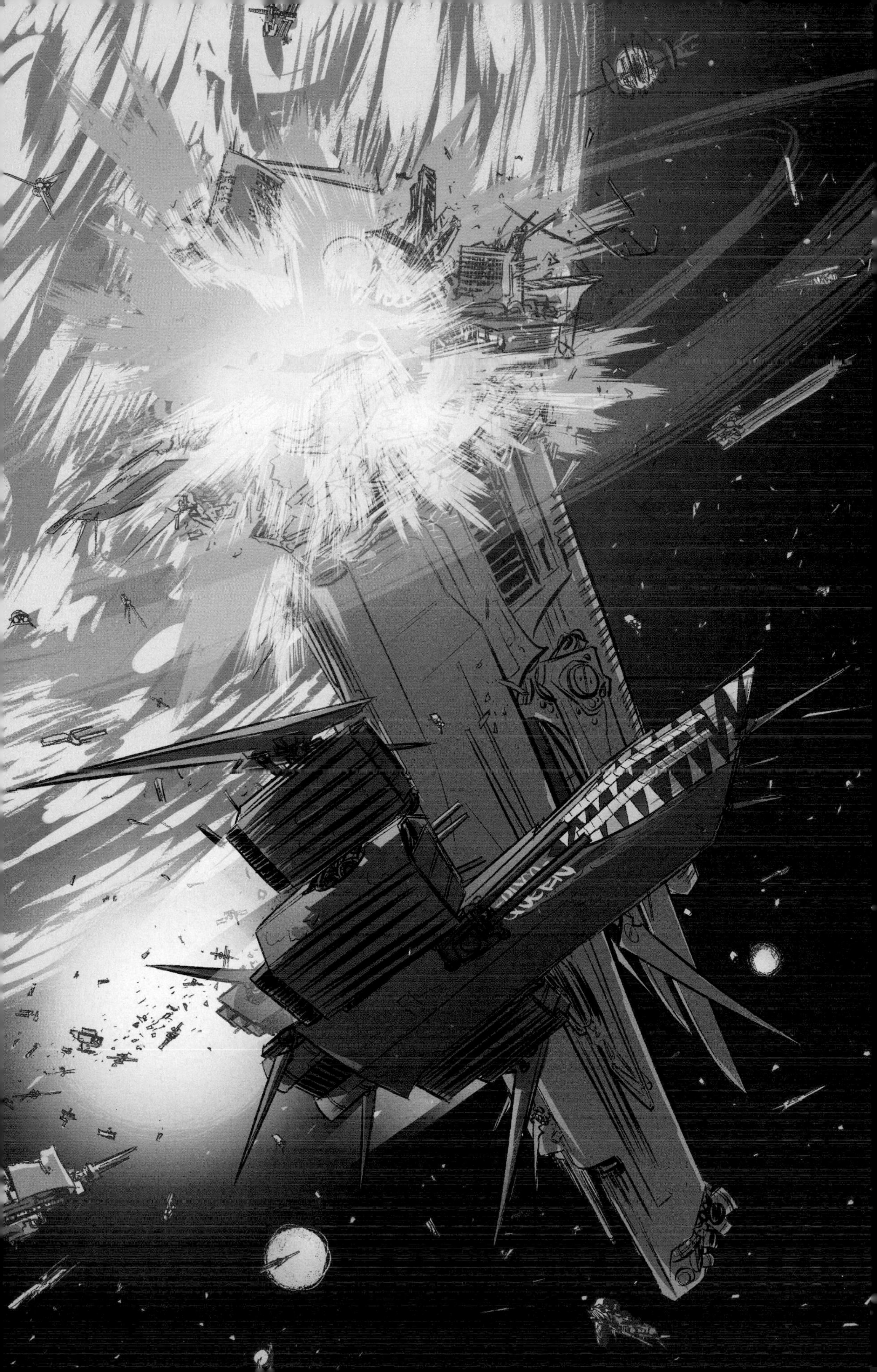

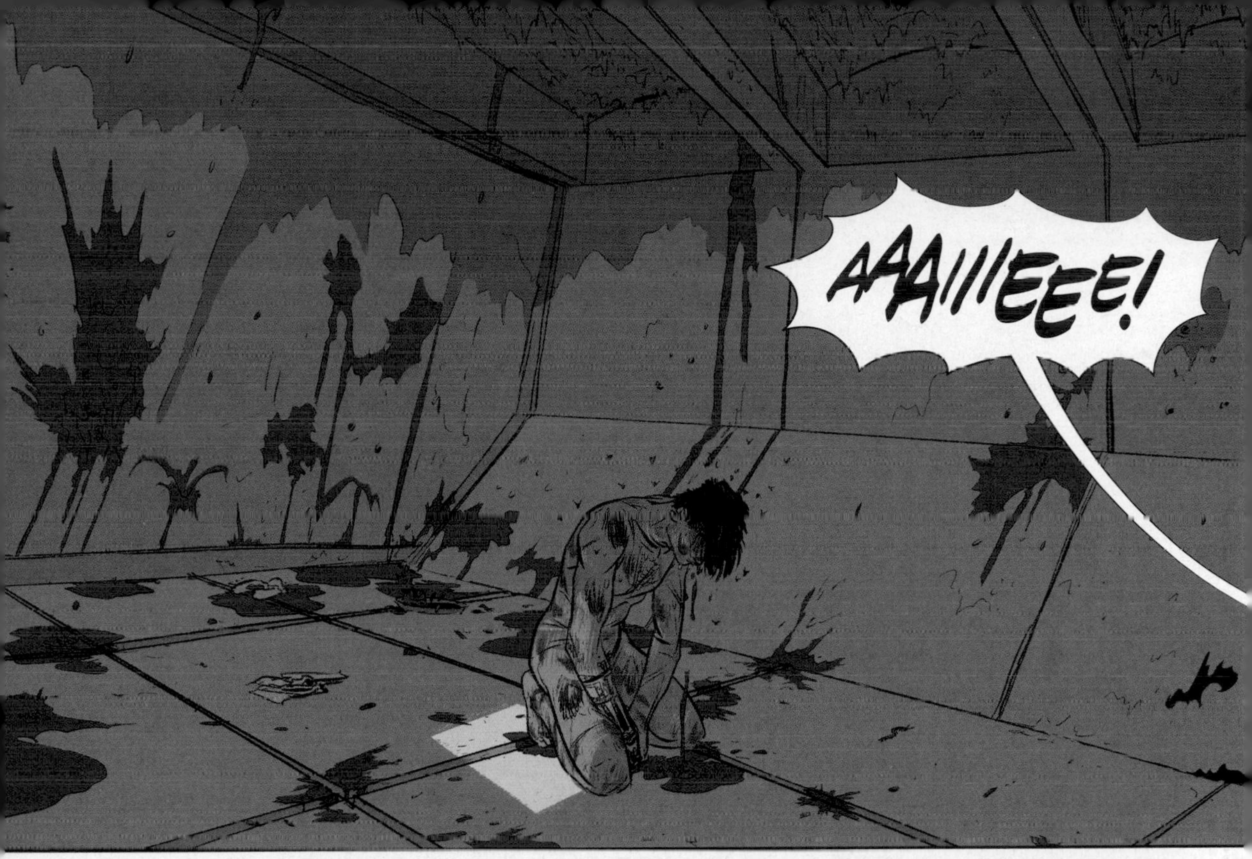
AAAIIIIEEEE!

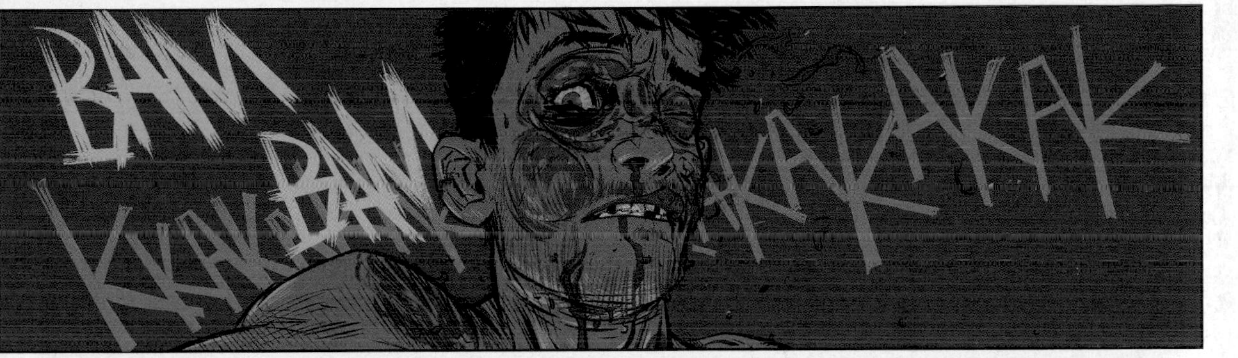
BAM
BAM
BAM
KKAKAKAKAKAKAKAK

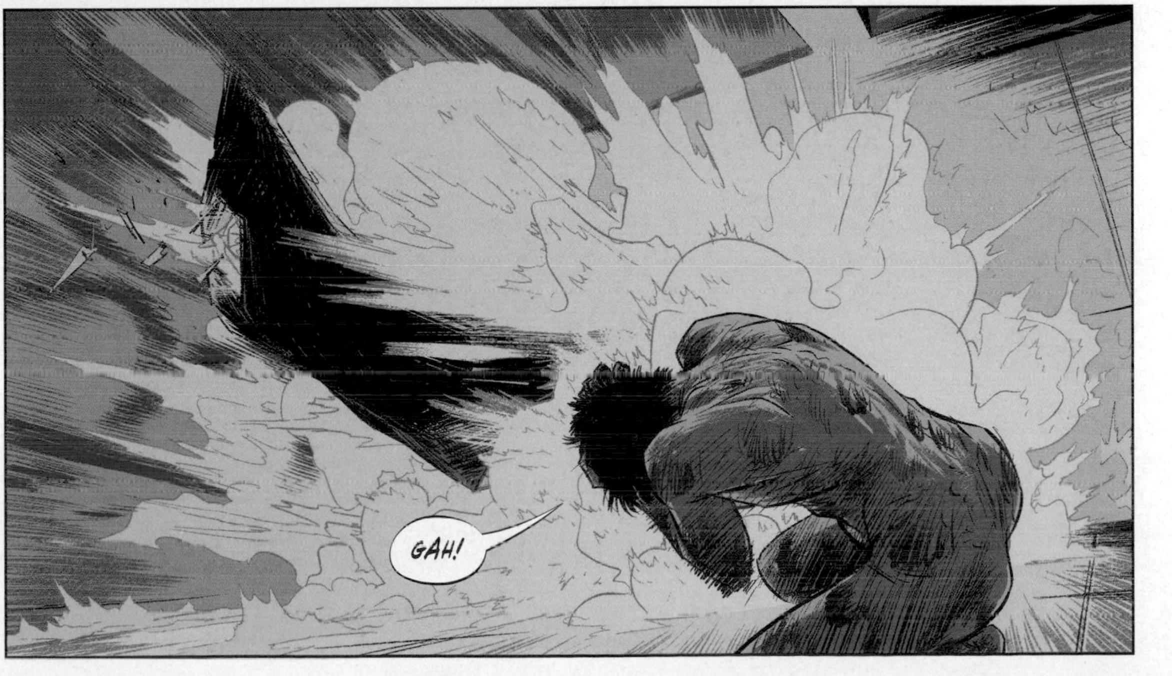
GAH!

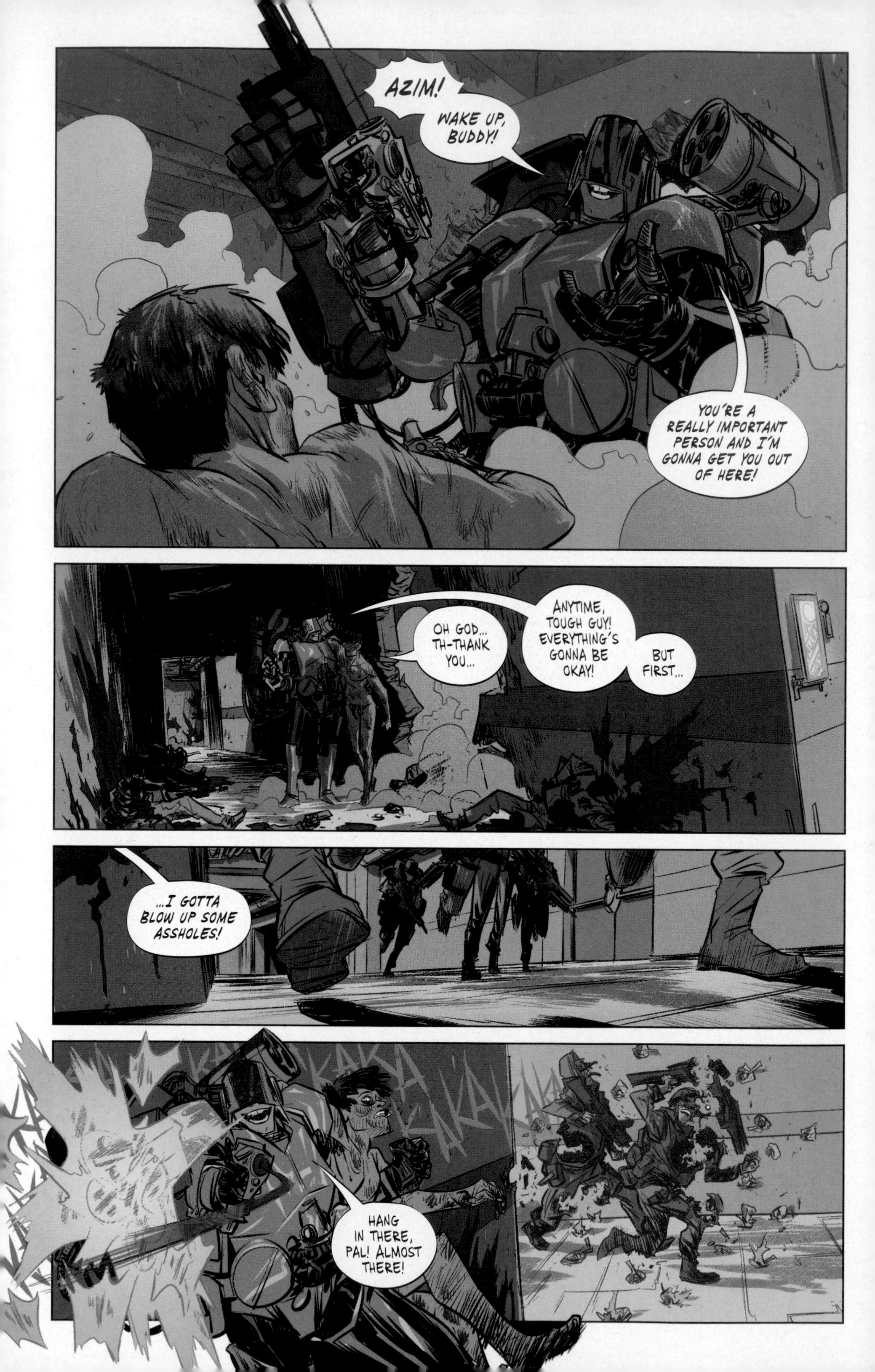
AZIM!
WAKE UP, BUDDY!
YOU'RE A REALLY IMPORTANT PERSON AND I'M GONNA GET YOU OUT OF HERE!
OH GOD... TH-THANK YOU...
ANYTIME, TOUGH GUY! EVERYTHING'S GONNA BE OKAY!
BUT FIRST...
...I GOTTA BLOW UP SOME ASSHOLES!
HANG IN THERE, PAL! ALMOST THERE!

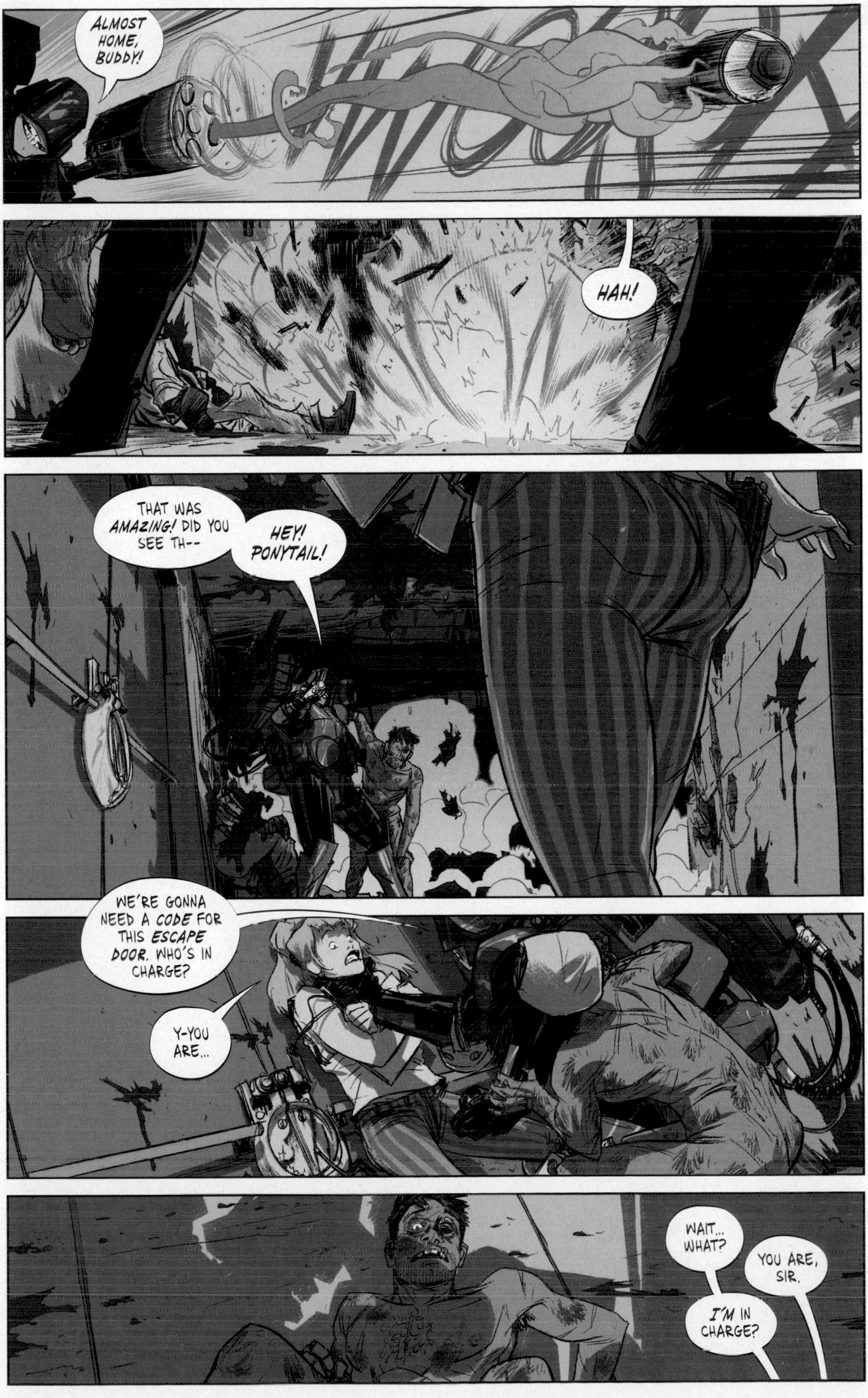
ALMOST HOME, BUDDY!
HAH!
THAT WAS AMAZING! DID YOU SEE TH--
HEY! PONYTAIL!
WE'RE GONNA NEED A CODE FOR THIS ESCAPE DOOR. WHO'S IN CHARGE?
Y-YOU ARE...
WAIT... WHAT?
YOU ARE, SIR.
I'M IN CHARGE?

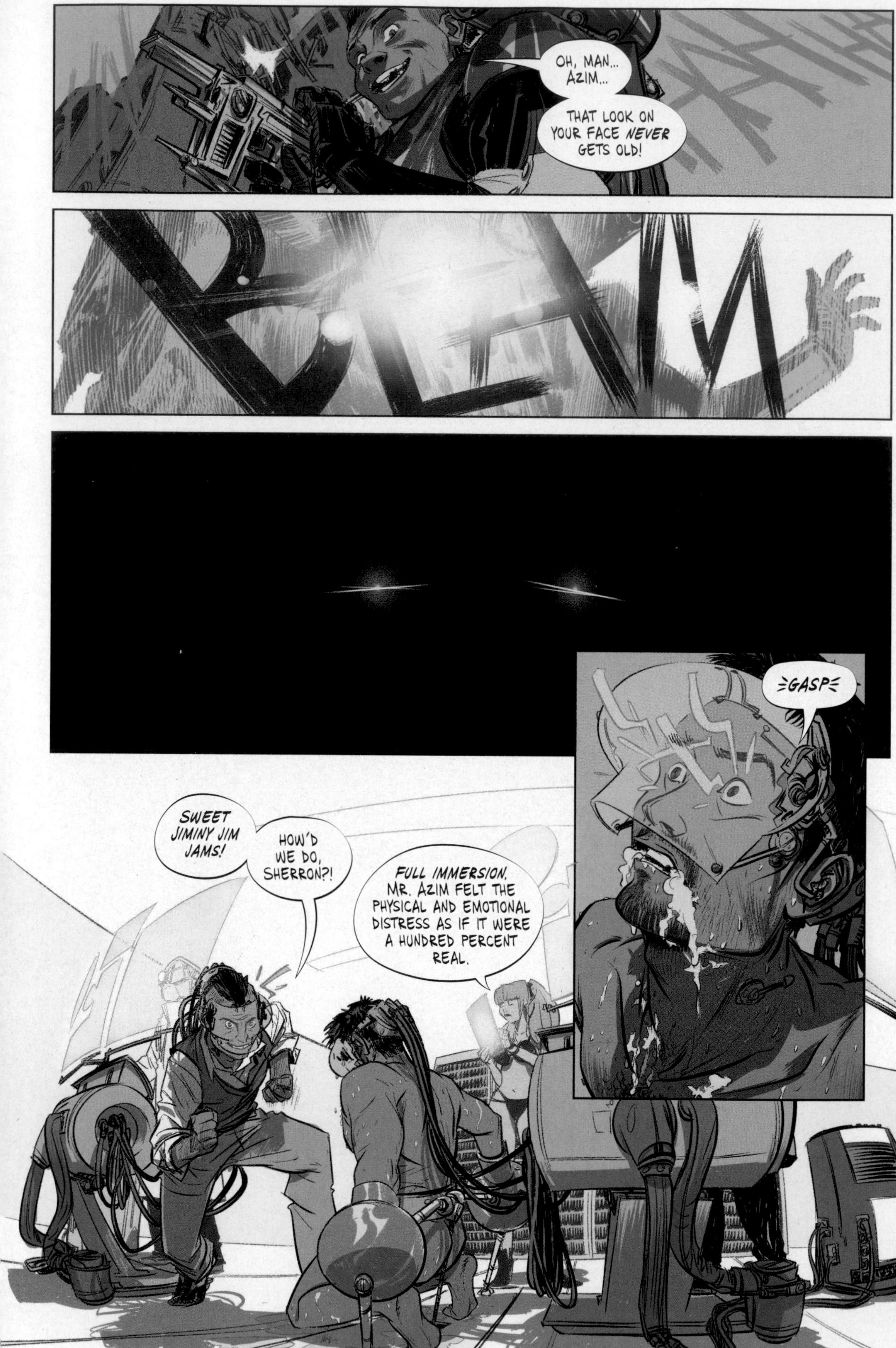
OH, MAN... AZIM...
THAT LOOK ON YOUR FACE NEVER GETS OLD!
GASP
SWEET JIMINY JIM JAMS!
HOW'D WE DO, SHERRON?!
FULL IMMERSION. MR. AZIM FELT THE PHYSICAL AND EMOTIONAL DISTRESS AS IF IT WERE A HUNDRED PERCENT REAL.

AND THE PAIN OF DEATH?!

LIKE IT ACTUALLY HAPPENED.

OUTSTANDING! TWENTY-FIFTH TIME'S THE CHARM!

HOW YA FEELIN', CHAMP? NOT SO GOOD, HUH?

YEAH, JUST A LITTLE SOMETHIN' MY GUYS'VE BEEN WORKING ON.

ADAPTED FROM RECENT DEVELOPMENTS IN THE PORN INDUSTRY. *FINE WORK* THOSE FOLKS ARE DOING.

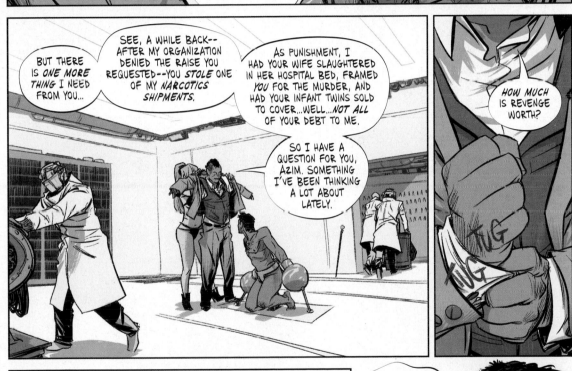

BUT THERE IS *ONE MORE THING* I NEED FROM YOU...

SEE, A WHILE BACK-- AFTER MY ORGANIZATION DENIED THE RAISE YOU REQUESTED--YOU *STOLE* ONE OF MY *NARCOTICS SHIPMENTS.*

AS PUNISHMENT, I HAD YOUR WIFE SLAUGHTERED IN HER HOSPITAL BED, FRAMED *YOU* FOR THE MURDER, AND HAD YOUR INFANT TWINS SOLD TO COVER...WELL...*NOT ALL* OF YOUR DEBT TO ME.

SO I HAVE A QUESTION FOR YOU, AZIM. SOMETHING I'VE BEEN THINKING A LOT ABOUT LATELY.

HOW MUCH IS REVENGE WORTH?

WH-WHAT...?

I MEAN LET'S PUT A NUMBER ON IT. IF I WERE TO LET YOU GO...

IF I WERE TO SIGN MY *SIZABLE* FORTUNE OVER TO YOU, WHAT AMOUNT OF MONEY WOULD YOU PAY TO SEE ME DEAD?

A *MILLION* PLUGOS? A *BILLION?*

ALL OF IT. E-EVERYTHING I OWN AND MORE...

THAT'S WHAT I THOUGHT.

FORTUNATELY FOR MY BOTTOM LINE...

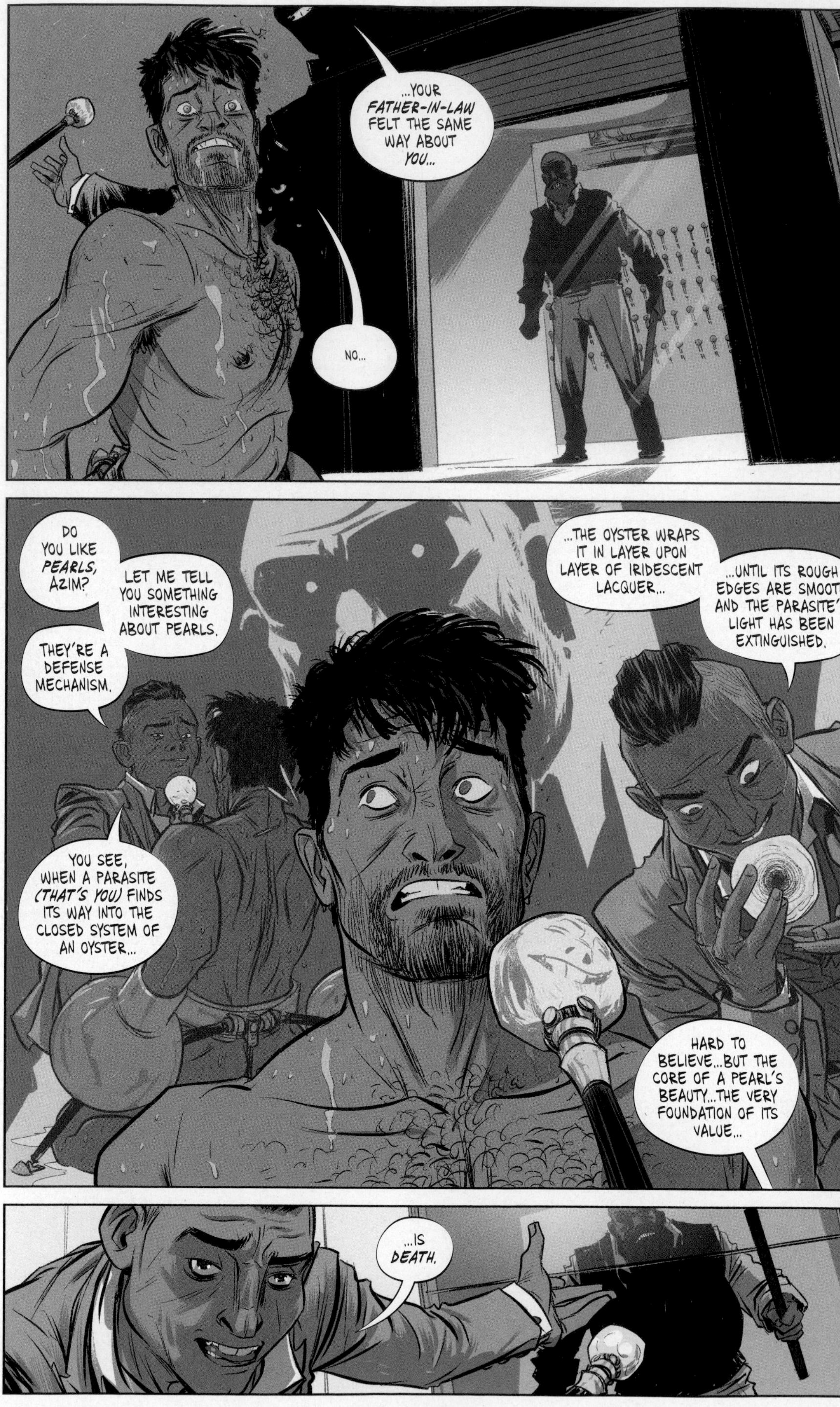
...YOUR *FATHER-IN-LAW* FELT THE SAME WAY ABOUT *YOU*...
NO...
DO YOU LIKE *PEARLS*, AZIM?
LET ME TELL YOU SOMETHING INTERESTING ABOUT PEARLS.
THEY'RE A DEFENSE MECHANISM.
YOU SEE, WHEN A PARASITE *(THAT'S YOU)* FINDS ITS WAY INTO THE CLOSED SYSTEM OF AN OYSTER...
...THE OYSTER WRAPS IT IN LAYER UPON LAYER OF IRIDESCENT LACQUER...
...UNTIL ITS ROUGH EDGES ARE SMOOTH AND THE PARASITE'S LIGHT HAS BEEN EXTINGUISHED.
HARD TO BELIEVE...BUT THE CORE OF A PEARL'S BEAUTY...THE VERY FOUNDATION OF ITS VALUE...
...IS *DEATH*.

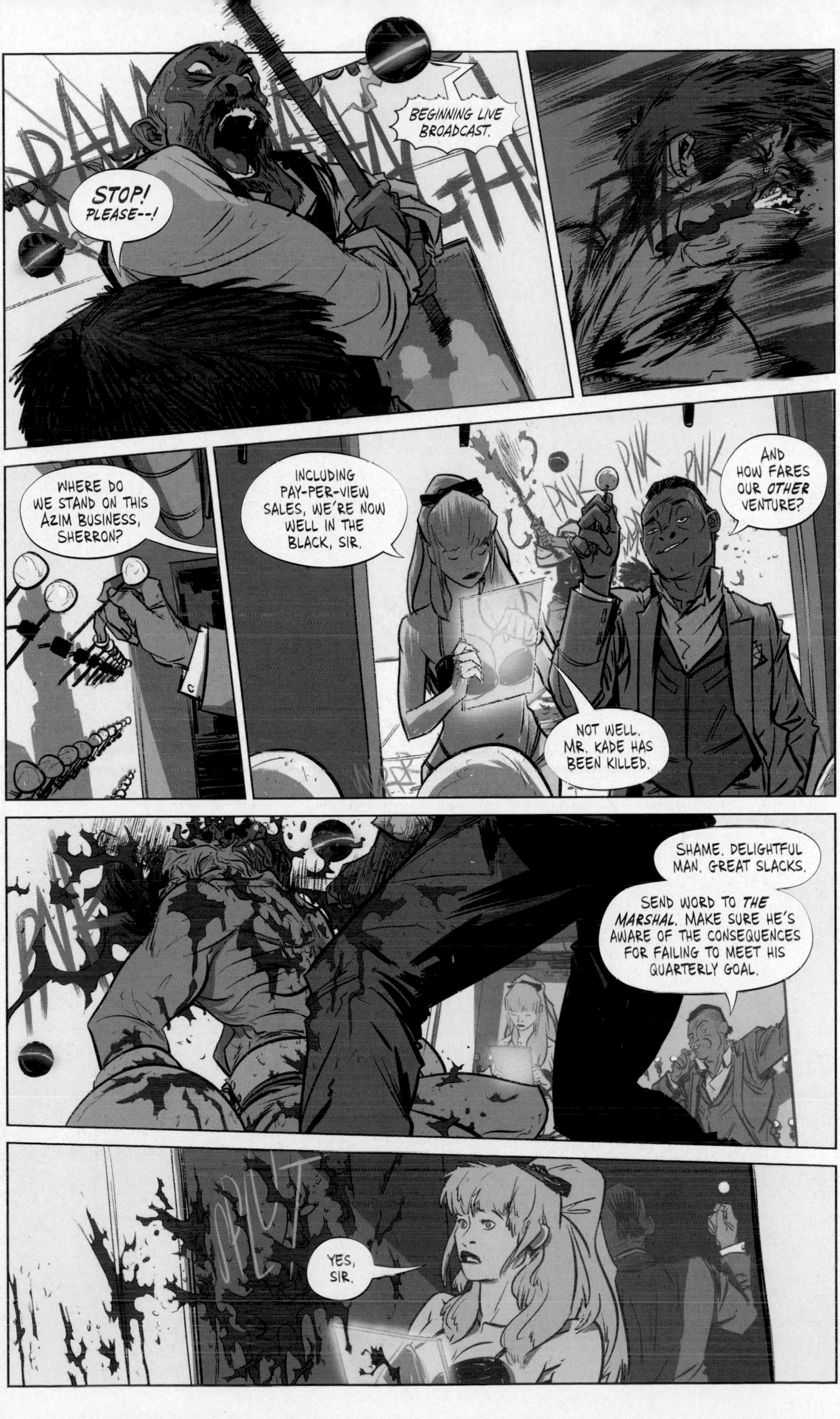
BEGINNING LIVE BROADCAST.
STOP! PLEASE--!
WHERE DO WE STAND ON THIS AZIM BUSINESS, SHERRON?
INCLUDING PAY-PER-VIEW SALES, WE'RE NOW WELL IN THE BLACK, SIR.
AND HOW FARES OUR *OTHER* VENTURE?
NOT WELL. MR. KADE HAS BEEN KILLED.
SHAME. DELIGHTFUL MAN. GREAT SLACKS.
SEND WORD TO *THE MARSHAL*. MAKE SURE HE'S AWARE OF THE CONSEQUENCES FOR FAILING TO MEET HIS QUARTERLY GOAL.
YES, SIR.

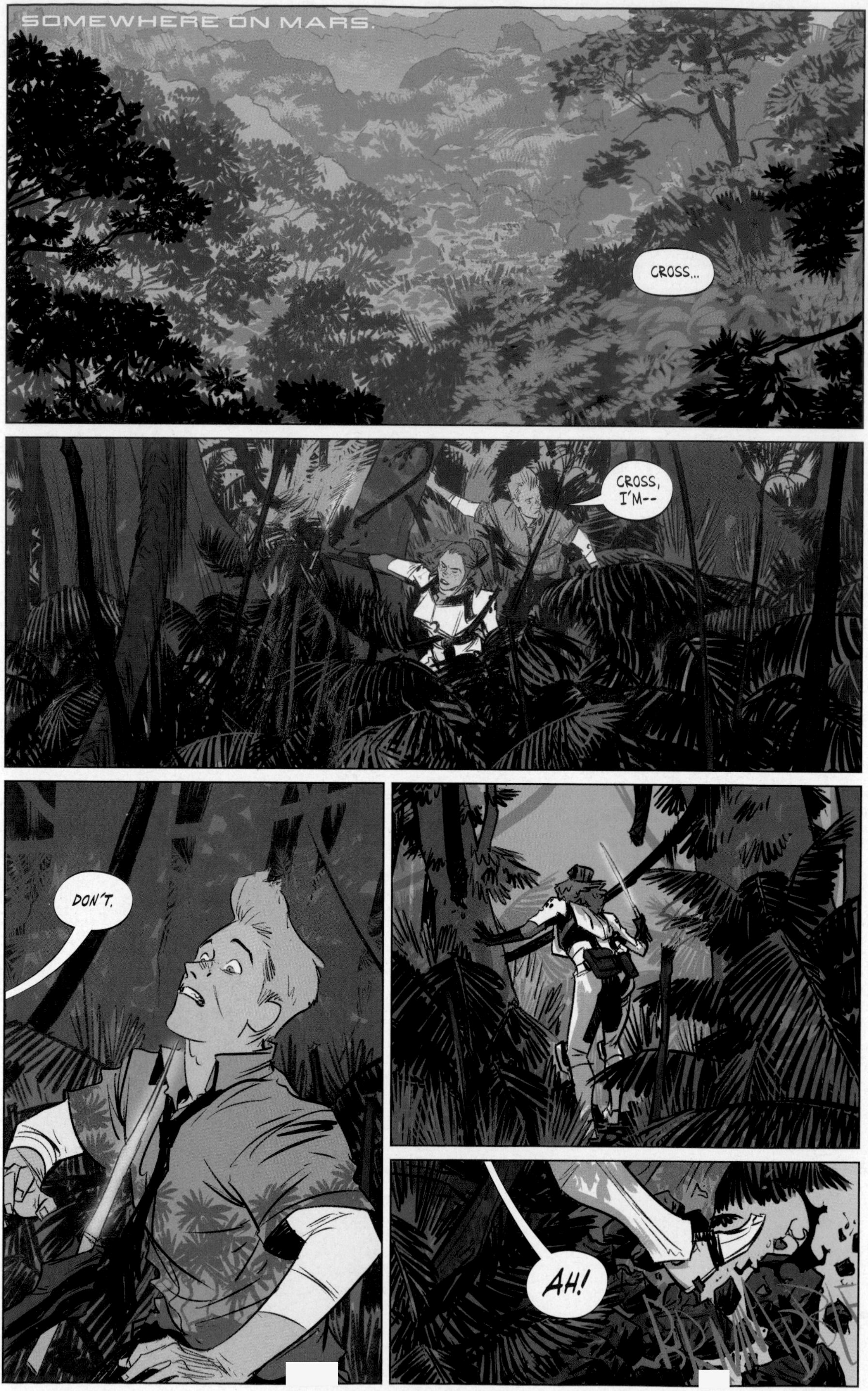
SOMEWHERE ON MARS.
CROSS...
CROSS, I'M--
DON'T.
AH!

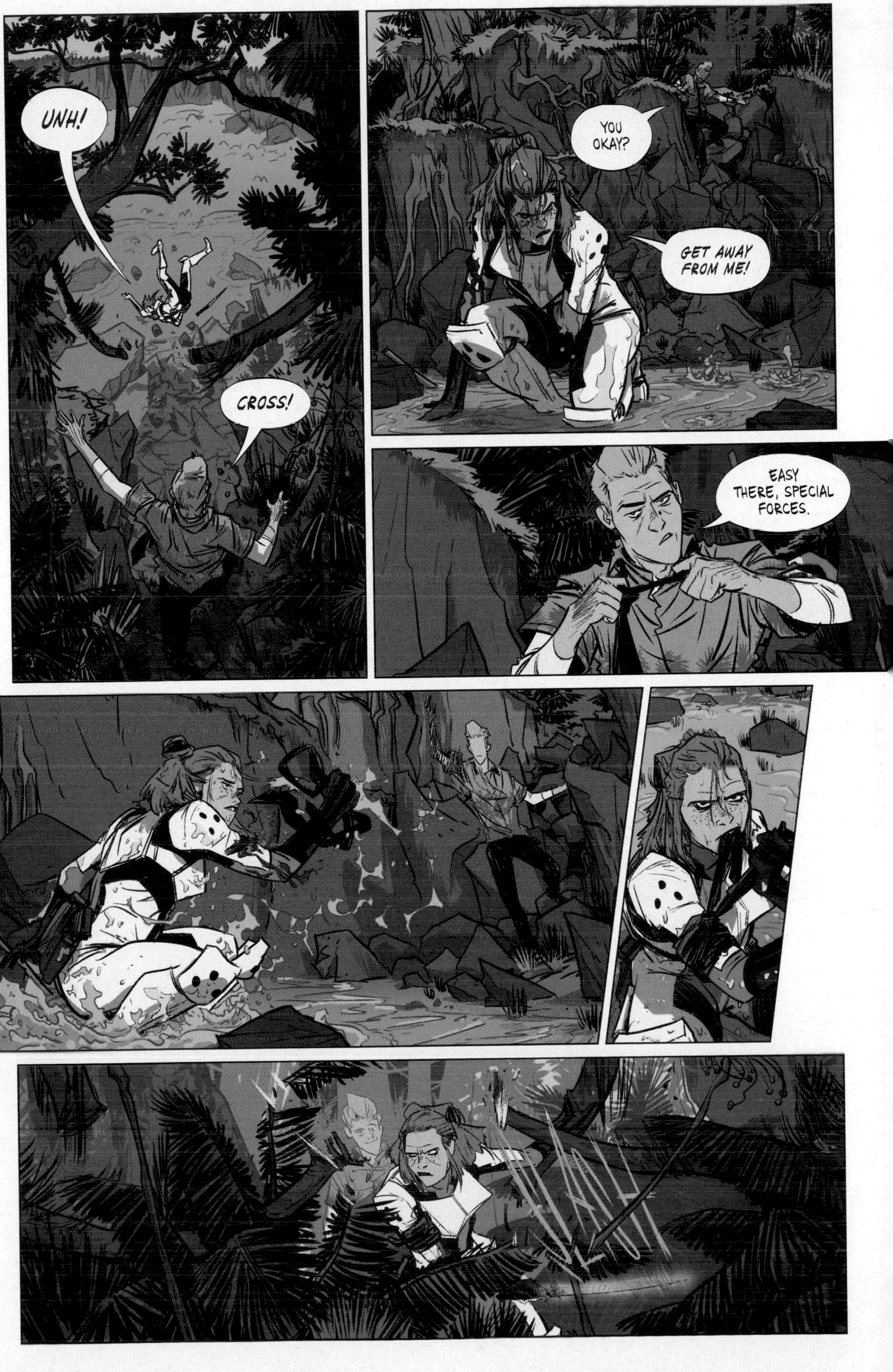
UNH!
CROSS!
YOU OKAY?
GET AWAY FROM ME!
EASY THERE, SPECIAL FORCES.

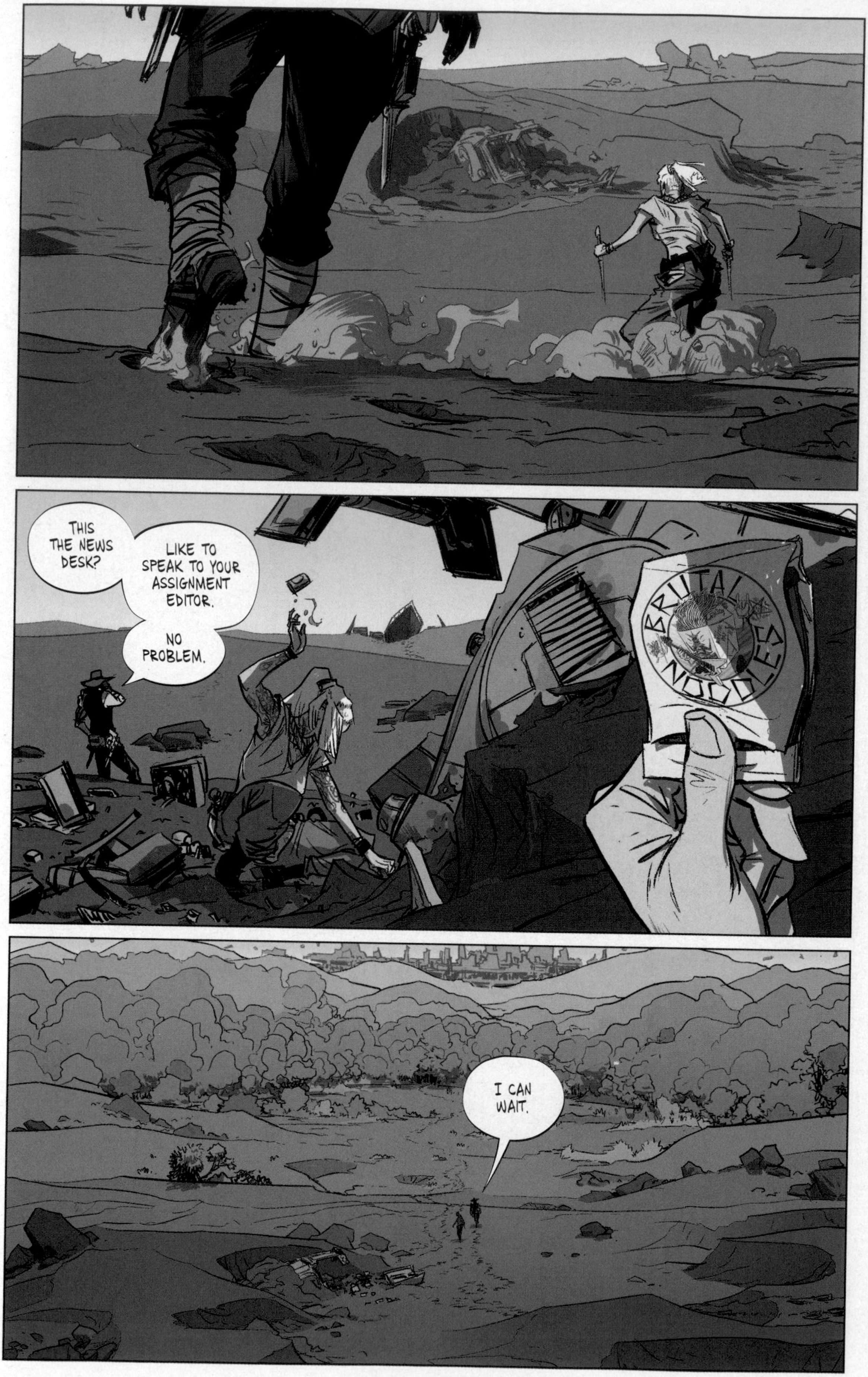
THIS THE NEWS DESK?
LIKE TO SPEAK TO YOUR ASSIGNMENT EDITOR.
NO PROBLEM.
BRUTAL NOODLES
I CAN WAIT.

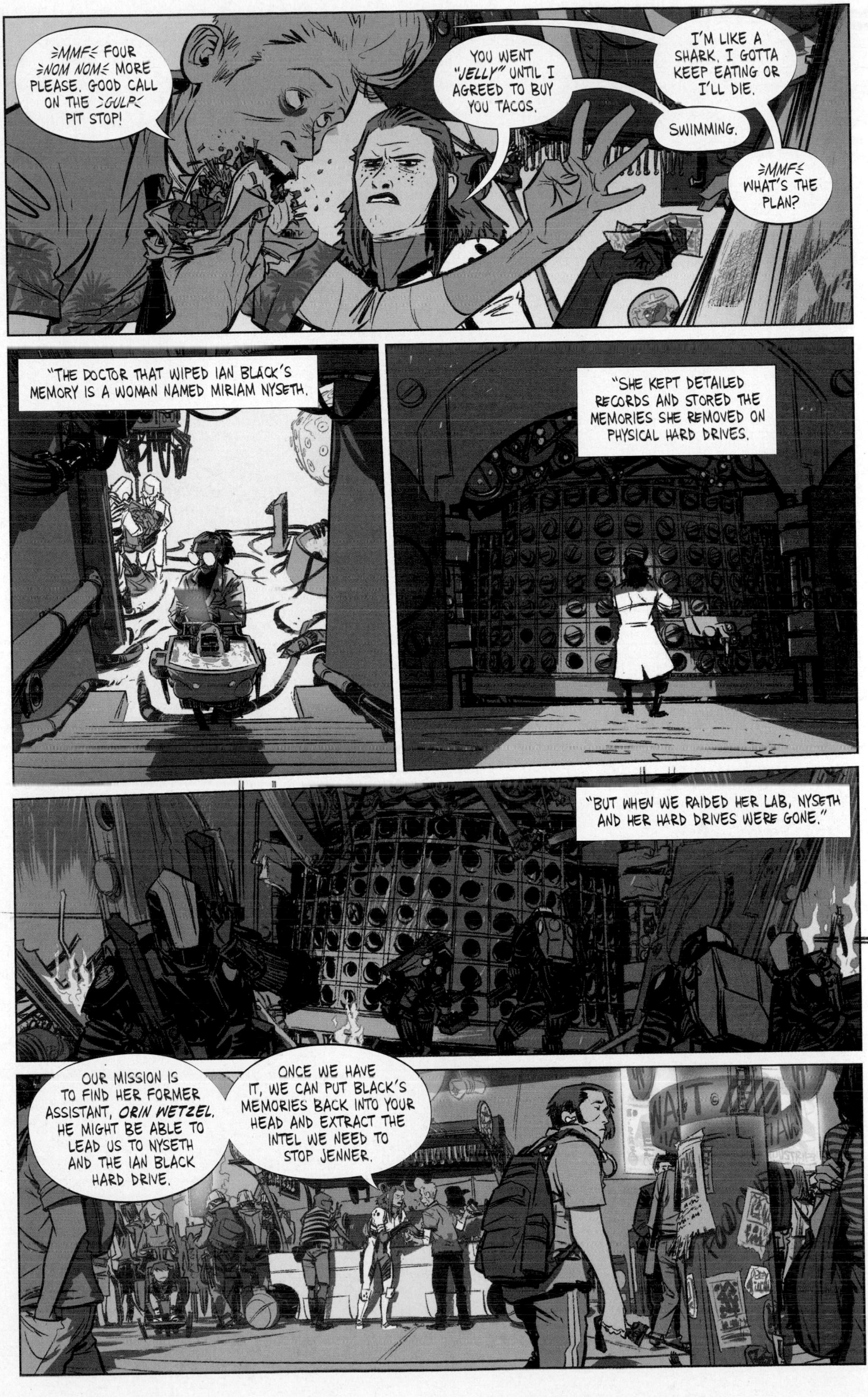

>MMF< FOUR >NOM NOM< MORE PLEASE. GOOD CALL ON THE >GULP< PIT STOP!
YOU WENT "JELLY" UNTIL I AGREED TO BUY YOU TACOS.
I'M LIKE A SHARK. I GOTTA KEEP EATING OR I'LL DIE.
SWIMMING.
>MMF< WHAT'S THE PLAN?
"THE DOCTOR THAT WIPED IAN BLACK'S MEMORY IS A WOMAN NAMED MIRIAM NYSETH.
"SHE KEPT DETAILED RECORDS AND STORED THE MEMORIES SHE REMOVED ON PHYSICAL HARD DRIVES.
"BUT WHEN WE RAIDED HER LAB, NYSETH AND HER HARD DRIVES WERE GONE."
OUR MISSION IS TO FIND HER FORMER ASSISTANT, ORIN WETZEL. HE MIGHT BE ABLE TO LEAD US TO NYSETH AND THE IAN BLACK HARD DRIVE.
ONCE WE HAVE IT, WE CAN PUT BLACK'S MEMORIES BACK INTO YOUR HEAD AND EXTRACT THE INTEL WE NEED TO STOP JENNER.

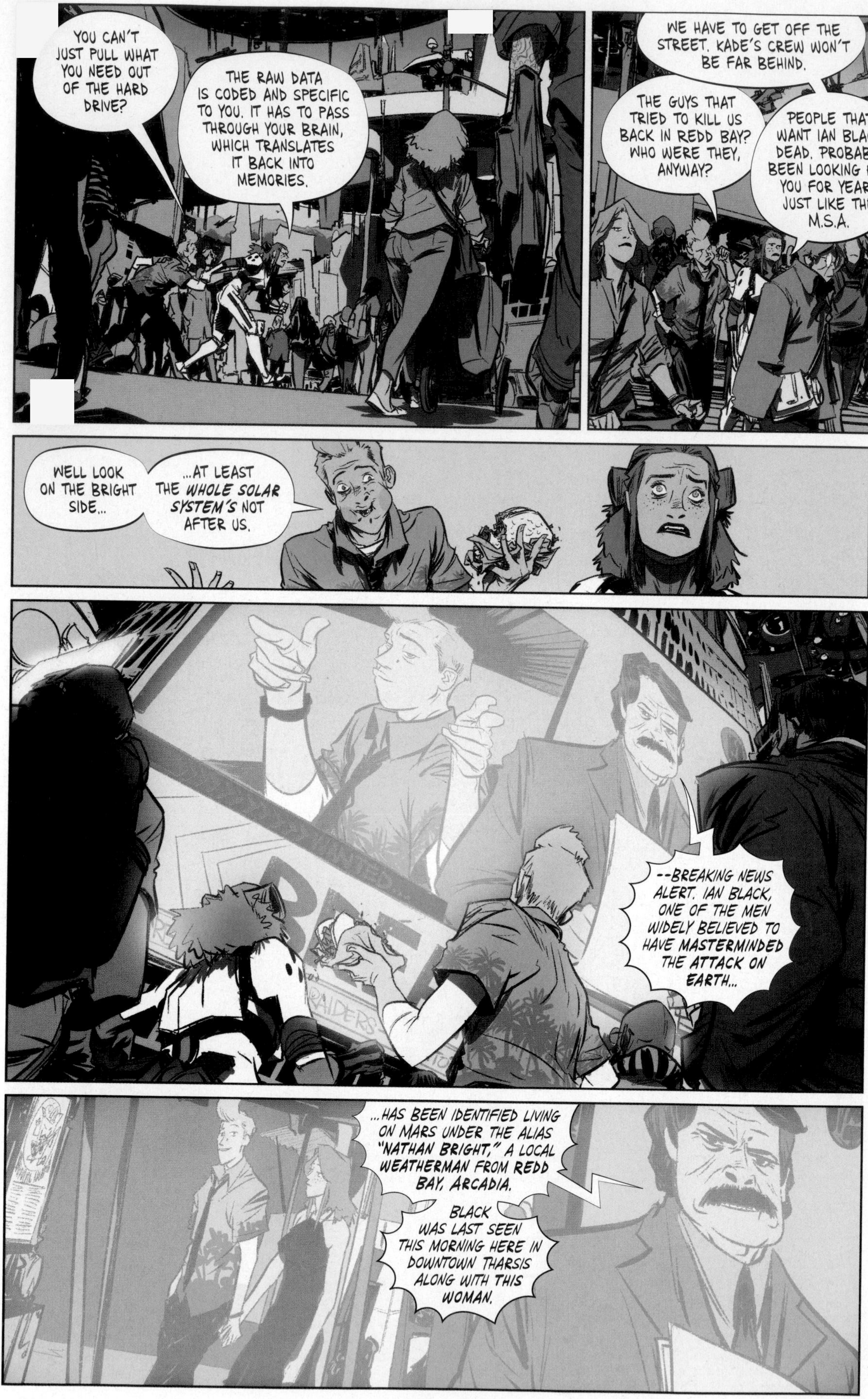
YOU CAN'T JUST PULL WHAT YOU NEED OUT OF THE HARD DRIVE?
THE RAW DATA IS CODED AND SPECIFIC TO YOU. IT HAS TO PASS THROUGH YOUR BRAIN, WHICH TRANSLATES IT BACK INTO MEMORIES.
WE HAVE TO GET OFF THE STREET. KADE'S CREW WON'T BE FAR BEHIND.
THE GUYS THAT TRIED TO KILL US BACK IN REDD BAY? WHO WERE THEY, ANYWAY?
PEOPLE THAT WANT IAN BLACK DEAD. PROBABLY BEEN LOOKING FOR YOU FOR YEARS JUST LIKE THE M.S.A.
WELL LOOK ON THE BRIGHT SIDE...
...AT LEAST THE WHOLE SOLAR SYSTEM'S NOT AFTER US.
--BREAKING NEWS ALERT. IAN BLACK, ONE OF THE MEN WIDELY BELIEVED TO HAVE MASTERMINDED THE ATTACK ON EARTH...
...HAS BEEN IDENTIFIED LIVING ON MARS UNDER THE ALIAS "NATHAN BRIGHT," A LOCAL WEATHERMAN FROM REDD BAY, ARCADIA.
BLACK WAS LAST SEEN THIS MORNING HERE IN DOWNTOWN THARSIS ALONG WITH THIS WOMAN.

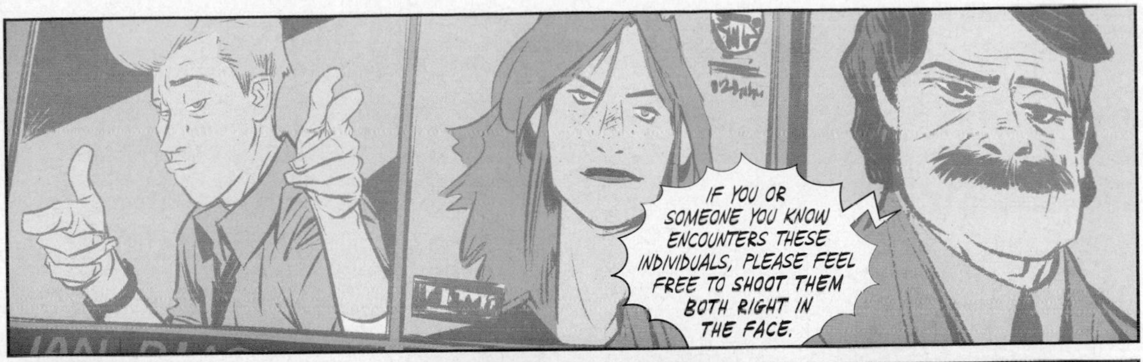
IF YOU OR SOMEONE YOU KNOW ENCOUNTERS THESE INDIVIDUALS, PLEASE FEEL FREE TO SHOOT THEM BOTH RIGHT IN THE FACE.

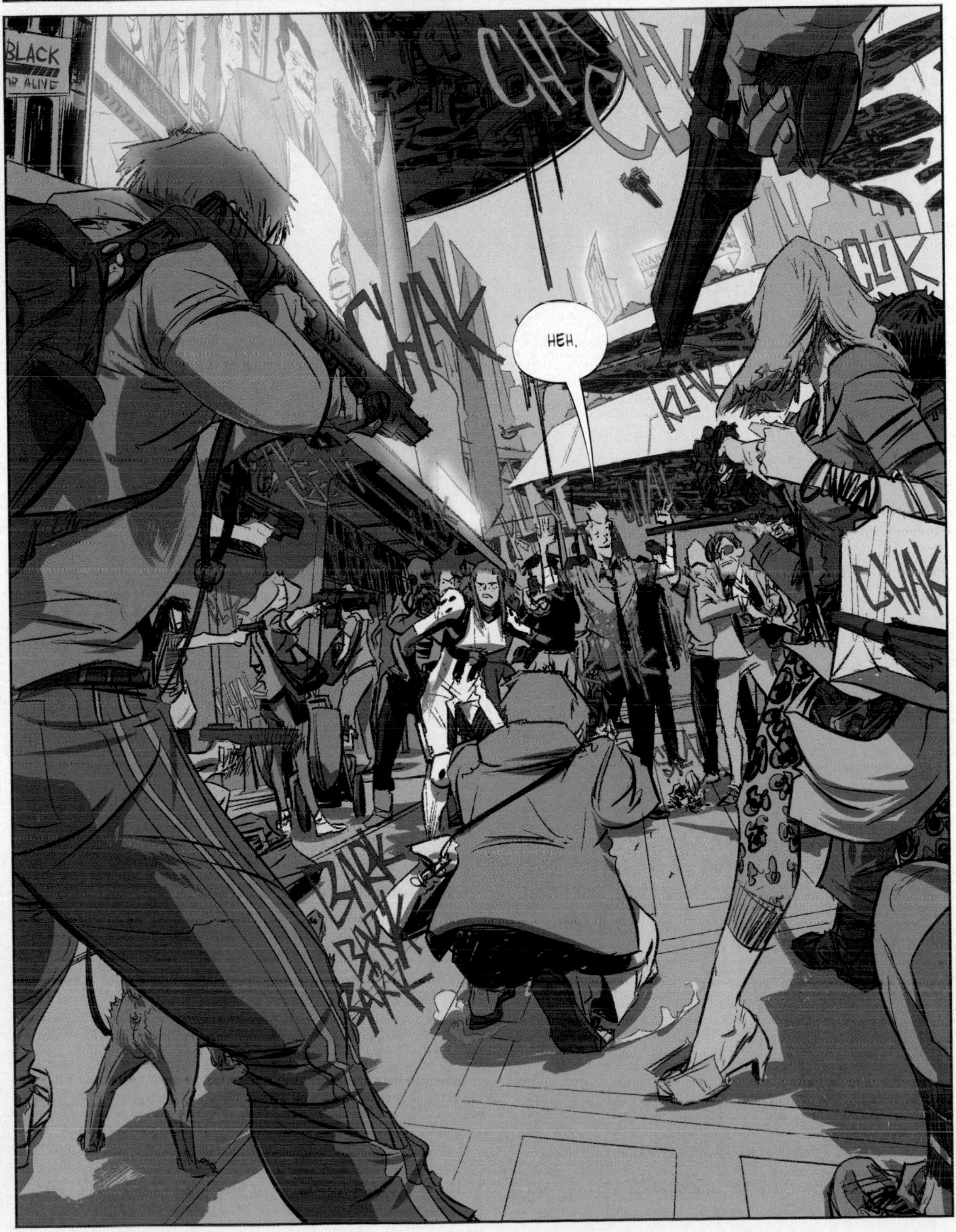
BLACK
CHAK
CLIK
KLAK
HEH.
CHAK
BARK
BARK
BARK

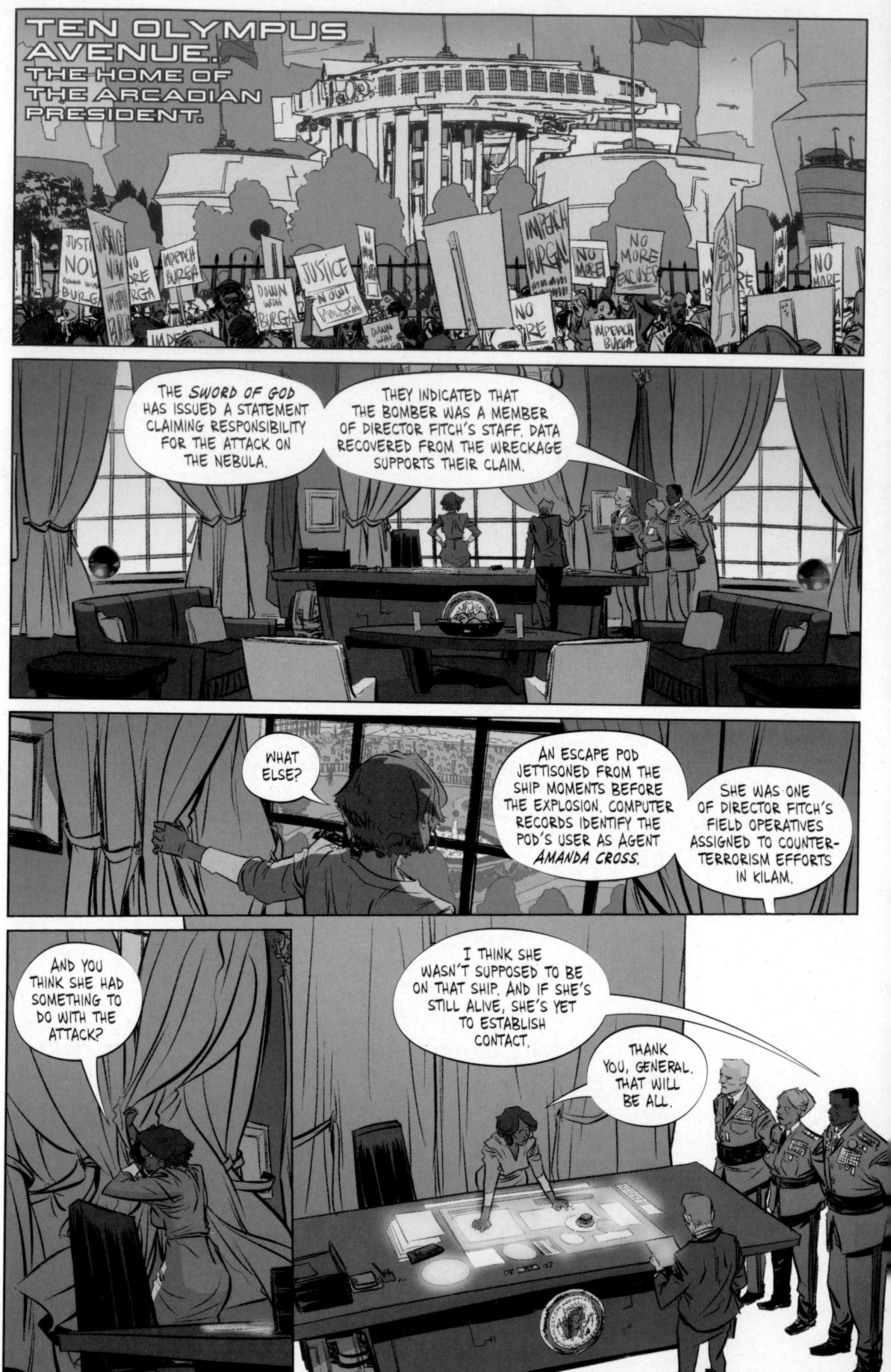
TEN OLYMPUS AVENUE. THE HOME OF THE ARCADIAN PRESIDENT.
JUSTICE NOW
JUSTICE NOW
IMPEACH BURGA
DOWN WITH BURGA
JUSTICE NOW!
IMPEACH BURGA
NO MORE
NO MORE EXCUSES
NO MORE
IMPEACH BURGA
THE *SWORD OF GOD* HAS ISSUED A STATEMENT CLAIMING RESPONSIBILITY FOR THE ATTACK ON THE NEBULA.
THEY INDICATED THAT THE BOMBER WAS A MEMBER OF DIRECTOR FITCH'S STAFF. DATA RECOVERED FROM THE WRECKAGE SUPPORTS THEIR CLAIM.
WHAT ELSE?
AN ESCAPE POD JETTISONED FROM THE SHIP MOMENTS BEFORE THE EXPLOSION. COMPUTER RECORDS IDENTIFY THE POD'S USER AS AGENT *AMANDA CROSS.*
SHE WAS ONE OF DIRECTOR FITCH'S FIELD OPERATIVES ASSIGNED TO COUNTER-TERRORISM EFFORTS IN KILAM.
AND YOU THINK SHE HAD SOMETHING TO DO WITH THE ATTACK?
I THINK SHE WASN'T SUPPOSED TO BE ON THAT SHIP. AND IF SHE'S STILL ALIVE, SHE'S YET TO ESTABLISH CONTACT.
THANK YOU, GENERAL. THAT WILL BE ALL.

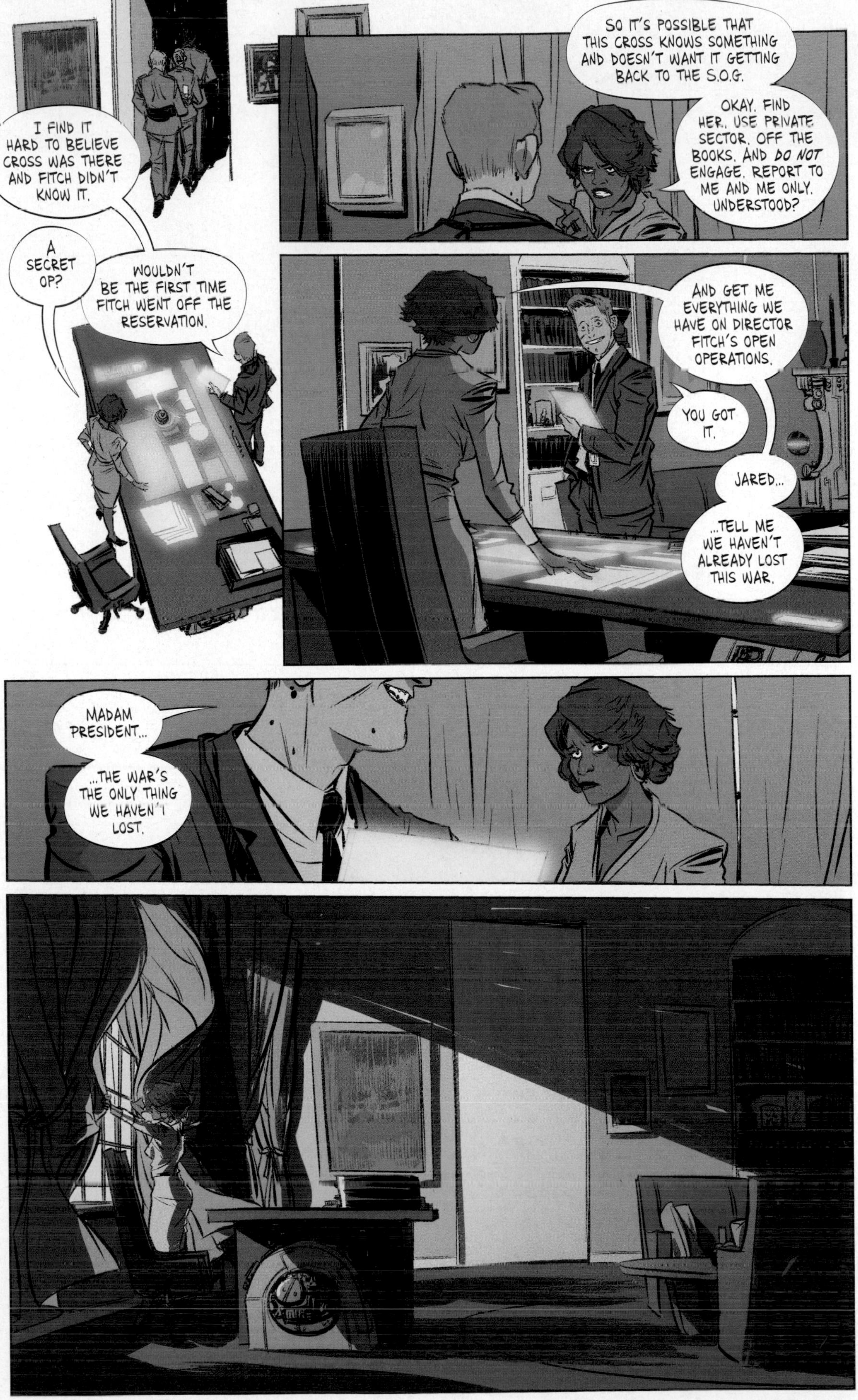
I FIND IT HARD TO BELIEVE CROSS WAS THERE AND FITCH DIDN'T KNOW IT.
A SECRET OP?
WOULDN'T BE THE FIRST TIME FITCH WENT OFF THE RESERVATION.
SO IT'S POSSIBLE THAT THIS CROSS KNOWS SOMETHING AND DOESN'T WANT IT GETTING BACK TO THE S.O.G.
OKAY. FIND HER. USE PRIVATE SECTOR. OFF THE BOOKS. AND *DO NOT* ENGAGE. REPORT TO ME AND ME ONLY. UNDERSTOOD?
AND GET ME EVERYTHING WE HAVE ON DIRECTOR FITCH'S OPEN OPERATIONS.
YOU GOT IT.
JARED...
...TELL ME WE HAVEN'T ALREADY LOST THIS WAR.
MADAM PRESIDENT...
...THE WAR'S THE ONLY THING WE HAVEN'T LOST.

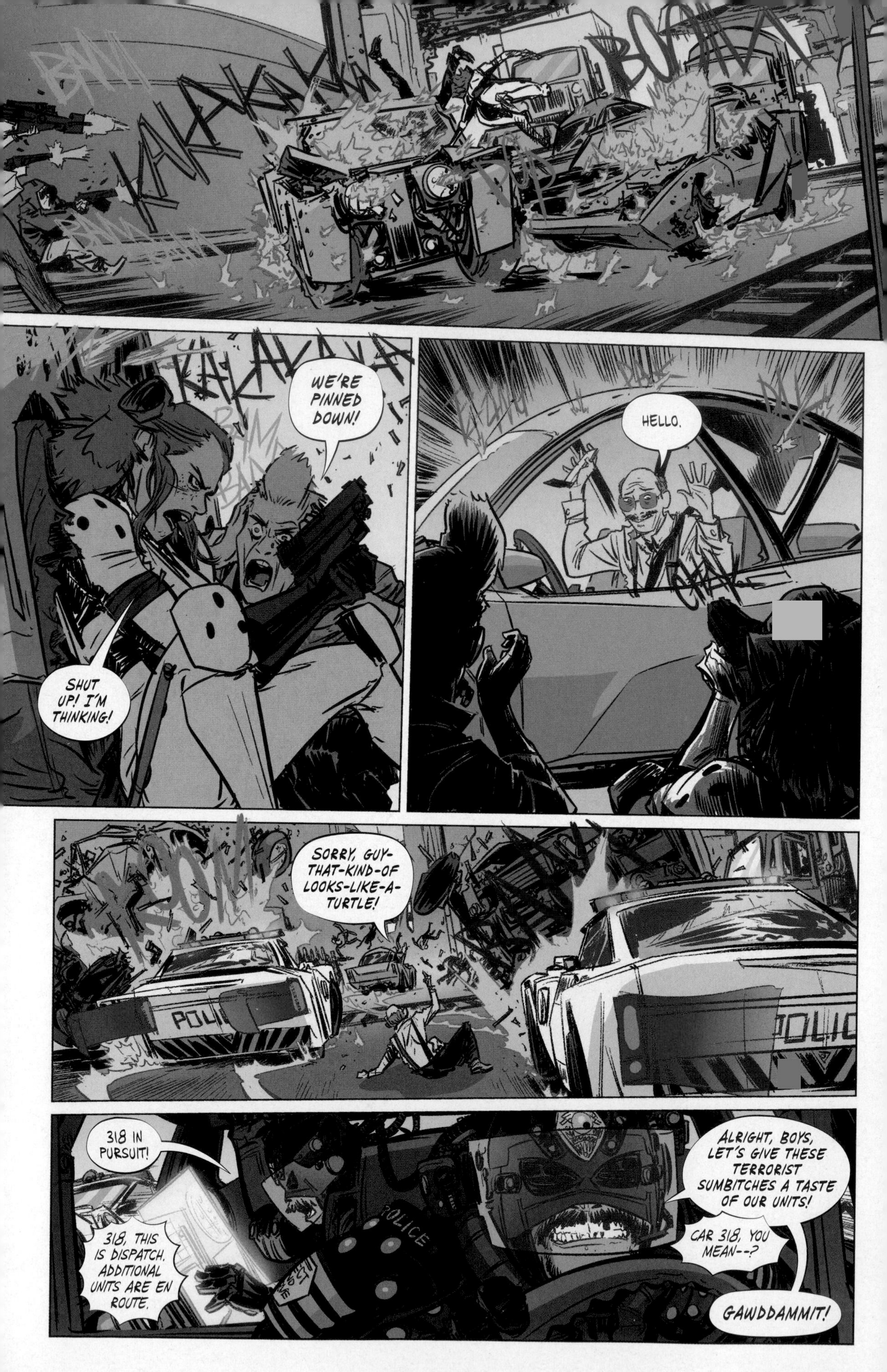
WE'RE PINNED DOWN!
SHUT UP! I'M THINKING!
HELLO.
SORRY, GUY-THAT-KIND-OF-LOOKS-LIKE-A-TURTLE!
318 IN PURSUIT!
318, THIS IS DISPATCH. ADDITIONAL UNITS ARE EN ROUTE.
ALRIGHT, BOYS, LET'S GIVE THESE TERRORIST SUMBITCHES A TASTE OF OUR UNITS!
CAR 318, YOU MEAN--?
GAWDDAMMIT!
POLICE

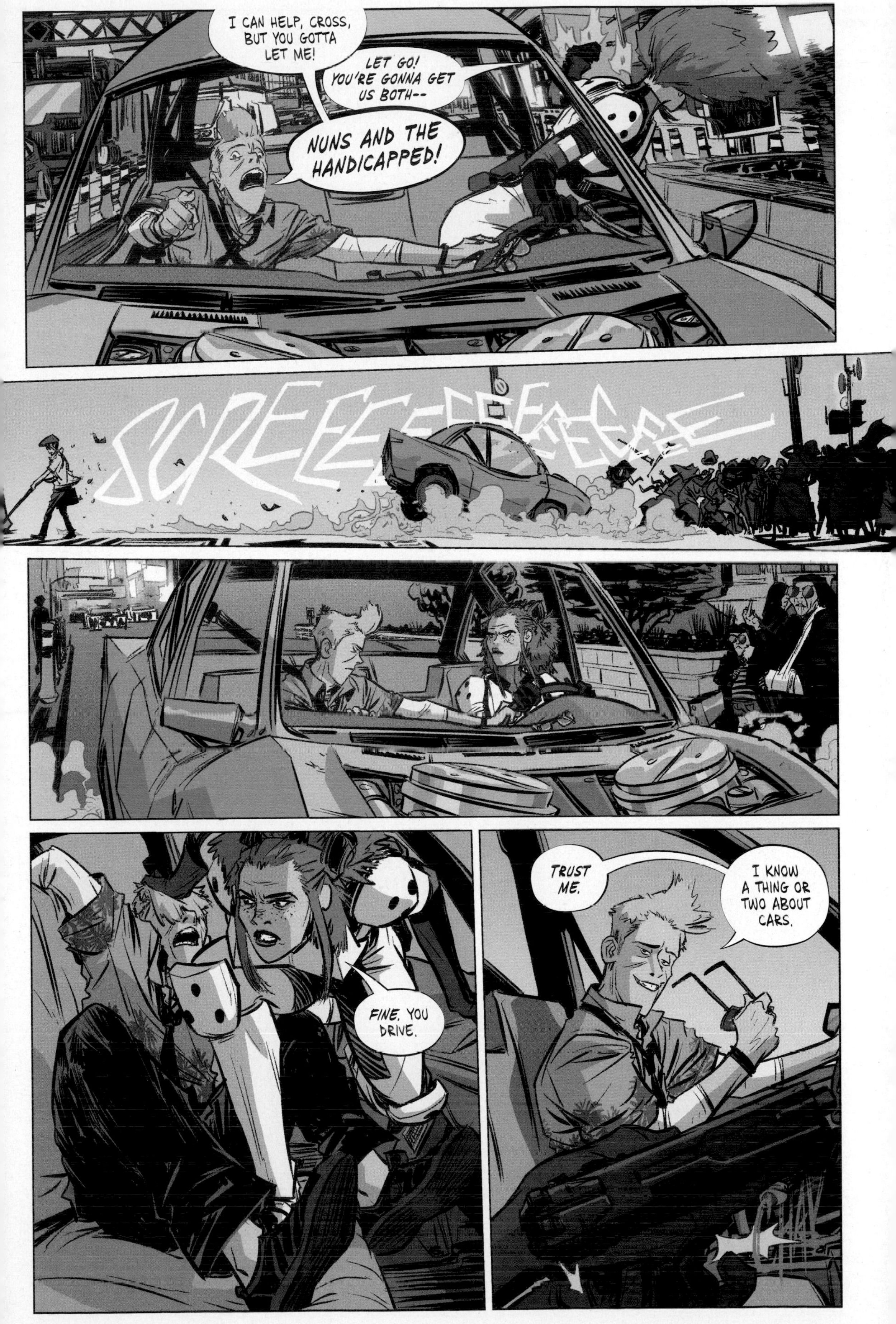
I CAN HELP, CROSS, BUT YOU GOTTA LET ME!
LET GO! YOU'RE GONNA GET US BOTH--
NUNS AND THE HANDICAPPED!
SCREEEEEEEEEEEE
FINE. YOU DRIVE.
TRUST ME.
I KNOW A THING OR TWO ABOUT CARS.

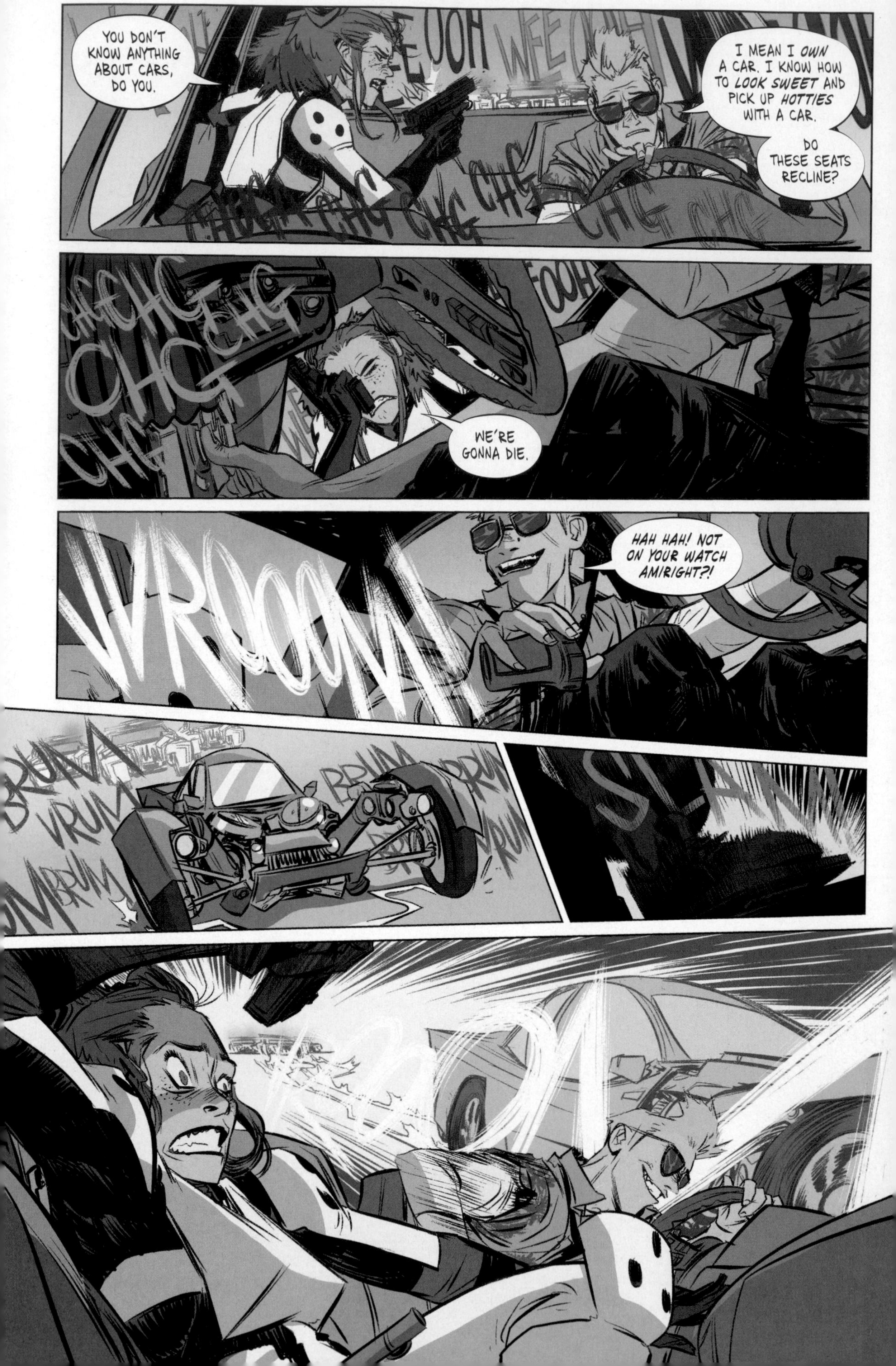
YOU DON'T KNOW ANYTHING ABOUT CARS, DO YOU.
I MEAN I OWN A CAR. I KNOW HOW TO LOOK SWEET AND PICK UP HOTTIES WITH A CAR.
DO THESE SEATS RECLINE?
WE'RE GONNA DIE.
VROOOOM
HAH HAH! NOT ON YOUR WATCH AMIRIGHT?!
VRUM

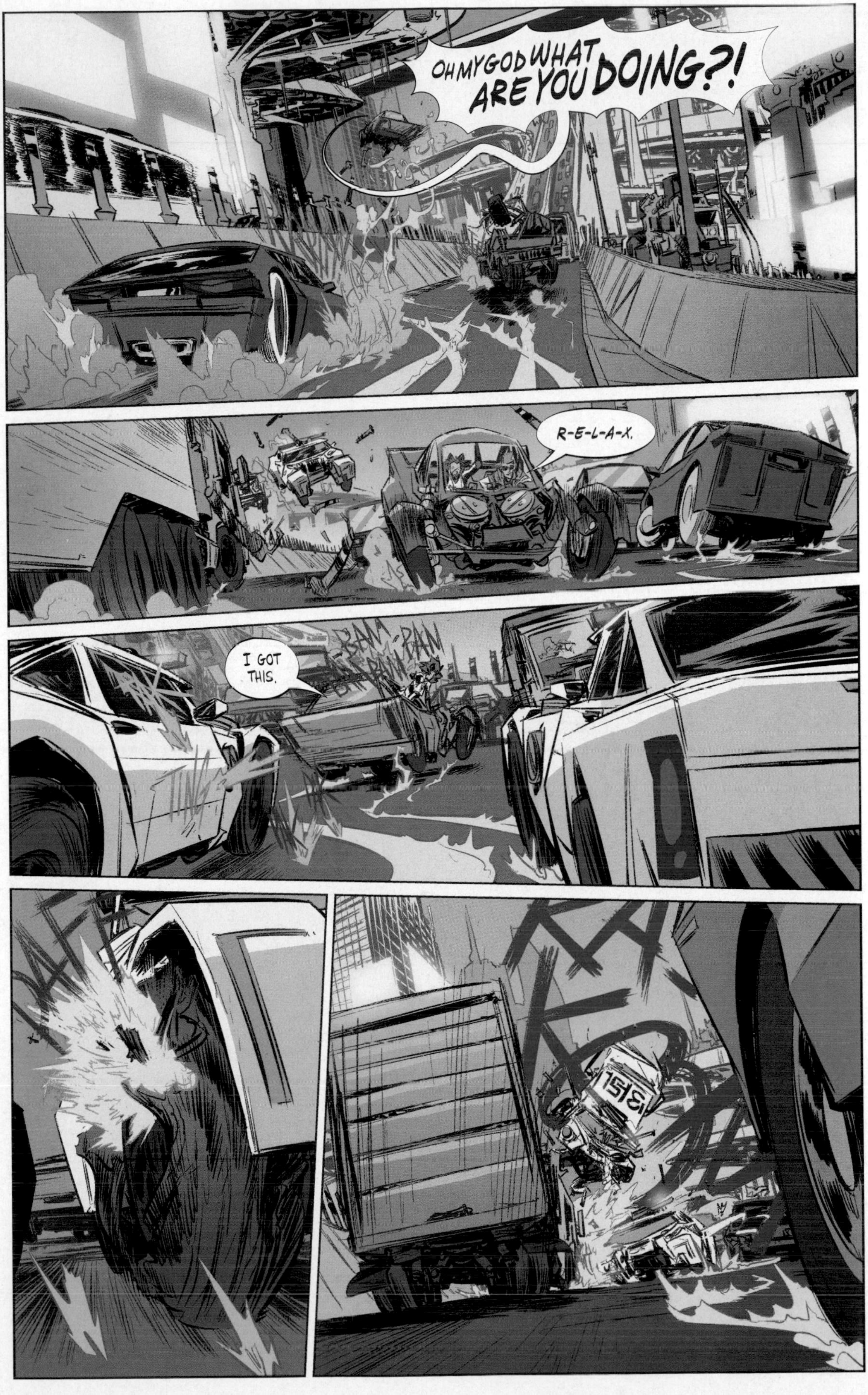
OH MY GOD WHAT ARE YOU DOING?!
R-E-L-A-X.
I GOT THIS.

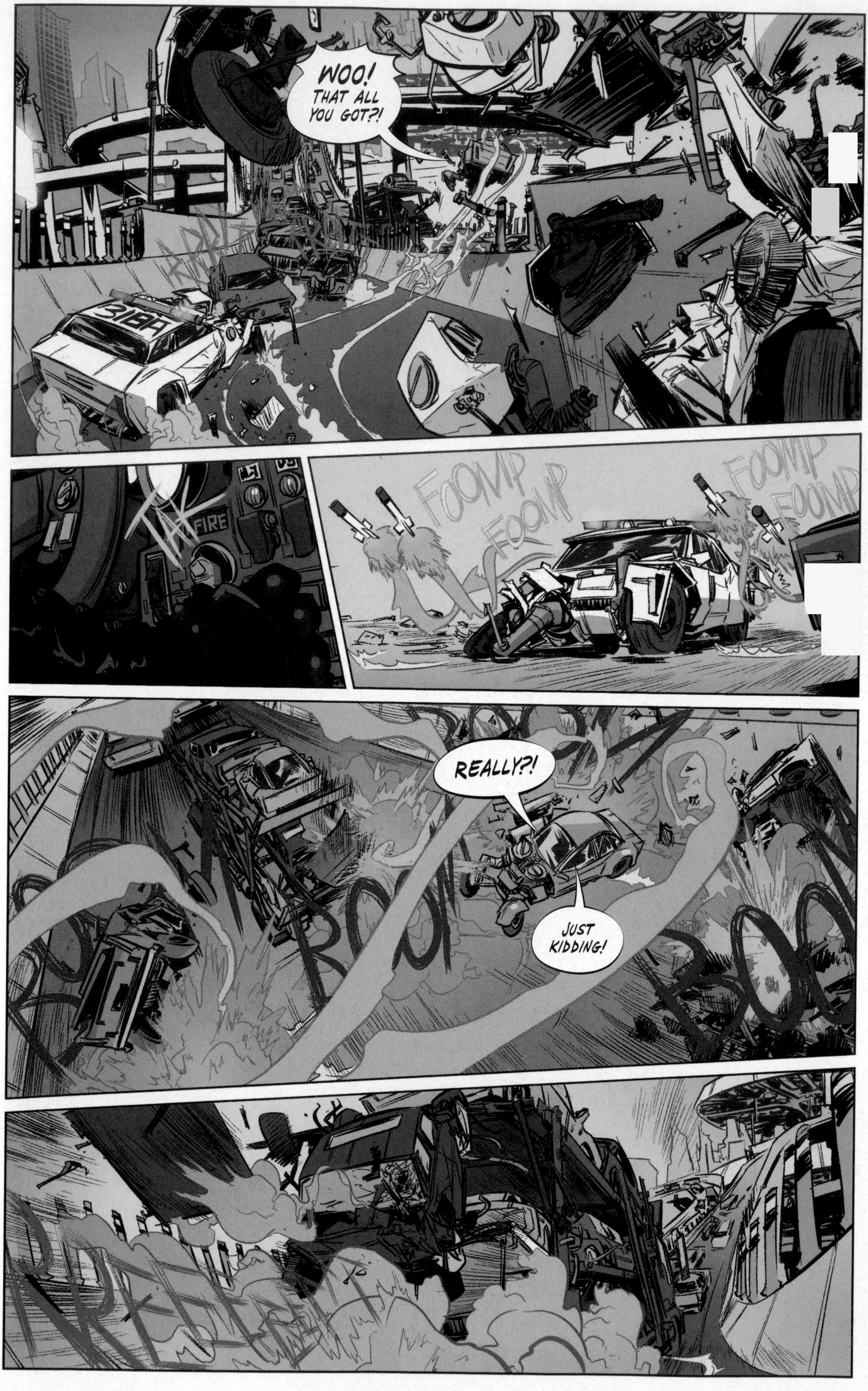
WOO! THAT ALL YOU GOT?!
FIRE
FOOMP
FOOMP
FOOMP
FOOMP
REALLY?!
JUST KIDDING!

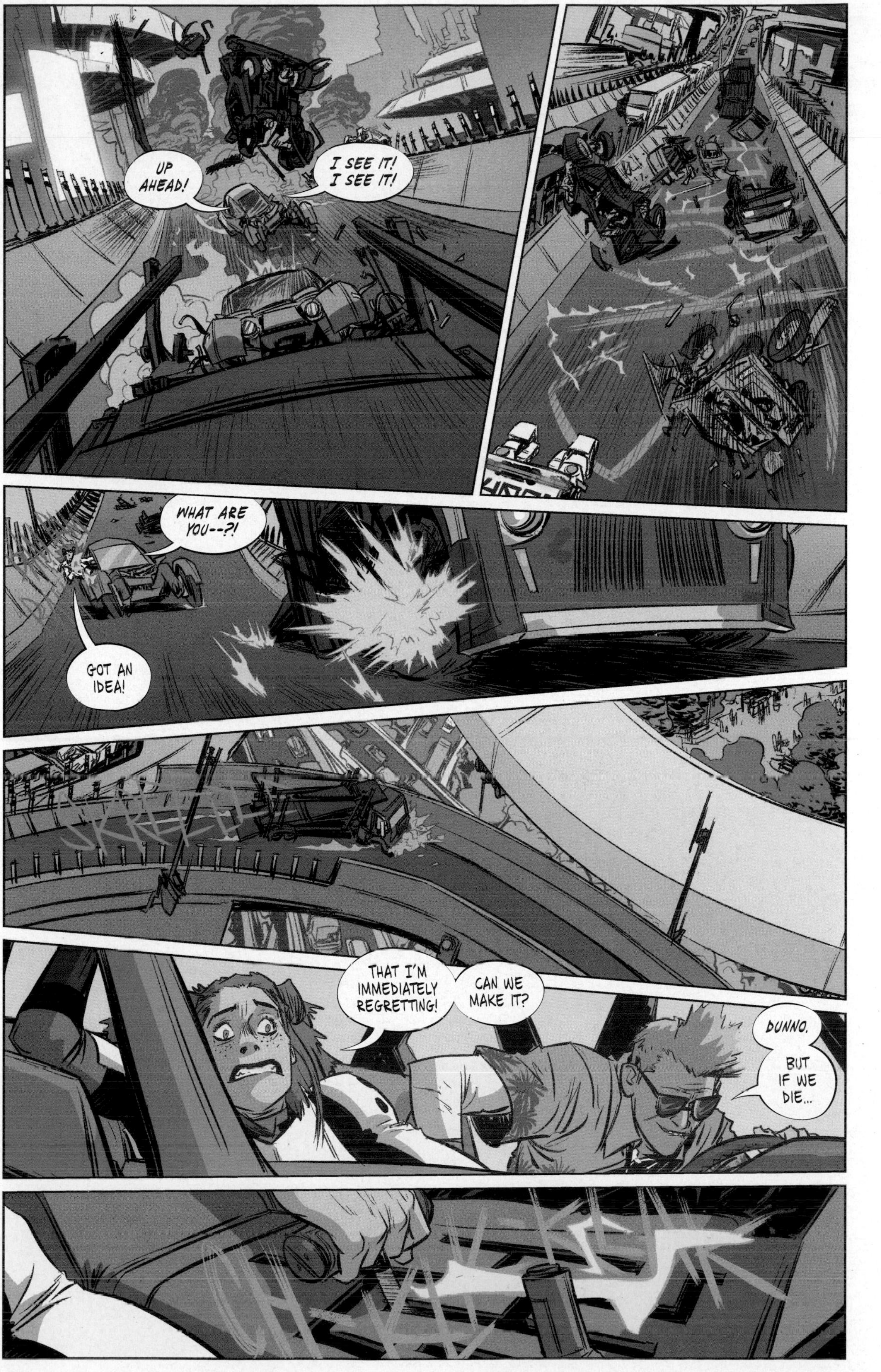
UP AHEAD!
I SEE IT! I SEE IT!
WHAT ARE YOU--?!
GOT AN IDEA!
THAT I'M IMMEDIATELY REGRETTING!
CAN WE MAKE IT?
DUNNO.
BUT IF WE DIE...

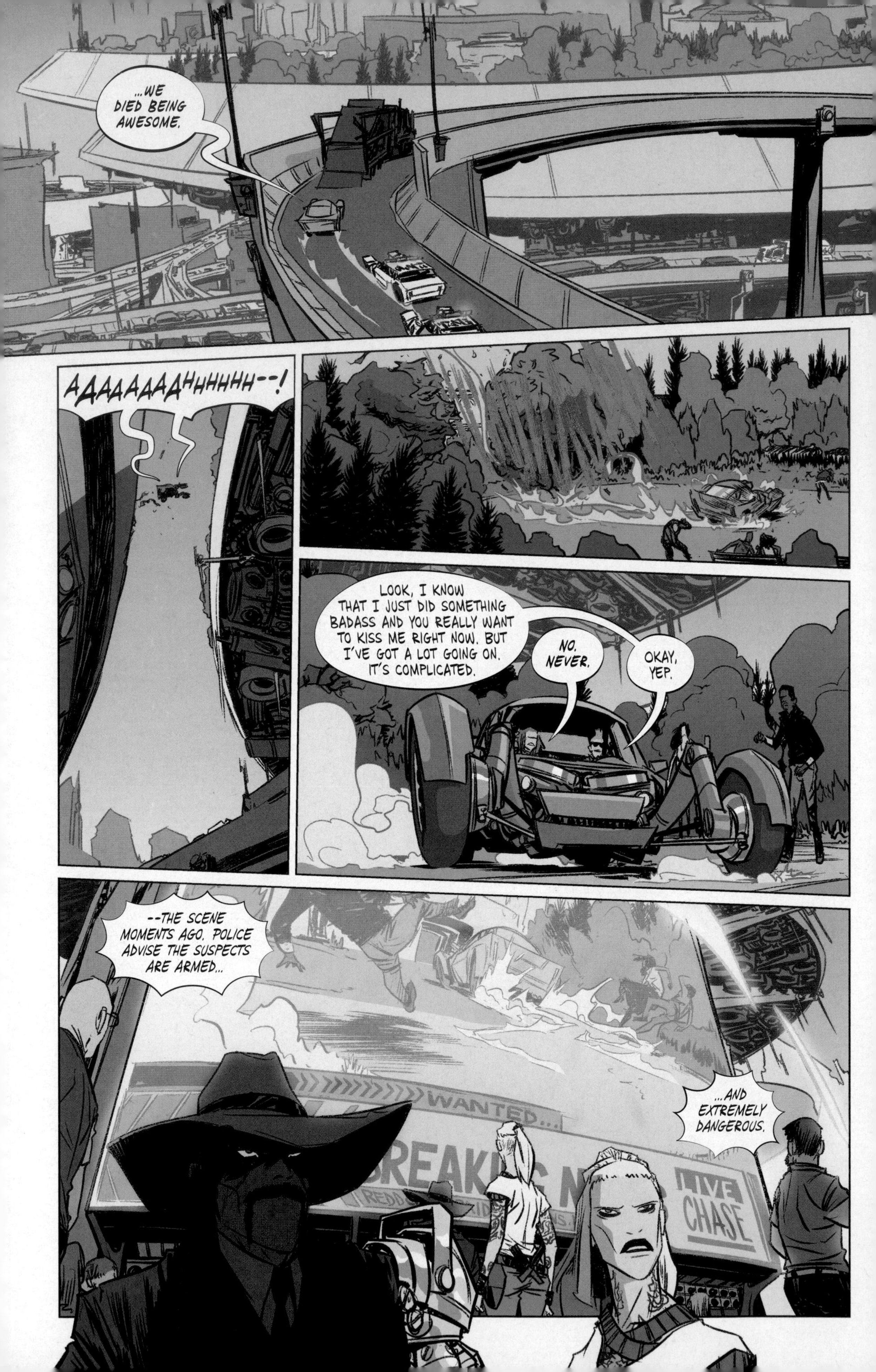
...WE DIED BEING AWESOME.
AAAAAAAHHHHHH--!
LOOK, I KNOW THAT I JUST DID SOMETHING BADASS AND YOU REALLY WANT TO KISS ME RIGHT NOW. BUT I'VE GOT A LOT GOING ON. IT'S COMPLICATED.
NO. NEVER.
OKAY, YEP.
--THE SCENE MOMENTS AGO. POLICE ADVISE THE SUSPECTS ARE ARMED...
WANTED...
LIVE CHASE
...AND EXTREMELY DANGEROUS.

FOUND THIS IN THE CAR, NOT THE MOST IDEAL COVER BUT IT'LL DO.

LOOKS LIKE AN OVERDOSE.

ON WHAT?

MNEMONIUM, ALSO KNOWN AS *"NEMO,"* IT'S EVERYWHERE NOW.

NEMO LETS YOU EXPERIENCE EVENTS FROM THE PAST AS IF THEY WERE HAPPENING ALL OVER AGAIN.

MOST FOLKS USE IT TO REMEMBER LOST LOVED ONES.

JUST MAKE SURE YOU'RE FOCUSING ON THE RIGHT MEMORY. IT'LL AMPLIFY BAD ONES AS WELL.

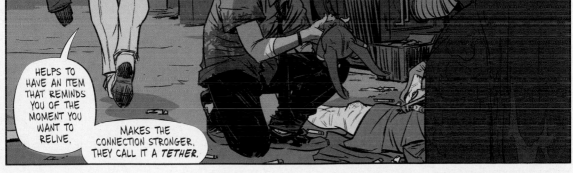

HELPS TO HAVE AN ITEM THAT REMINDS YOU OF THE MOMENT YOU WANT TO RELIVE.

MAKES THE CONNECTION STRONGER. THEY CALL IT A *TETHER.*

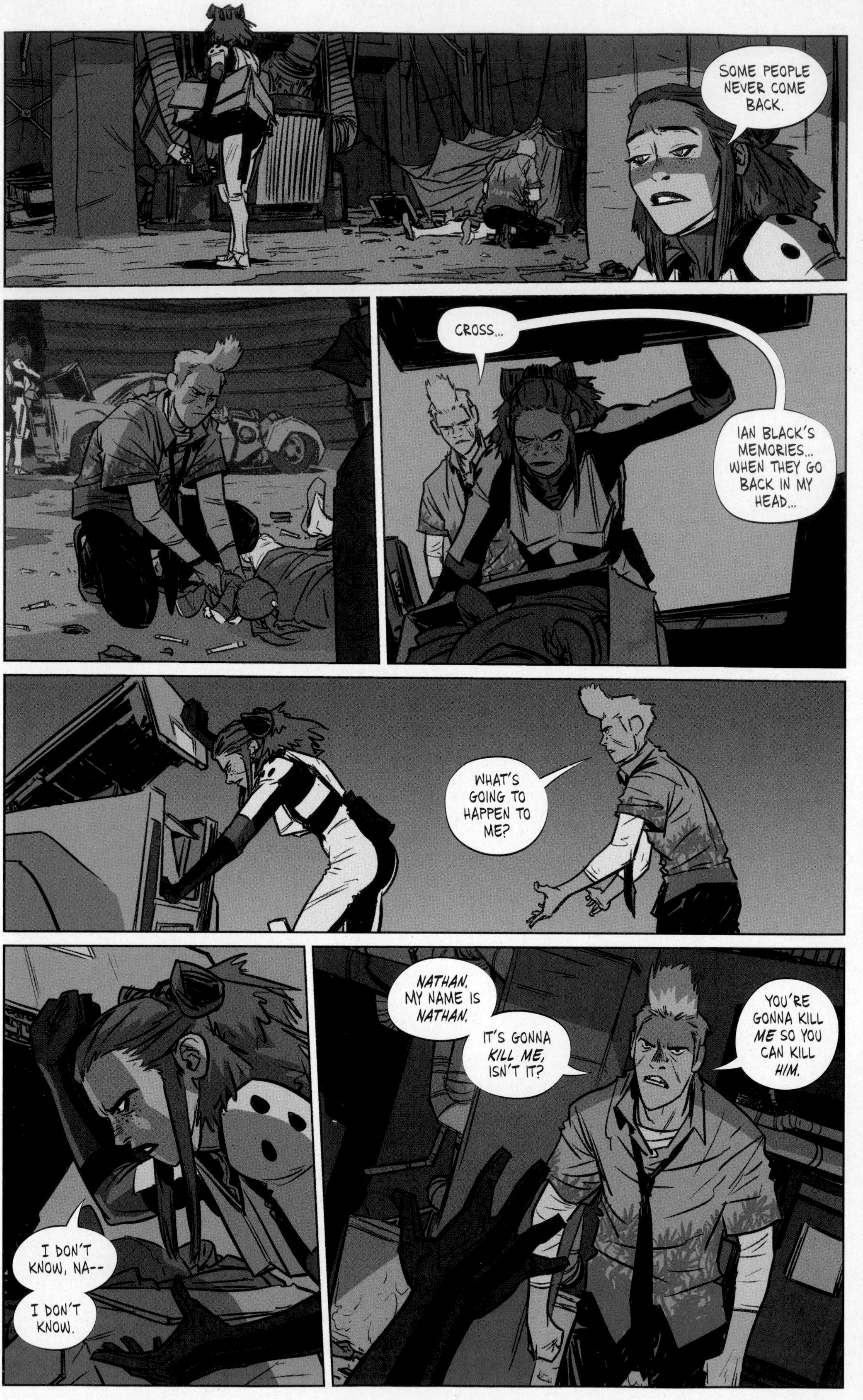
SOME PEOPLE NEVER COME BACK.
CROSS...
IAN BLACK'S MEMORIES... WHEN THEY GO BACK IN MY HEAD...
WHAT'S GOING TO HAPPEN TO ME?
NATHAN. MY NAME IS NATHAN.
IT'S GONNA KILL ME, ISN'T IT?
YOU'RE GONNA KILL ME SO YOU CAN KILL HIM.
I DON'T KNOW, NA--
I DON'T KNOW.

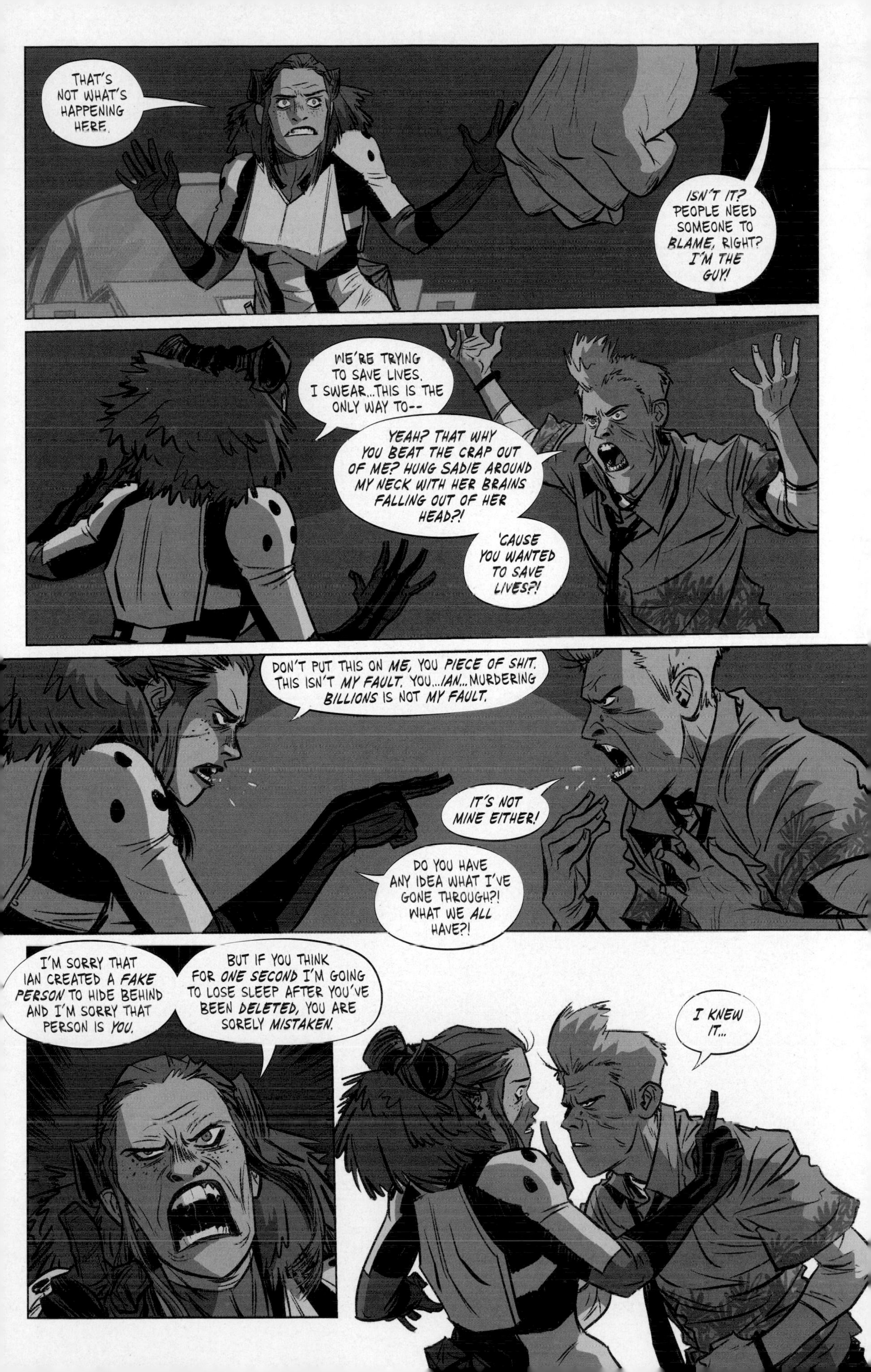
THAT'S NOT WHAT'S HAPPENING HERE.
ISN'T IT? PEOPLE NEED SOMEONE TO BLAME, RIGHT? I'M THE GUY!
WE'RE TRYING TO SAVE LIVES. I SWEAR...THIS IS THE ONLY WAY TO--
YEAH? THAT WHY YOU BEAT THE CRAP OUT OF ME? HUNG SADIE AROUND MY NECK WITH HER BRAINS FALLING OUT OF HER HEAD?!
'CAUSE YOU WANTED TO SAVE LIVES?!
DON'T PUT THIS ON ME, YOU PIECE OF SHIT. THIS ISN'T MY FAULT. YOU...IAN...MURDERING BILLIONS IS NOT MY FAULT.
IT'S NOT MINE EITHER!
DO YOU HAVE ANY IDEA WHAT I'VE GONE THROUGH?! WHAT WE ALL HAVE?!
I'M SORRY THAT IAN CREATED A FAKE PERSON TO HIDE BEHIND AND I'M SORRY THAT PERSON IS YOU.
BUT IF YOU THINK FOR ONE SECOND I'M GOING TO LOSE SLEEP AFTER YOU'VE BEEN DELETED, YOU ARE SORELY MISTAKEN.
I KNEW IT...

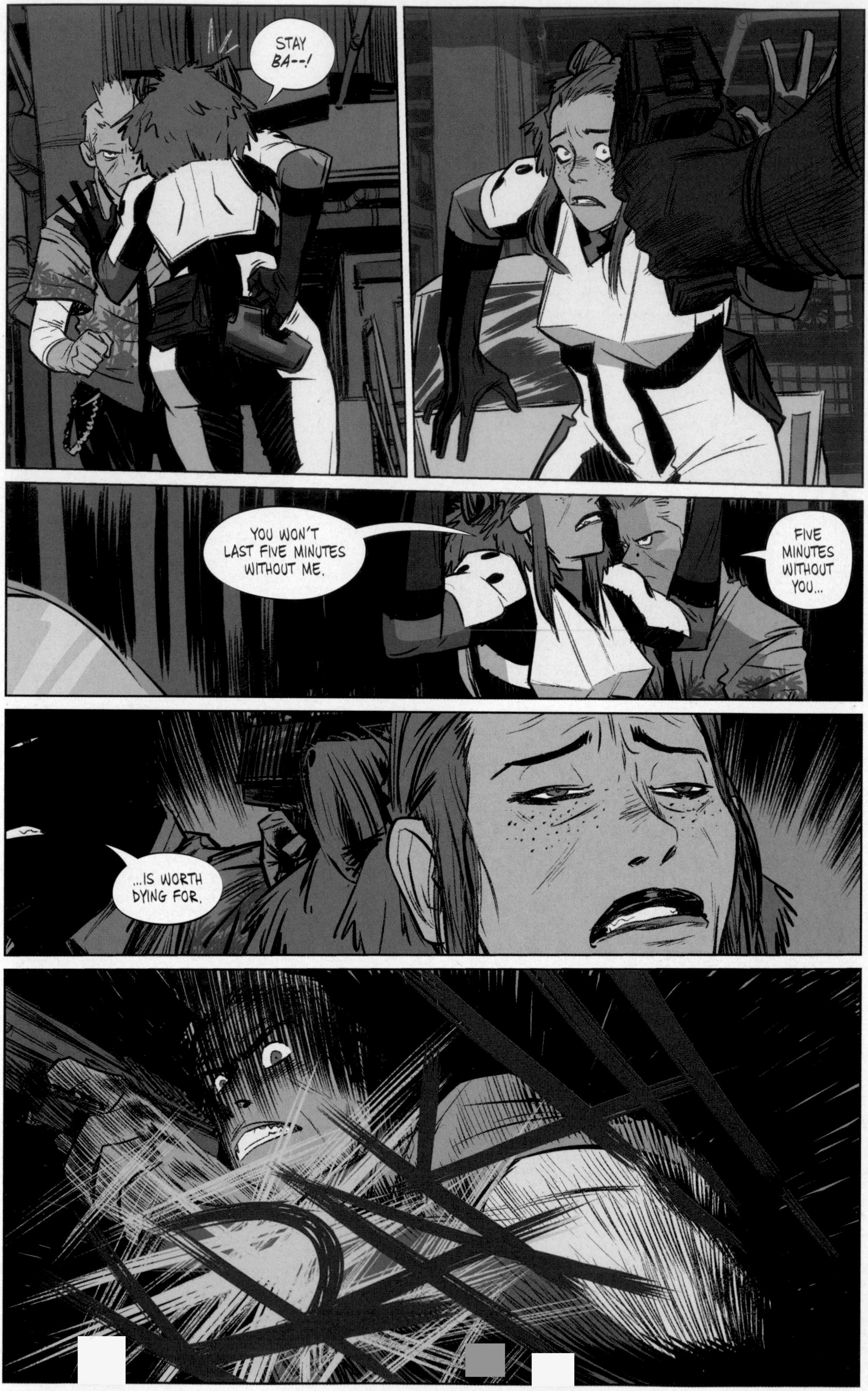
STAY BA--!
YOU WON'T LAST FIVE MINUTES WITHOUT ME.
FIVE MINUTES WITHOUT YOU...
...IS WORTH DYING FOR.

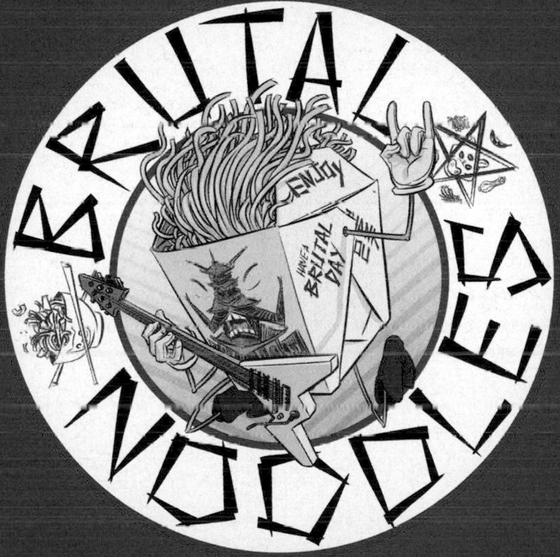
BRUTAL NOODLES
ENJOY
HAVE A BRUTAL DAY

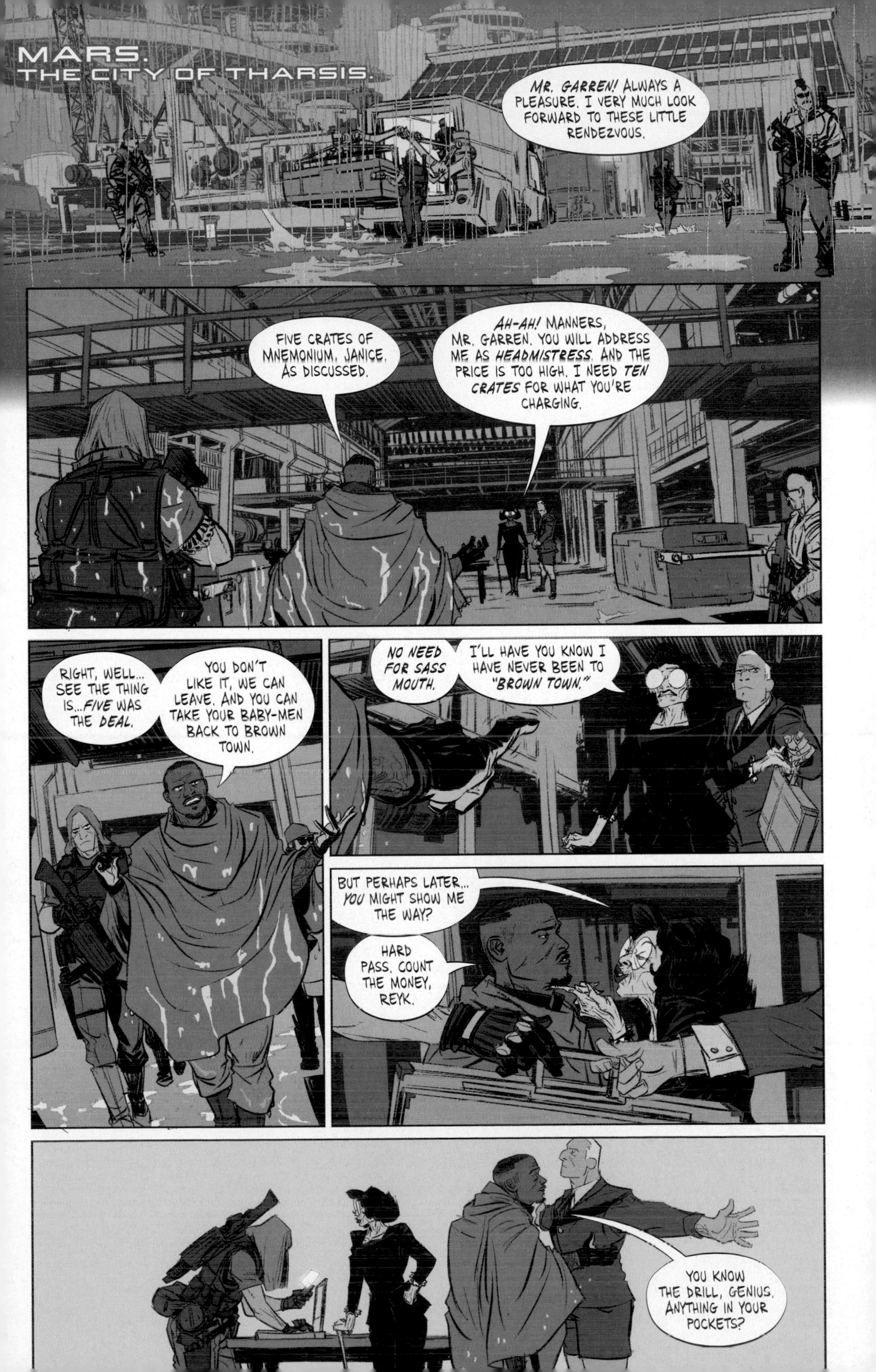
MARS.
THE CITY OF THARSIS.
MR. GARREN! ALWAYS A PLEASURE. I VERY MUCH LOOK FORWARD TO THESE LITTLE RENDEZVOUS.
FIVE CRATES OF MNEMONIUM, JANICE. AS DISCUSSED.
AH-AH! MANNERS, MR. GARREN. YOU WILL ADDRESS ME AS HEADMISTRESS. AND THE PRICE IS TOO HIGH. I NEED TEN CRATES FOR WHAT YOU'RE CHARGING.
RIGHT, WELL... SEE THE THING IS...FIVE WAS THE DEAL.
YOU DON'T LIKE IT, WE CAN LEAVE. AND YOU CAN TAKE YOUR BABY-MEN BACK TO BROWN TOWN.
NO NEED FOR SASS MOUTH.
I'LL HAVE YOU KNOW I HAVE NEVER BEEN TO "BROWN TOWN."
BUT PERHAPS LATER... YOU MIGHT SHOW ME THE WAY?
HARD PASS. COUNT THE MONEY, REYK.
YOU KNOW THE DRILL, GENIUS. ANYTHING IN YOUR POCKETS?

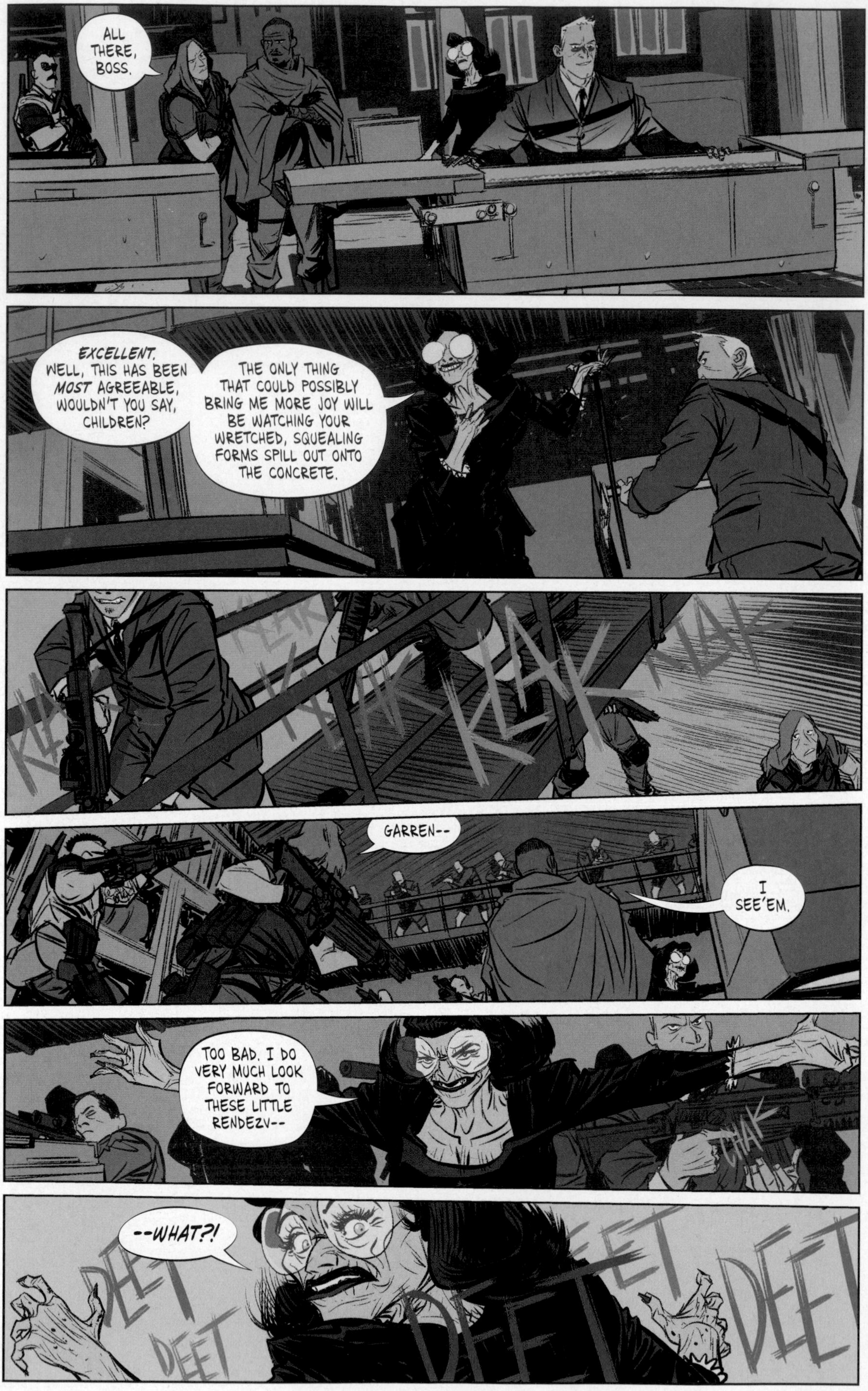
ALL THERE, BOSS.
EXCELLENT. WELL, THIS HAS BEEN MOST AGREEABLE, WOULDN'T YOU SAY, CHILDREN?
THE ONLY THING THAT COULD POSSIBLY BRING ME MORE JOY WILL BE WATCHING YOUR WRETCHED, SQUEALING FORMS SPILL OUT ONTO THE CONCRETE.
KLAK KLAK KLAK KLAK KLAK KLAK
GARREN--
I SEE'EM.
TOO BAD. I DO VERY MUCH LOOK FORWARD TO THESE LITTLE RENDEZV--
CHAK
--WHAT?!
DEET DEET DEET DEET DEET

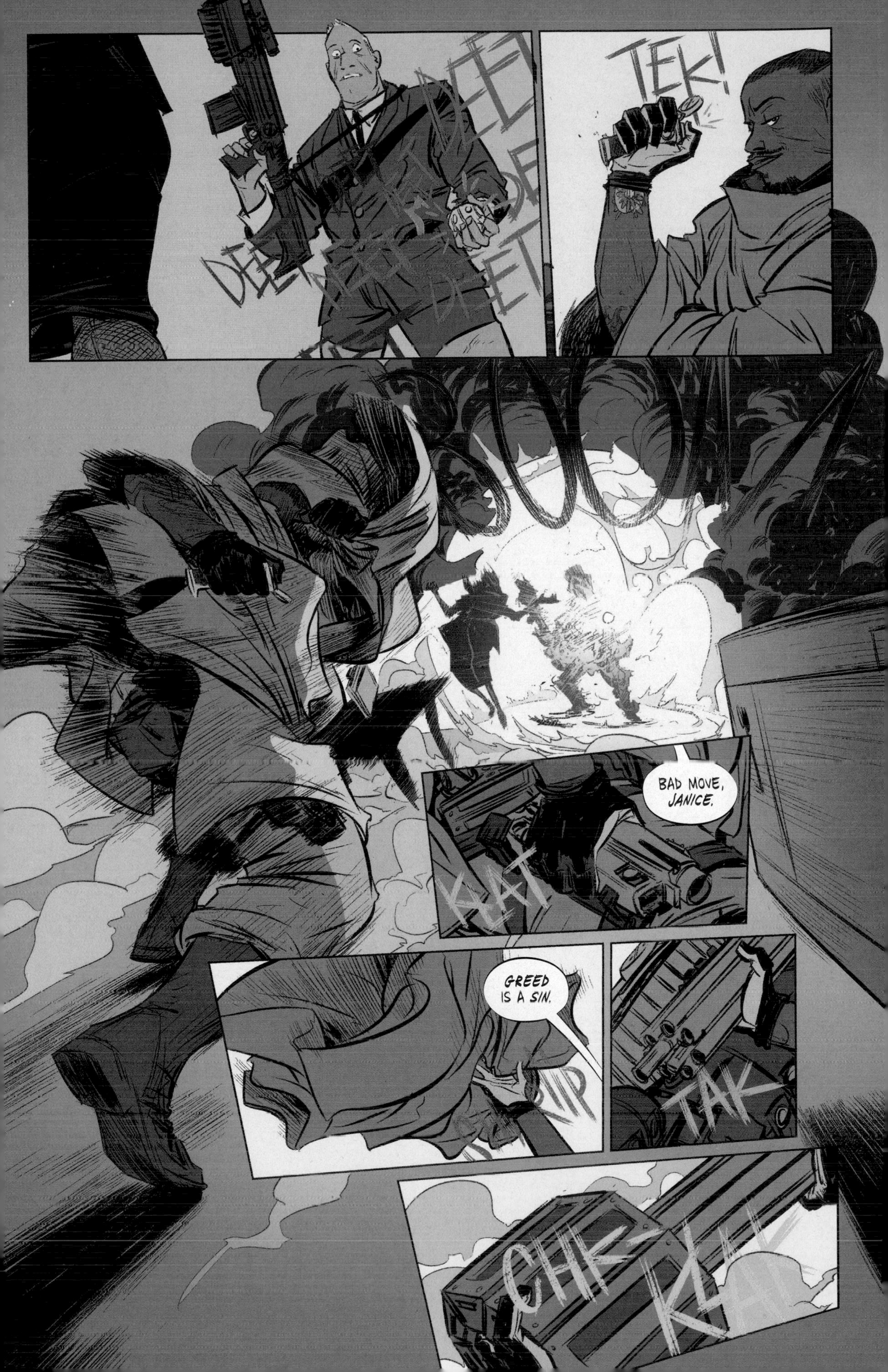
DEET
TEK!
BAD MOVE, JANICE.
KLAT
GREED IS A SIN.
TAK
CHK-KLAK

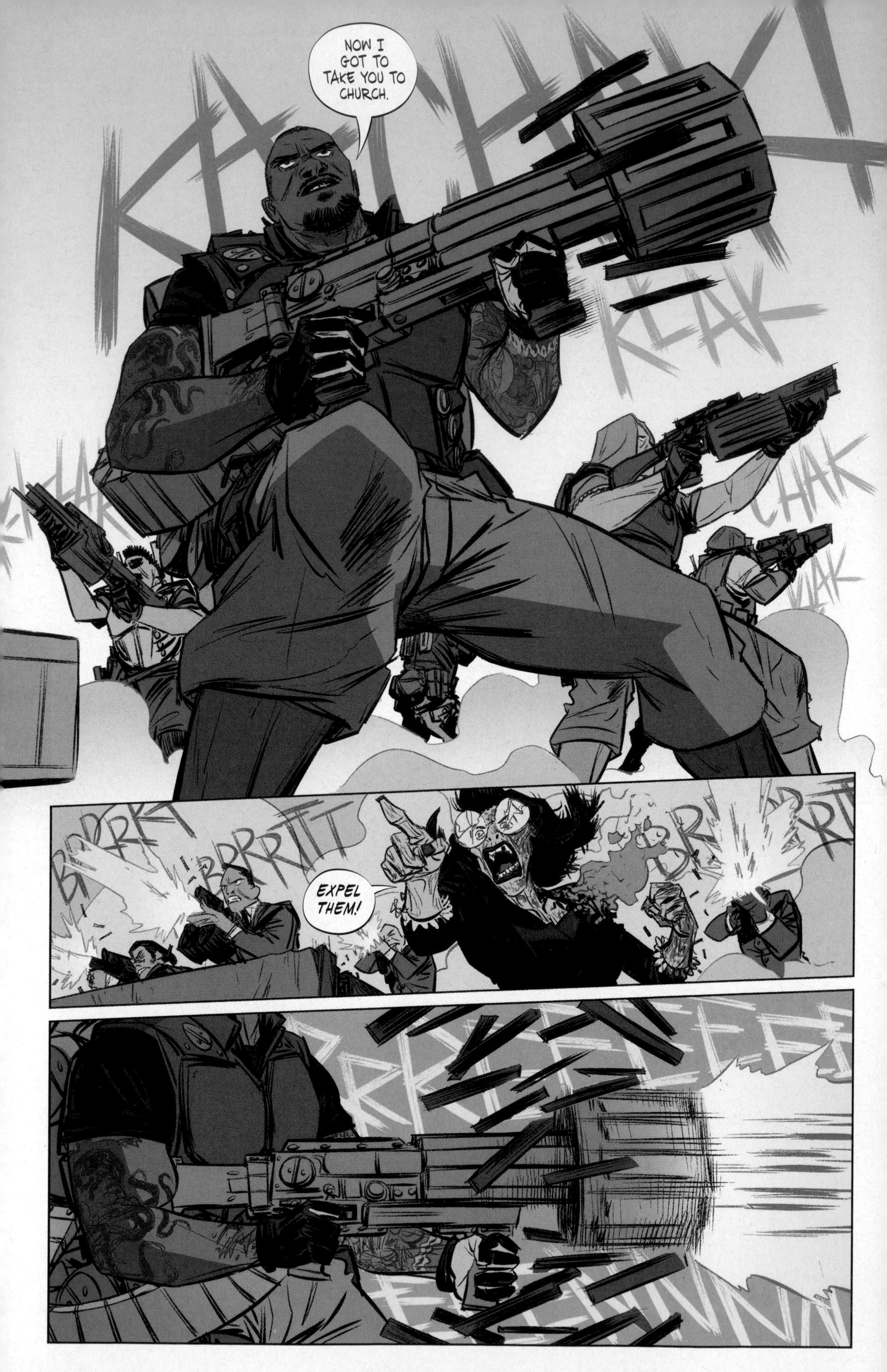
NOW I GOT TO TAKE YOU TO CHURCH.
KLAK
CHAK
EXPEL THEM!
BRRRTTT

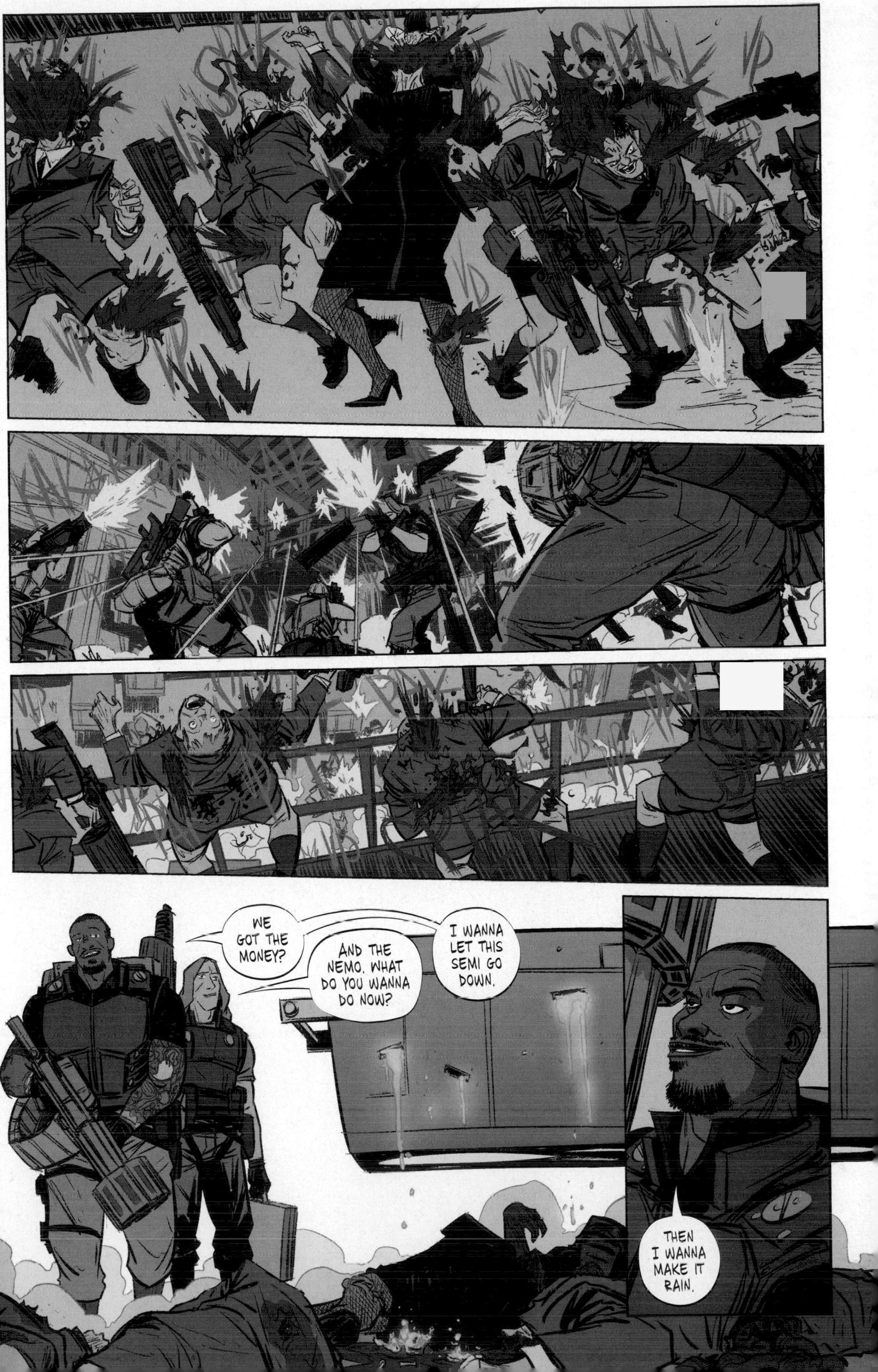
WE GOT THE MONEY?
AND THE NEMO. WHAT DO YOU WANNA DO NOW?
I WANNA LET THIS SEMI GO DOWN.
THEN I WANNA MAKE IT RAIN.

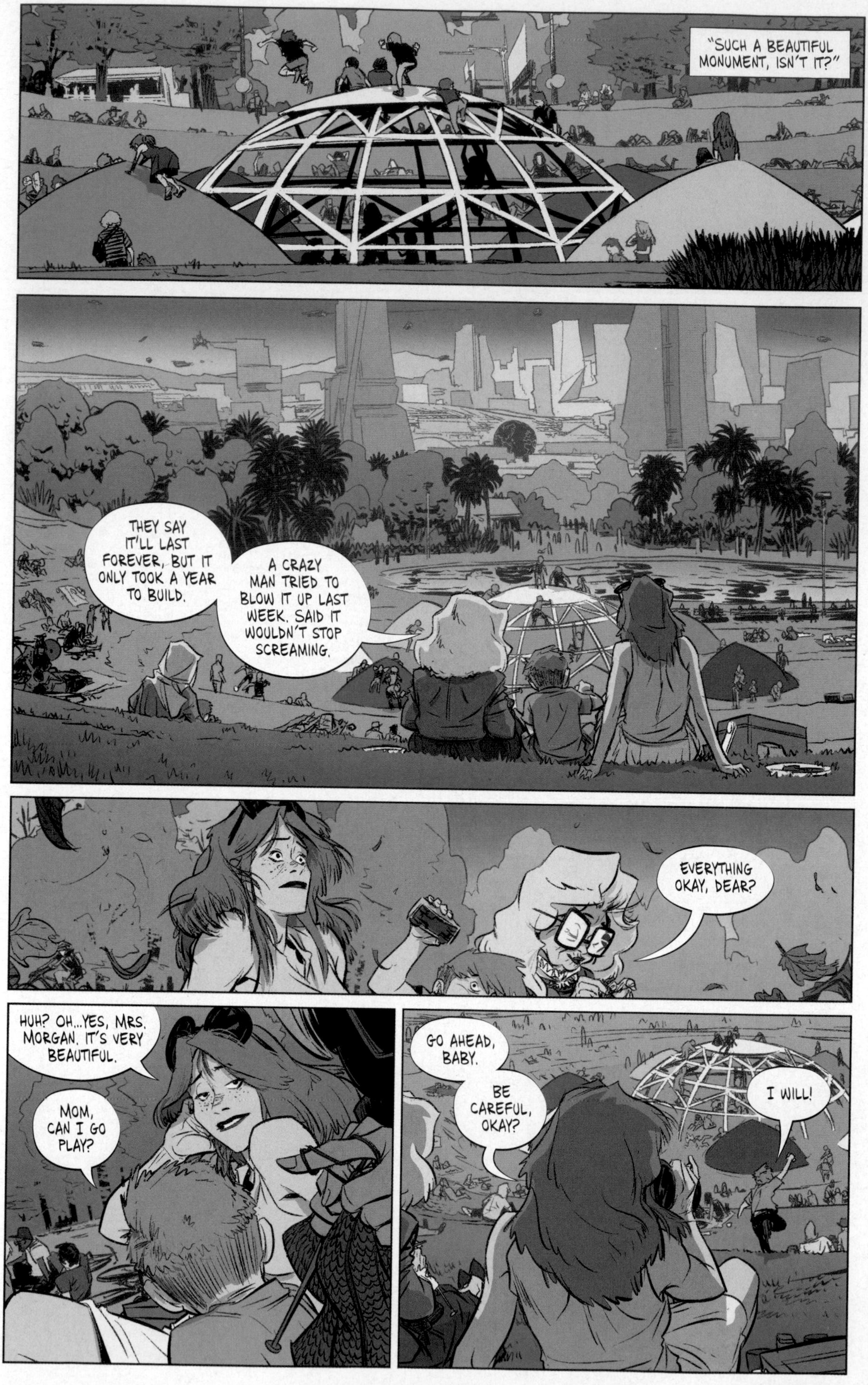
"SUCH A BEAUTIFUL MONUMENT, ISN'T IT?"
THEY SAY IT'LL LAST FOREVER, BUT IT ONLY TOOK A YEAR TO BUILD.
A CRAZY MAN TRIED TO BLOW IT UP LAST WEEK. SAID IT WOULDN'T STOP SCREAMING.
EVERYTHING OKAY, DEAR?
HUH? OH...YES, MRS. MORGAN. IT'S VERY BEAUTIFUL.
MOM, CAN I GO PLAY?
GO AHEAD, BABY.
BE CAREFUL, OKAY?
I WILL!

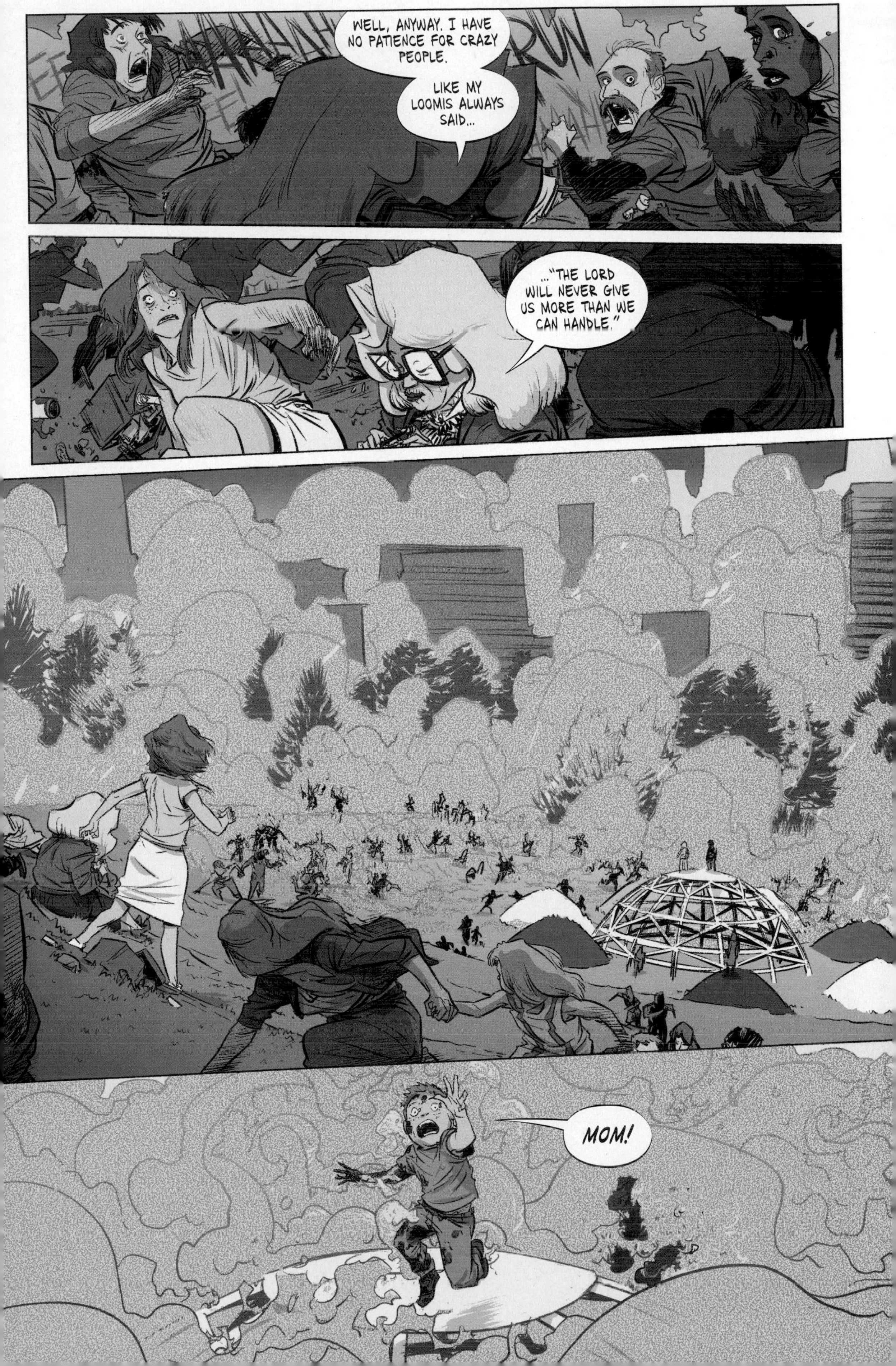
WELL, ANYWAY. I HAVE NO PATIENCE FOR CRAZY PEOPLE.
LIKE MY LOOMIS ALWAYS SAID...
..."THE LORD WILL NEVER GIVE US MORE THAN WE CAN HANDLE."
MOM!

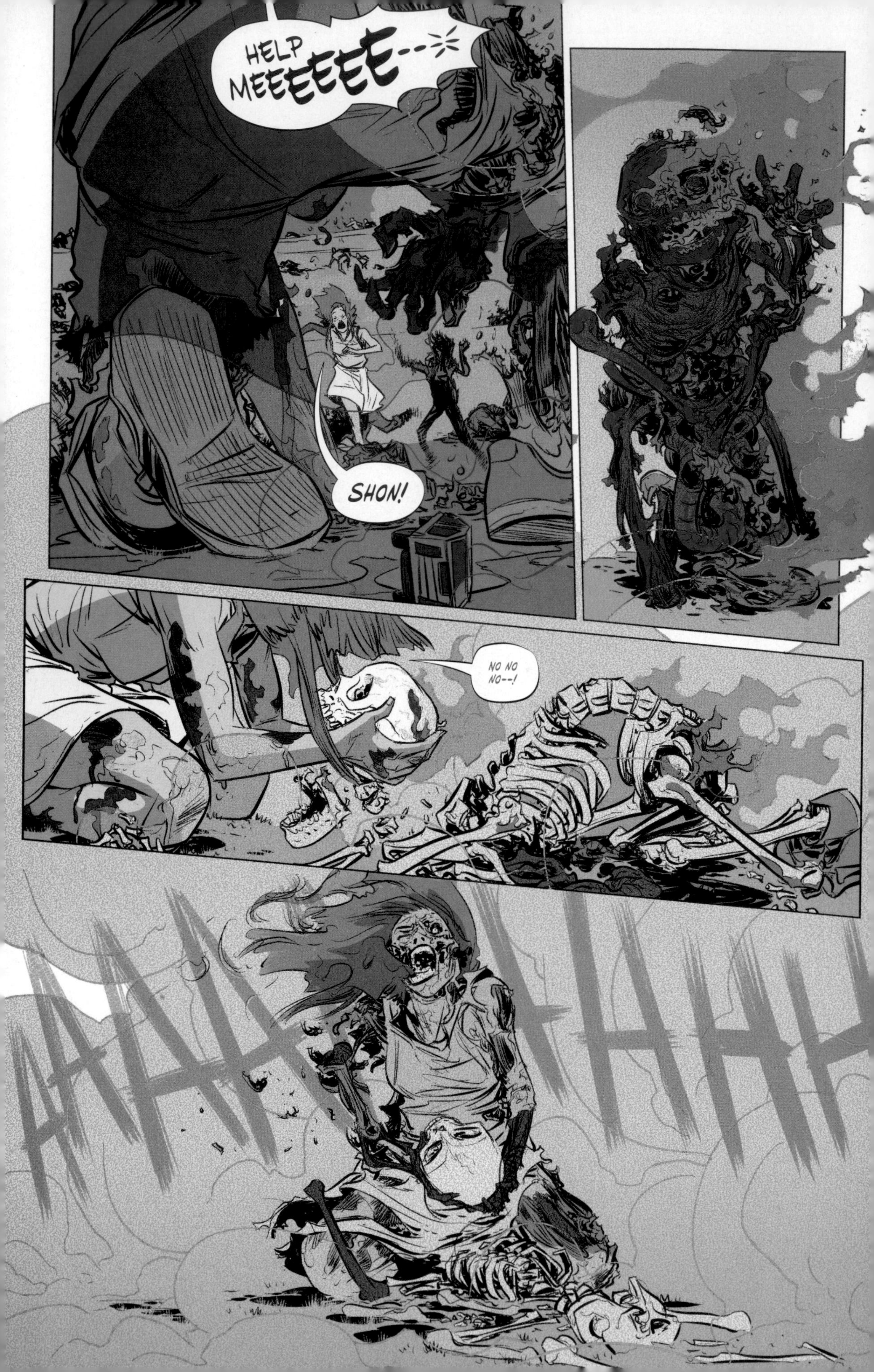
HELP MEEEEEEE--
SHON!
NO NO NO--!
AAAAHHH

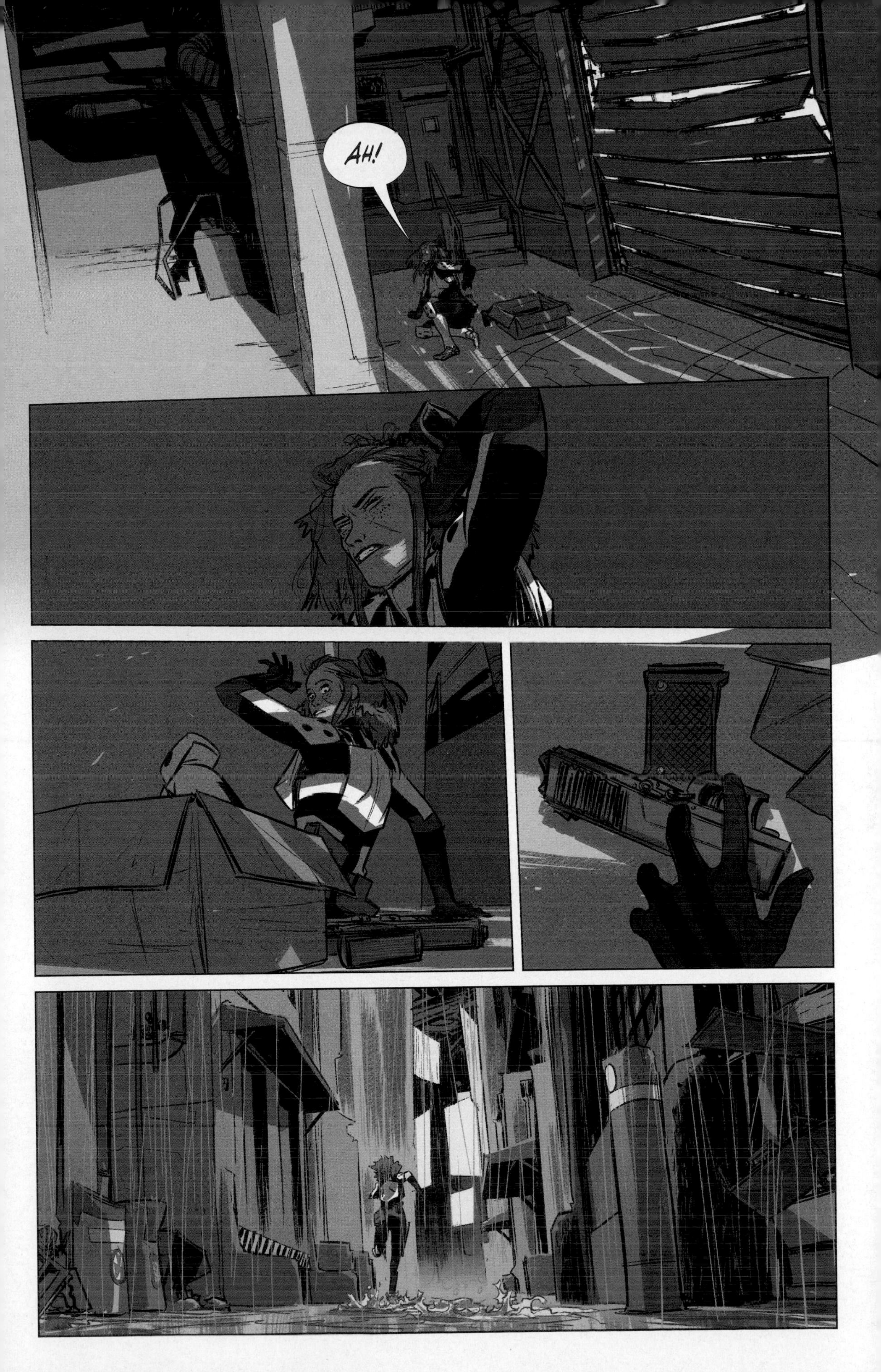
AH!

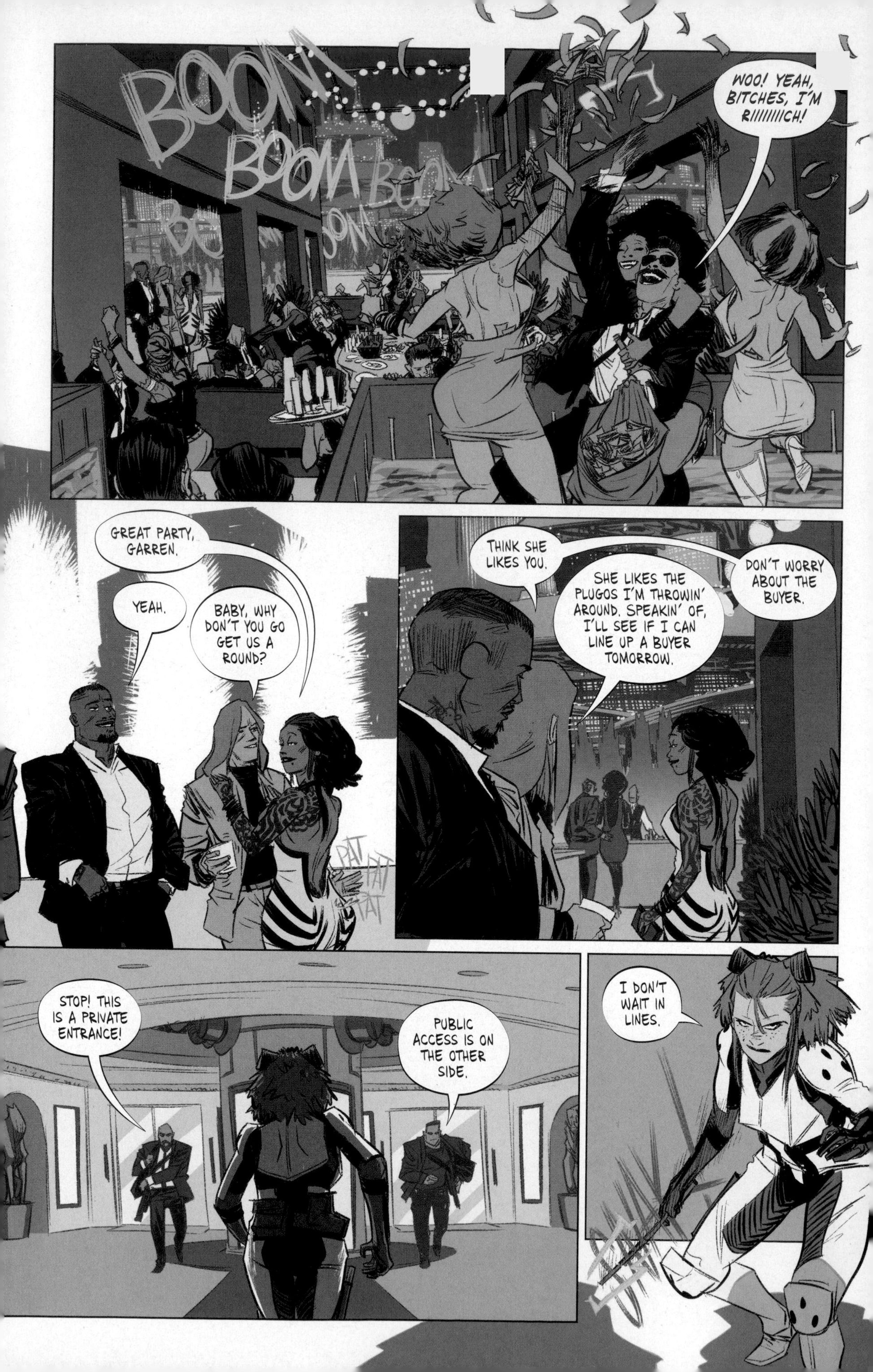
BOOM
BOOM
BOOM
BOOM
WOO! YEAH, BITCHES, I'M RIIIIIIICH!
GREAT PARTY, GARREN.
YEAH.
BABY, WHY DON'T YOU GO GET US A ROUND?
PAT PAT PAT
THINK SHE LIKES YOU.
SHE LIKES THE PLUGOS I'M THROWIN' AROUND. SPEAKIN' OF, I'LL SEE IF I CAN LINE UP A BUYER TOMORROW.
DON'T WORRY ABOUT THE BUYER.
STOP! THIS IS A PRIVATE ENTRANCE!
PUBLIC ACCESS IS ON THE OTHER SIDE.
I DON'T WAIT IN LINES.

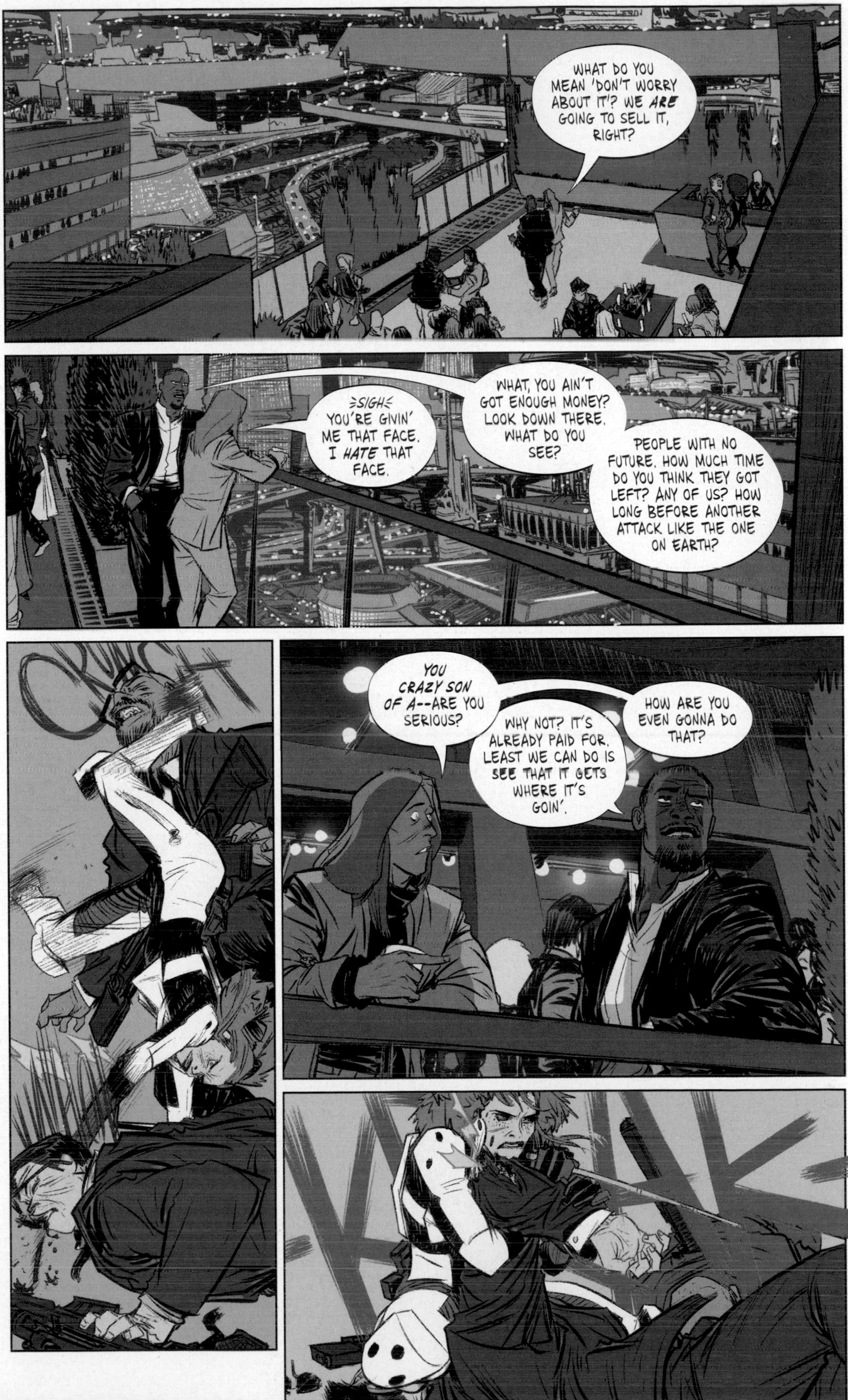
WHAT DO YOU MEAN 'DON'T WORRY ABOUT IT'? WE *ARE* GOING TO SELL IT, RIGHT?
SIGH YOU'RE GIVIN' ME THAT FACE. I *HATE* THAT FACE.
WHAT, YOU AIN'T GOT ENOUGH MONEY? LOOK DOWN THERE. WHAT DO YOU SEE?
PEOPLE WITH NO FUTURE. HOW MUCH TIME DO YOU THINK THEY GOT LEFT? ANY OF US? HOW LONG BEFORE ANOTHER ATTACK LIKE THE ONE ON EARTH?
YOU *CRAZY SON OF A*--ARE YOU SERIOUS?
WHY NOT? IT'S ALREADY PAID FOR. LEAST WE CAN DO IS SEE THAT IT GETS WHERE IT'S GOIN'.
HOW ARE YOU EVEN GONNA DO THAT?

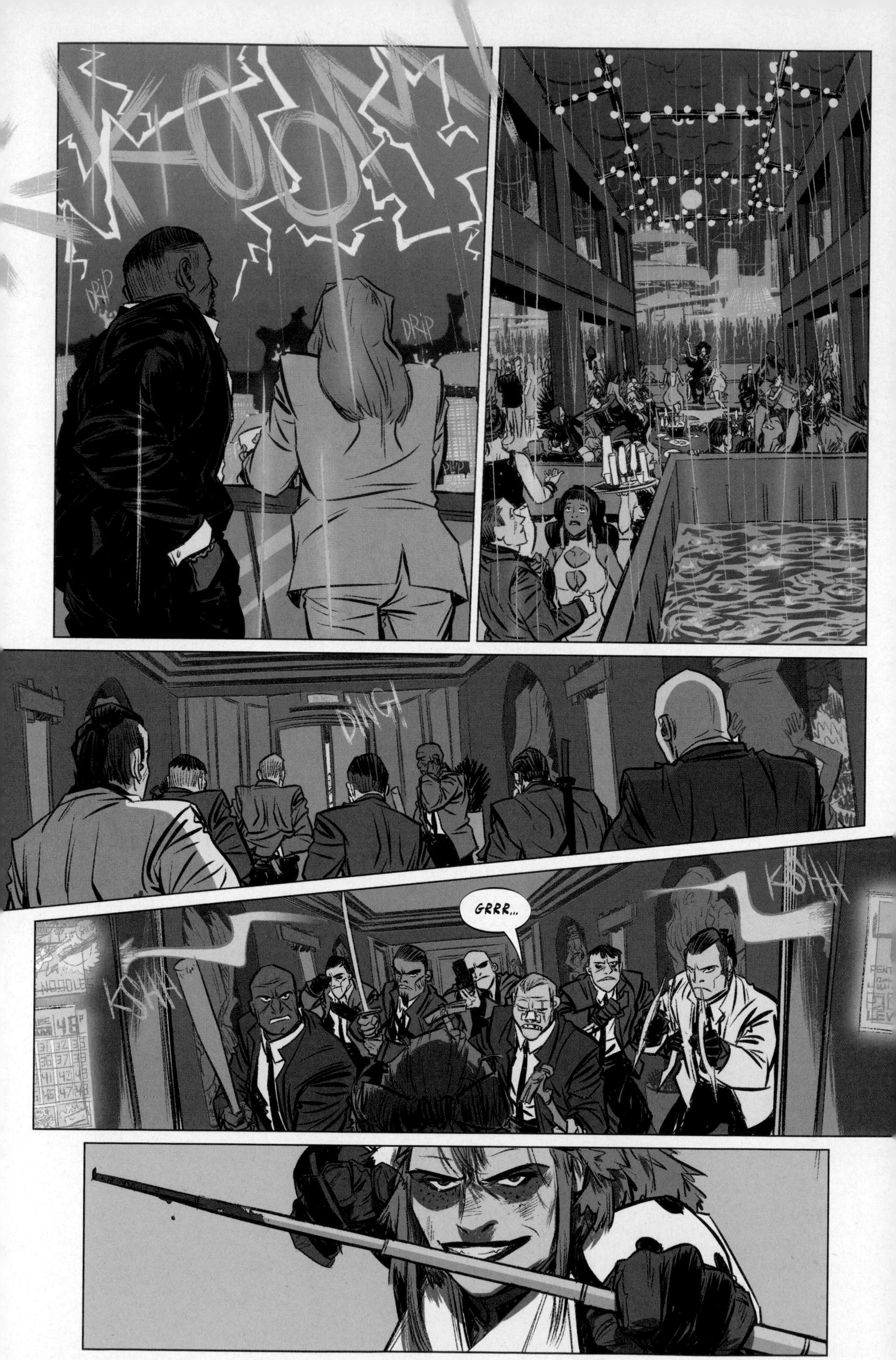
DRIP
DRIP
DING!
GRRR...
KSHH
KSHH

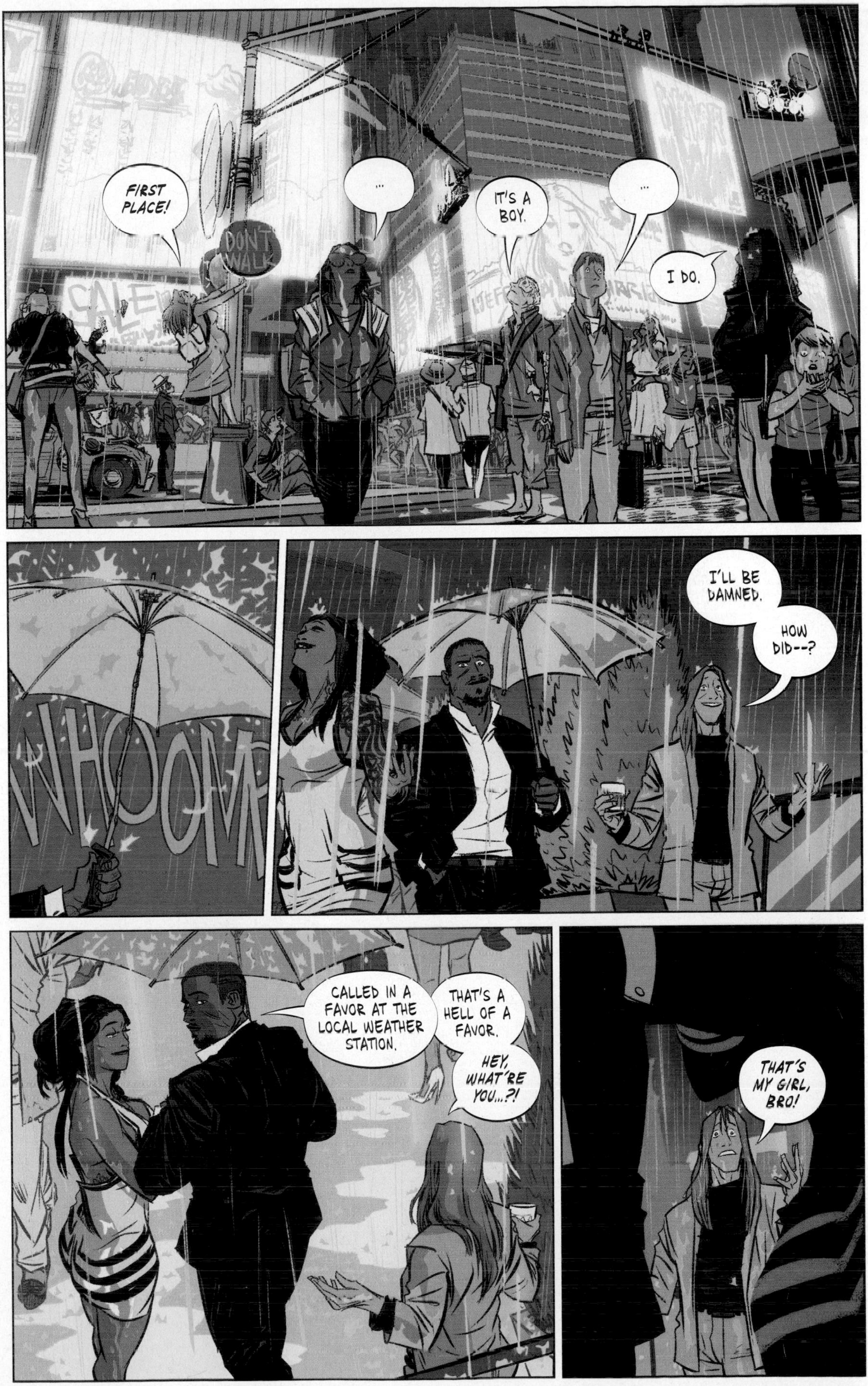
FIRST PLACE!
...
IT'S A BOY.
...
I DO.
DON'T WALK
SALE
WHOOM
I'LL BE DAMNED.
HOW DID--?
CALLED IN A FAVOR AT THE LOCAL WEATHER STATION.
THAT'S A HELL OF A FAVOR.
HEY, WHAT'RE YOU...?!
THAT'S MY GIRL, BRO!

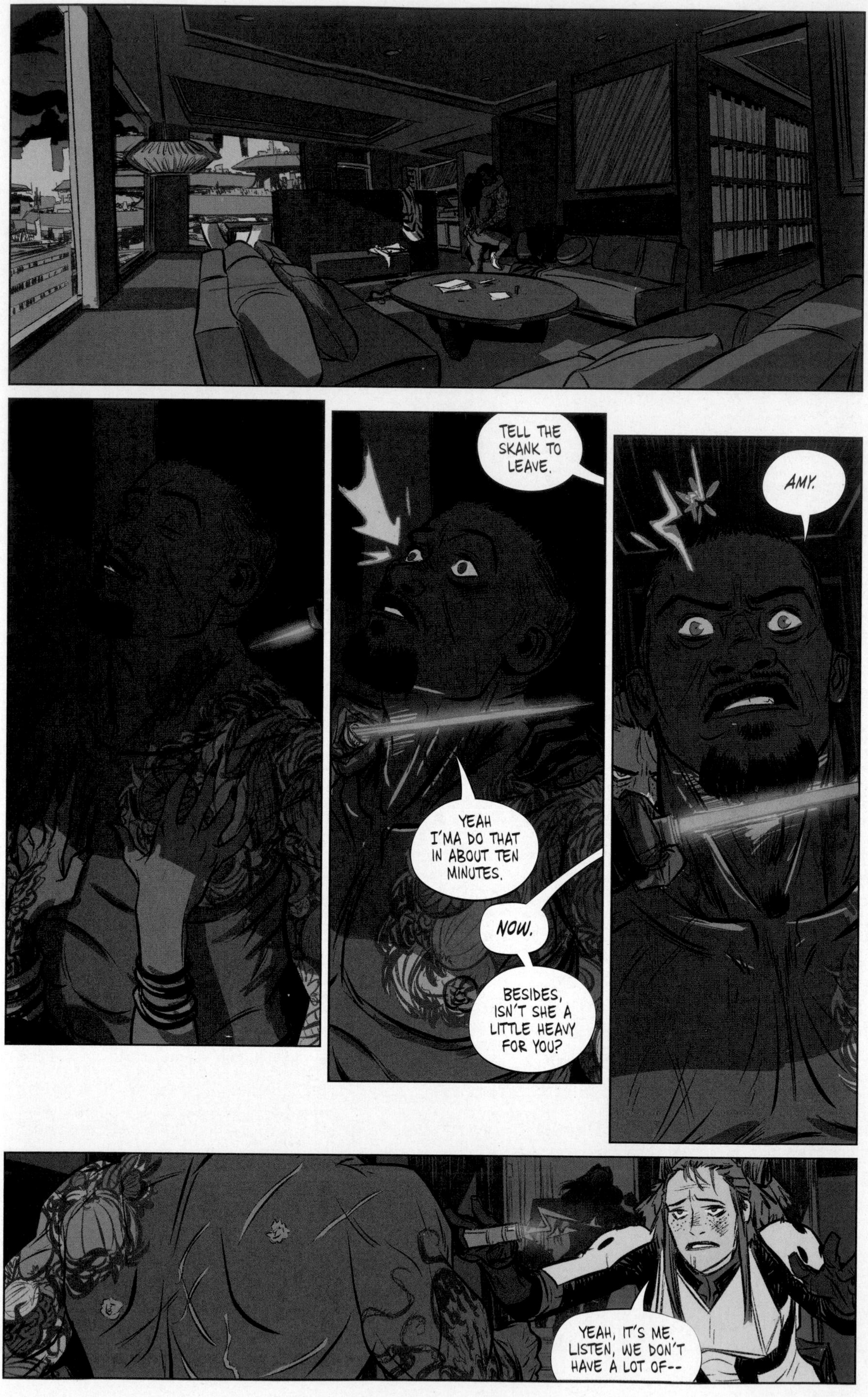
TELL THE SKANK TO LEAVE.
YEAH I'MA DO THAT IN ABOUT TEN MINUTES.
NOW.
BESIDES, ISN'T SHE A LITTLE HEAVY FOR YOU?
AMY.
YEAH, IT'S ME. LISTEN, WE DON'T HAVE A LOT OF--

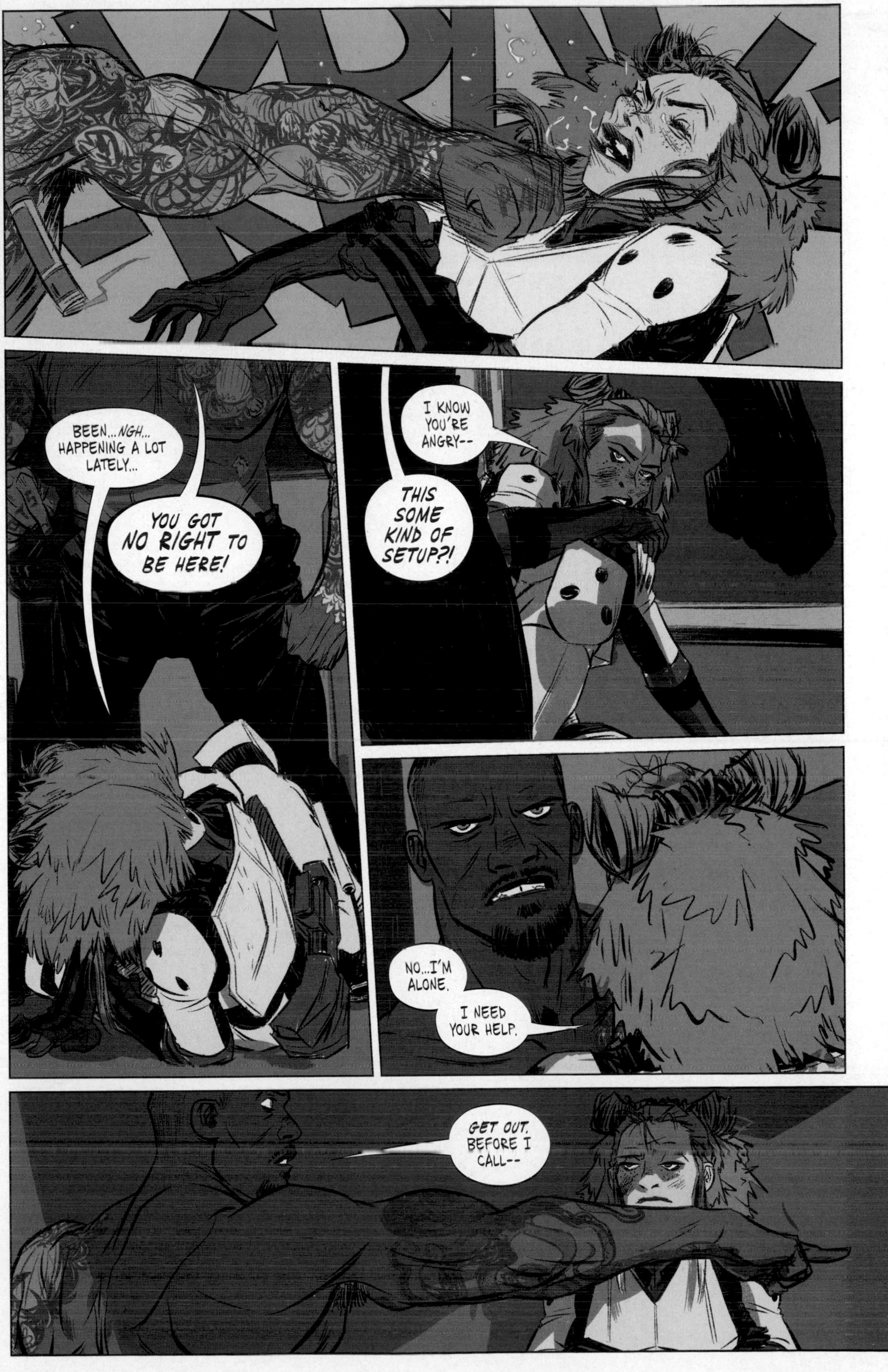
BEEN...NGH... HAPPENING A LOT LATELY...
YOU GOT NO RIGHT TO BE HERE!
I KNOW YOU'RE ANGRY--
THIS SOME KIND OF SETUP?!
NO...I'M ALONE.
I NEED YOUR HELP.
GET OUT. BEFORE I CALL--

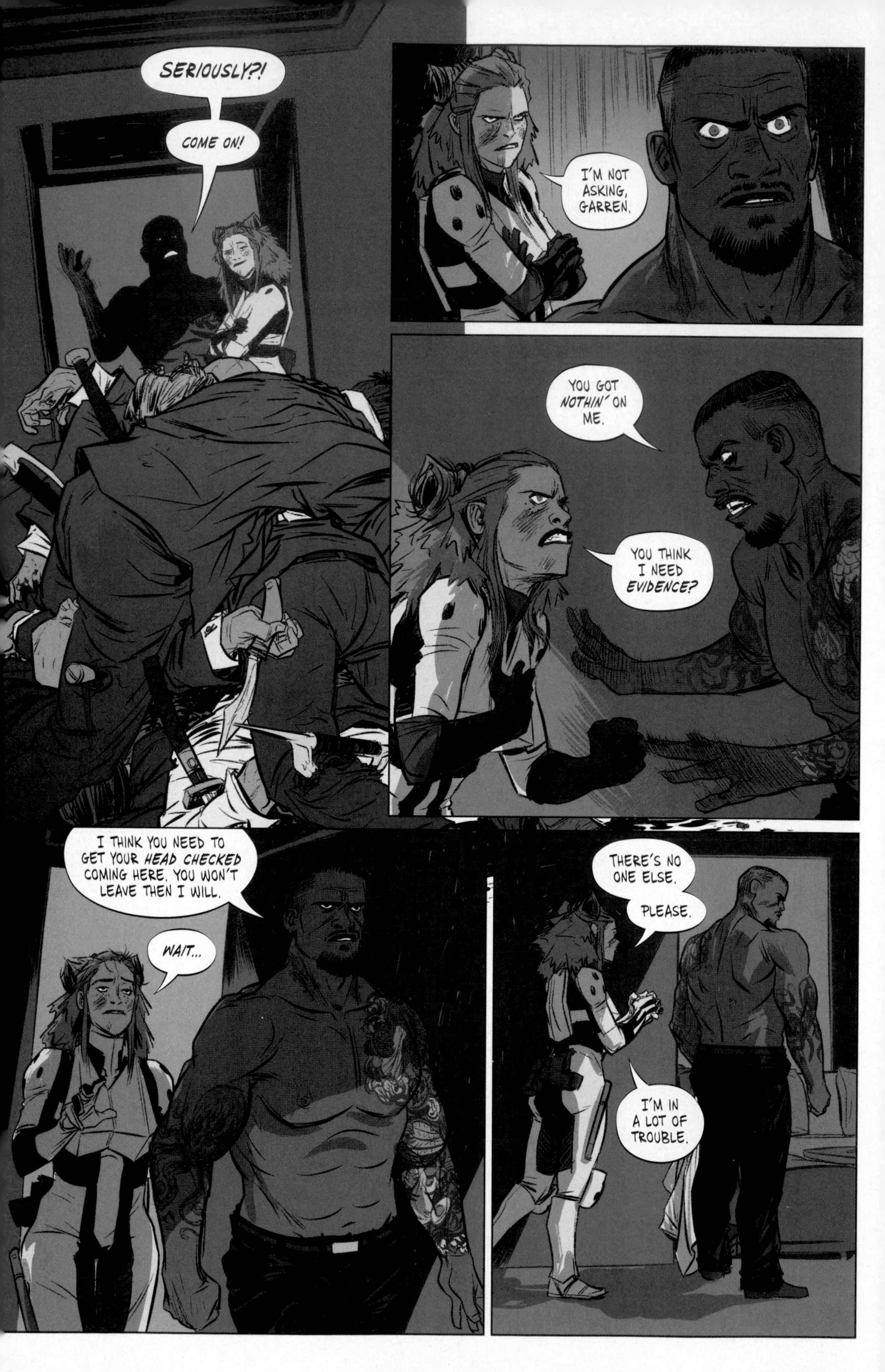
SERIOUSLY?!
COME ON!
I'M NOT ASKING, GARREN.
YOU GOT *NOTHIN'* ON ME.
YOU THINK I NEED *EVIDENCE?*
I THINK YOU NEED TO GET YOUR *HEAD CHECKED* COMING HERE. YOU WON'T LEAVE THEN I WILL.
WAIT...
THERE'S NO ONE ELSE.
PLEASE.
I'M IN A LOT OF TROUBLE.

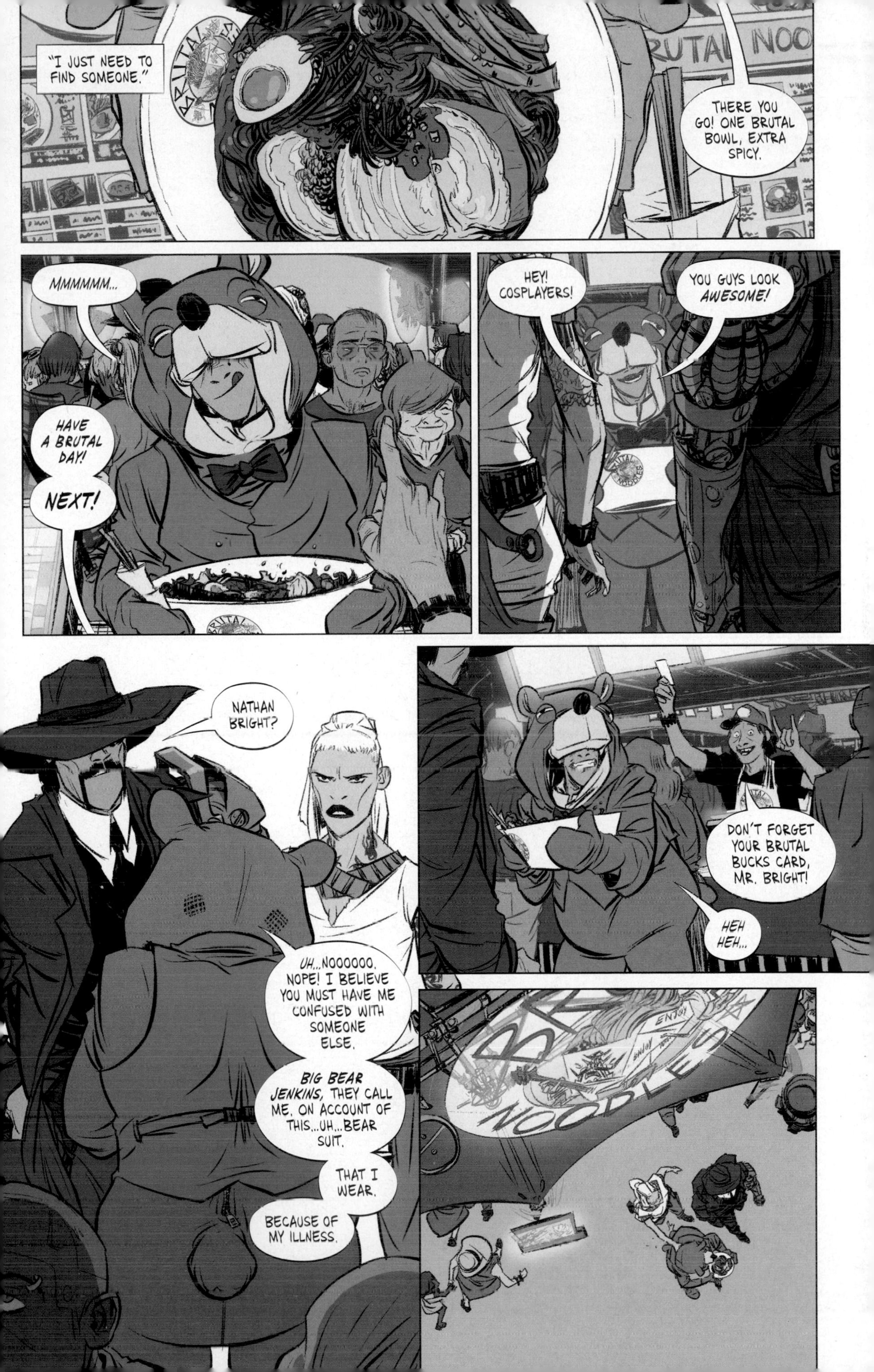
"I JUST NEED TO FIND SOMEONE."
THERE YOU GO! ONE BRUTAL BOWL, EXTRA SPICY.
BRUTAL NOO
MMMMMM...
HAVE A BRUTAL DAY!
NEXT!
HEY! COSPLAYERS!
YOU GUYS LOOK *AWESOME!*
NATHAN BRIGHT?
UH...NOOOOOO. NOPE! I BELIEVE YOU MUST HAVE ME CONFUSED WITH SOMEONE ELSE.
BIG BEAR JENKINS, THEY CALL ME, ON ACCOUNT OF THIS...UH...BEAR SUIT.
THAT I WEAR.
BECAUSE OF MY ILLNESS.
DON'T FORGET YOUR BRUTAL BUCKS CARD, MR. BRIGHT!
HEH HEH...
NOODLES

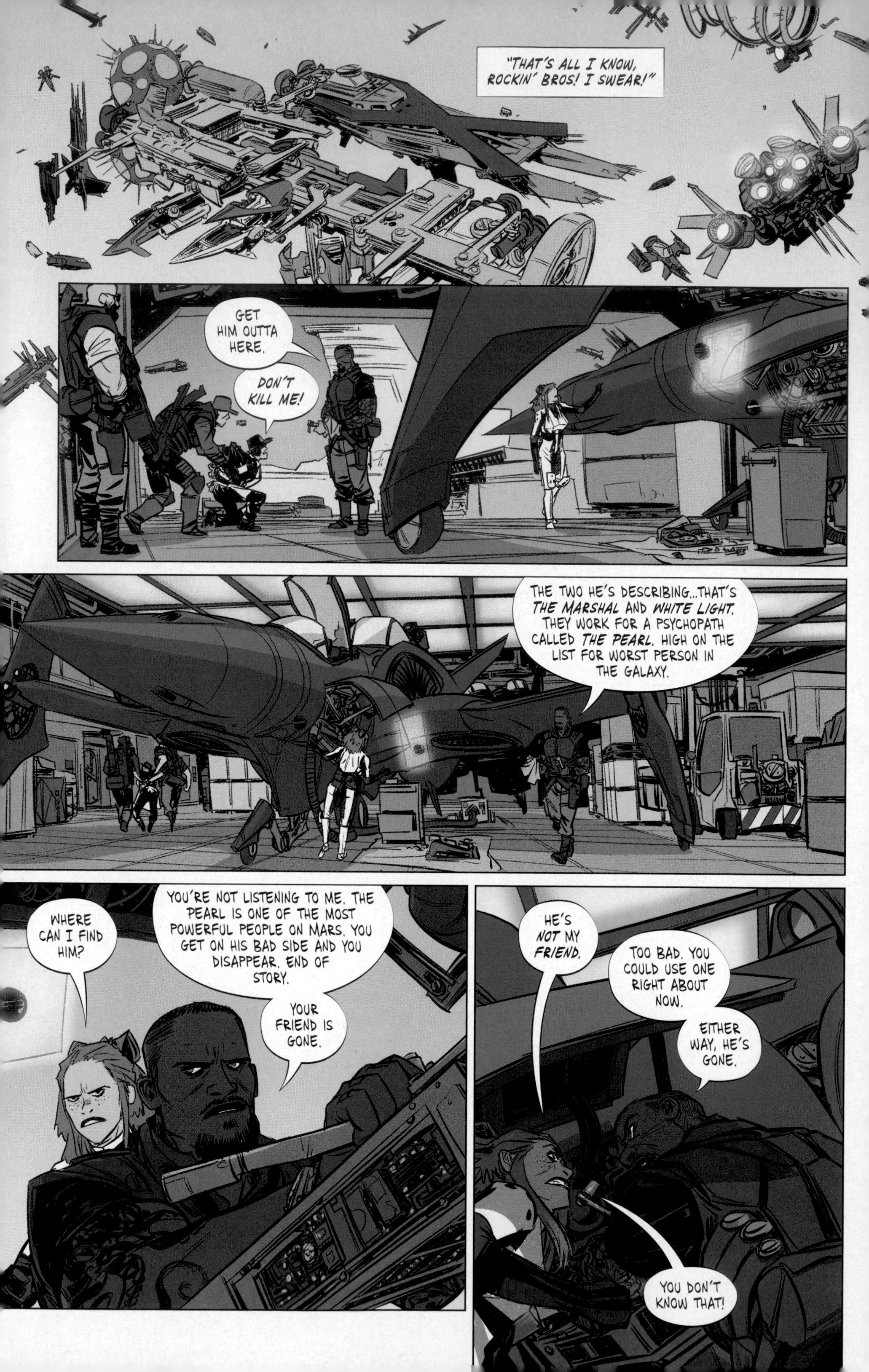
"THAT'S ALL I KNOW, ROCKIN' BROS! I SWEAR!"
GET HIM OUTTA HERE.
DON'T KILL ME!
THE TWO HE'S DESCRIBING...THAT'S THE MARSHAL AND WHITE LIGHT. THEY WORK FOR A PSYCHOPATH CALLED THE PEARL. HIGH ON THE LIST FOR WORST PERSON IN THE GALAXY.
WHERE CAN I FIND HIM?
YOU'RE NOT LISTENING TO ME. THE PEARL IS ONE OF THE MOST POWERFUL PEOPLE ON MARS. YOU GET ON HIS BAD SIDE AND YOU DISAPPEAR. END OF STORY.
YOUR FRIEND IS GONE.
HE'S NOT MY FRIEND.
TOO BAD. YOU COULD USE ONE RIGHT ABOUT NOW.
EITHER WAY, HE'S GONE.
YOU DON'T KNOW THAT!

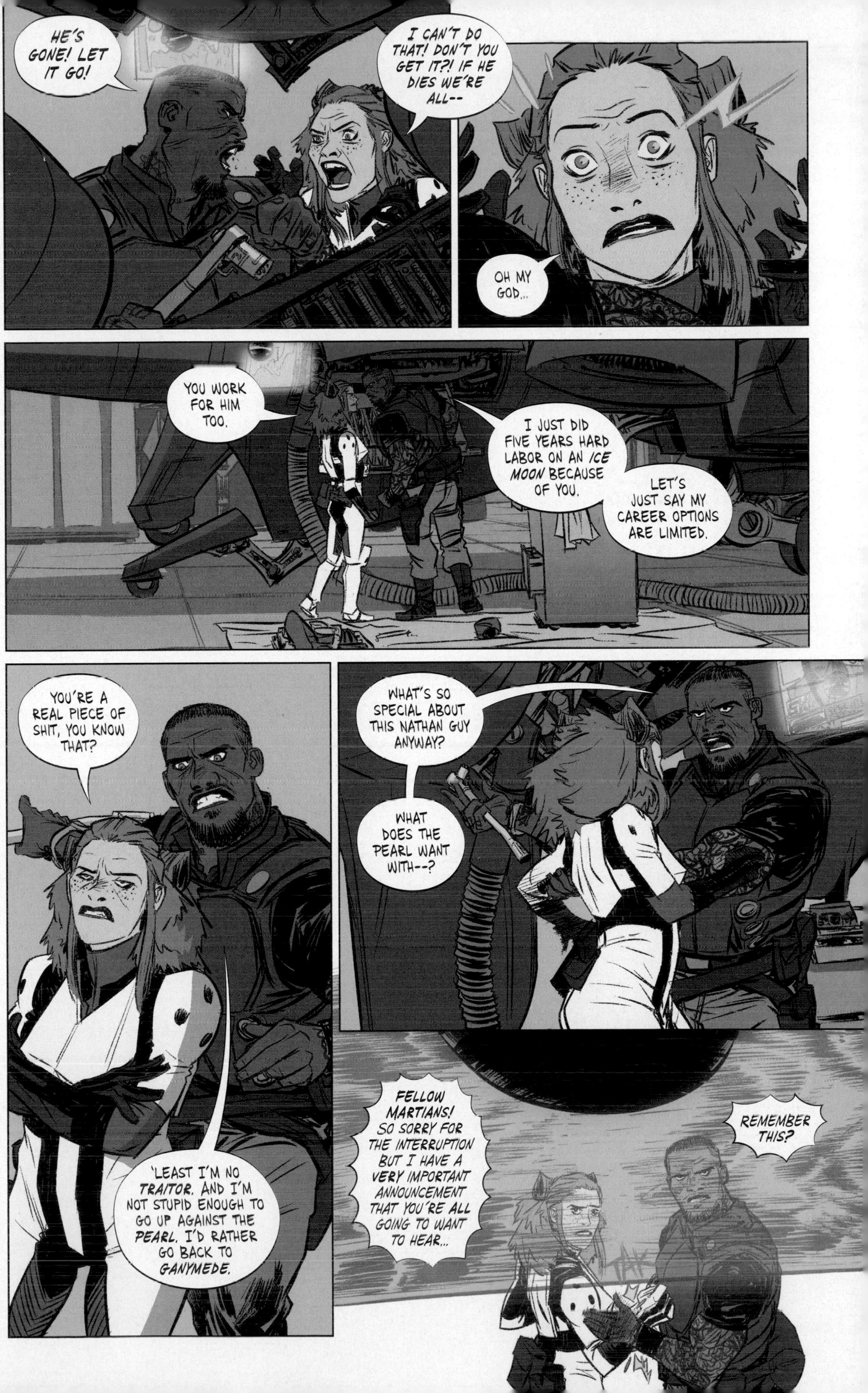
HE'S GONE! LET IT GO!
I CAN'T DO THAT! DON'T YOU GET IT?! IF HE DIES WE'RE ALL--
OH MY GOD...
YOU WORK FOR HIM TOO.
I JUST DID FIVE YEARS HARD LABOR ON AN ICE MOON BECAUSE OF YOU.
LET'S JUST SAY MY CAREER OPTIONS ARE LIMITED.
YOU'RE A REAL PIECE OF SHIT, YOU KNOW THAT?
'LEAST I'M NO TRAITOR. AND I'M NOT STUPID ENOUGH TO GO UP AGAINST THE PEARL. I'D RATHER GO BACK TO GANYMEDE.
WHAT'S SO SPECIAL ABOUT THIS NATHAN GUY ANYWAY?
WHAT DOES THE PEARL WANT WITH--?
FELLOW MARTIANS! SO SORRY FOR THE INTERRUPTION BUT I HAVE A VERY IMPORTANT ANNOUNCEMENT THAT YOU'RE ALL GOING TO WANT TO HEAR...
REMEMBER THIS?

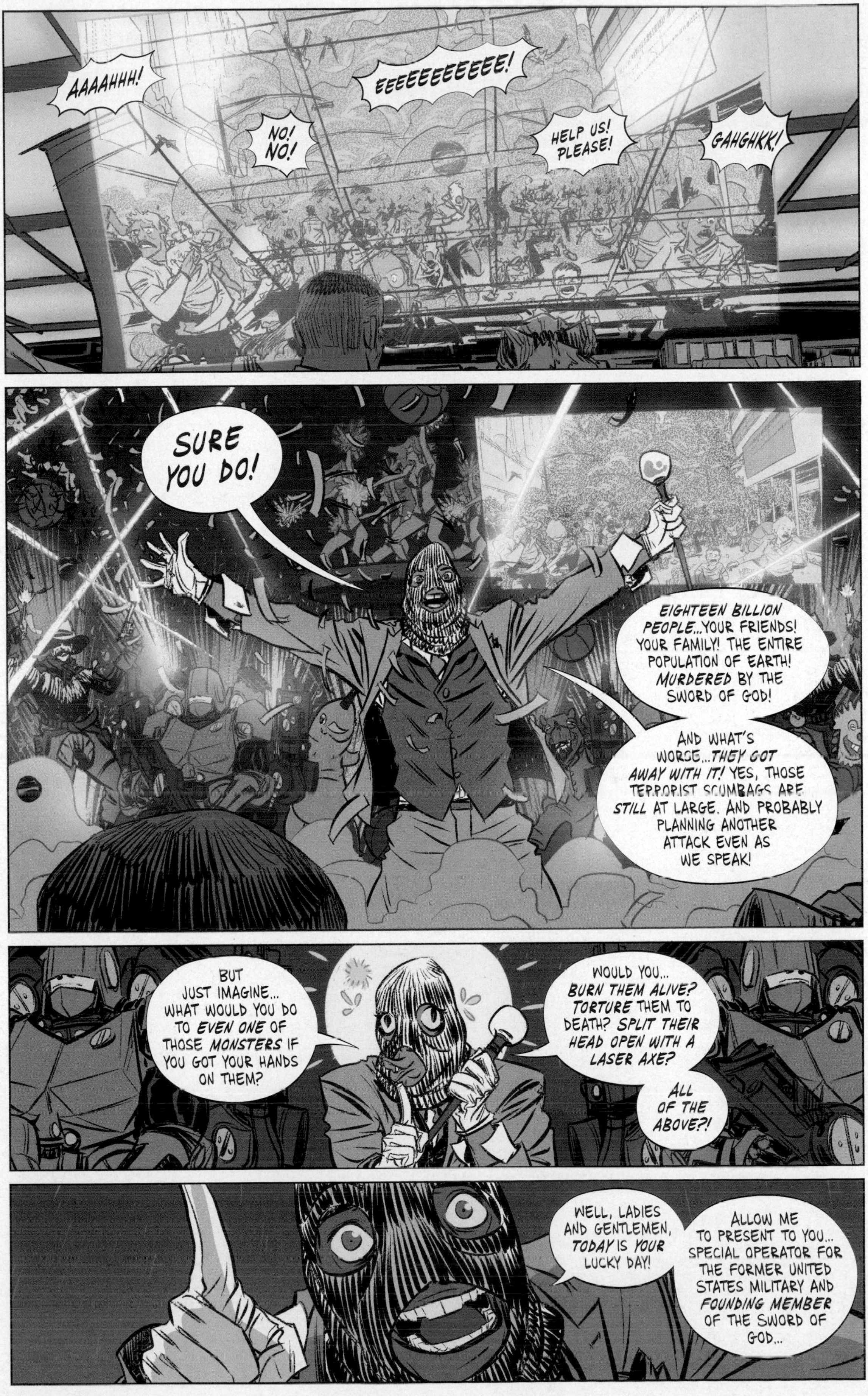
AAAAHHH!
EEEEEEEEEEE!
NO! NO!
HELP US! PLEASE!
GAHGHKK!
SURE YOU DO!
EIGHTEEN BILLION PEOPLE...YOUR FRIENDS! YOUR FAMILY! THE ENTIRE POPULATION OF EARTH! MURDERED BY THE SWORD OF GOD!
AND WHAT'S WORSE...THEY GOT AWAY WITH IT! YES, THOSE TERRORIST SCUMBAGS ARE STILL AT LARGE. AND PROBABLY PLANNING ANOTHER ATTACK EVEN AS WE SPEAK!
BUT JUST IMAGINE... WHAT WOULD YOU DO TO EVEN ONE OF THOSE MONSTERS IF YOU GOT YOUR HANDS ON THEM?
WOULD YOU... BURN THEM ALIVE? TORTURE THEM TO DEATH? SPLIT THEIR HEAD OPEN WITH A LASER AXE?
ALL OF THE ABOVE?!
WELL, LADIES AND GENTLEMEN, TODAY IS YOUR LUCKY DAY!
ALLOW ME TO PRESENT TO YOU... SPECIAL OPERATOR FOR THE FORMER UNITED STATES MILITARY AND FOUNDING MEMBER OF THE SWORD OF GOD...

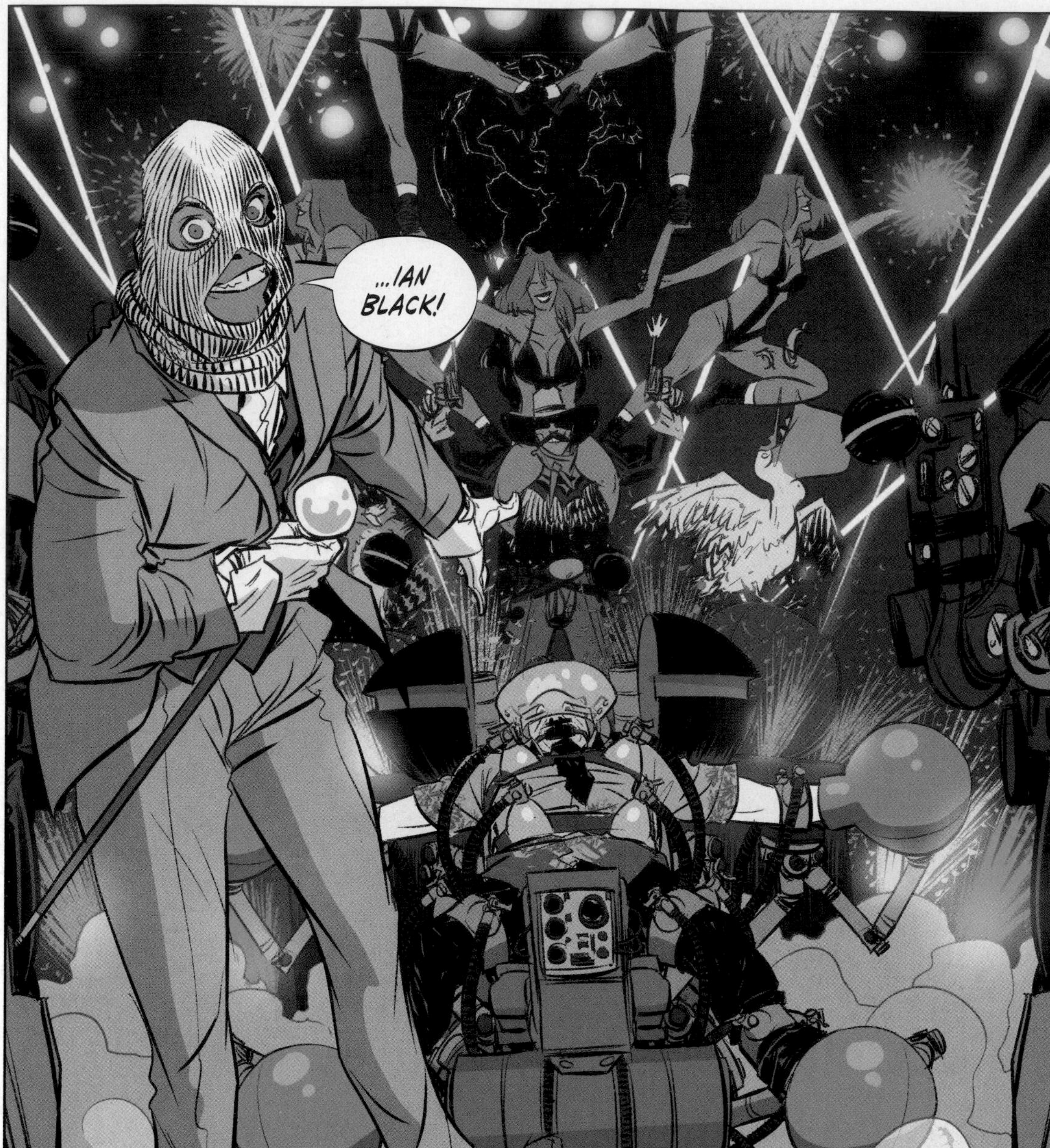
...IAN BLACK!

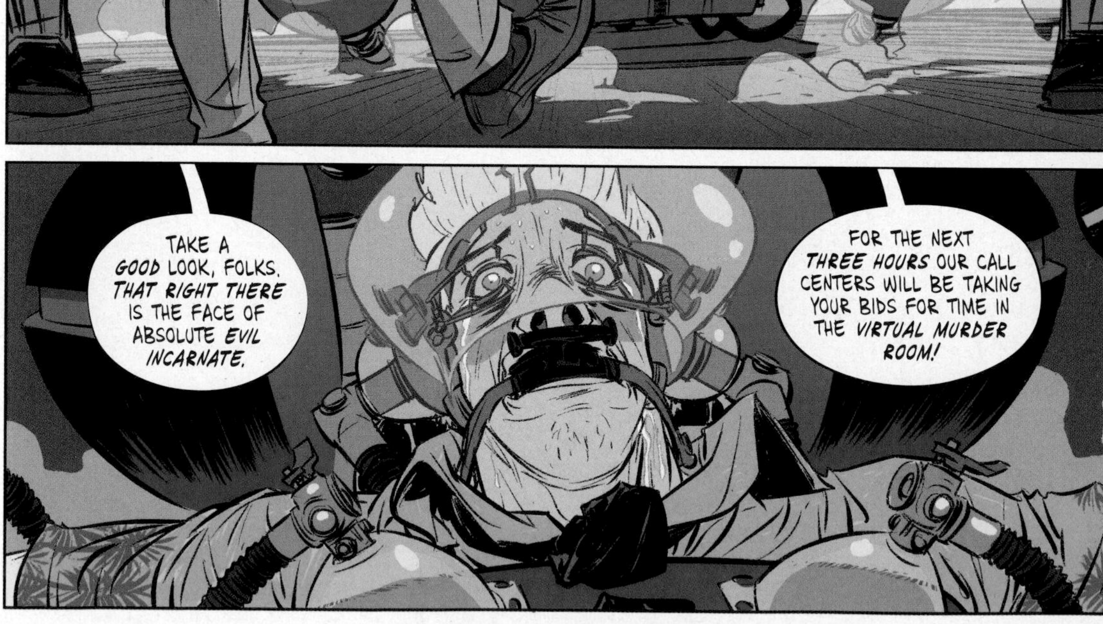
TAKE A GOOD LOOK, FOLKS. THAT RIGHT THERE IS THE FACE OF ABSOLUTE EVIL INCARNATE.
FOR THE NEXT THREE HOURS OUR CALL CENTERS WILL BE TAKING YOUR BIDS FOR TIME IN THE VIRTUAL MURDER ROOM!

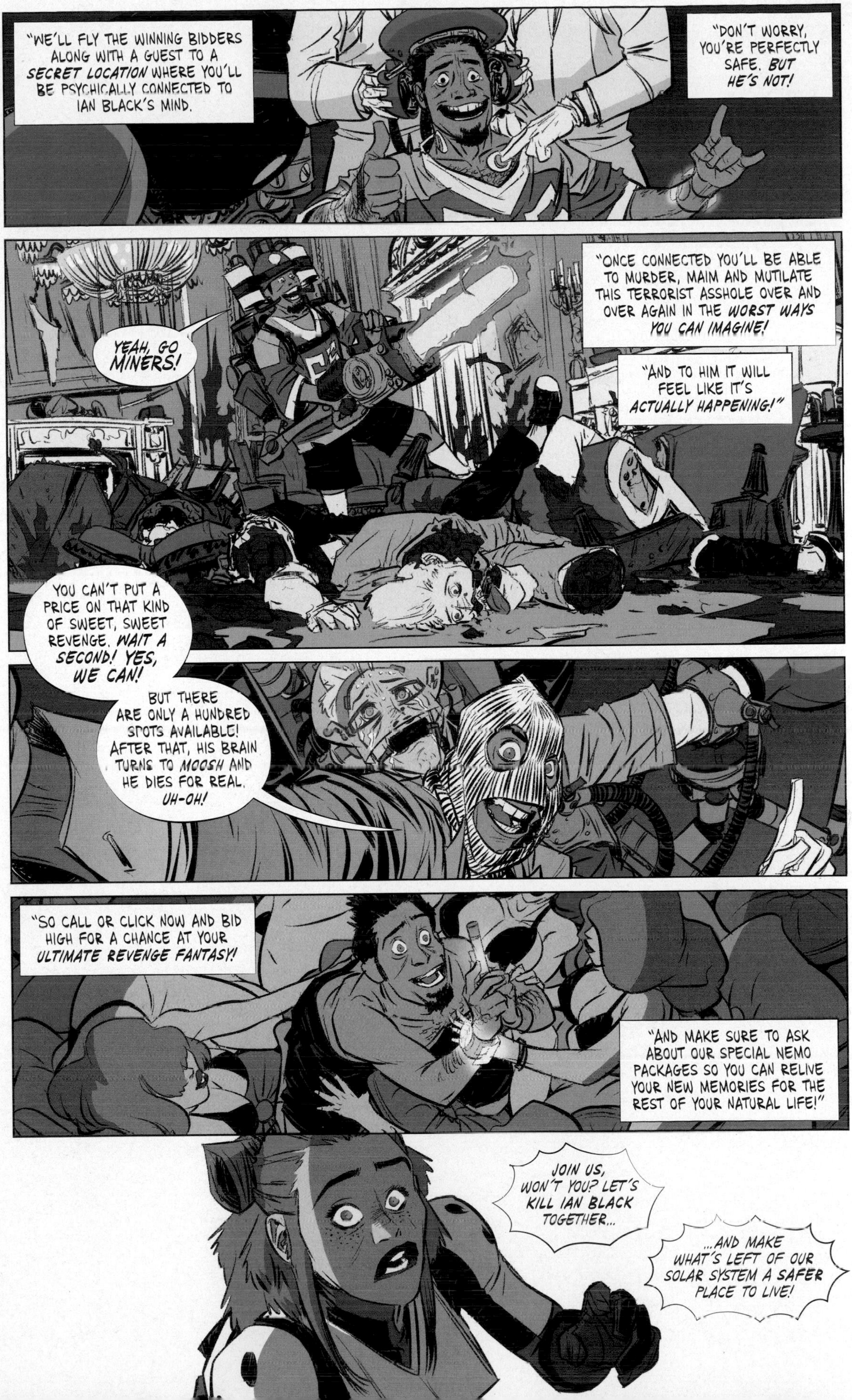
"WE'LL FLY THE WINNING BIDDERS ALONG WITH A GUEST TO A *SECRET LOCATION* WHERE YOU'LL BE PSYCHICALLY CONNECTED TO IAN BLACK'S MIND.
"DON'T WORRY, YOU'RE PERFECTLY SAFE. *BUT HE'S NOT!*
"ONCE CONNECTED YOU'LL BE ABLE TO MURDER, MAIM AND MUTILATE THIS TERRORIST ASSHOLE OVER AND OVER AGAIN IN THE *WORST WAYS YOU CAN IMAGINE!*
YEAH, GO MINERS!
"AND TO HIM IT WILL FEEL LIKE IT'S *ACTUALLY HAPPENING!"*
YOU CAN'T PUT A PRICE ON THAT KIND OF SWEET, SWEET REVENGE. *WAIT A SECOND! YES, WE CAN!*
BUT THERE ARE ONLY A HUNDRED SPOTS AVAILABLE! AFTER THAT, HIS BRAIN TURNS TO *MOOSH* AND HE DIES FOR REAL. *UH-OH!*
"SO CALL OR CLICK NOW AND BID HIGH FOR A CHANCE AT YOUR *ULTIMATE REVENGE FANTASY!*
"AND MAKE SURE TO ASK ABOUT OUR SPECIAL NEMO PACKAGES SO YOU CAN RELIVE YOUR NEW MEMORIES FOR THE REST OF YOUR NATURAL LIFE!"
JOIN US, WON'T YOU? LET'S KILL IAN BLACK TOGETHER...
...AND MAKE WHAT'S LEFT OF OUR SOLAR SYSTEM A SAFER PLACE TO LIVE!

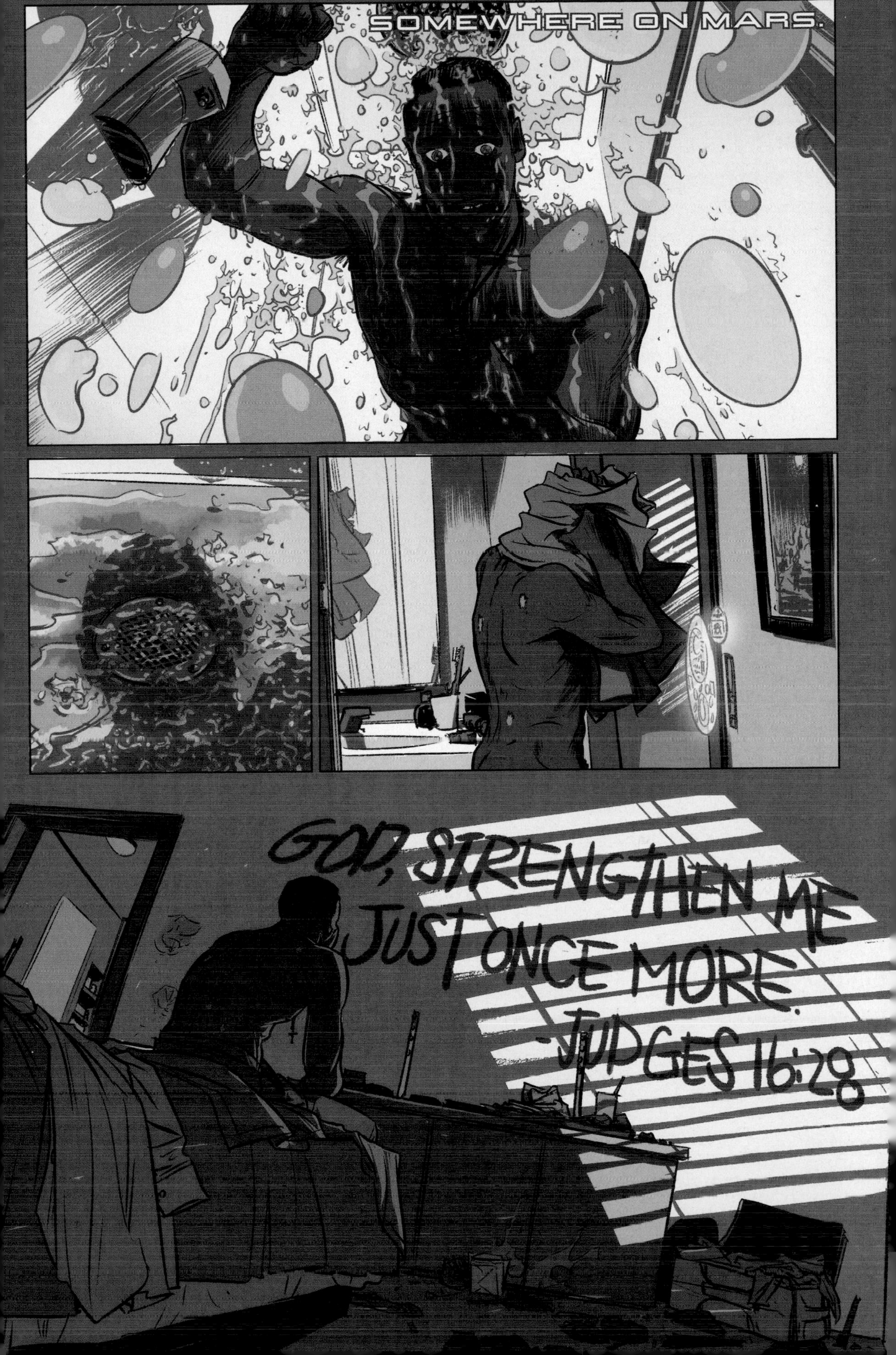
SOMEWHERE ON MARS.
GOD, STRENGTHEN ME JUST ONCE MORE.
-JUDGES 16:28

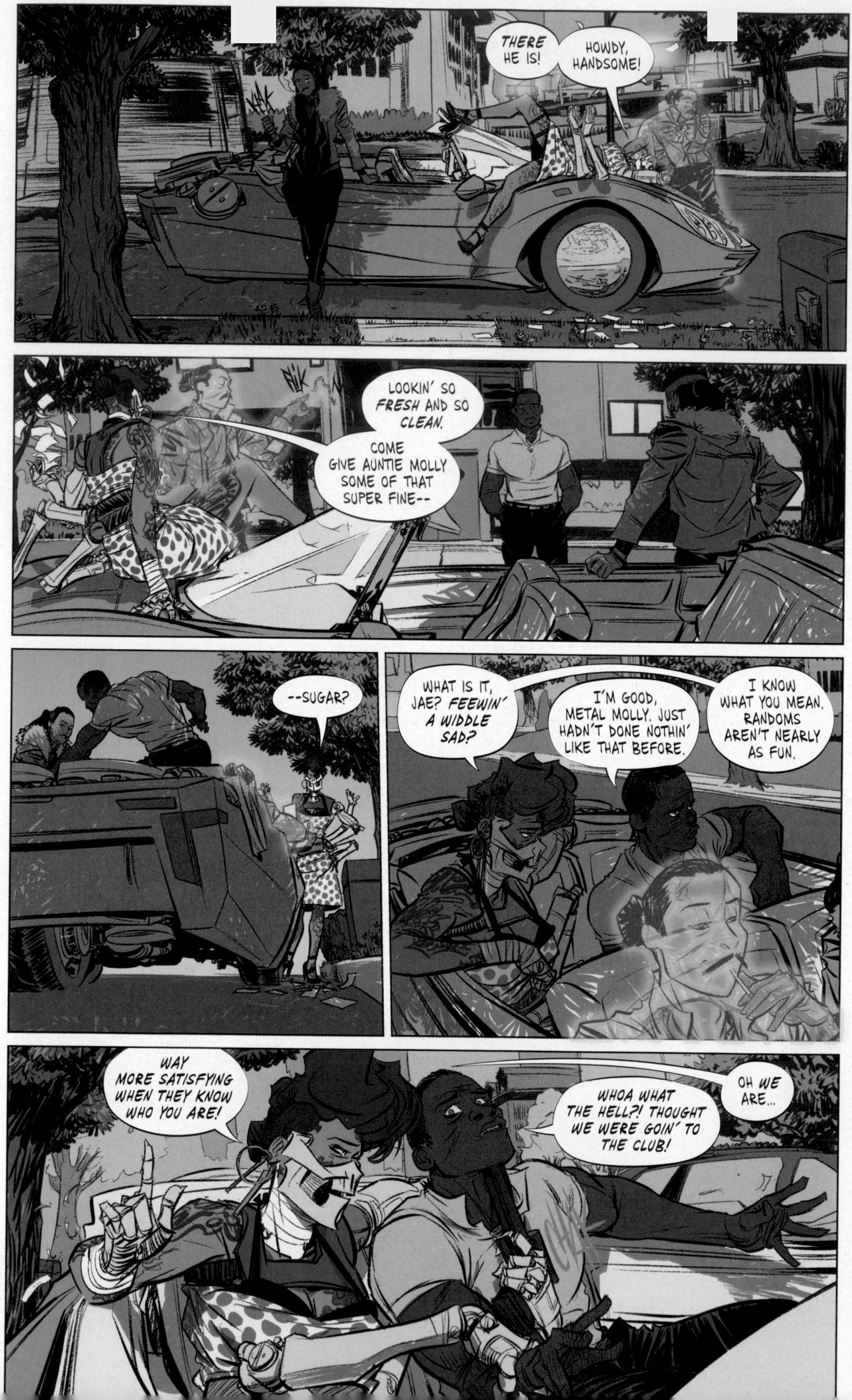
THERE HE IS!
HOWDY, HANDSOME!
LOOKIN' SO FRESH AND SO CLEAN.
COME GIVE AUNTIE MOLLY SOME OF THAT SUPER FINE--
--SUGAR?
WHAT IS IT, JAE? FEEWIN' A WIDDLE SAD?
I'M GOOD, METAL MOLLY. JUST HADN'T DONE NOTHIN' LIKE THAT BEFORE.
I KNOW WHAT YOU MEAN. RANDOMS AREN'T NEARLY AS FUN.
WAY MORE SATISFYING WHEN THEY KNOW WHO YOU ARE!
WHOA WHAT THE HELL?! THOUGHT WE WERE GOIN' TO THE CLUB!
OH WE ARE...

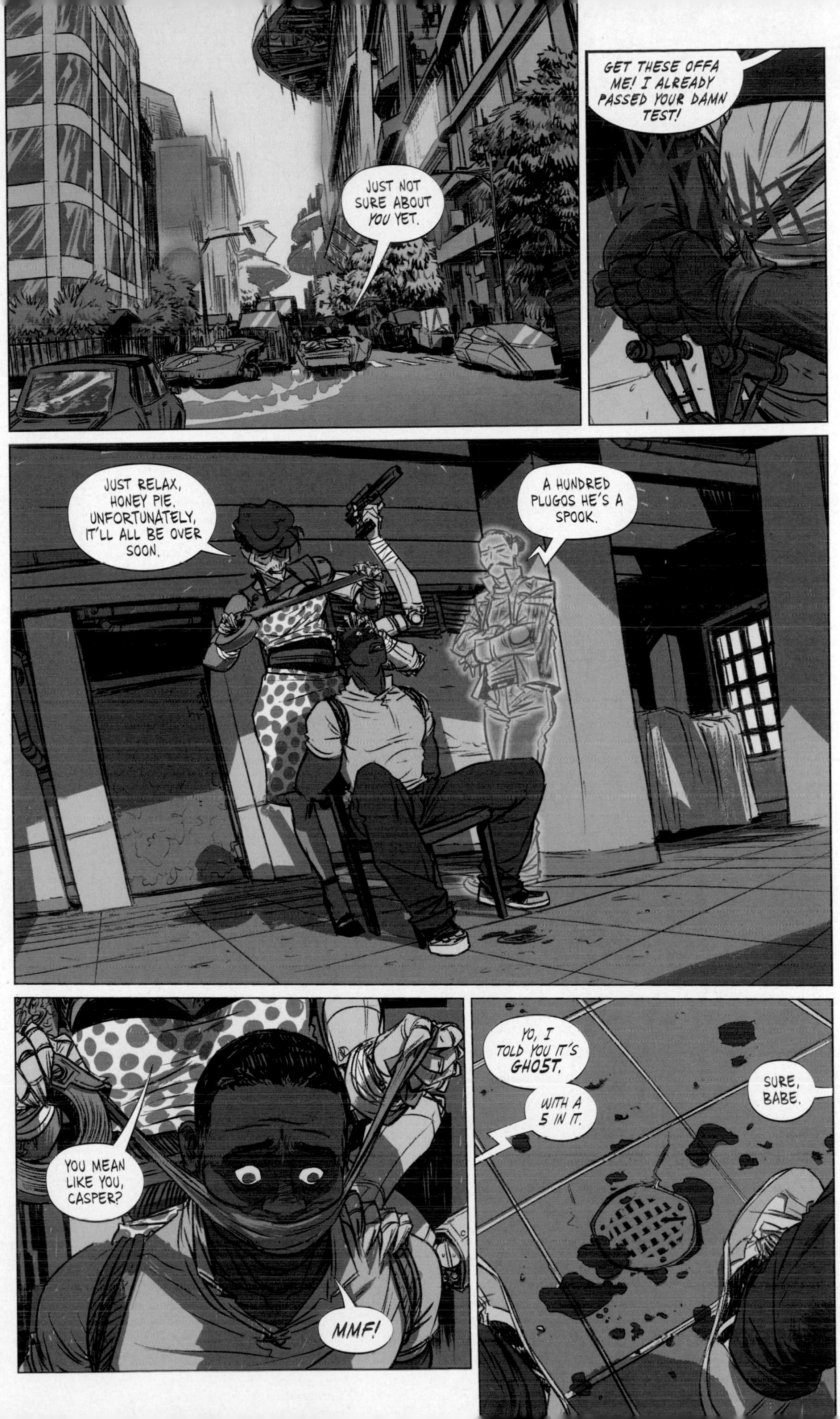
JUST NOT SURE ABOUT YOU YET.
GET THESE OFFA ME! I ALREADY PASSED YOUR DAMN TEST!
JUST RELAX, HONEY PIE. UNFORTUNATELY, IT'LL ALL BE OVER SOON.
A HUNDRED PLUGOS HE'S A SPOOK.
YOU MEAN LIKE YOU, CASPER?
MMF!
YO, I TOLD YOU IT'S GHO5T.
WITH A 5 IN IT.
SURE, BABE.

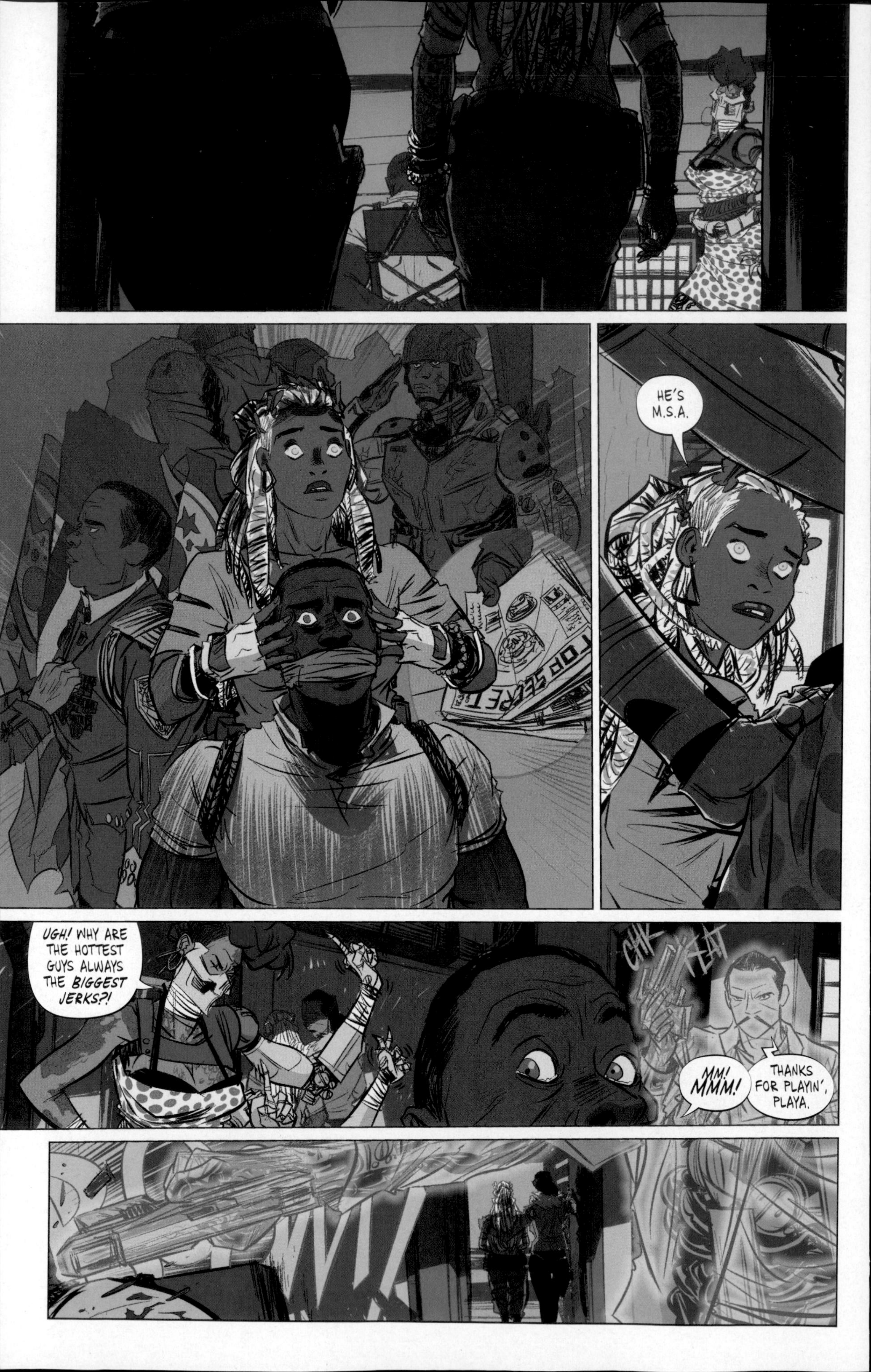
TOP SECRET
HE'S M.S.A.
UGH! WHY ARE THE HOTTEST GUYS ALWAYS THE *BIGGEST JERKS?!*
MM! MMM!
THANKS FOR PLAYIN', PLAYA.

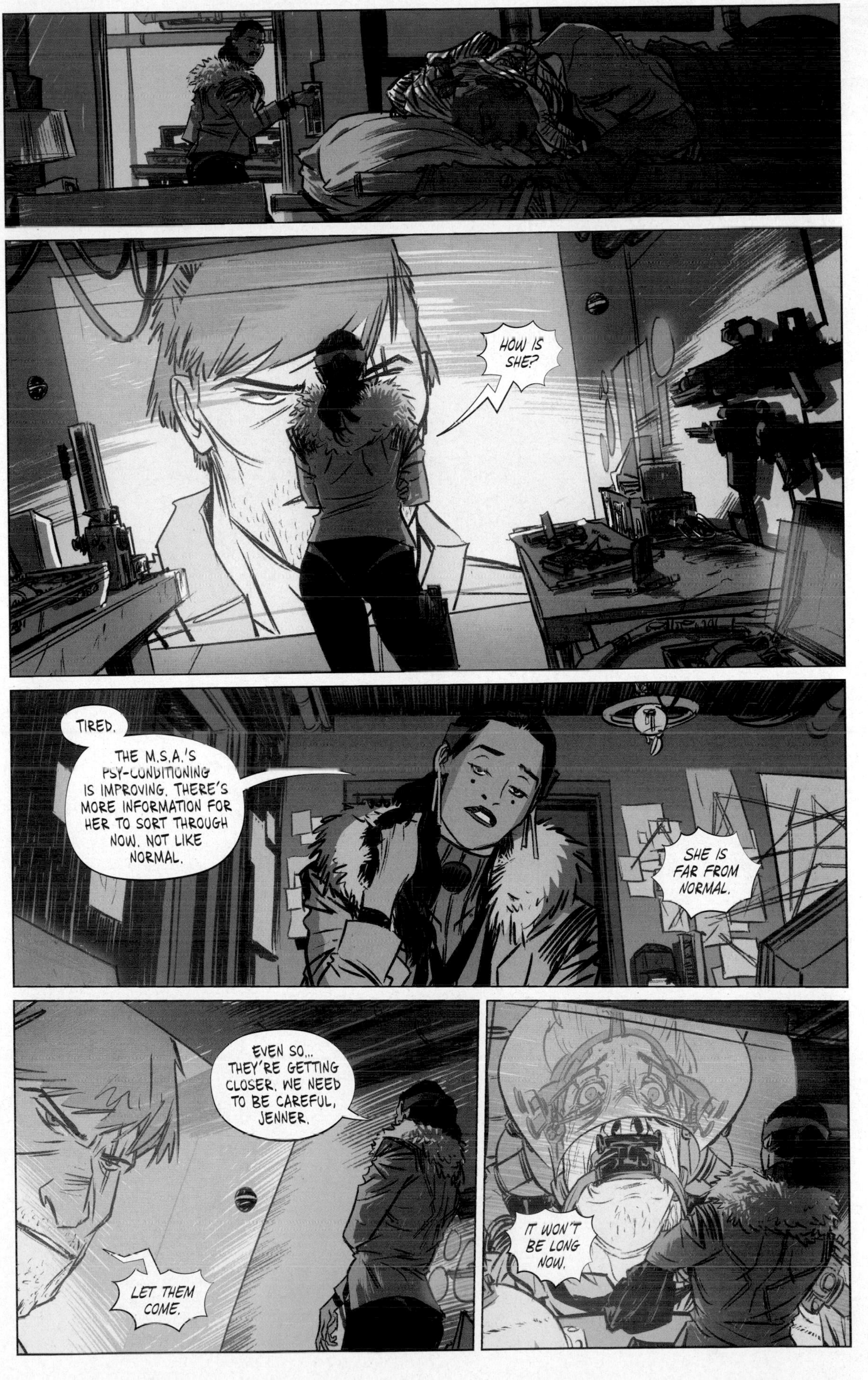
HOW IS SHE?
TIRED.
THE M.S.A.'S PSY-CONDITIONING IS IMPROVING. THERE'S MORE INFORMATION FOR HER TO SORT THROUGH NOW. NOT LIKE NORMAL.
SHE IS FAR FROM NORMAL.
EVEN SO... THEY'RE GETTING CLOSER. WE NEED TO BE CAREFUL, JENNER.
LET THEM COME.
IT WON'T BE LONG NOW.

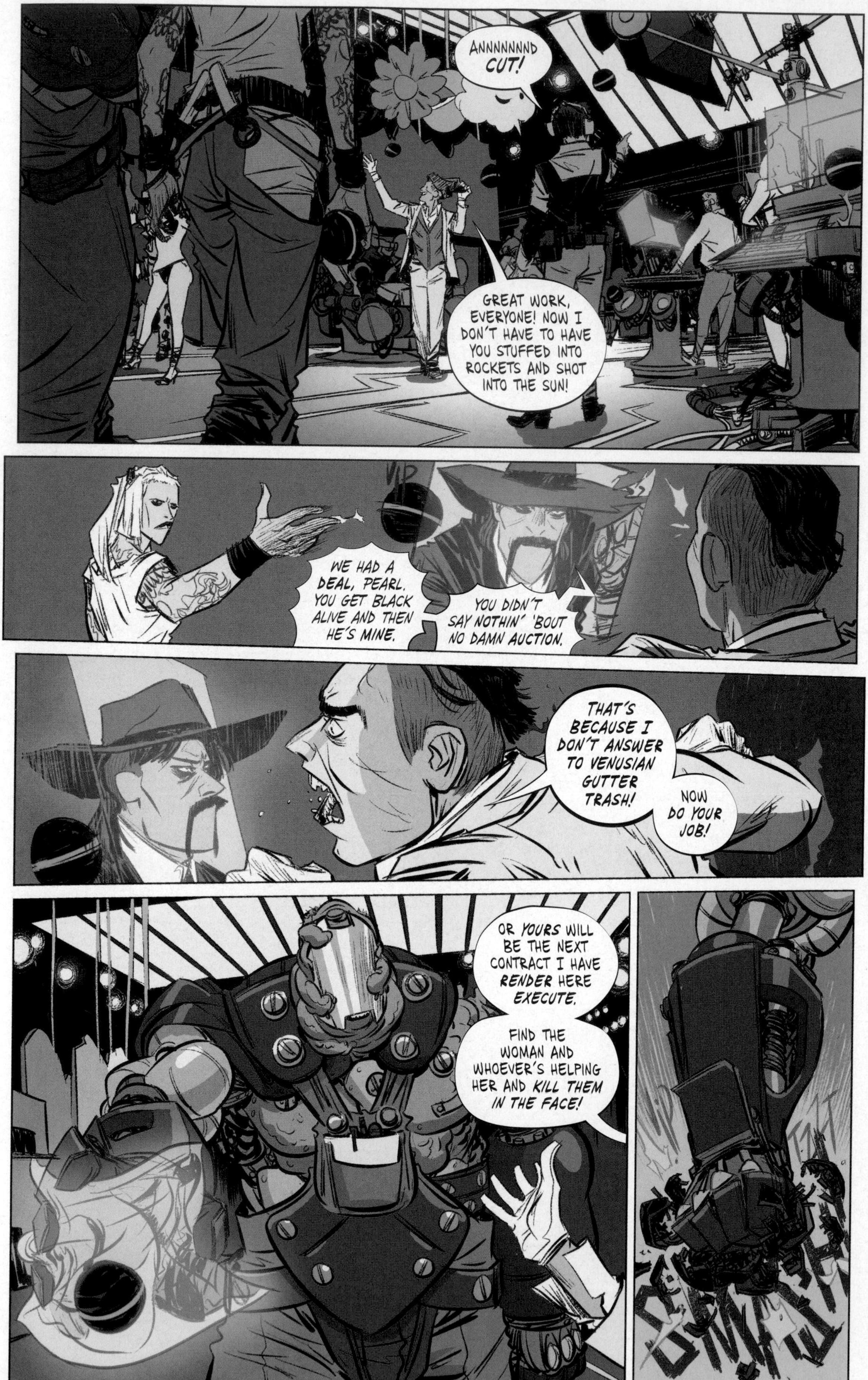
ANNNNNND CUT!
GREAT WORK, EVERYONE! NOW I DON'T HAVE TO HAVE YOU STUFFED INTO ROCKETS AND SHOT INTO THE SUN!
WE HAD A DEAL, PEARL. YOU GET BLACK ALIVE AND THEN HE'S MINE.
YOU DIDN'T SAY NOTHIN' 'BOUT NO DAMN AUCTION.
THAT'S BECAUSE I DON'T ANSWER TO VENUSIAN GUTTER TRASH!
NOW DO YOUR JOB!
OR YOURS WILL BE THE NEXT CONTRACT I HAVE RENDER HERE EXECUTE.
FIND THE WOMAN AND WHOEVER'S HELPING HER AND KILL THEM IN THE FACE!

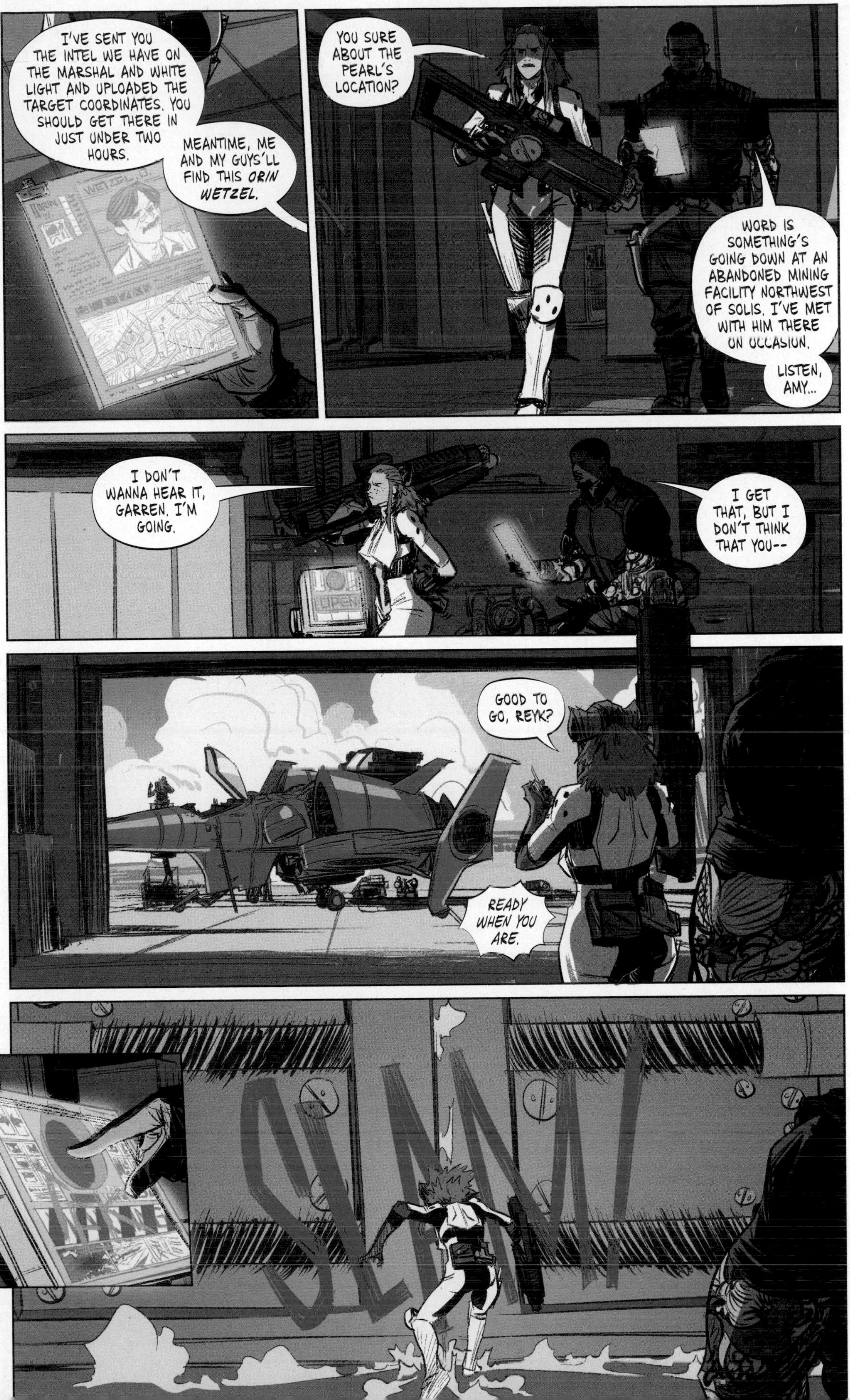
I'VE SENT YOU THE INTEL WE HAVE ON THE MARSHAL AND WHITE LIGHT AND UPLOADED THE TARGET COORDINATES. YOU SHOULD GET THERE IN JUST UNDER TWO HOURS.
MEANTIME, ME AND MY GUYS'LL FIND THIS ORIN WETZEL.
YOU SURE ABOUT THE PEARL'S LOCATION?
WORD IS SOMETHING'S GOING DOWN AT AN ABANDONED MINING FACILITY NORTHWEST OF SOLIS. I'VE MET WITH HIM THERE ON OCCASION.
LISTEN, AMY...
I DON'T WANNA HEAR IT, GARREN. I'M GOING.
I GET THAT, BUT I DON'T THINK THAT YOU--
OPEN
GOOD TO GO, REYK?
READY WHEN YOU ARE.
SLAM!

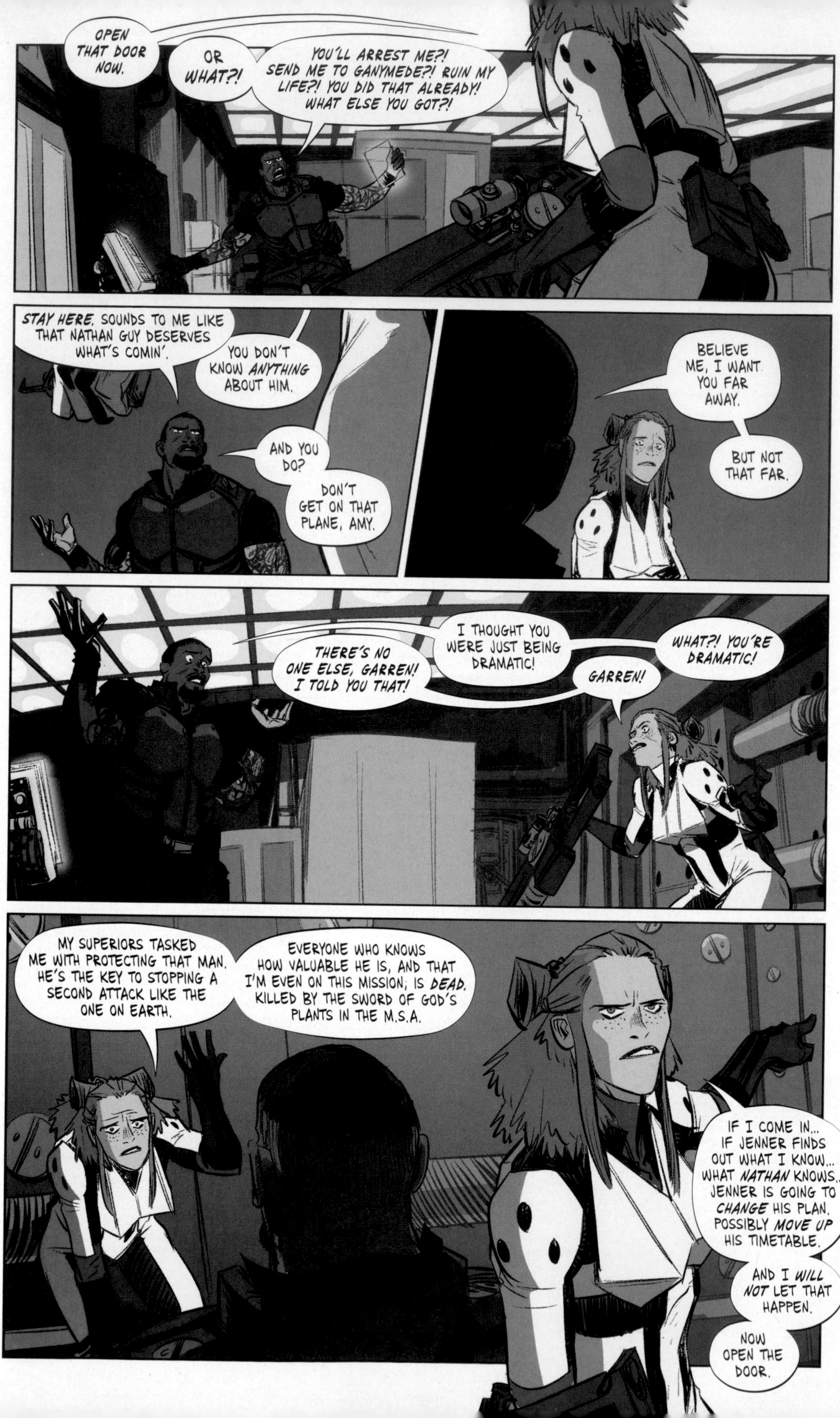
OPEN THAT DOOR NOW.
OR WHAT?!
YOU'LL ARREST ME?! SEND ME TO GANYMEDE?! RUIN MY LIFE?! YOU DID THAT ALREADY! WHAT ELSE YOU GOT?!
STAY HERE. SOUNDS TO ME LIKE THAT NATHAN GUY DESERVES WHAT'S COMIN'.
YOU DON'T KNOW ANYTHING ABOUT HIM.
AND YOU DO?
DON'T GET ON THAT PLANE, AMY.
BELIEVE ME, I WANT YOU FAR AWAY.
BUT NOT THAT FAR.
THERE'S NO ONE ELSE, GARREN! I TOLD YOU THAT!
I THOUGHT YOU WERE JUST BEING DRAMATIC!
GARREN!
WHAT?! YOU'RE DRAMATIC!
MY SUPERIORS TASKED ME WITH PROTECTING THAT MAN. HE'S THE KEY TO STOPPING A SECOND ATTACK LIKE THE ONE ON EARTH.
EVERYONE WHO KNOWS HOW VALUABLE HE IS, AND THAT I'M EVEN ON THIS MISSION; IS DEAD. KILLED BY THE SWORD OF GOD'S PLANTS IN THE M.S.A.
IF I COME IN... IF JENNER FINDS OUT WHAT I KNOW... WHAT NATHAN KNOWS... JENNER IS GOING TO CHANGE HIS PLAN. POSSIBLY MOVE UP HIS TIMETABLE.
AND I WILL NOT LET THAT HAPPEN.
NOW OPEN THE DOOR.

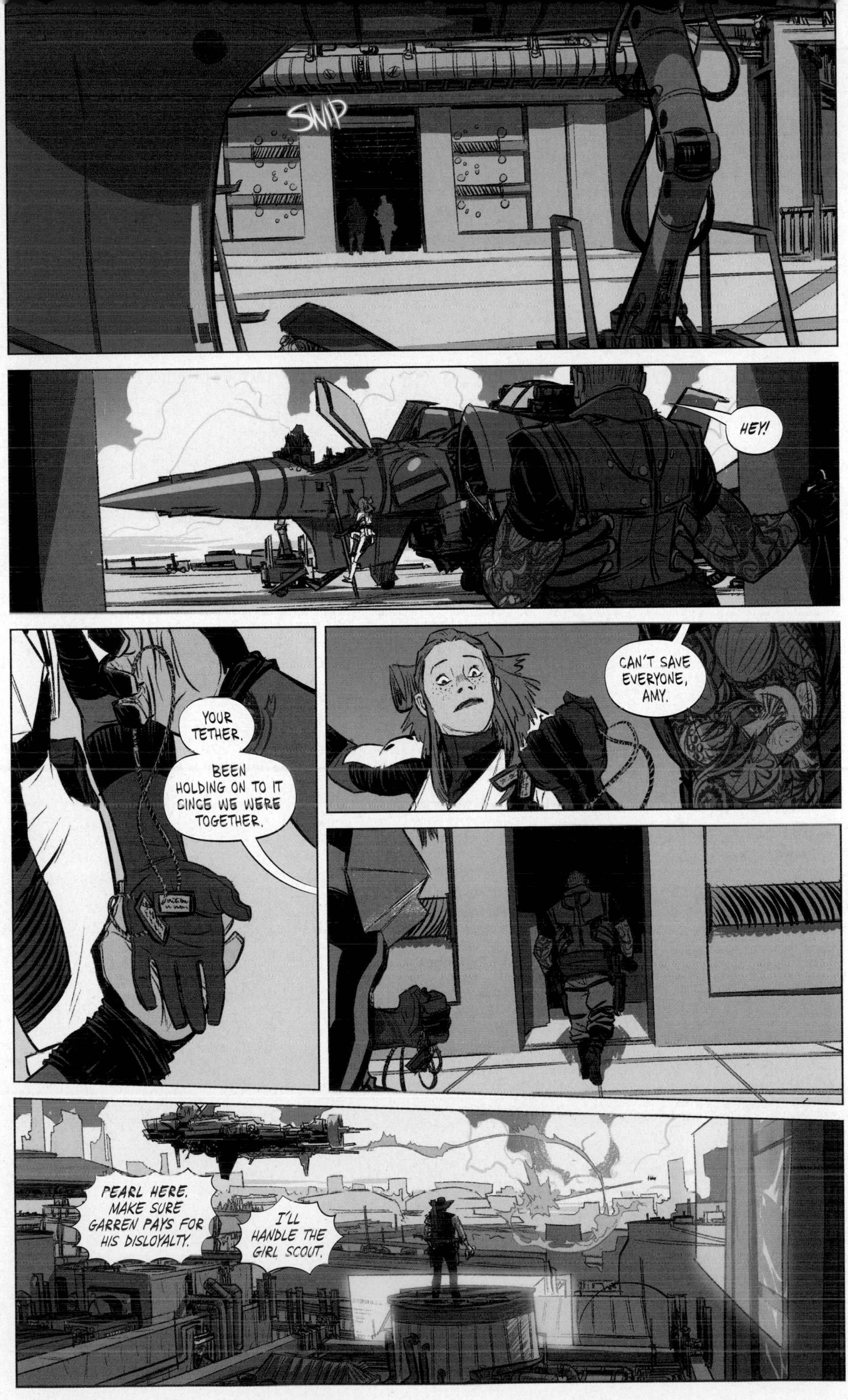
SWIP
HEY!
YOUR TETHER.
BEEN HOLDING ON TO IT SINCE WE WERE TOGETHER.
CAN'T SAVE EVERYONE, AMY.
PEARL HERE. MAKE SURE GARREN PAYS FOR HIS DISLOYALTY.
I'LL HANDLE THE GIRL SCOUT.

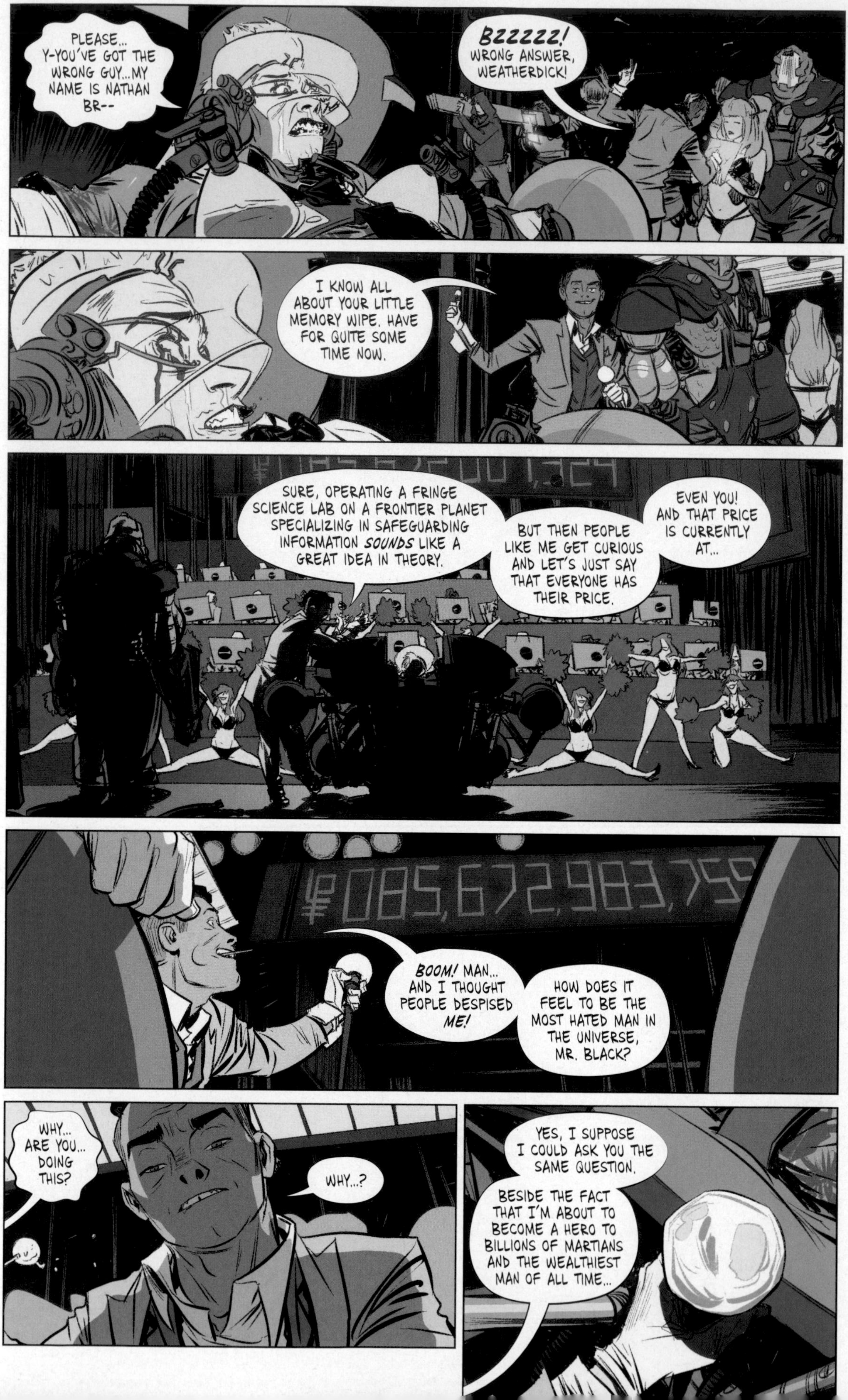
PLEASE... Y-YOU'VE GOT THE WRONG GUY...MY NAME IS NATHAN BR--
BZZZZZ! WRONG ANSWER, WEATHERDICK!
I KNOW ALL ABOUT YOUR LITTLE MEMORY WIPE. HAVE FOR QUITE SOME TIME NOW.
SURE, OPERATING A FRINGE SCIENCE LAB ON A FRONTIER PLANET SPECIALIZING IN SAFEGUARDING INFORMATION SOUNDS LIKE A GREAT IDEA IN THEORY.
BUT THEN PEOPLE LIKE ME GET CURIOUS AND LET'S JUST SAY THAT EVERYONE HAS THEIR PRICE.
EVEN YOU! AND THAT PRICE IS CURRENTLY AT...
₩085,672,983,75
BOOM! MAN... AND I THOUGHT PEOPLE DESPISED ME!
HOW DOES IT FEEL TO BE THE MOST HATED MAN IN THE UNIVERSE, MR. BLACK?
WHY... ARE YOU... DOING THIS?
WHY...?
YES, I SUPPOSE I COULD ASK YOU THE SAME QUESTION.
BESIDE THE FACT THAT I'M ABOUT TO BECOME A HERO TO BILLIONS OF MARTIANS AND THE WEALTHIEST MAN OF ALL TIME...

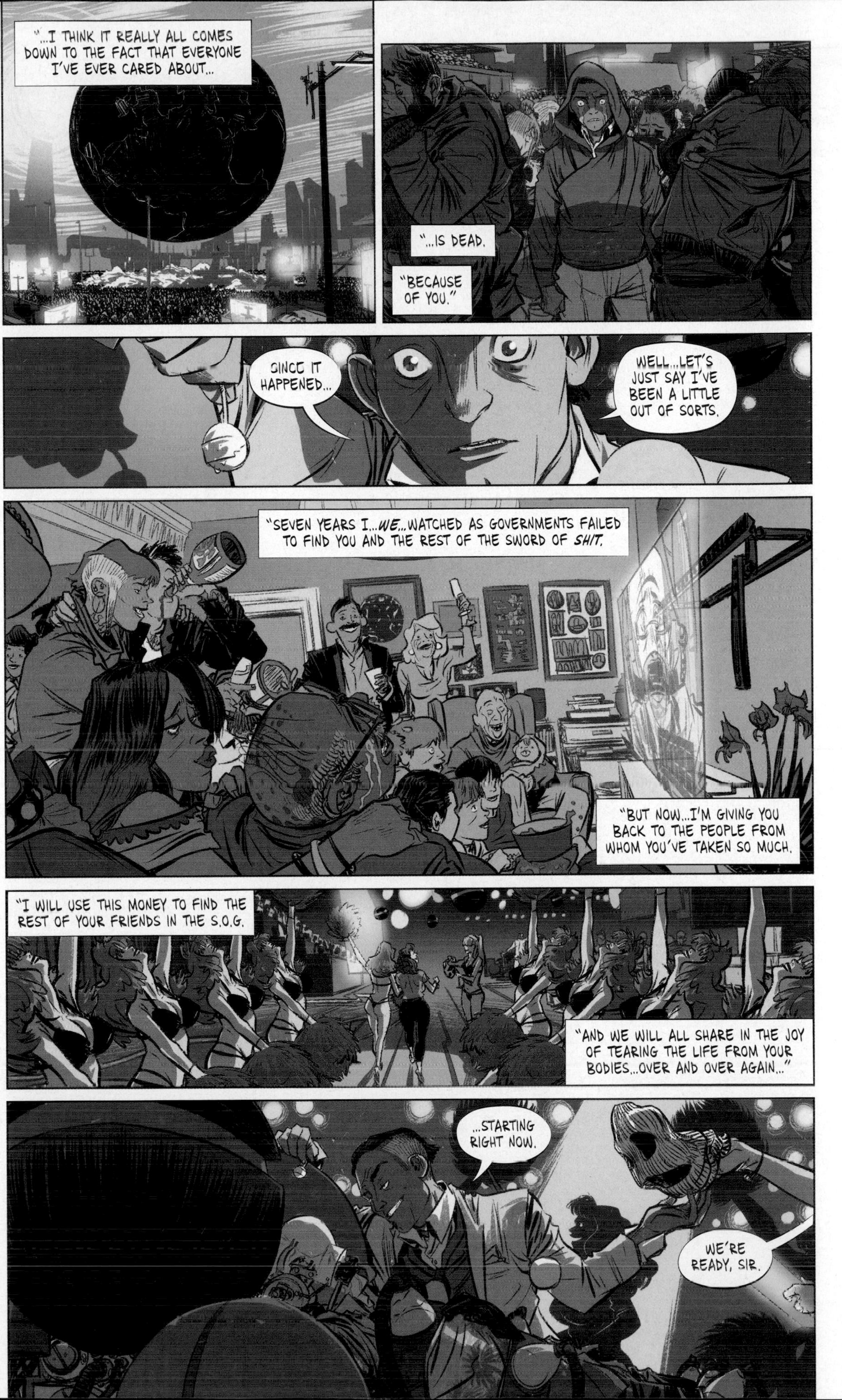
"...I THINK IT REALLY ALL COMES DOWN TO THE FACT THAT EVERYONE I'VE EVER CARED ABOUT...
"...IS DEAD.
"BECAUSE OF YOU."
SINCE IT HAPPENED...
WELL...LET'S JUST SAY I'VE BEEN A LITTLE OUT OF SORTS.
"SEVEN YEARS I...WE...WATCHED AS GOVERNMENTS FAILED TO FIND YOU AND THE REST OF THE SWORD OF SHIT.
"BUT NOW...I'M GIVING YOU BACK TO THE PEOPLE FROM WHOM YOU'VE TAKEN SO MUCH.
"I WILL USE THIS MONEY TO FIND THE REST OF YOUR FRIENDS IN THE S.O.G.
"AND WE WILL ALL SHARE IN THE JOY OF TEARING THE LIFE FROM YOUR BODIES...OVER AND OVER AGAIN..."
...STARTING RIGHT NOW.
WE'RE READY, SIR.

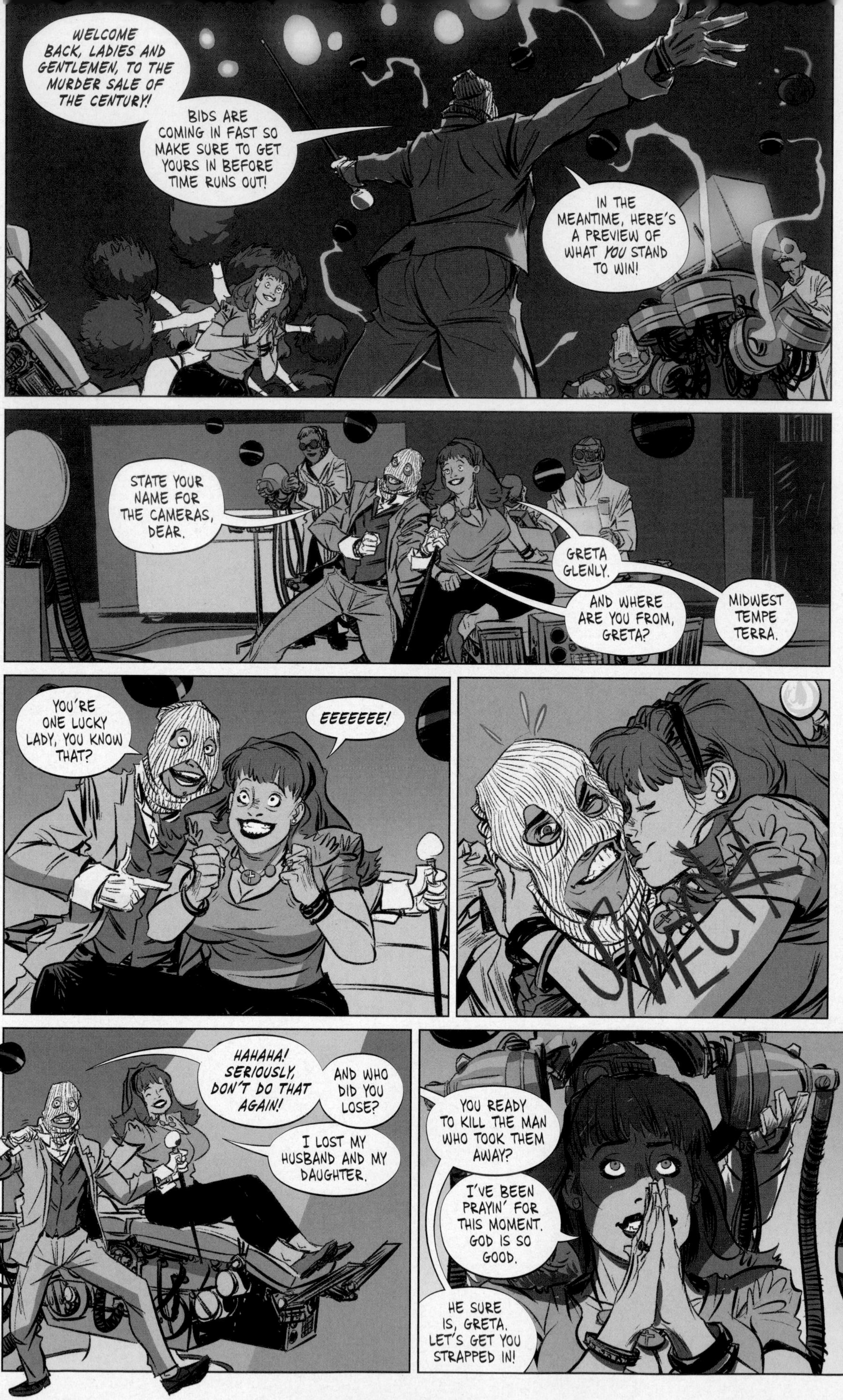
WELCOME BACK, LADIES AND GENTLEMEN, TO THE MURDER SALE OF THE CENTURY!
BIDS ARE COMING IN FAST SO MAKE SURE TO GET YOURS IN BEFORE TIME RUNS OUT!
IN THE MEANTIME, HERE'S A PREVIEW OF WHAT YOU STAND TO WIN!
STATE YOUR NAME FOR THE CAMERAS, DEAR.
GRETA GLENLY.
AND WHERE ARE YOU FROM, GRETA?
MIDWEST TEMPE TERRA.
YOU'RE ONE LUCKY LADY, YOU KNOW THAT?
EEEEEEE!
SMECK
HAHAHA! SERIOUSLY, DON'T DO THAT AGAIN!
AND WHO DID YOU LOSE?
I LOST MY HUSBAND AND MY DAUGHTER.
YOU READY TO KILL THE MAN WHO TOOK THEM AWAY?
I'VE BEEN PRAYIN' FOR THIS MOMENT. GOD IS SO GOOD.
HE SURE IS, GRETA. LET'S GET YOU STRAPPED IN!

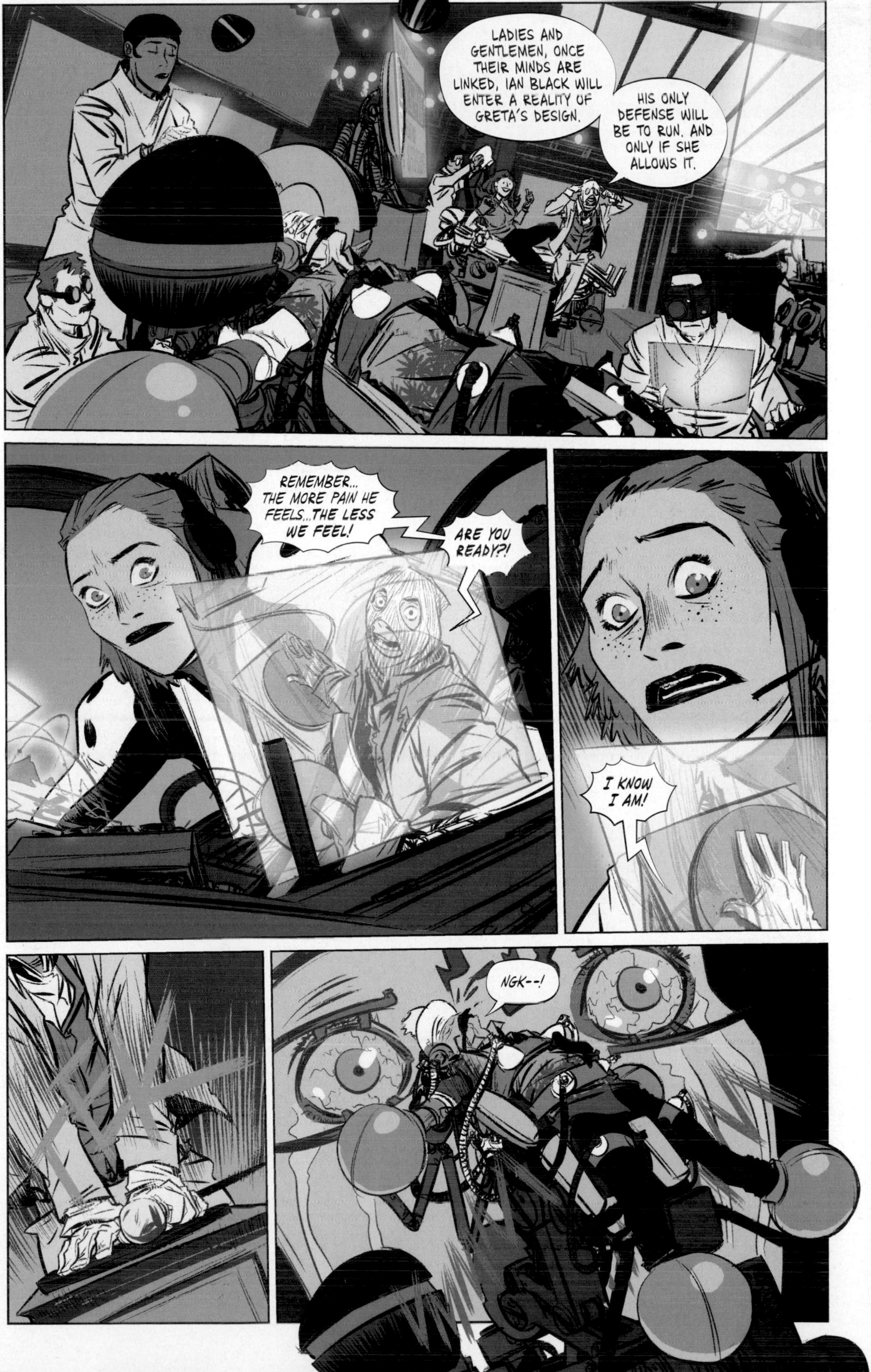
LADIES AND GENTLEMEN, ONCE THEIR MINDS ARE LINKED, IAN BLACK WILL ENTER A REALITY OF GRETA'S DESIGN.
HIS ONLY DEFENSE WILL BE TO RUN. AND ONLY IF SHE ALLOWS IT.
REMEMBER... THE MORE PAIN HE FEELS...THE LESS WE FEEL!
ARE YOU READY?!
I KNOW I AM!
NGK--!

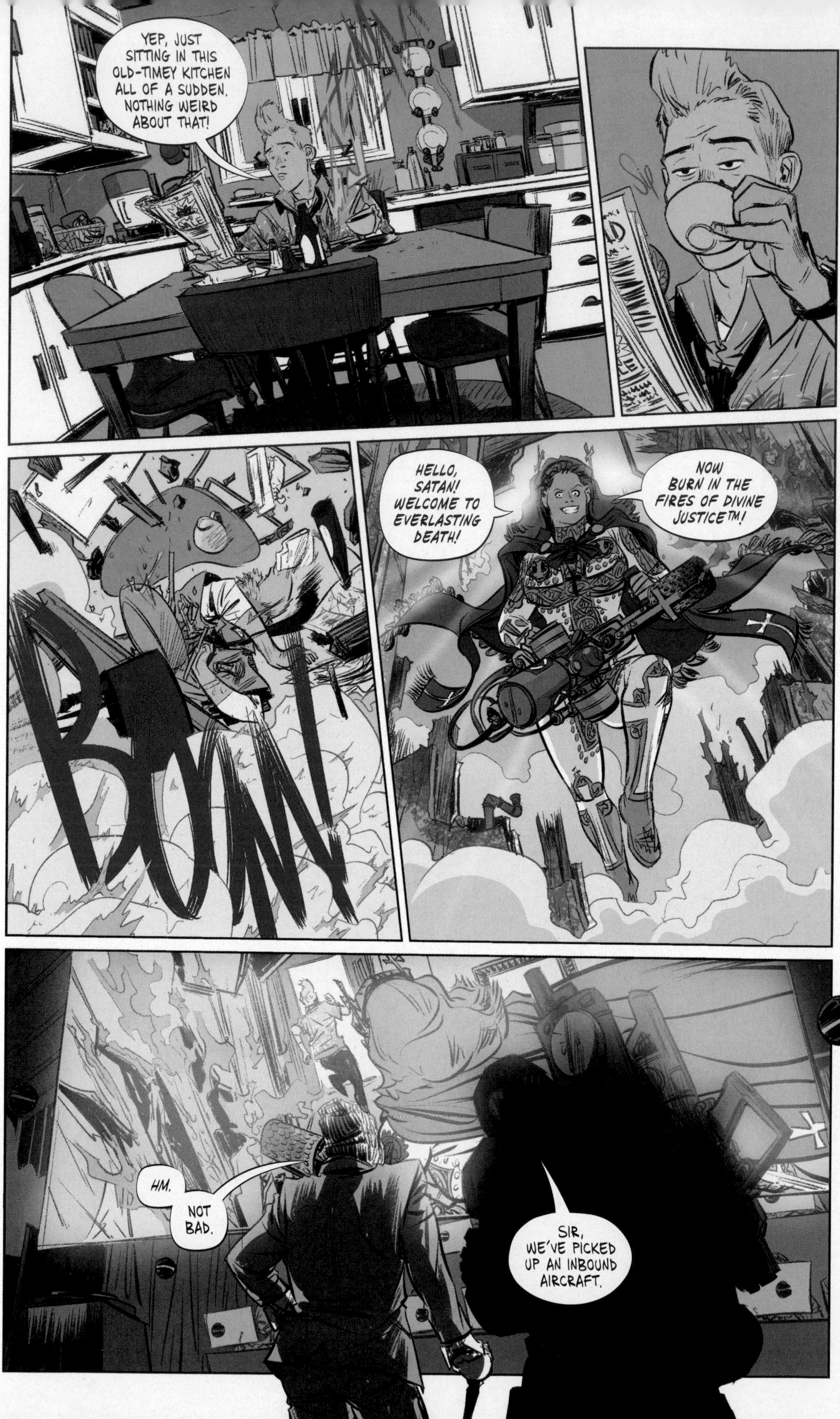
YEP, JUST SITTING IN THIS OLD-TIMEY KITCHEN ALL OF A SUDDEN. NOTHING WEIRD ABOUT THAT!
BOOM
HELLO, SATAN! WELCOME TO EVERLASTING DEATH!
NOW BURN IN THE FIRES OF DIVINE JUSTICE™!
HM.
NOT BAD.
SIR, WE'VE PICKED UP AN INBOUND AIRCRAFT.

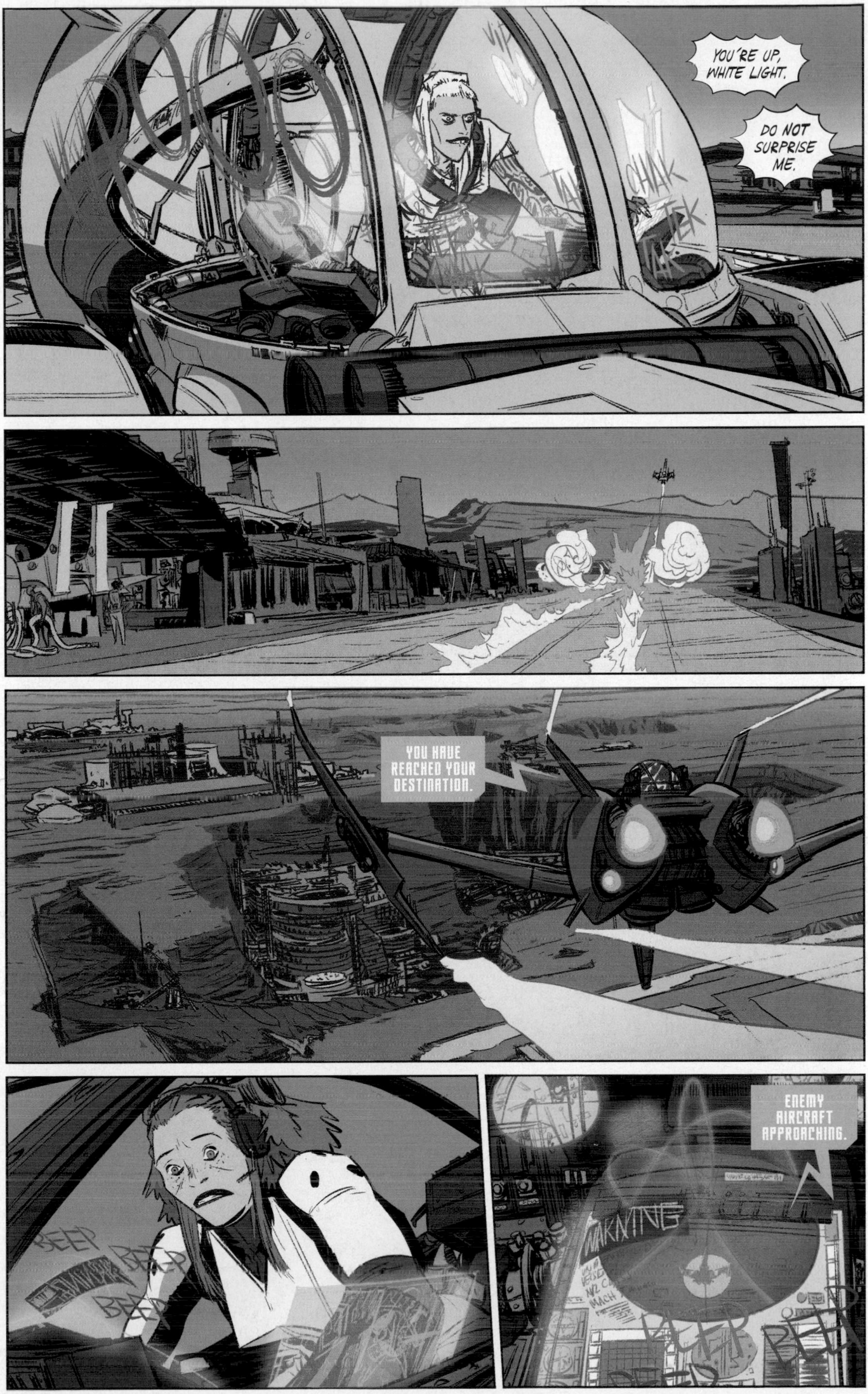

YOU'RE UP, WHITE LIGHT.
DO NOT SURPRISE ME.
YOU HAVE REACHED YOUR DESTINATION.
BEEP BEEP BEEP
ENEMY AIRCRAFT APPROACHING.
WARNING
BEEP BEEP BEEP

UNH!

KIK CHUNK

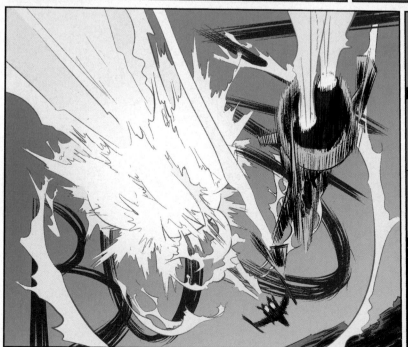

CHT

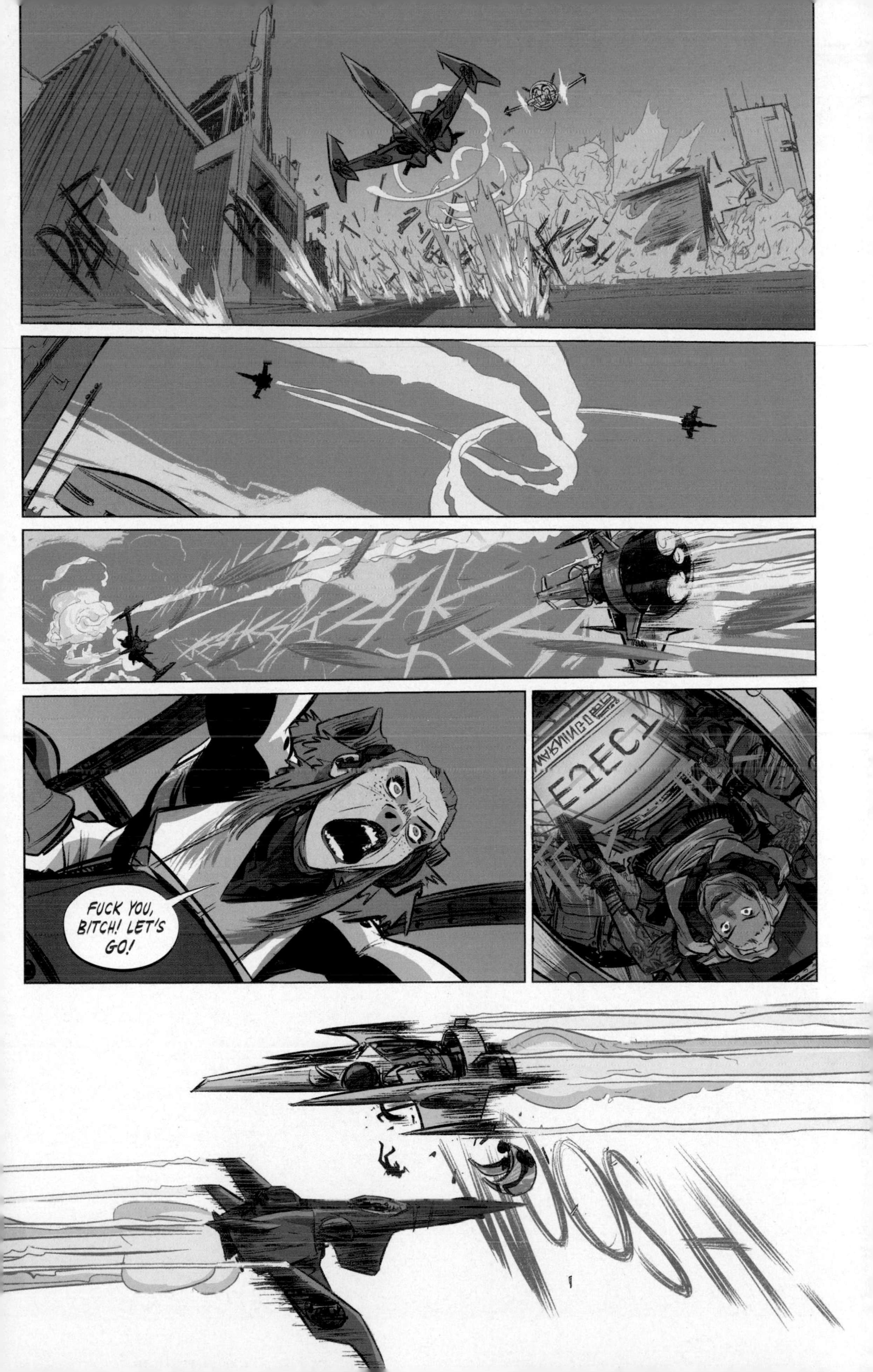
FUCK YOU, BITCH! LET'S GO!
WHOOSH

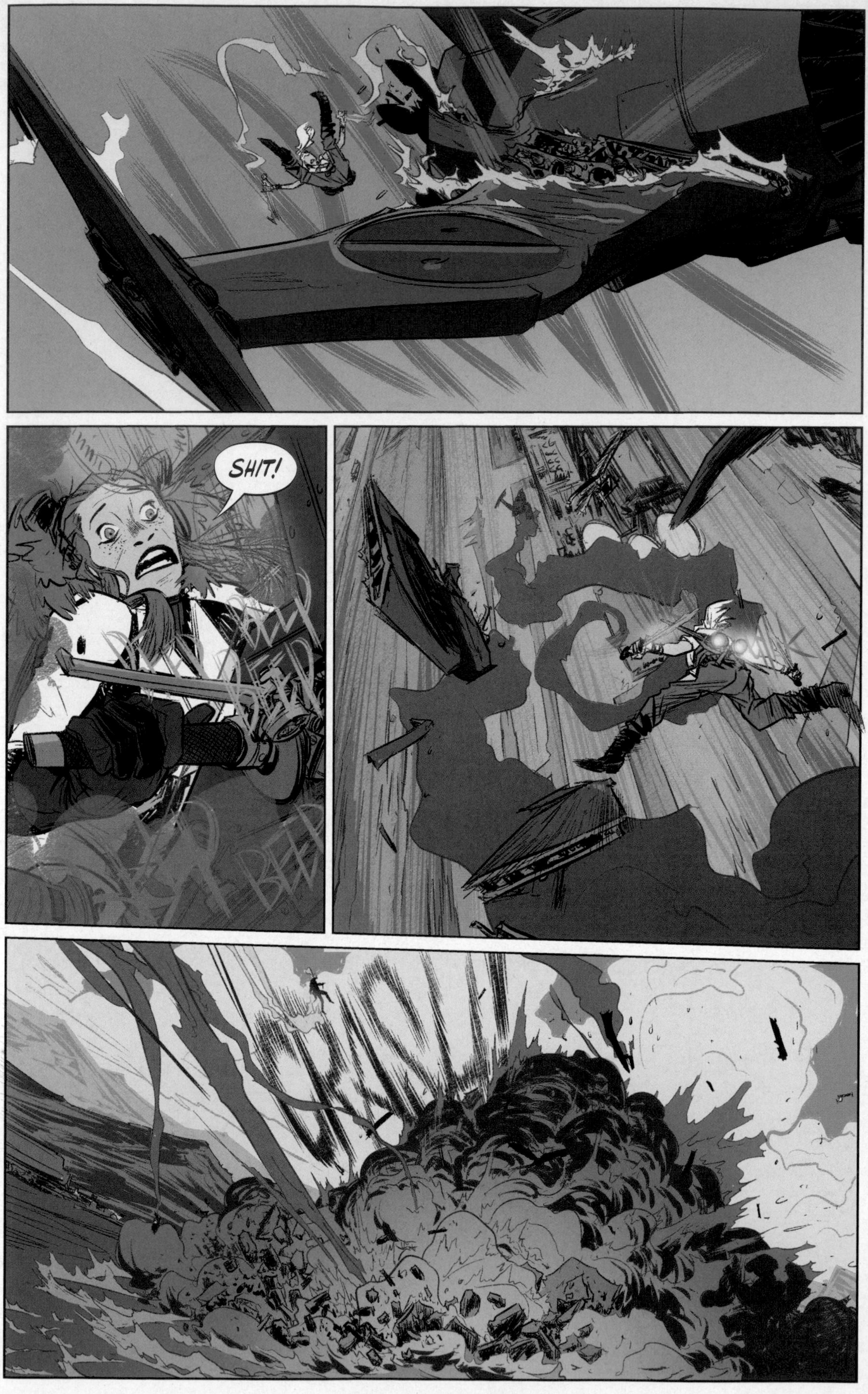
SHIT!

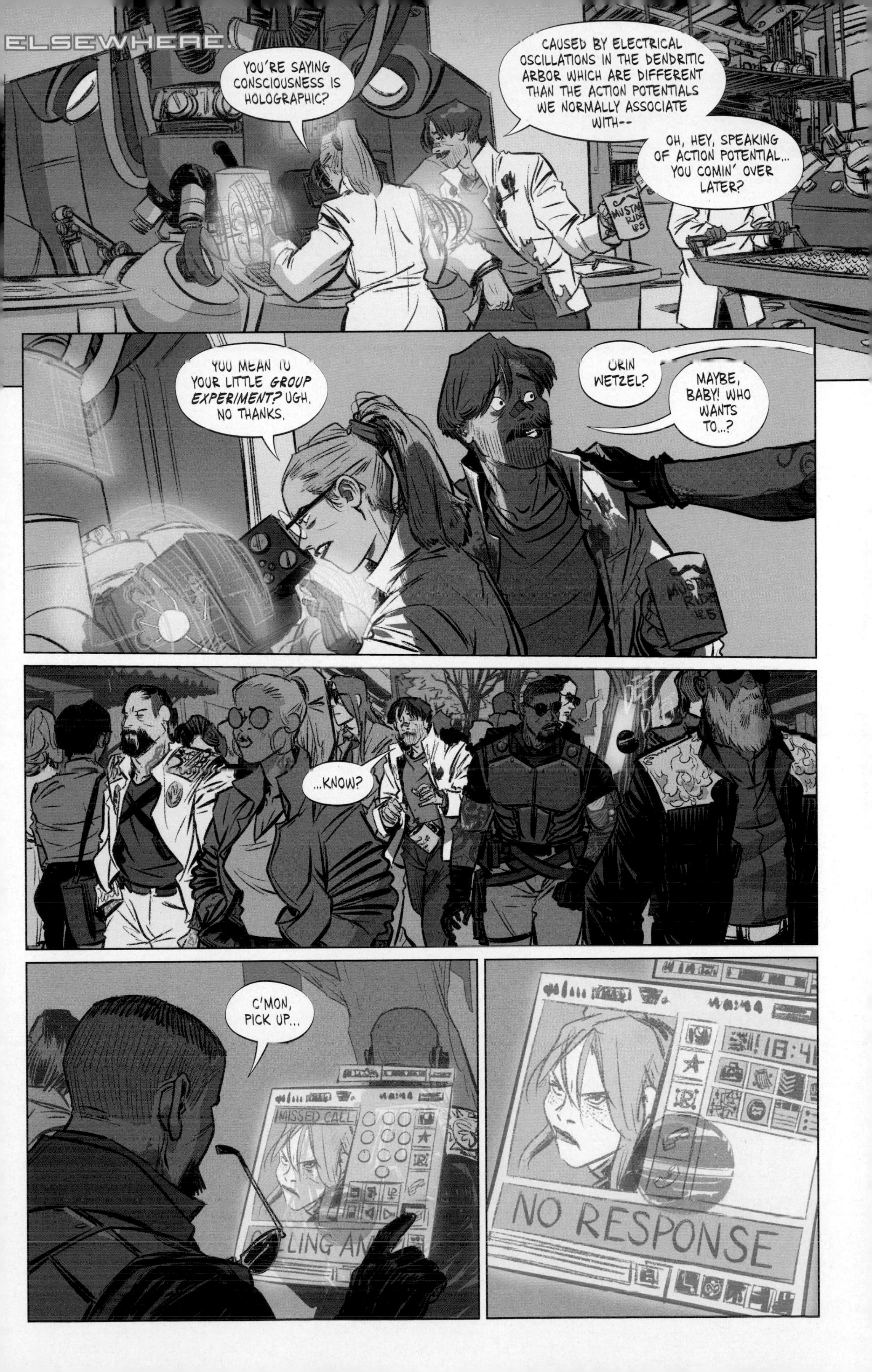
ELSEWHERE.
YOU'RE SAYING CONSCIOUSNESS IS HOLOGRAPHIC?
CAUSED BY ELECTRICAL OSCILLATIONS IN THE DENDRITIC ARBOR WHICH ARE DIFFERENT THAN THE ACTION POTENTIALS WE NORMALLY ASSOCIATE WITH--
OH, HEY, SPEAKING OF ACTION POTENTIAL... YOU COMIN' OVER LATER?
YOU MEAN TO YOUR LITTLE *GROUP EXPERIMENT?* UGH. NO THANKS.
ORIN WETZEL?
MAYBE, BABY! WHO WANTS TO...?
...KNOW?
C'MON, PICK UP...
MISSED CALL
NO RESPONSE

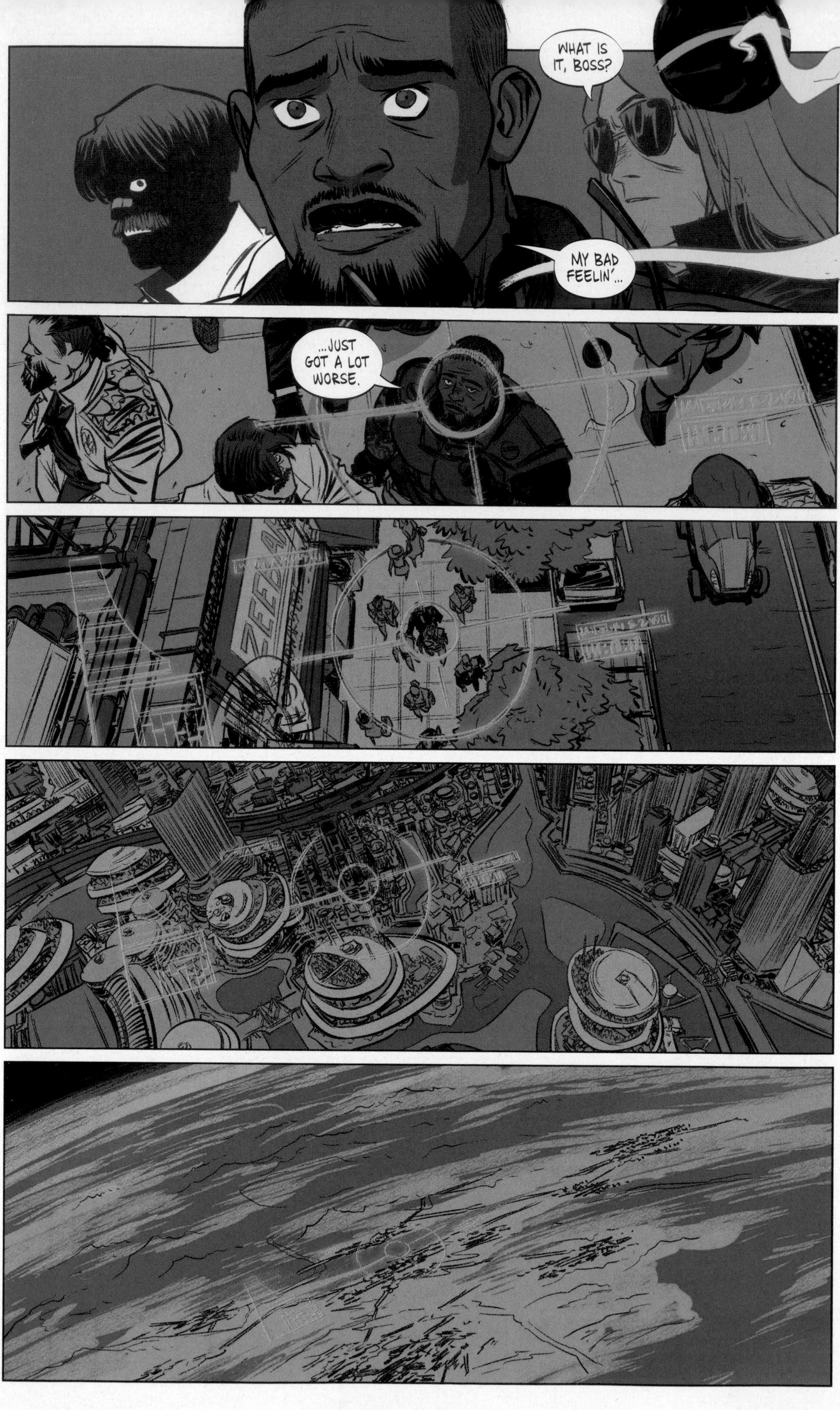
WHAT IS IT, BOSS?
MY BAD FEELIN'...
...JUST GOT A LOT WORSE.

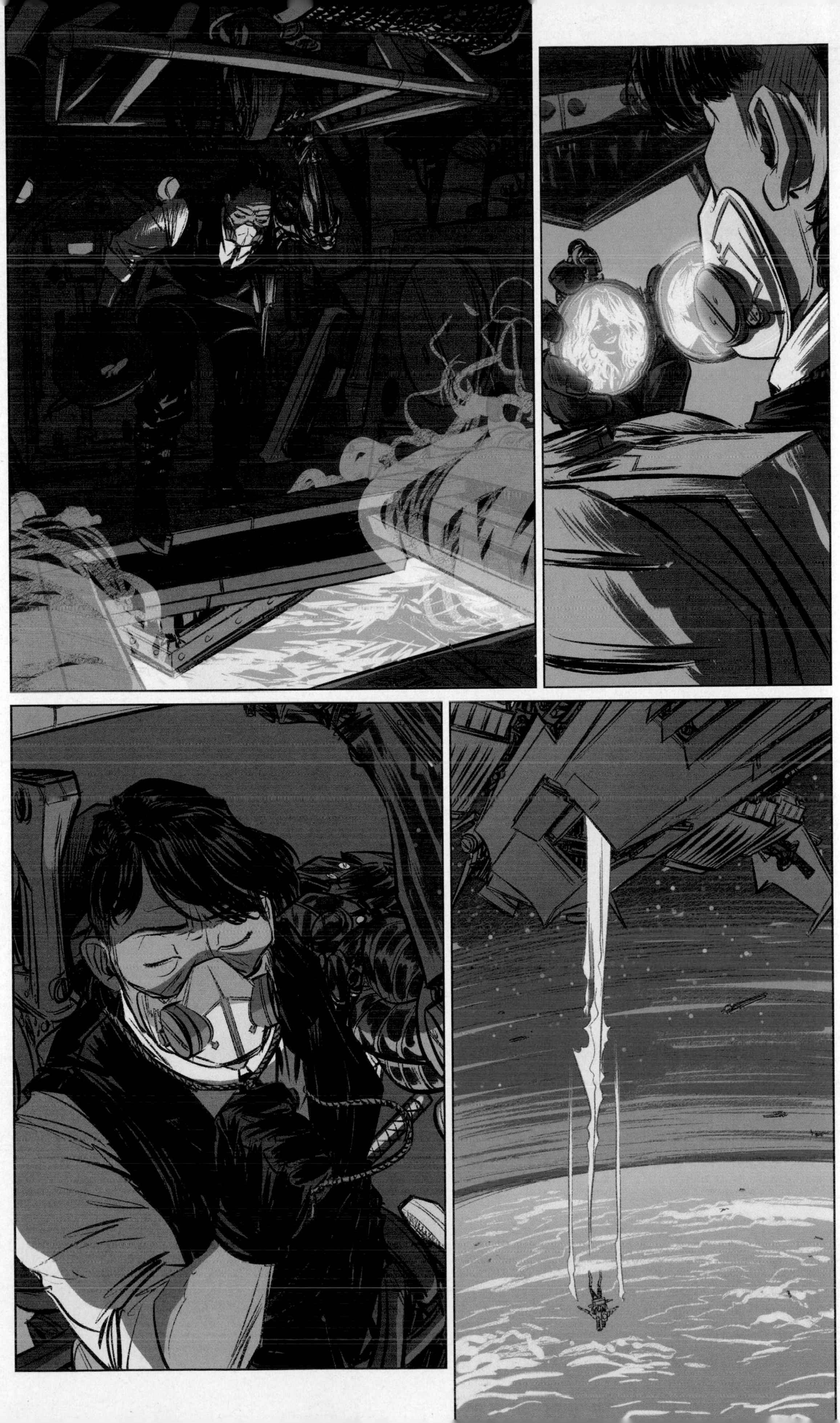

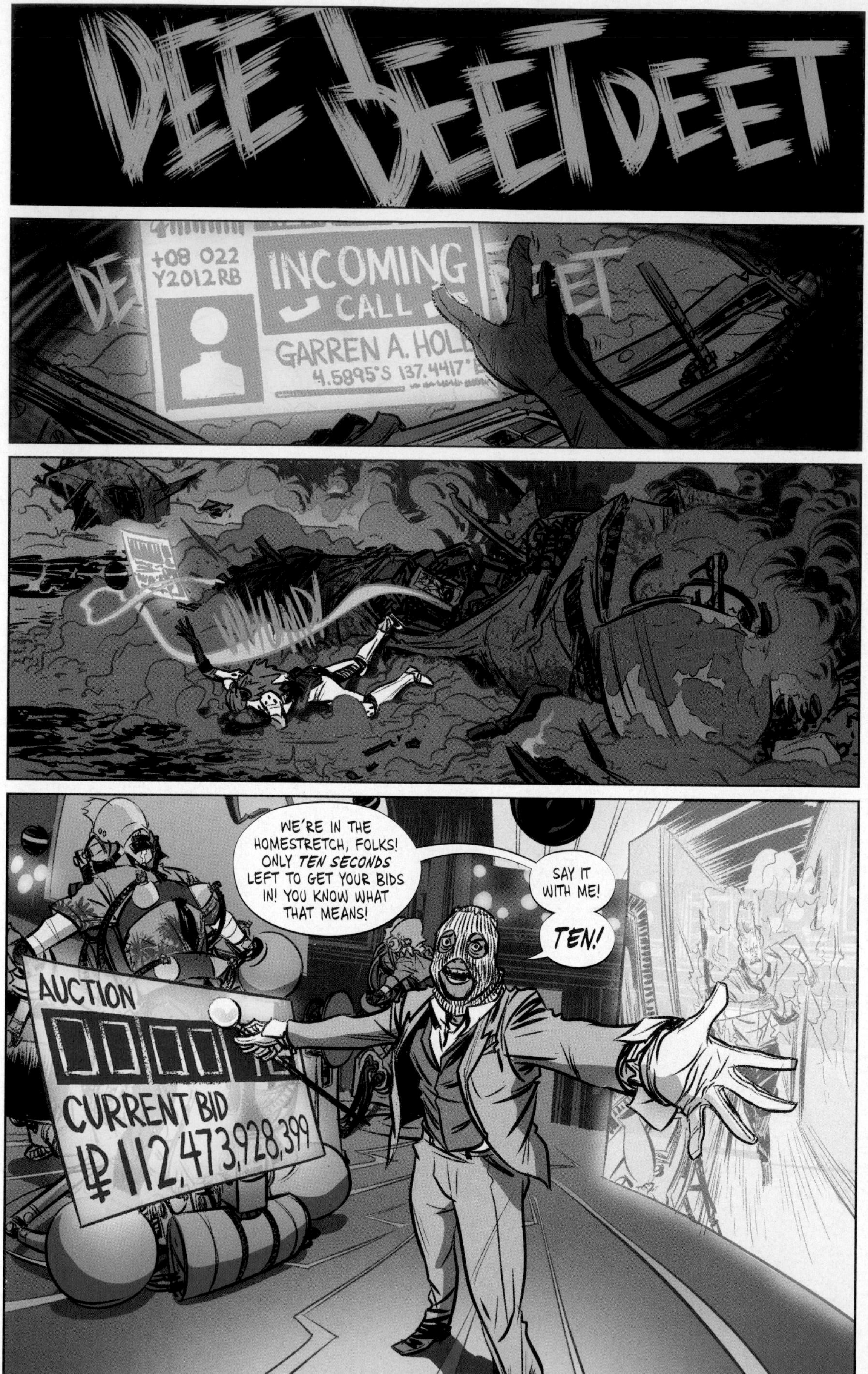
DEET DEET DEET
+08 022
Y2012RB
INCOMING CALL
GARREN A. HOLL
4.5895°S 137.4417°E
WHOMP
WE'RE IN THE HOMESTRETCH, FOLKS! ONLY TEN SECONDS LEFT TO GET YOUR BIDS IN! YOU KNOW WHAT THAT MEANS!
SAY IT WITH ME!
TEN!
AUCTION
CURRENT BID
₽ 112,473,928,399

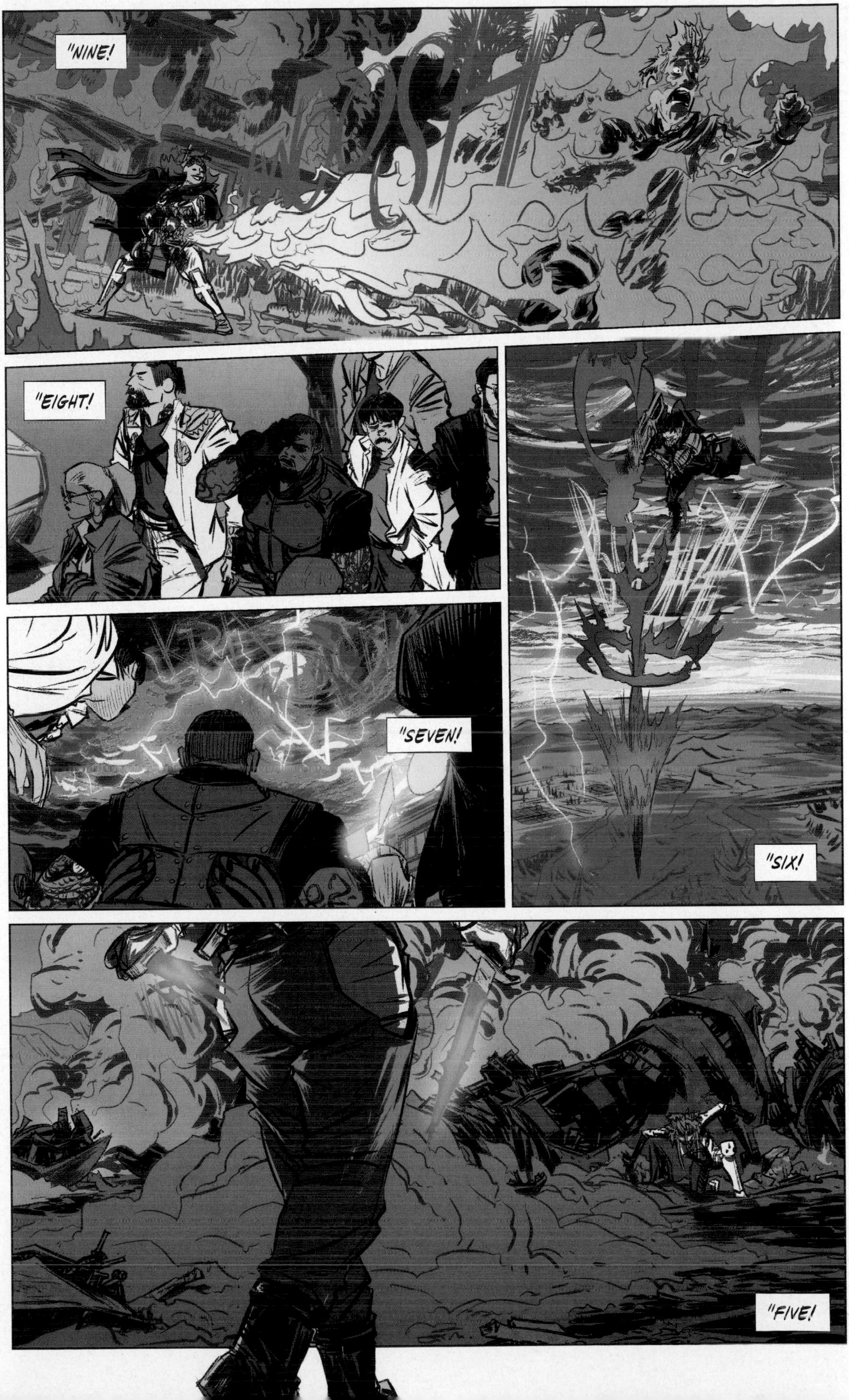
"NINE!
"EIGHT!
"SEVEN!
"SIX!
"FIVE!

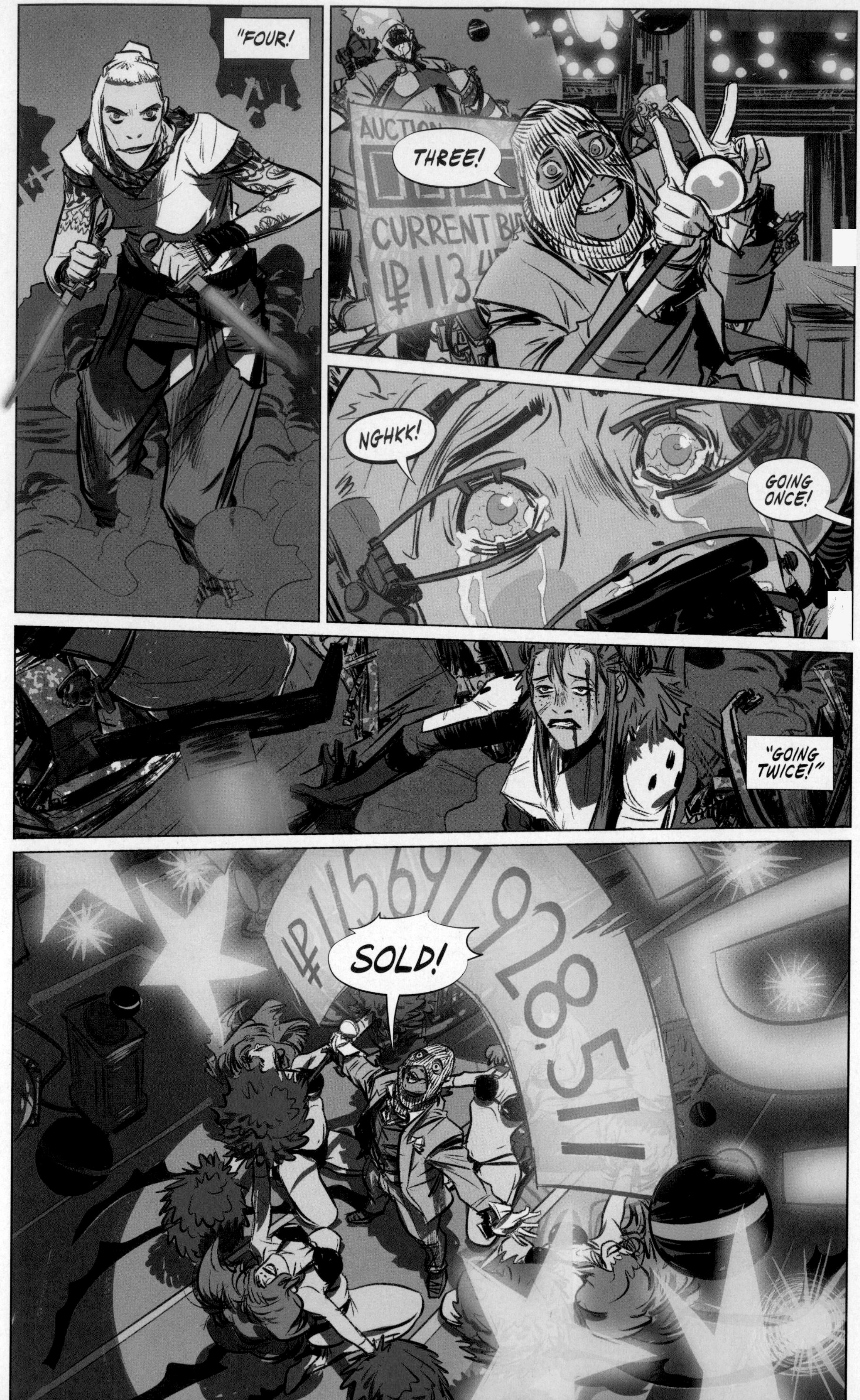
"FOUR!
AUCTION
CURRENT BID
₰113
THREE!
NGHKK!
GOING ONCE!
"GOING TWICE!"
₰115697928.517
SOLD!

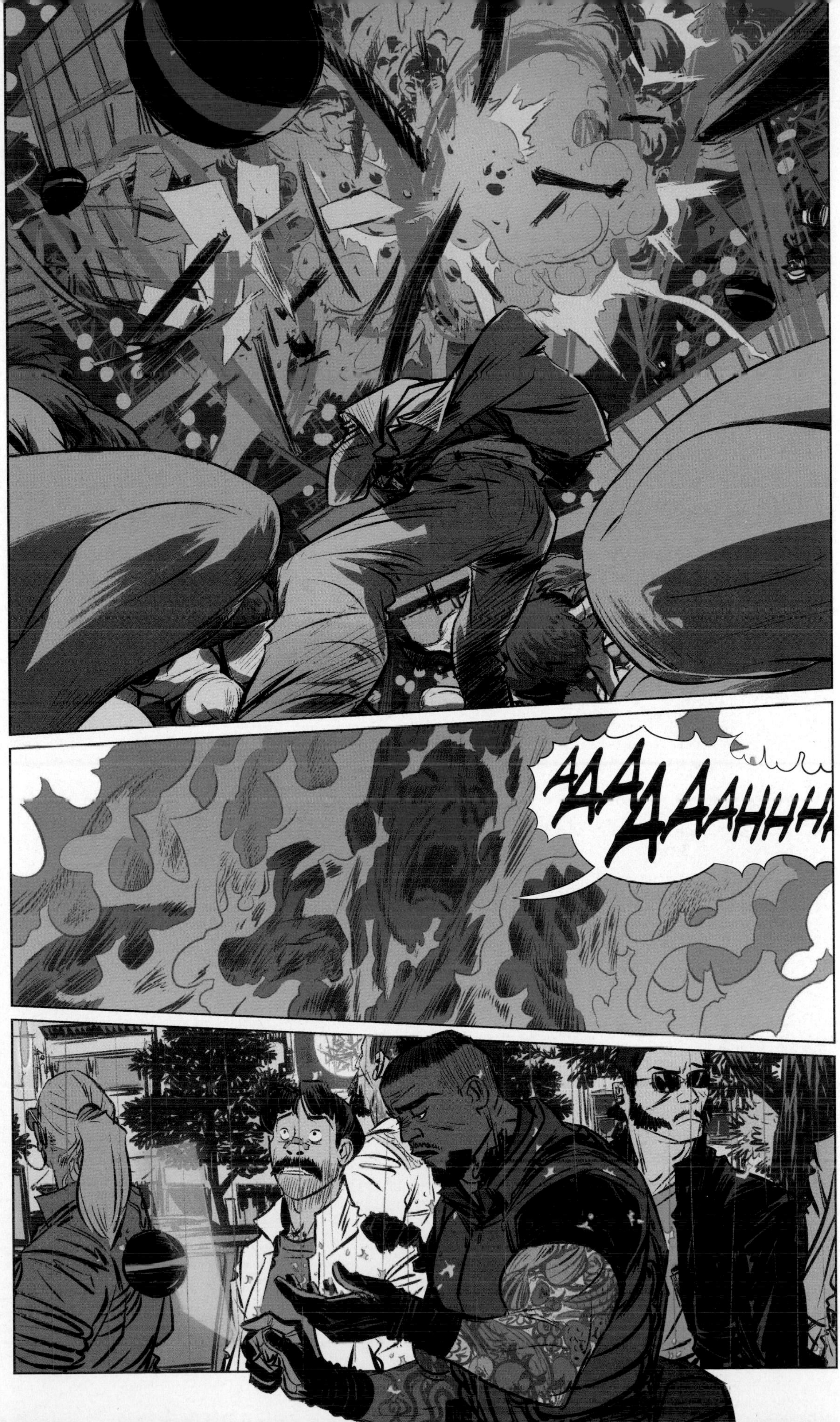
AAAAAAHHHH

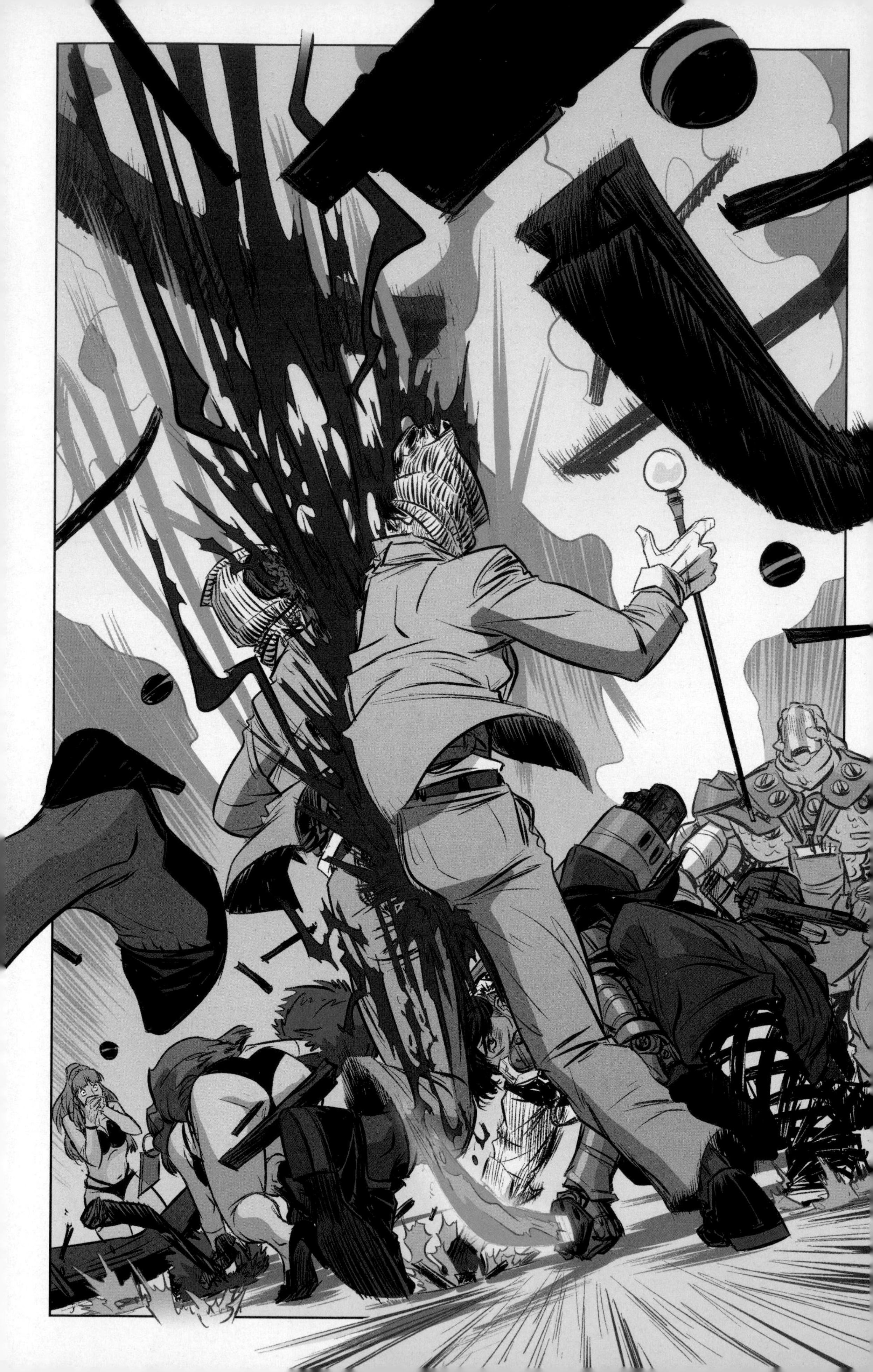

BRUTAL NOODLES

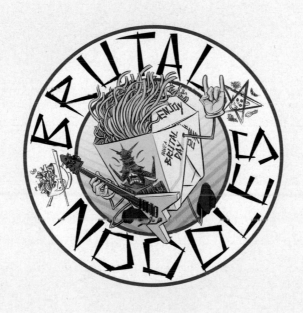

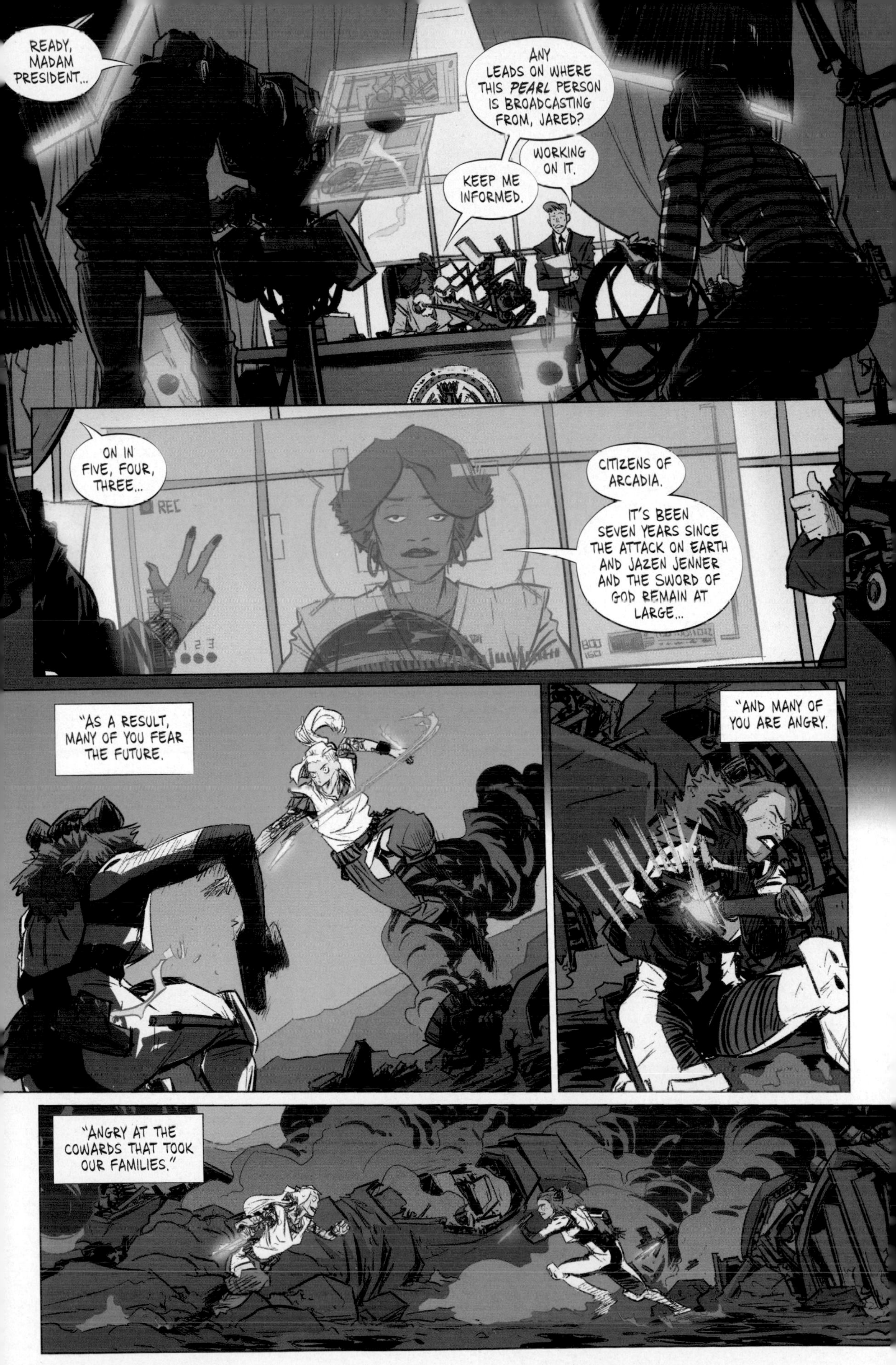
READY, MADAM PRESIDENT...
ANY LEADS ON WHERE THIS PEARL PERSON IS BROADCASTING FROM, JARED?
WORKING ON IT.
KEEP ME INFORMED.
ON IN FIVE, FOUR, THREE...
CITIZENS OF ARCADIA.
IT'S BEEN SEVEN YEARS SINCE THE ATTACK ON EARTH AND JAZEN JENNER AND THE SWORD OF GOD REMAIN AT LARGE...
"AS A RESULT, MANY OF YOU FEAR THE FUTURE.
"AND MANY OF YOU ARE ANGRY.
"ANGRY AT THE COWARDS THAT TOOK OUR FAMILIES."

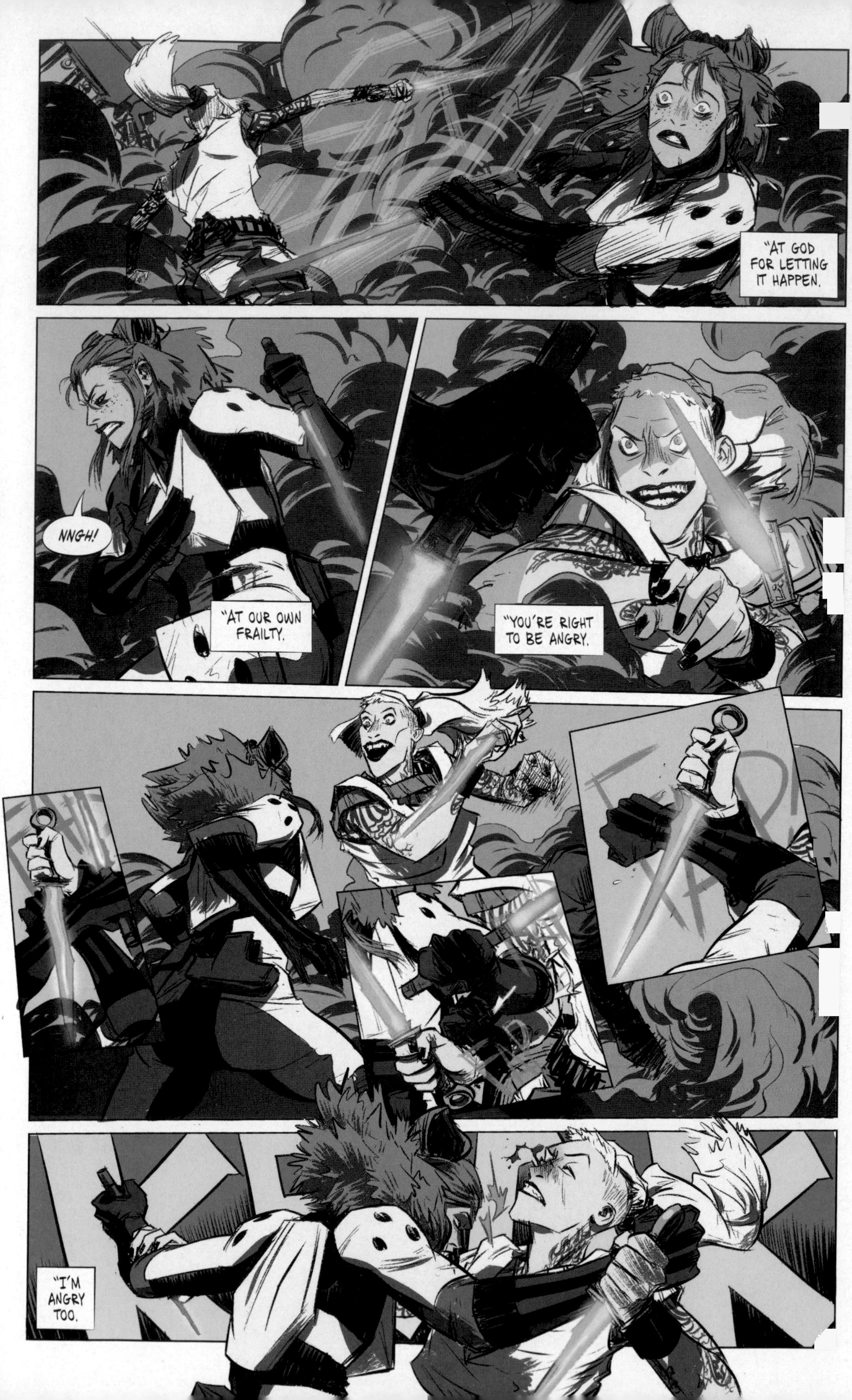
"AT GOD FOR LETTING IT HAPPEN.
NNGH!
"AT OUR OWN FRAILTY.
"YOU'RE RIGHT TO BE ANGRY.
"I'M ANGRY TOO.

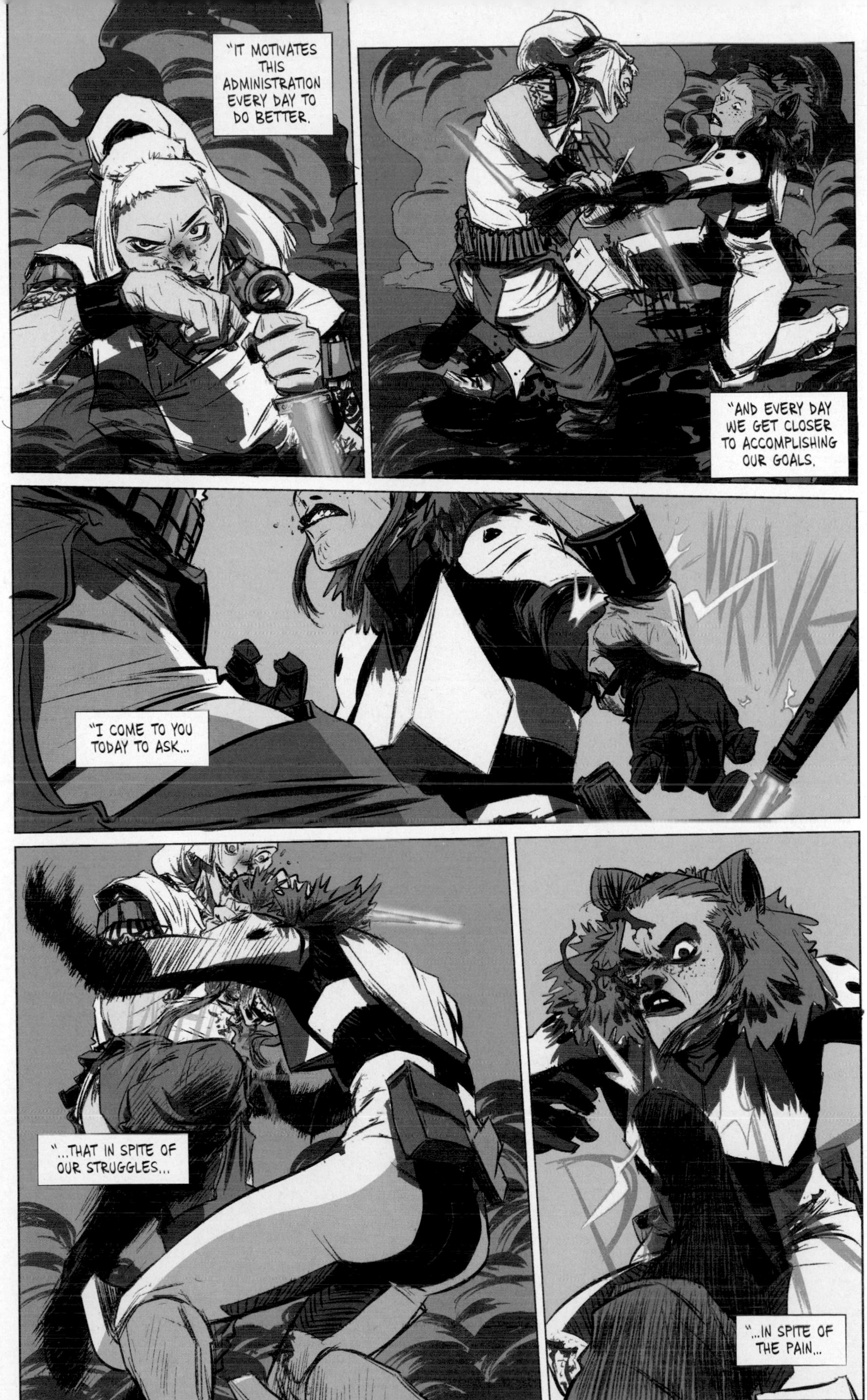
"IT MOTIVATES THIS ADMINISTRATION EVERY DAY TO DO BETTER.
"AND EVERY DAY WE GET CLOSER TO ACCOMPLISHING OUR GOALS.
"I COME TO YOU TODAY TO ASK...
WRNK
"...THAT IN SPITE OF OUR STRUGGLES...
"...IN SPITE OF THE PAIN...

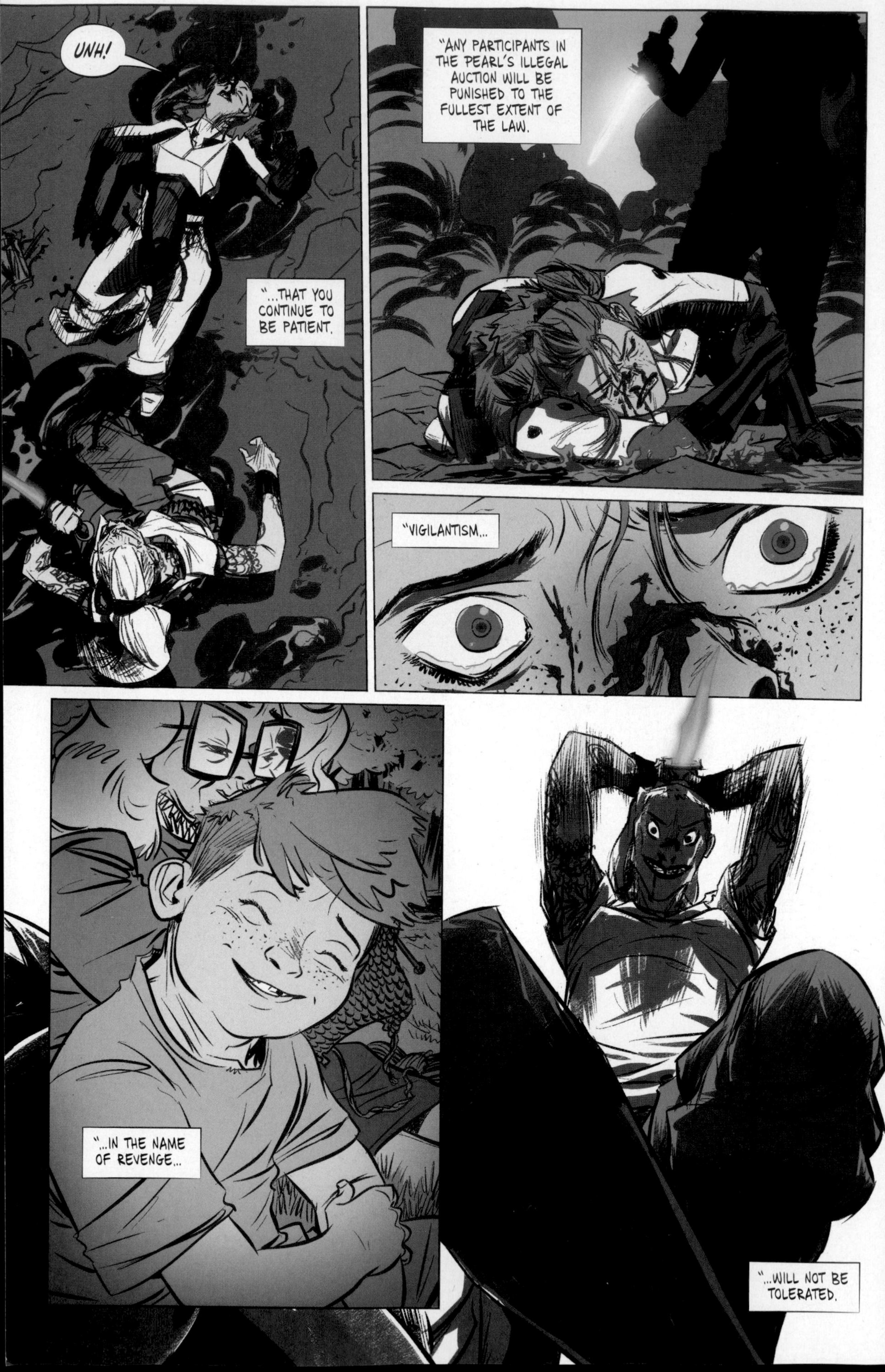
UNH!
"...THAT YOU CONTINUE TO BE PATIENT.
"ANY PARTICIPANTS IN THE PEARL'S ILLEGAL AUCTION WILL BE PUNISHED TO THE FULLEST EXTENT OF THE LAW.
"VIGILANTISM...
"...IN THE NAME OF REVENGE...
"...WILL NOT BE TOLERATED.

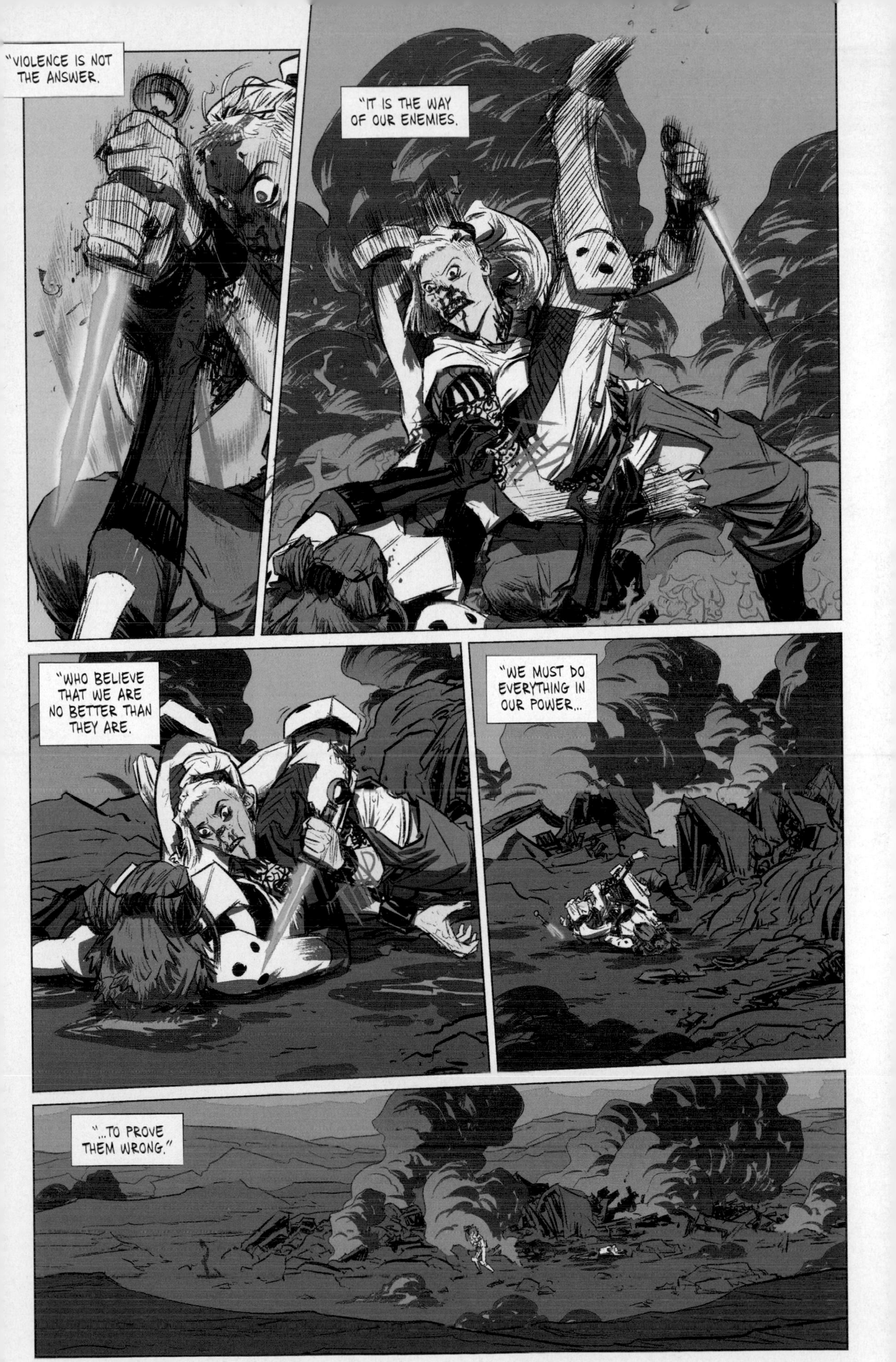
"VIOLENCE IS NOT THE ANSWER.
"IT IS THE WAY OF OUR ENEMIES.
"WHO BELIEVE THAT WE ARE NO BETTER THAN THEY ARE.
"WE MUST DO EVERYTHING IN OUR POWER...
"...TO PROVE THEM WRONG."

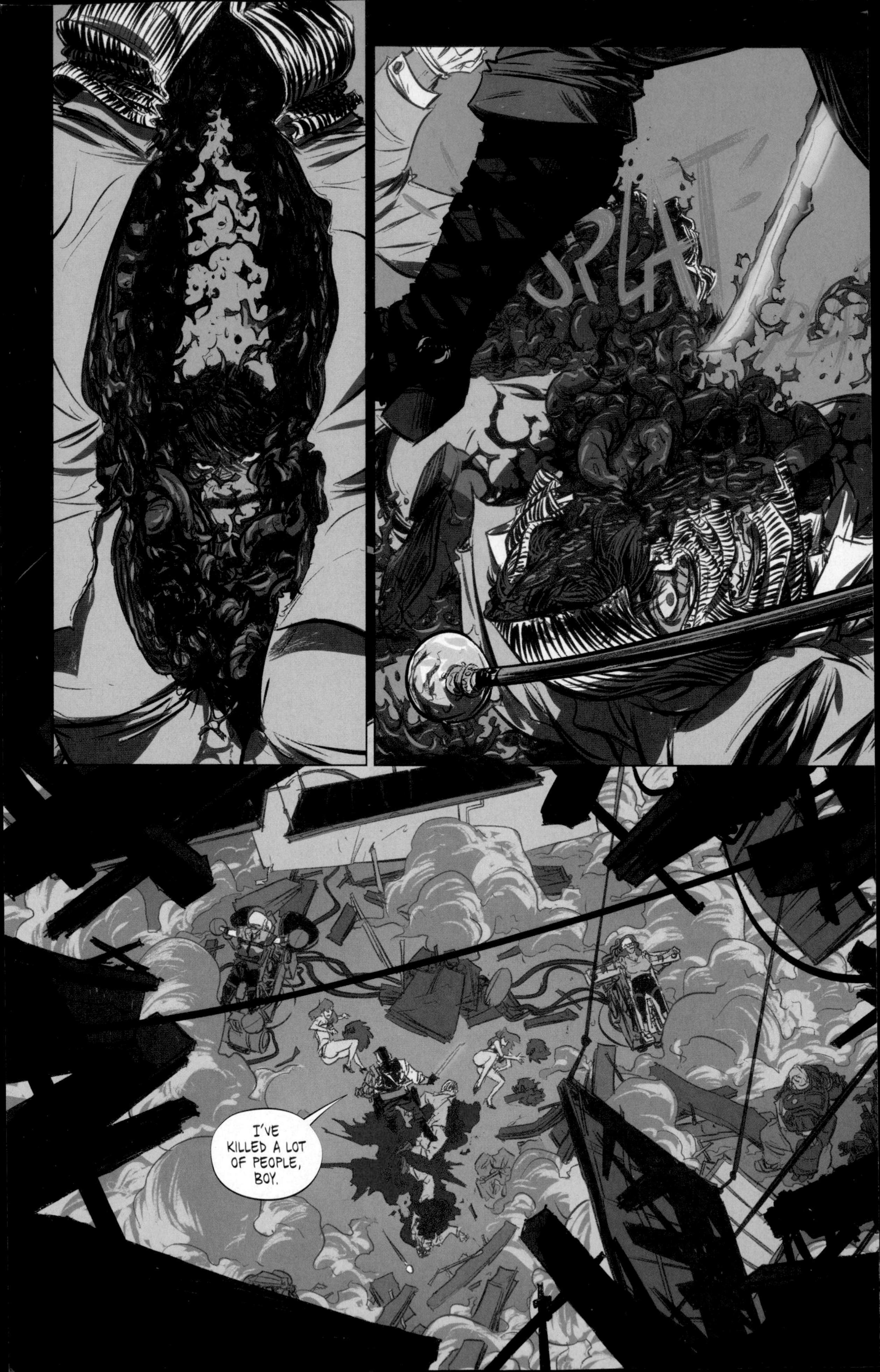
SPLAT
I'VE KILLED A LOT OF PEOPLE, BOY.

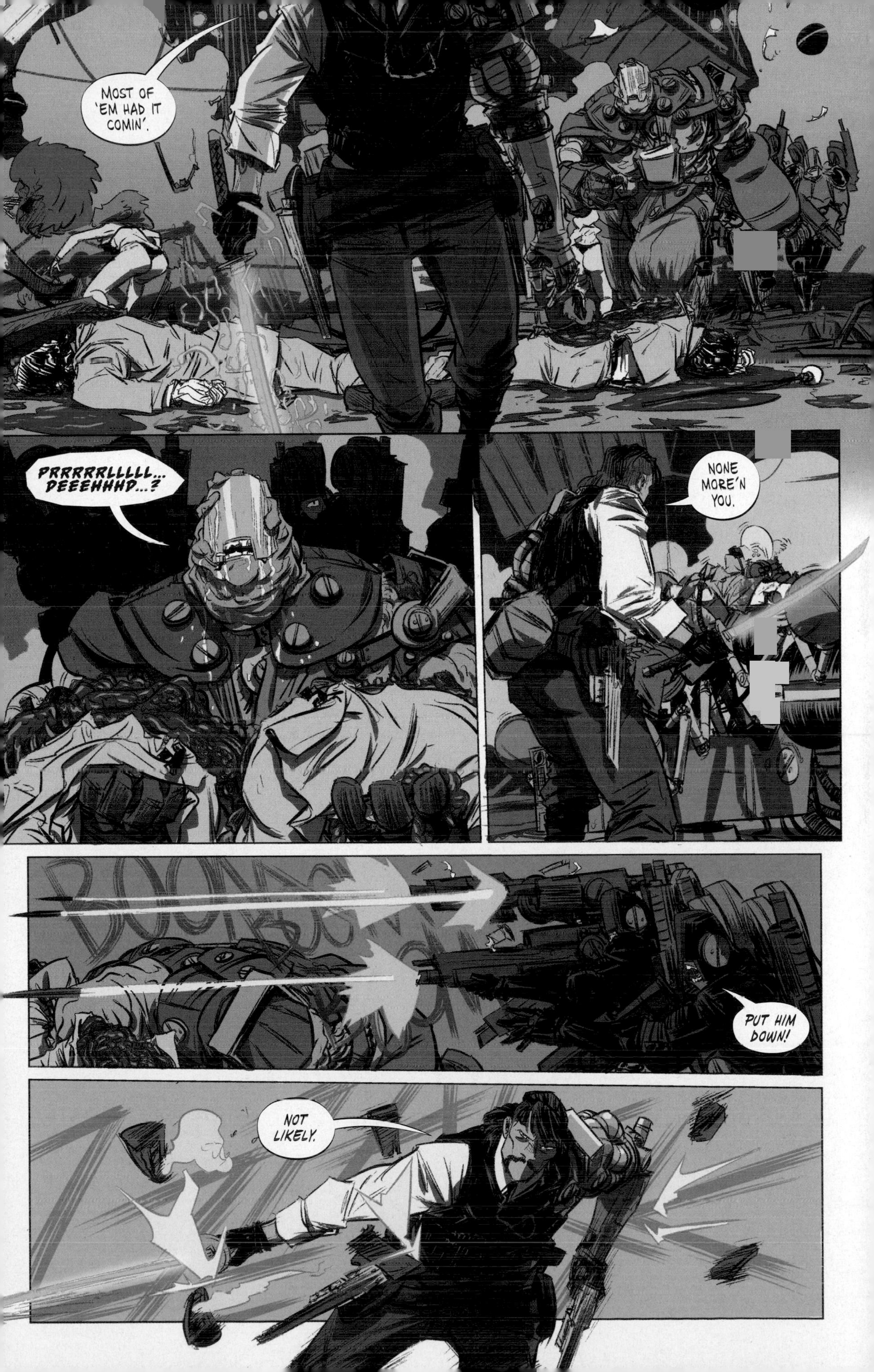
MOST OF 'EM HAD IT COMIN'.
PRRRRRLLLLLL... DEEEHHHD...?
NONE MORE'N YOU.
PUT HIM DOWN!
NOT LIKELY.

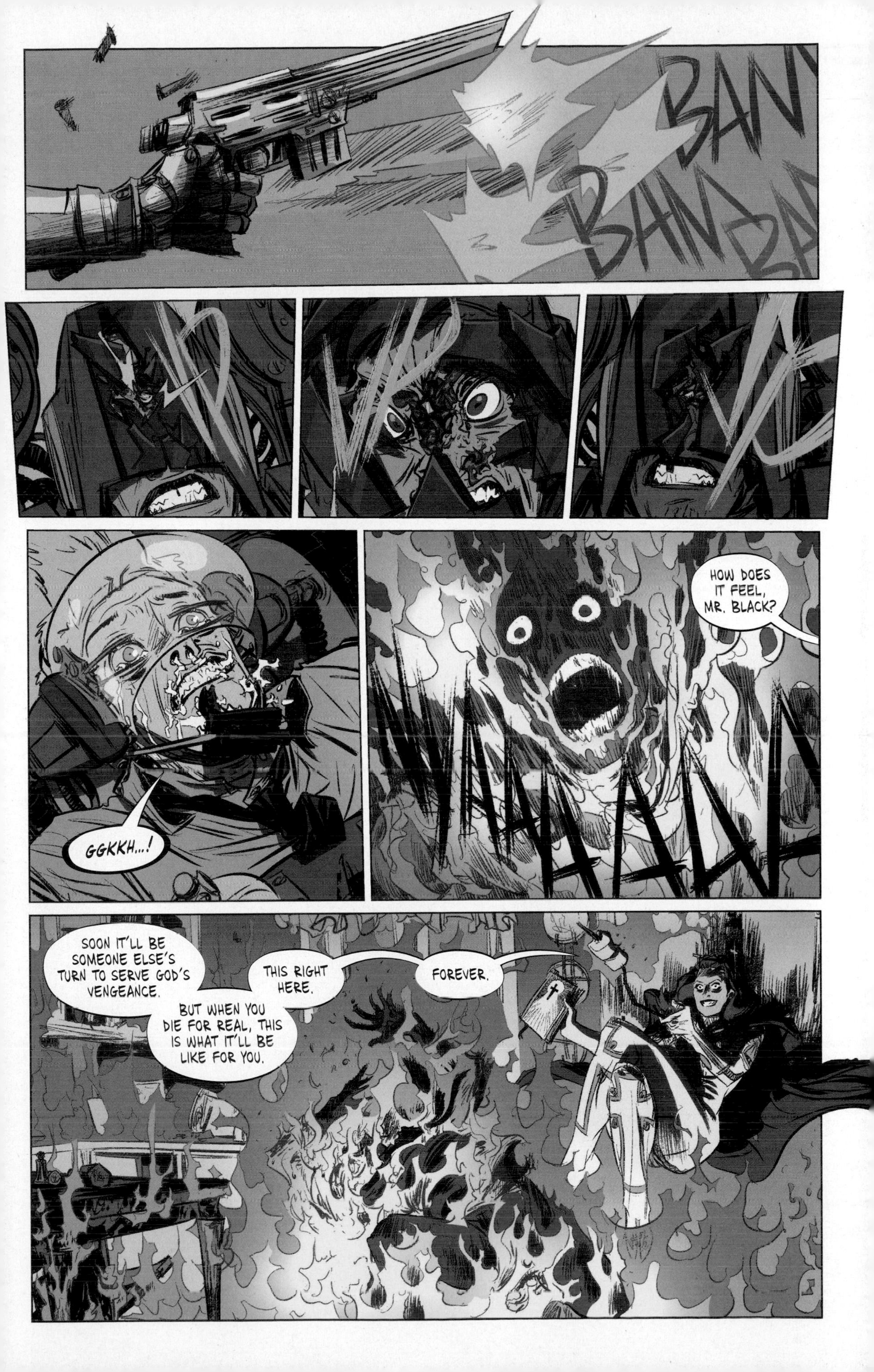
BAM
BAM BA
GGKKH...!
HOW DOES IT FEEL, MR. BLACK?
SOON IT'LL BE SOMEONE ELSE'S TURN TO SERVE GOD'S VENGEANCE.
BUT WHEN YOU DIE FOR REAL, THIS IS WHAT IT'LL BE LIKE FOR YOU.
THIS RIGHT HERE.
FOREVER.

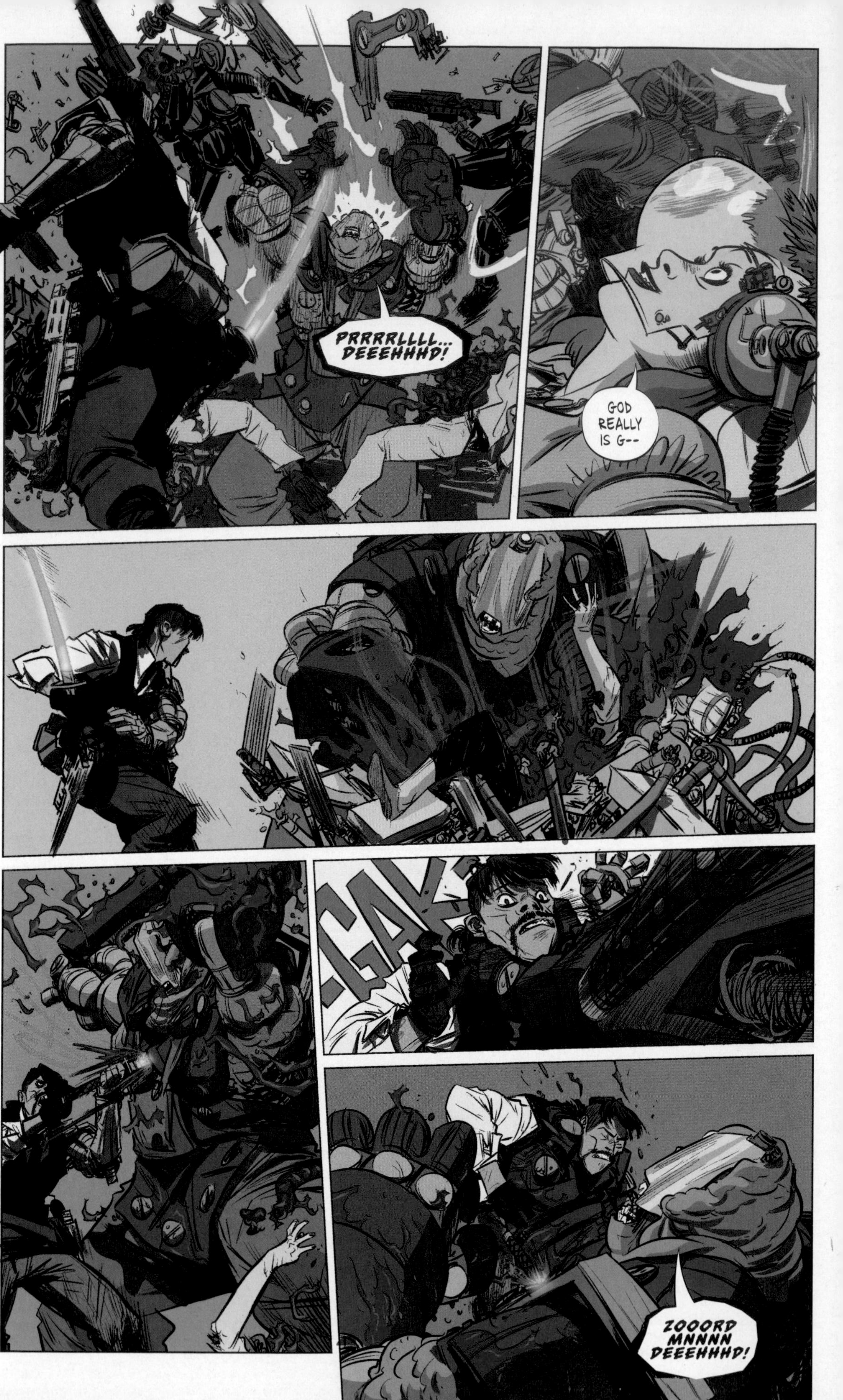
PRRRRLLLL...
DEEEHHHD!
GOD
REALLY
IS G--
ZOOORD
MNNNN
DEEEHHHD!

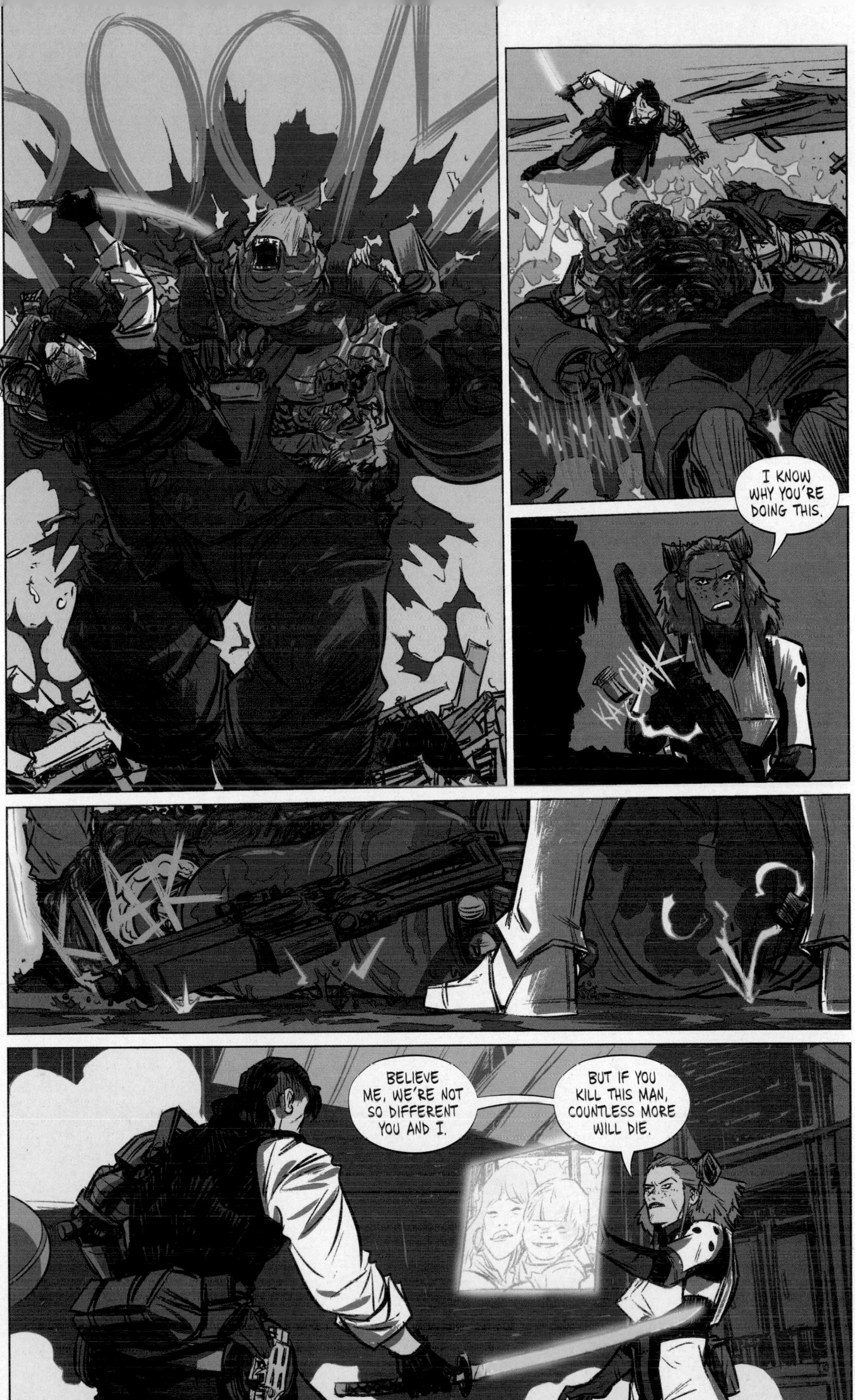
I KNOW WHY YOU'RE DOING THIS.
KA-CHAK
KAK
BELIEVE ME, WE'RE NOT SO DIFFERENT YOU AND I.
BUT IF YOU KILL THIS MAN, COUNTLESS MORE WILL DIE.

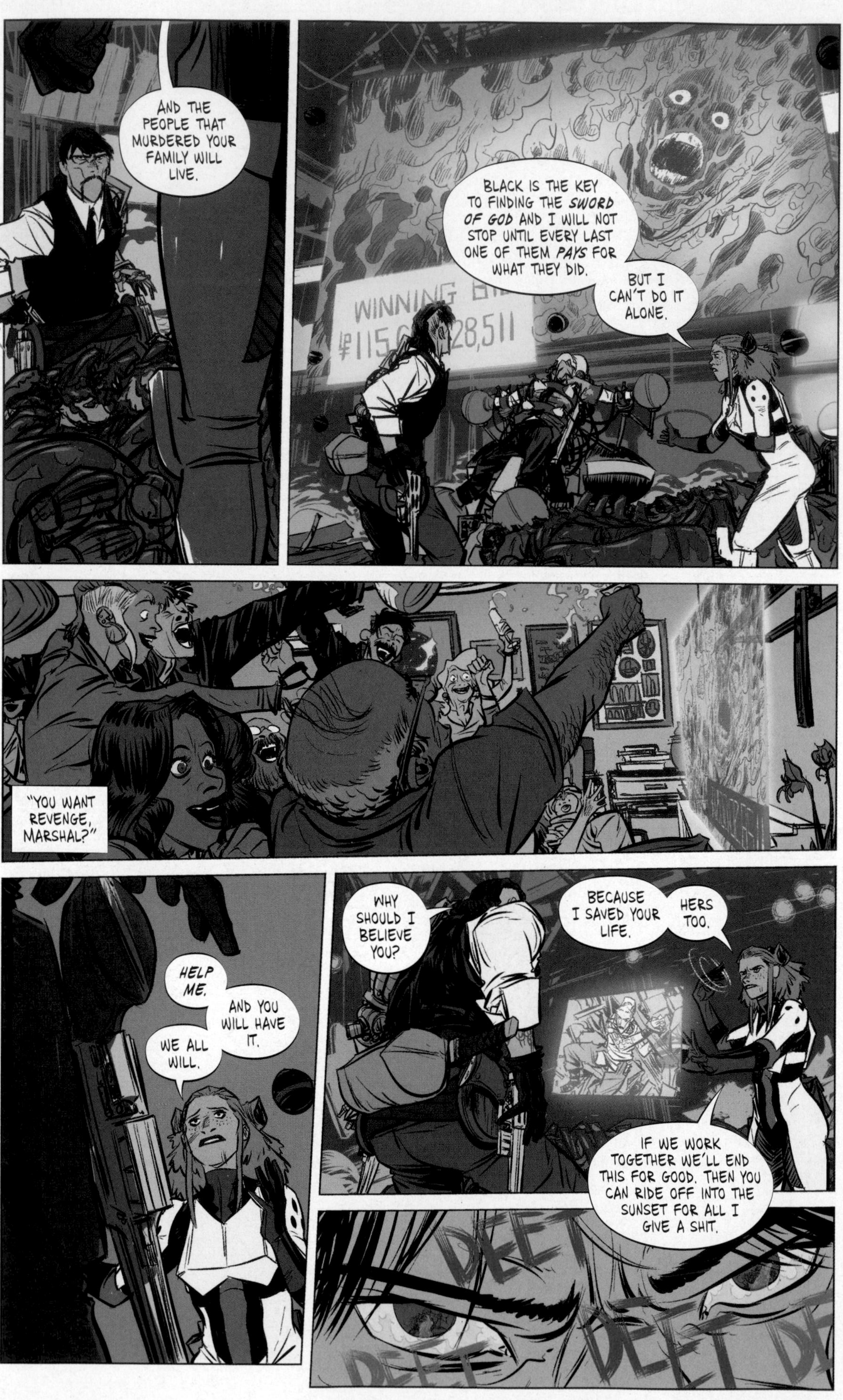

CHK
AND THE PEOPLE THAT MURDERED YOUR FAMILY WILL LIVE.
BLACK IS THE KEY TO FINDING THE *SWORD OF GOD* AND I WILL NOT STOP UNTIL EVERY LAST ONE OF THEM *PAYS* FOR WHAT THEY DID.
BUT I CAN'T DO IT ALONE.
"YOU WANT REVENGE, MARSHAL?"
HELP ME.
AND YOU WILL HAVE IT.
WE ALL WILL.
WHY SHOULD I BELIEVE YOU?
BECAUSE I SAVED YOUR LIFE.
HERS TOO.
IF WE WORK TOGETHER WE'LL END THIS FOR GOOD. THEN YOU CAN RIDE OFF INTO THE SUNSET FOR ALL I GIVE A SHIT.
DEET DEET DEET

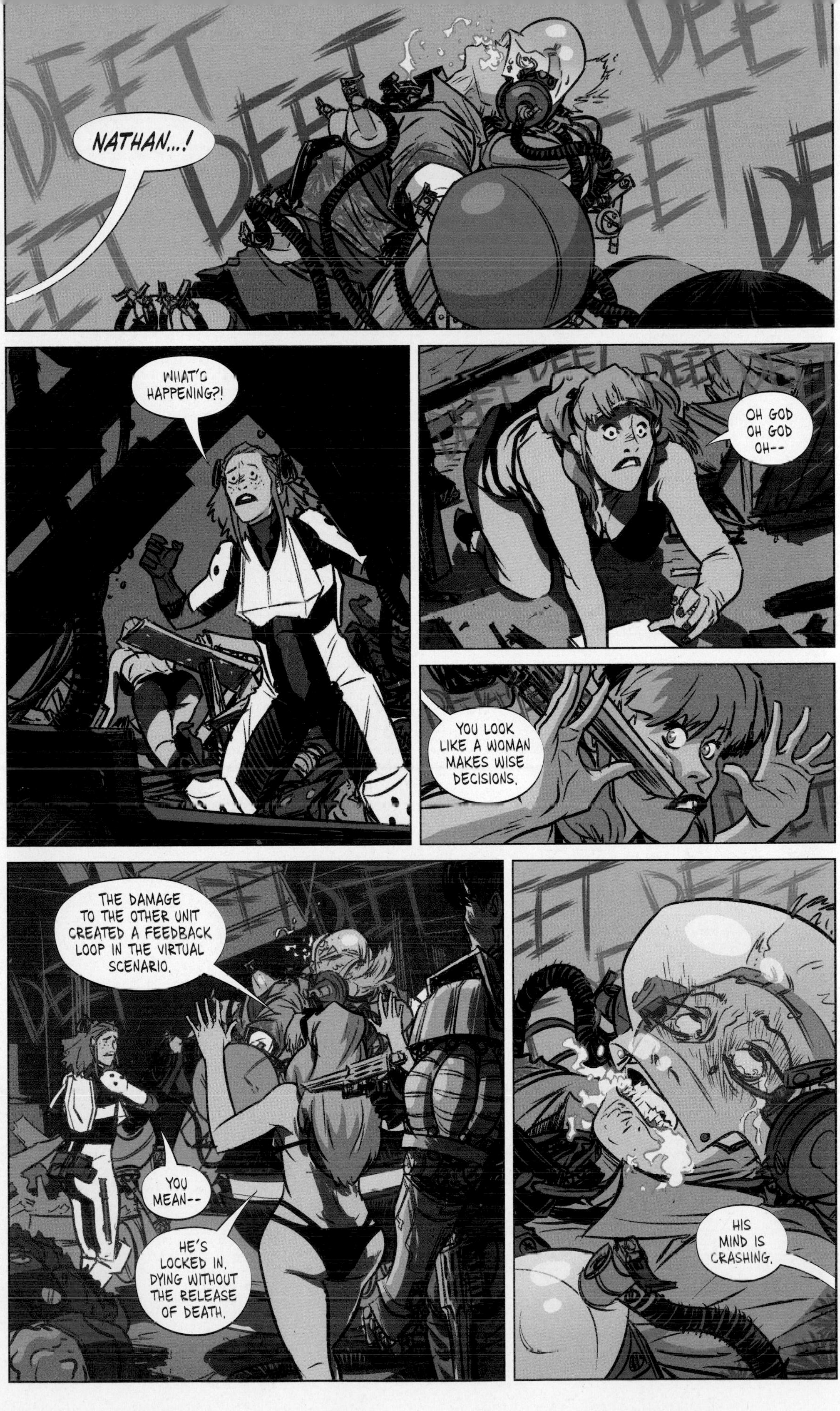

NATHAN...!
WHAT'S HAPPENING?!
OH GOD OH GOD OH--
YOU LOOK LIKE A WOMAN MAKES WISE DECISIONS.
THE DAMAGE TO THE OTHER UNIT CREATED A FEEDBACK LOOP IN THE VIRTUAL SCENARIO.
YOU MEAN--
HE'S LOCKED IN. DYING WITHOUT THE RELEASE OF DEATH.
HIS MIND IS CRASHING.

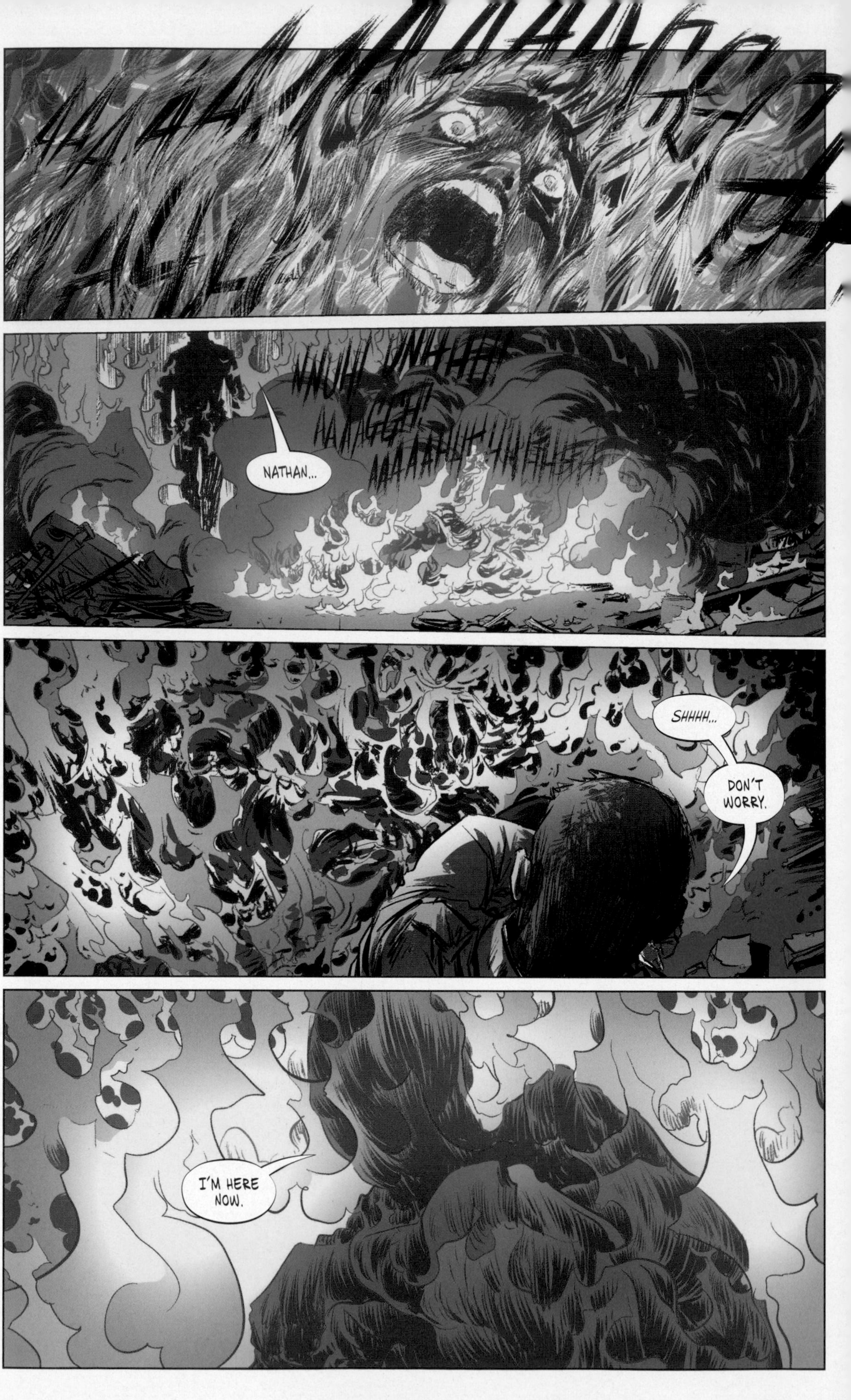
NATHAN...
SHHHH...
DON'T WORRY.
I'M HERE NOW.

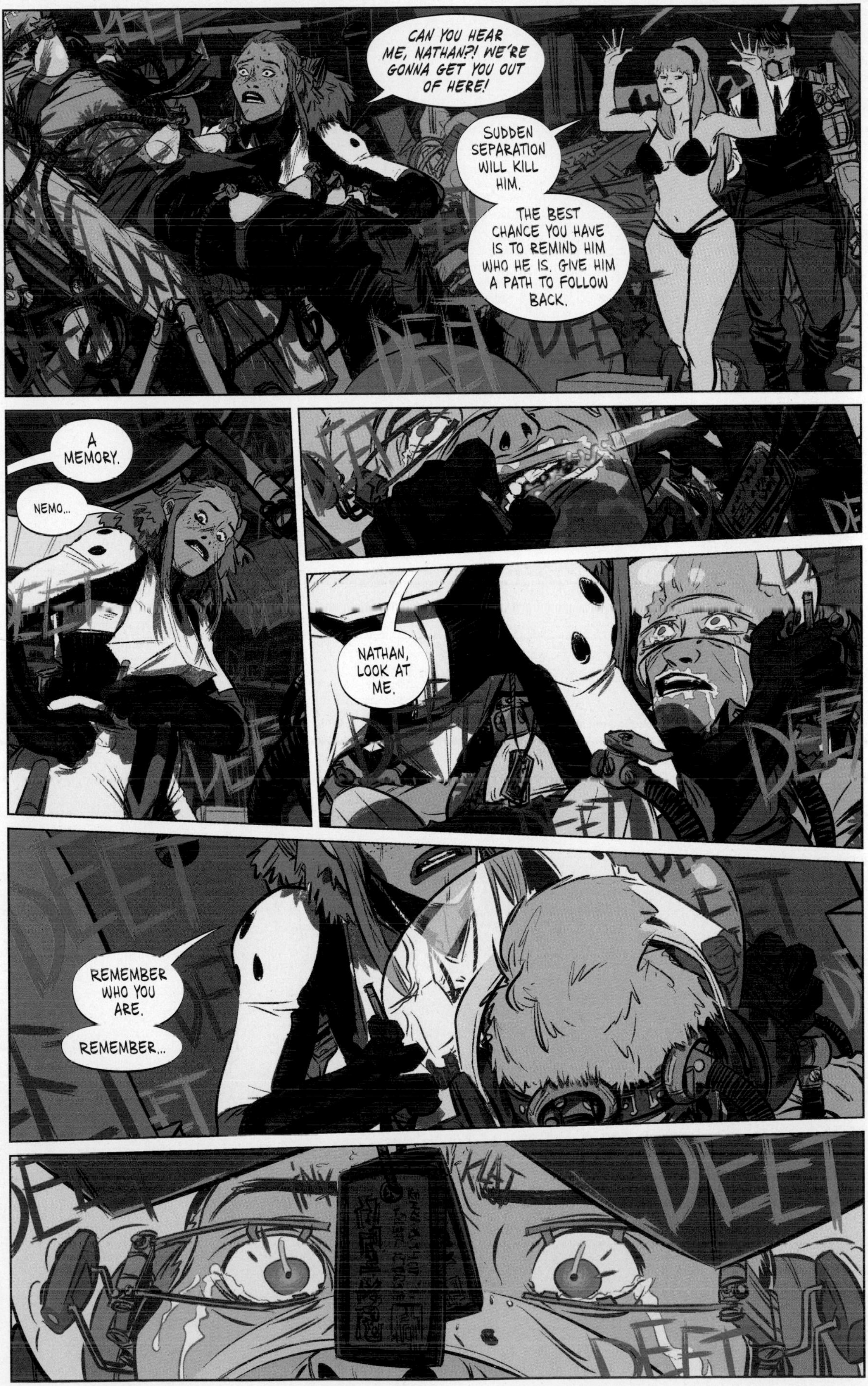
CAN YOU HEAR ME, NATHAN?! WE'RE GONNA GET YOU OUT OF HERE!
SUDDEN SEPARATION WILL KILL HIM.
THE BEST CHANCE YOU HAVE IS TO REMIND HIM WHO HE IS. GIVE HIM A PATH TO FOLLOW BACK.
DEET
DEET
A MEMORY.
NEMO...
NATHAN, LOOK AT ME.
REMEMBER WHO YOU ARE.
REMEMBER...
DEET
KLAT
DEET
DEET

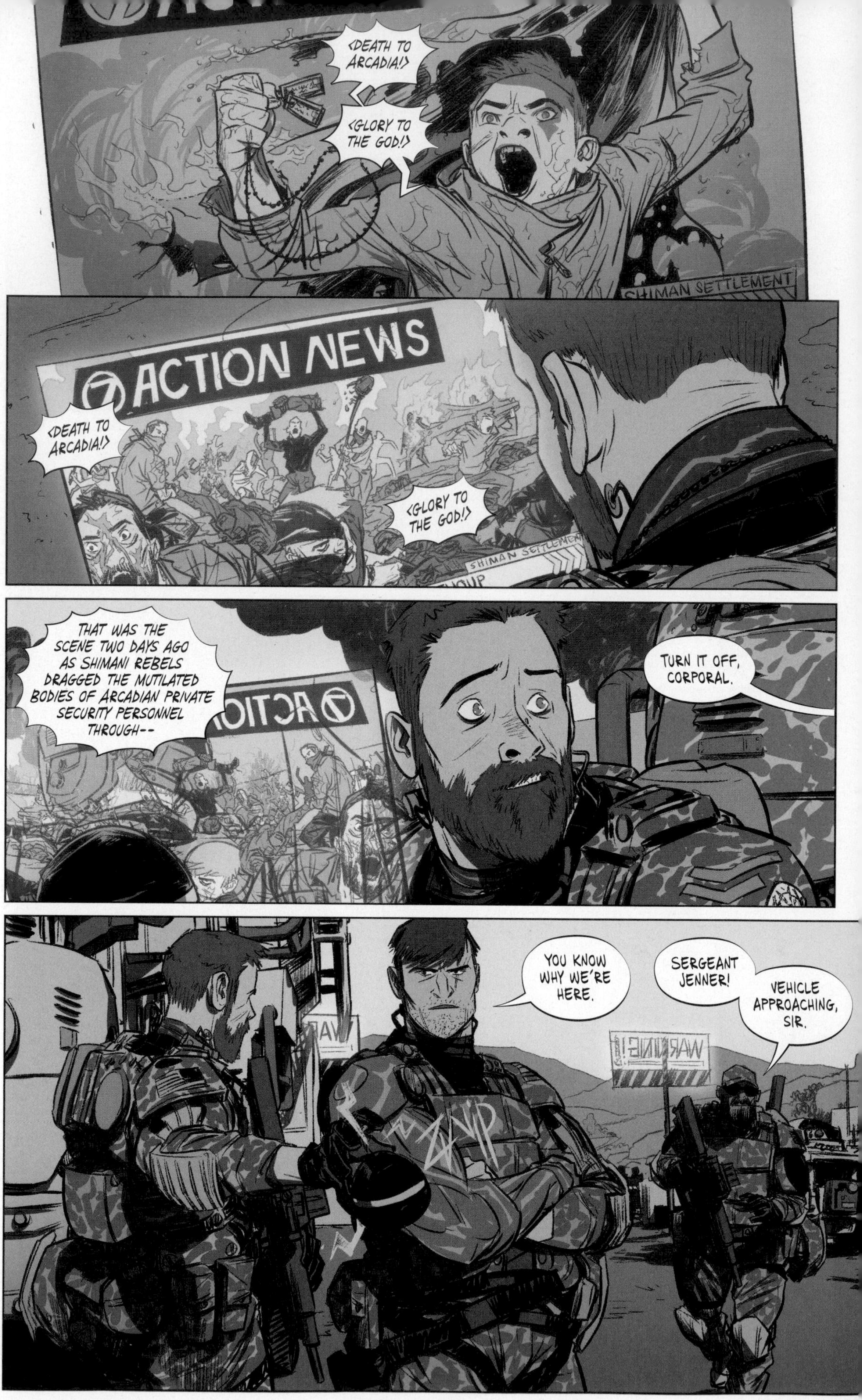

<DEATH TO ARCADIA!>
<GLORY TO THE GOD!>
SHIMAN SETTLEMENT
ACTION NEWS
<DEATH TO ARCADIA!>
<GLORY TO THE GOD!>
SHIMAN SETTLEMENT
THAT WAS THE SCENE TWO DAYS AGO AS SHIMANI REBELS DRAGGED THE MUTILATED BODIES OF ARCADIAN PRIVATE SECURITY PERSONNEL THROUGH--
TURN IT OFF, CORPORAL.
YOU KNOW WHY WE'RE HERE.
SERGEANT JENNER!
VEHICLE APPROACHING, SIR.

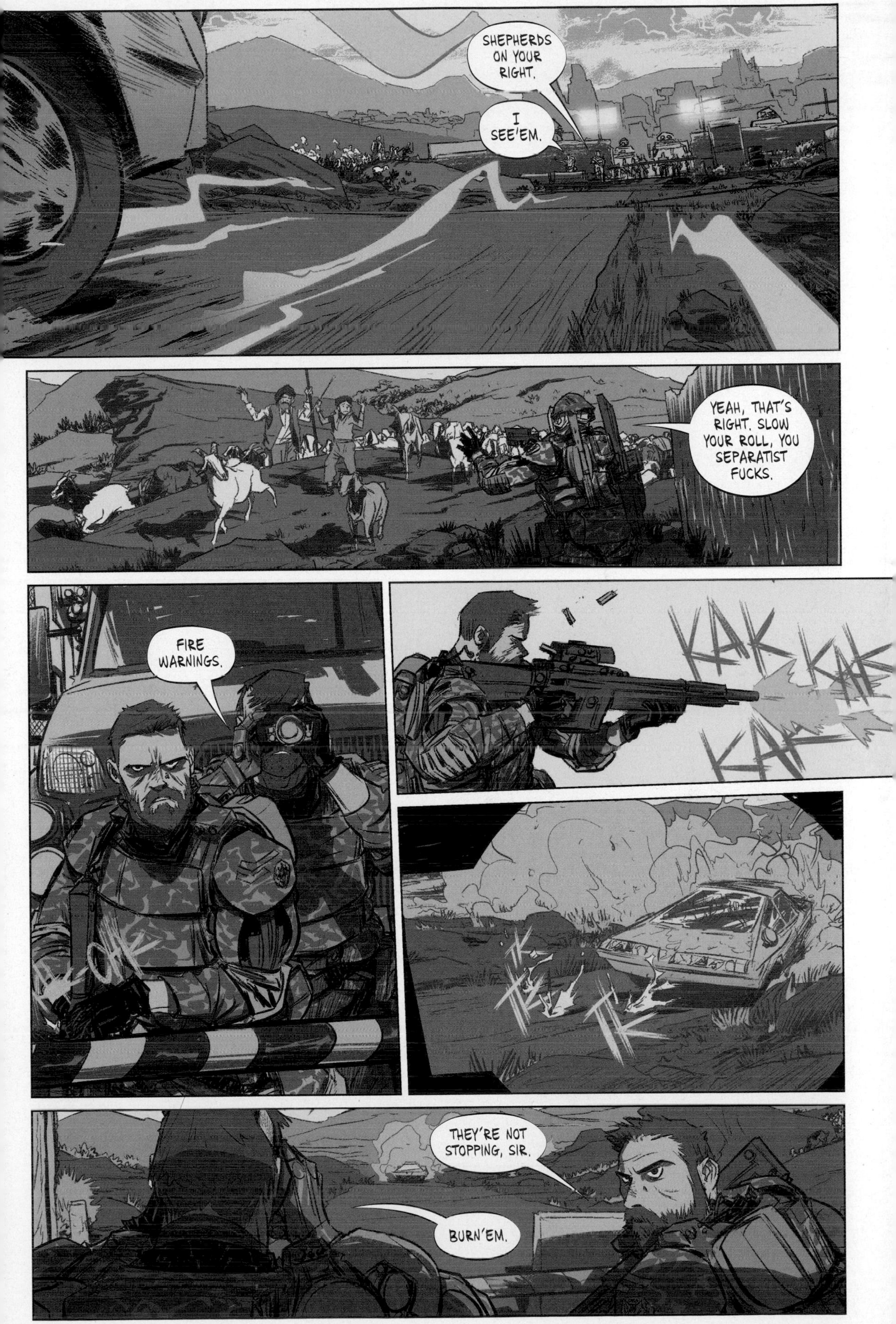
SHEPHERDS ON YOUR RIGHT.
I SEE'EM.
YEAH, THAT'S RIGHT. SLOW YOUR ROLL, YOU SEPARATIST FUCKS.
FIRE WARNINGS.
KAK KAK KAK
TK TK TK
THEY'RE NOT STOPPING, SIR.
BURN'EM.

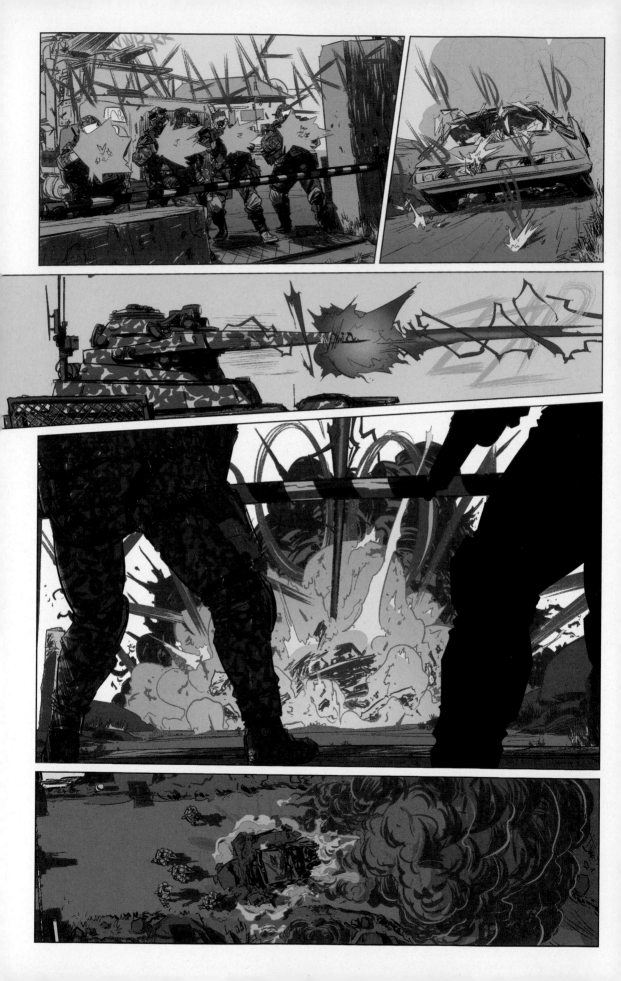

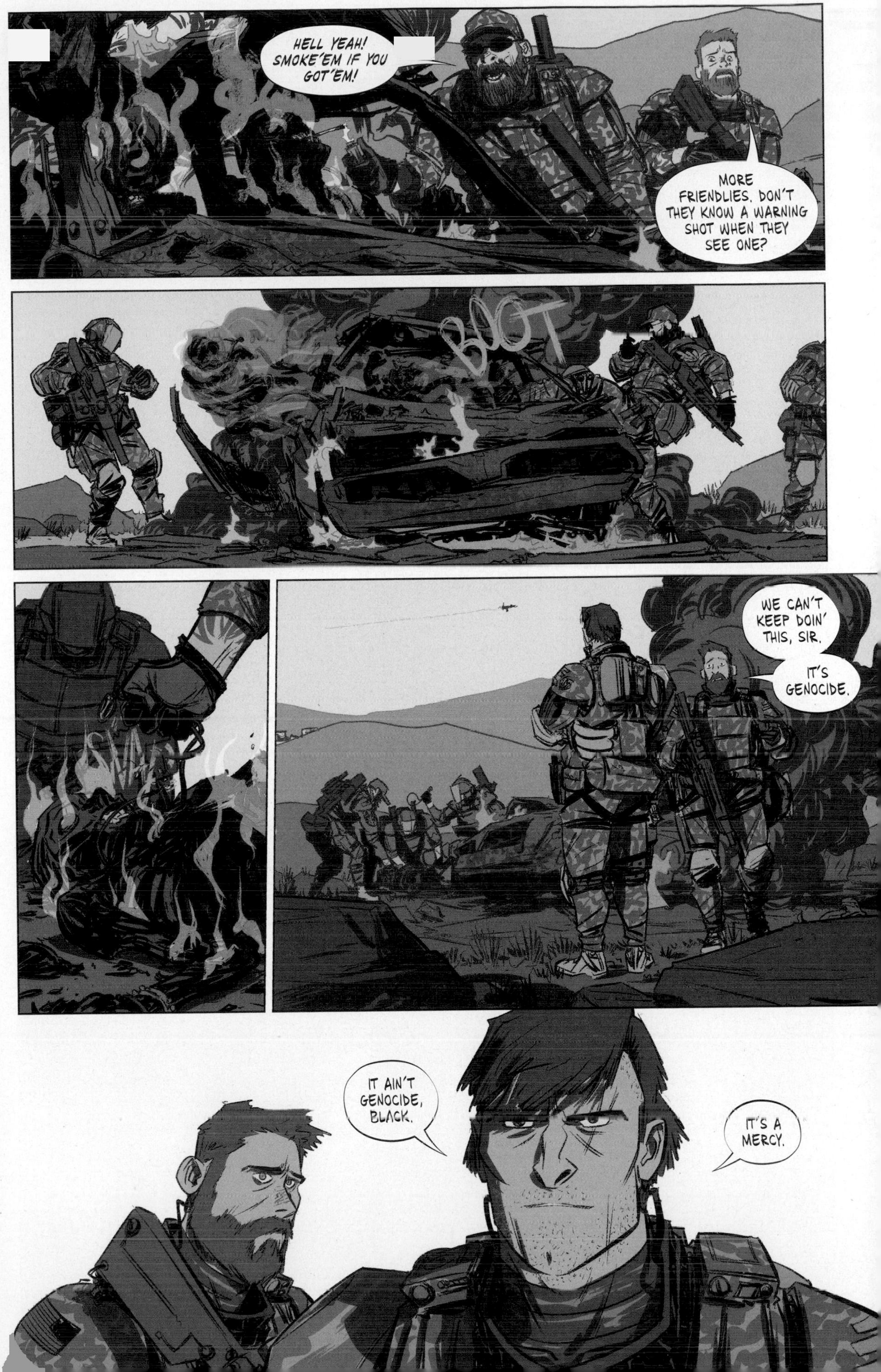
HELL YEAH! SMOKE'EM IF YOU GOT'EM!
MORE FRIENDLIES. DON'T THEY KNOW A WARNING SHOT WHEN THEY SEE ONE?
BOOT
WE CAN'T KEEP DOIN' THIS, SIR.
IT'S GENOCIDE.
IT AIN'T GENOCIDE, BLACK.
IT'S A MERCY.

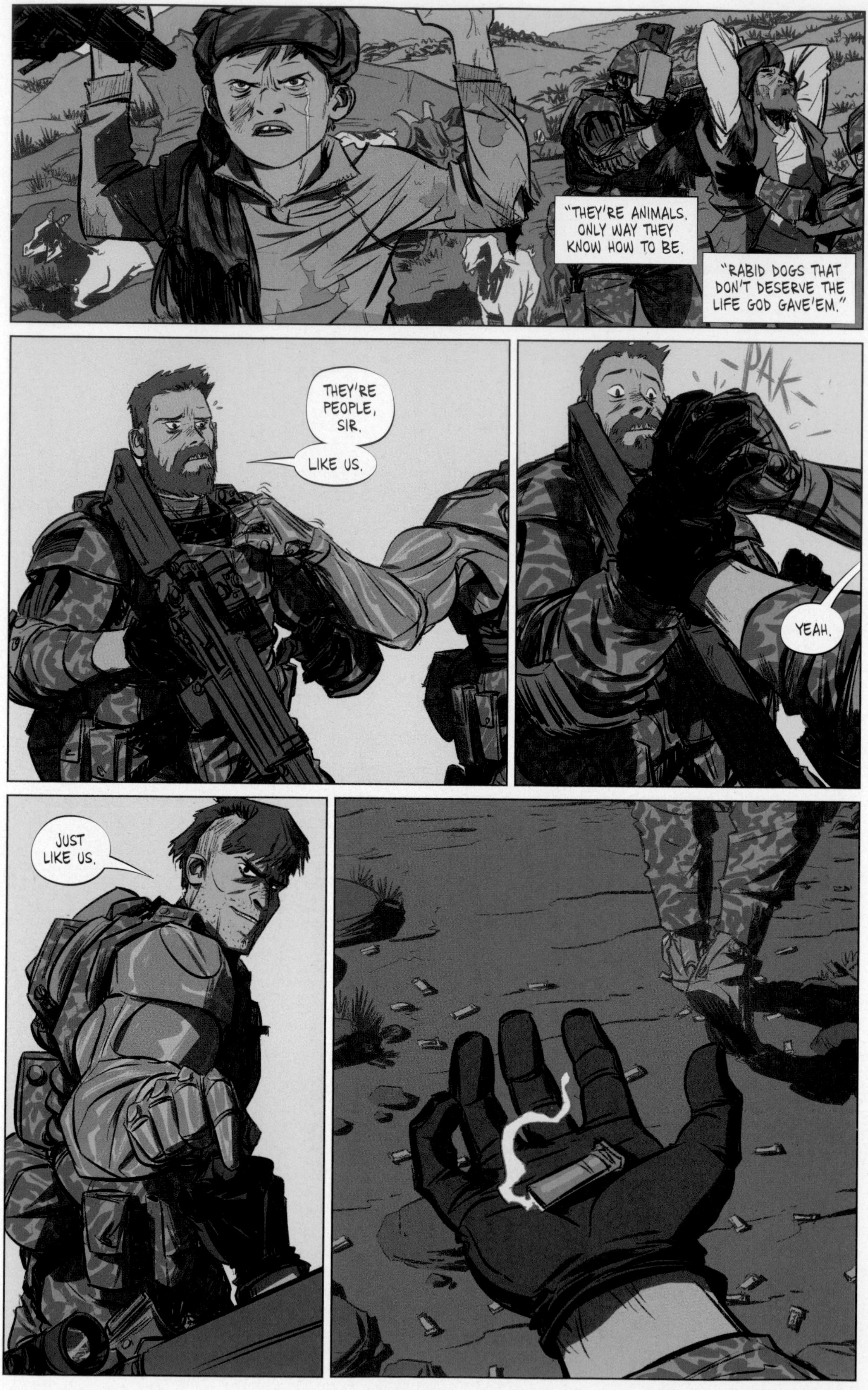
"THEY'RE ANIMALS. ONLY WAY THEY KNOW HOW TO BE.
"RABID DOGS THAT DON'T DESERVE THE LIFE GOD GAVE'EM."
THEY'RE PEOPLE, SIR.
LIKE US.
PAK
YEAH.
JUST LIKE US.

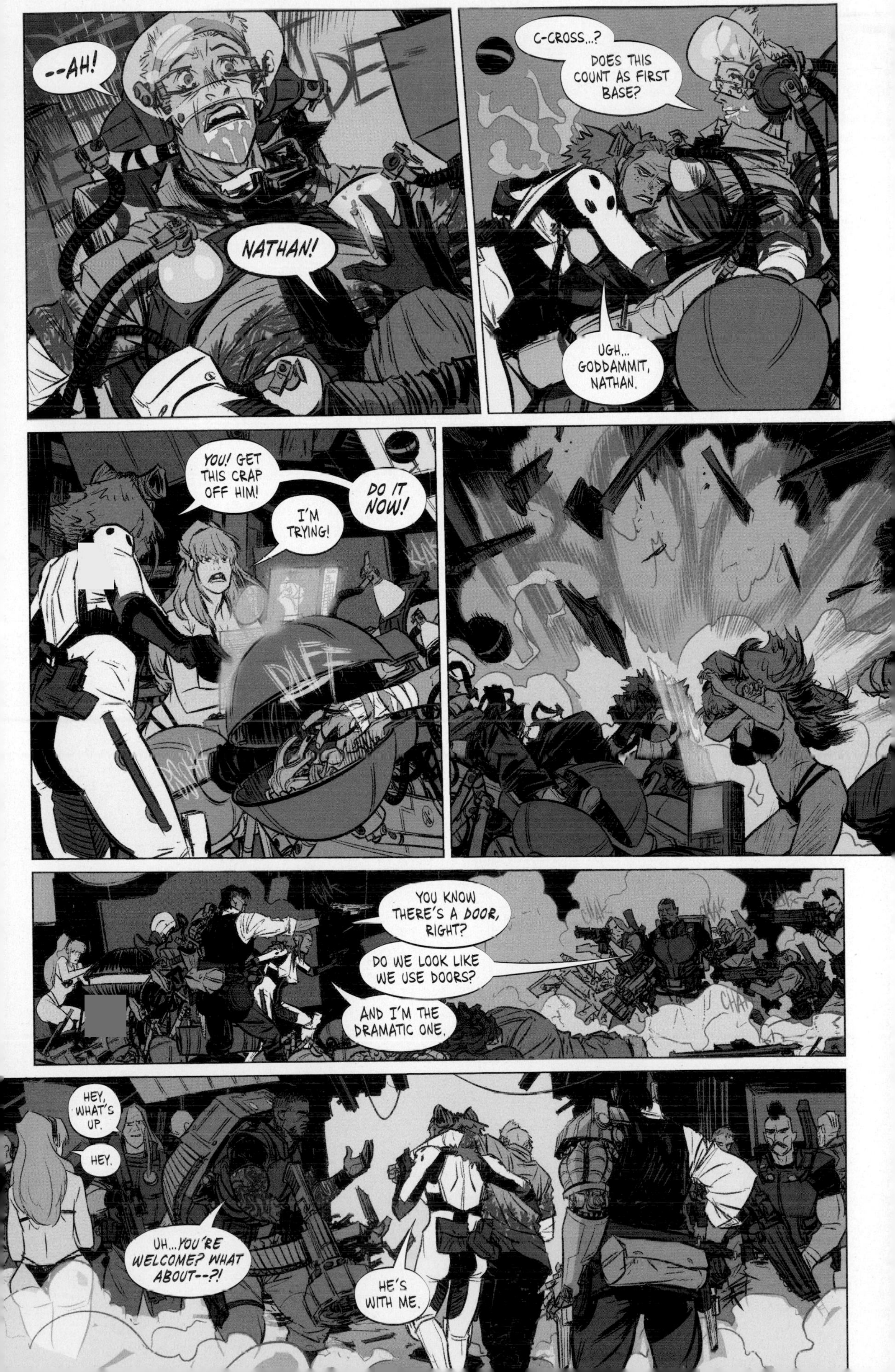

--AH!
NATHAN!
C-CROSS...?
DOES THIS COUNT AS FIRST BASE?
UGH... GODDAMMIT, NATHAN.
YOU! GET THIS CRAP OFF HIM!
DO IT NOW!
I'M TRYING!
YOU KNOW THERE'S A DOOR, RIGHT?
DO WE LOOK LIKE WE USE DOORS?
AND I'M THE DRAMATIC ONE.
HEY, WHAT'S UP.
HEY.
UH...YOU'RE WELCOME? WHAT ABOUT--?!
HE'S WITH ME.

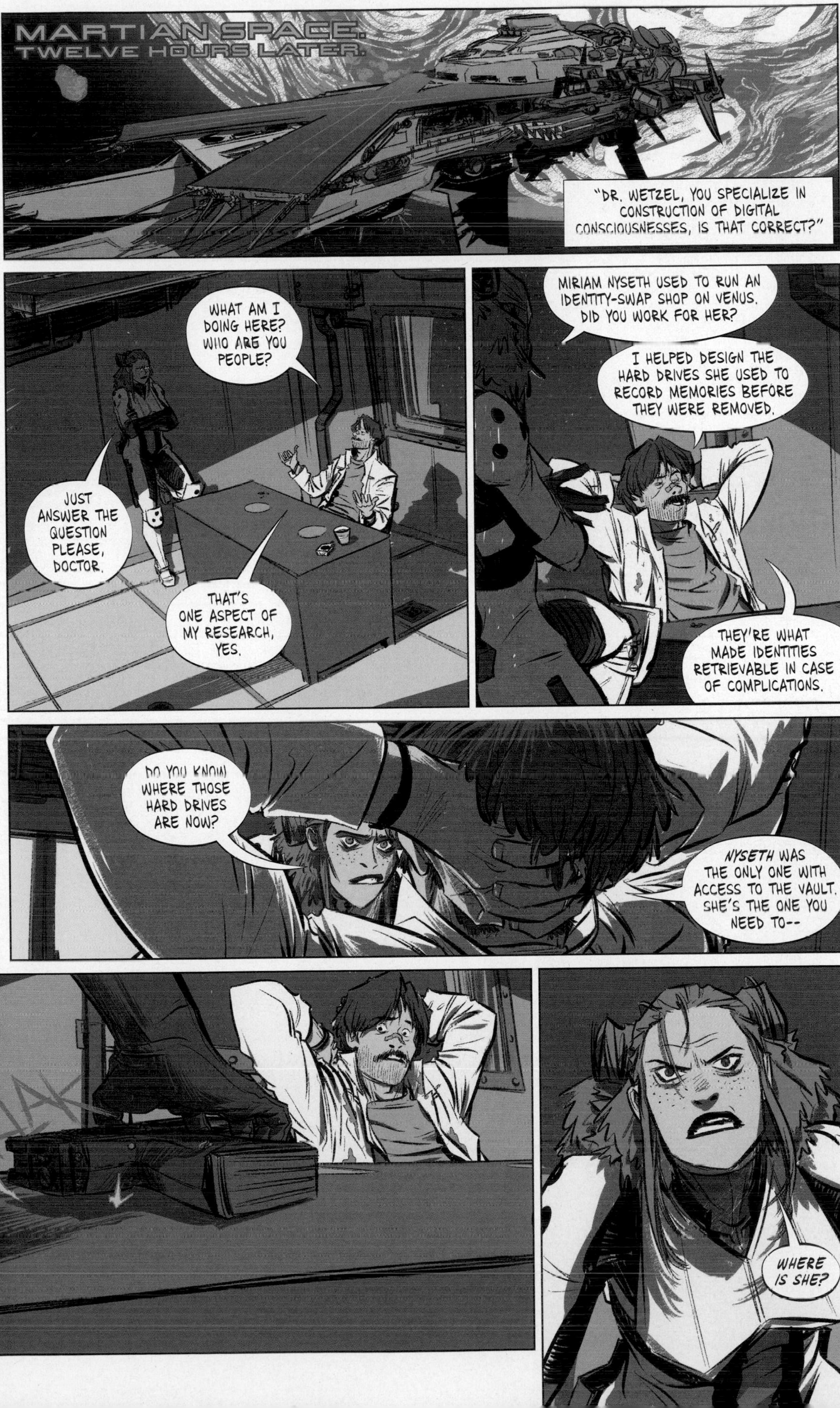
MARTIAN SPACE.
TWELVE HOURS LATER.
"DR. WETZEL, YOU SPECIALIZE IN CONSTRUCTION OF DIGITAL CONSCIOUSNESSES, IS THAT CORRECT?"
WHAT AM I DOING HERE? WHO ARE YOU PEOPLE?
JUST ANSWER THE QUESTION PLEASE, DOCTOR.
THAT'S ONE ASPECT OF MY RESEARCH, YES.
MIRIAM NYSETH USED TO RUN AN IDENTITY-SWAP SHOP ON VENUS. DID YOU WORK FOR HER?
I HELPED DESIGN THE HARD DRIVES SHE USED TO RECORD MEMORIES BEFORE THEY WERE REMOVED.
THEY'RE WHAT MADE IDENTITIES RETRIEVABLE IN CASE OF COMPLICATIONS.
DO YOU KNOW WHERE THOSE HARD DRIVES ARE NOW?
NYSETH WAS THE ONLY ONE WITH ACCESS TO THE VAULT. SHE'S THE ONE YOU NEED TO--
WHERE IS SHE?

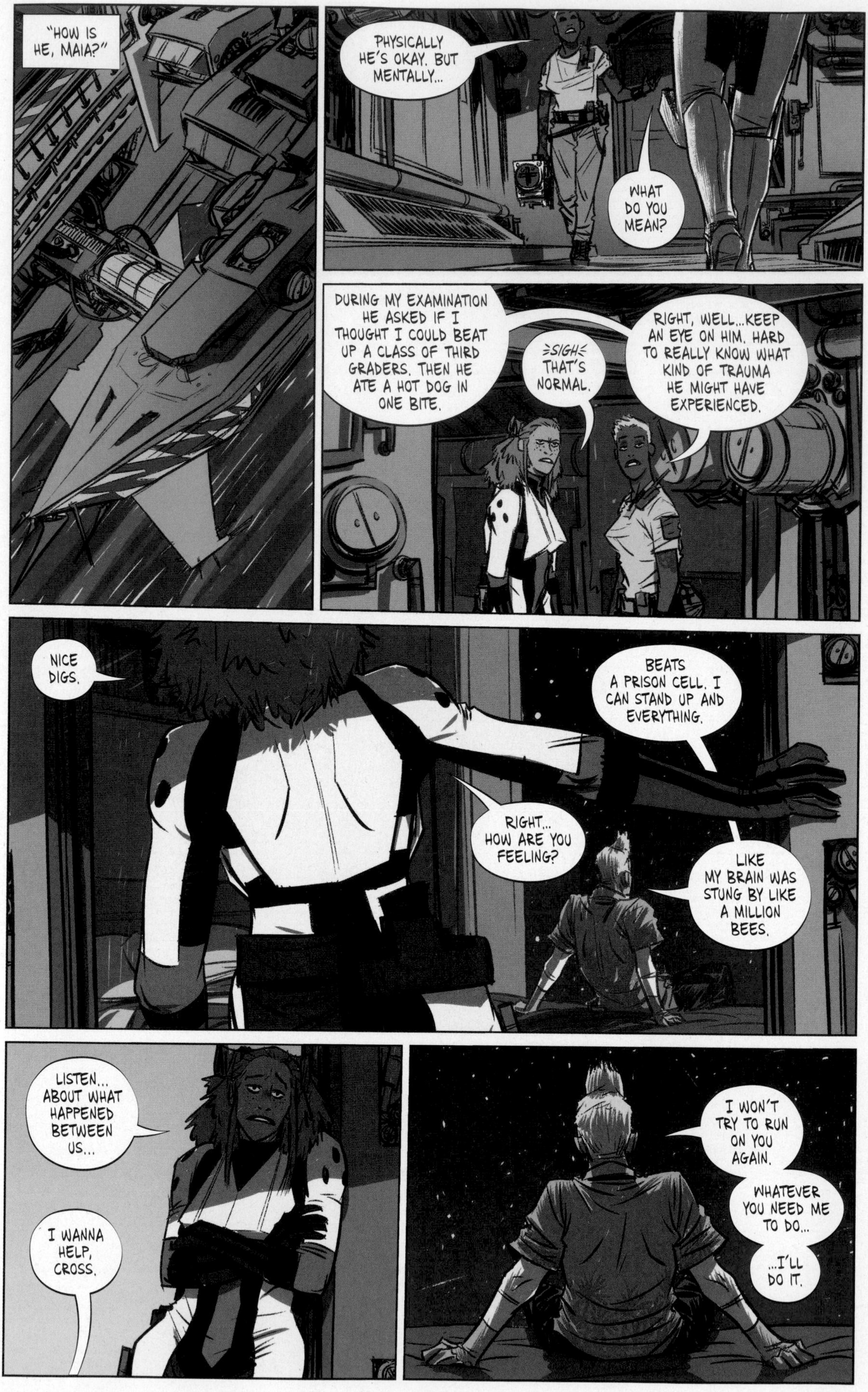
"HOW IS HE, MAIA?"
PHYSICALLY HE'S OKAY. BUT MENTALLY...
WHAT DO YOU MEAN?
DURING MY EXAMINATION HE ASKED IF I THOUGHT I COULD BEAT UP A CLASS OF THIRD GRADERS. THEN HE ATE A HOT DOG IN ONE BITE.
SIGH THAT'S NORMAL.
RIGHT, WELL...KEEP AN EYE ON HIM. HARD TO REALLY KNOW WHAT KIND OF TRAUMA HE MIGHT HAVE EXPERIENCED.
NICE DIGS.
BEATS A PRISON CELL. I CAN STAND UP AND EVERYTHING.
RIGHT... HOW ARE YOU FEELING?
LIKE MY BRAIN WAS STUNG BY LIKE A MILLION BEES.
LISTEN... ABOUT WHAT HAPPENED BETWEEN US...
I WANNA HELP, CROSS.
I WON'T TRY TO RUN ON YOU AGAIN.
WHATEVER YOU NEED ME TO DO...
...I'LL DO IT.

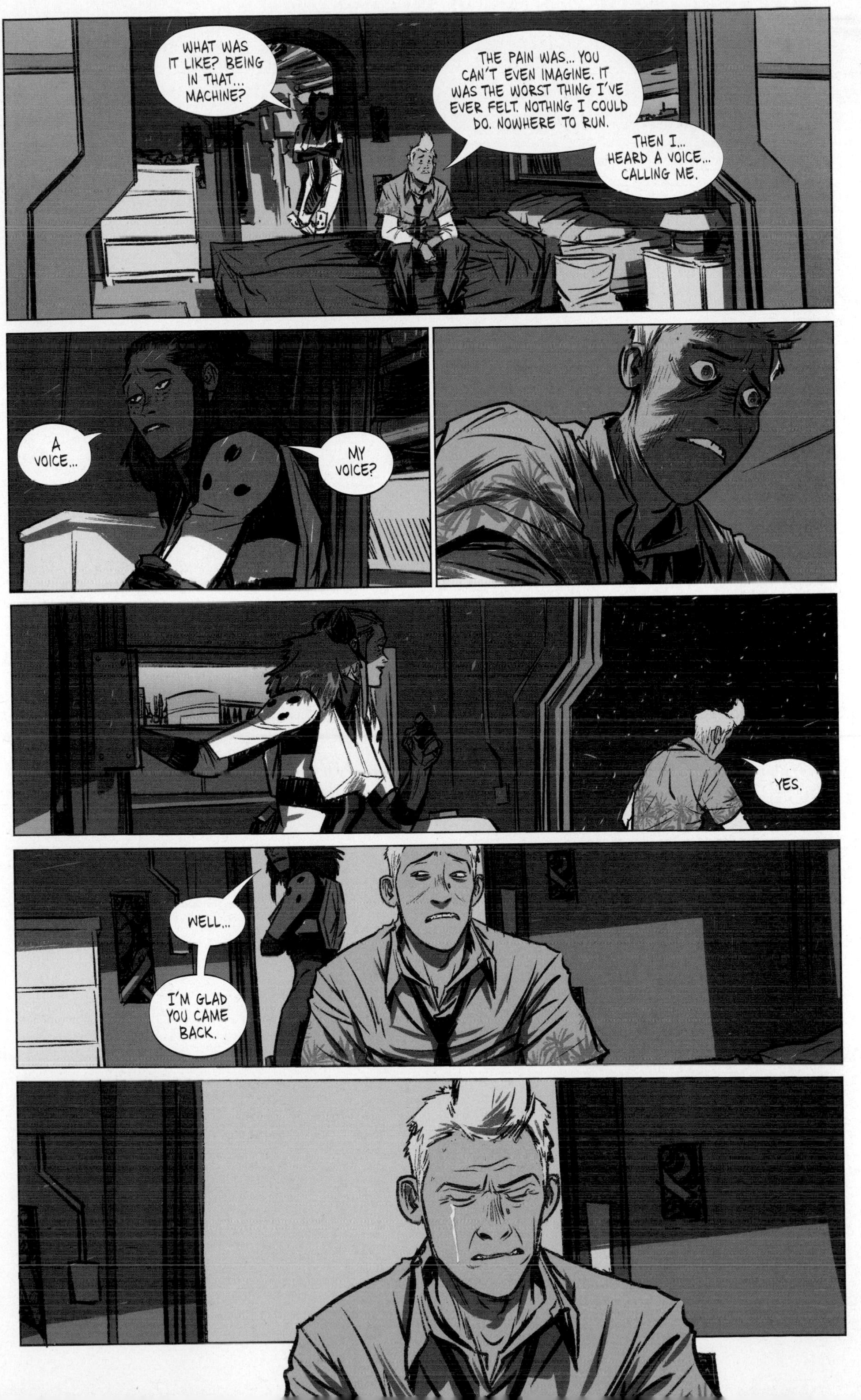
WHAT WAS IT LIKE? BEING IN THAT... MACHINE?
THE PAIN WAS... YOU CAN'T EVEN IMAGINE. IT WAS THE WORST THING I'VE EVER FELT. NOTHING I COULD DO. NOWHERE TO RUN.
THEN I... HEARD A VOICE... CALLING ME.
A VOICE...
MY VOICE?
YES.
WELL...
I'M GLAD YOU CAME BACK.

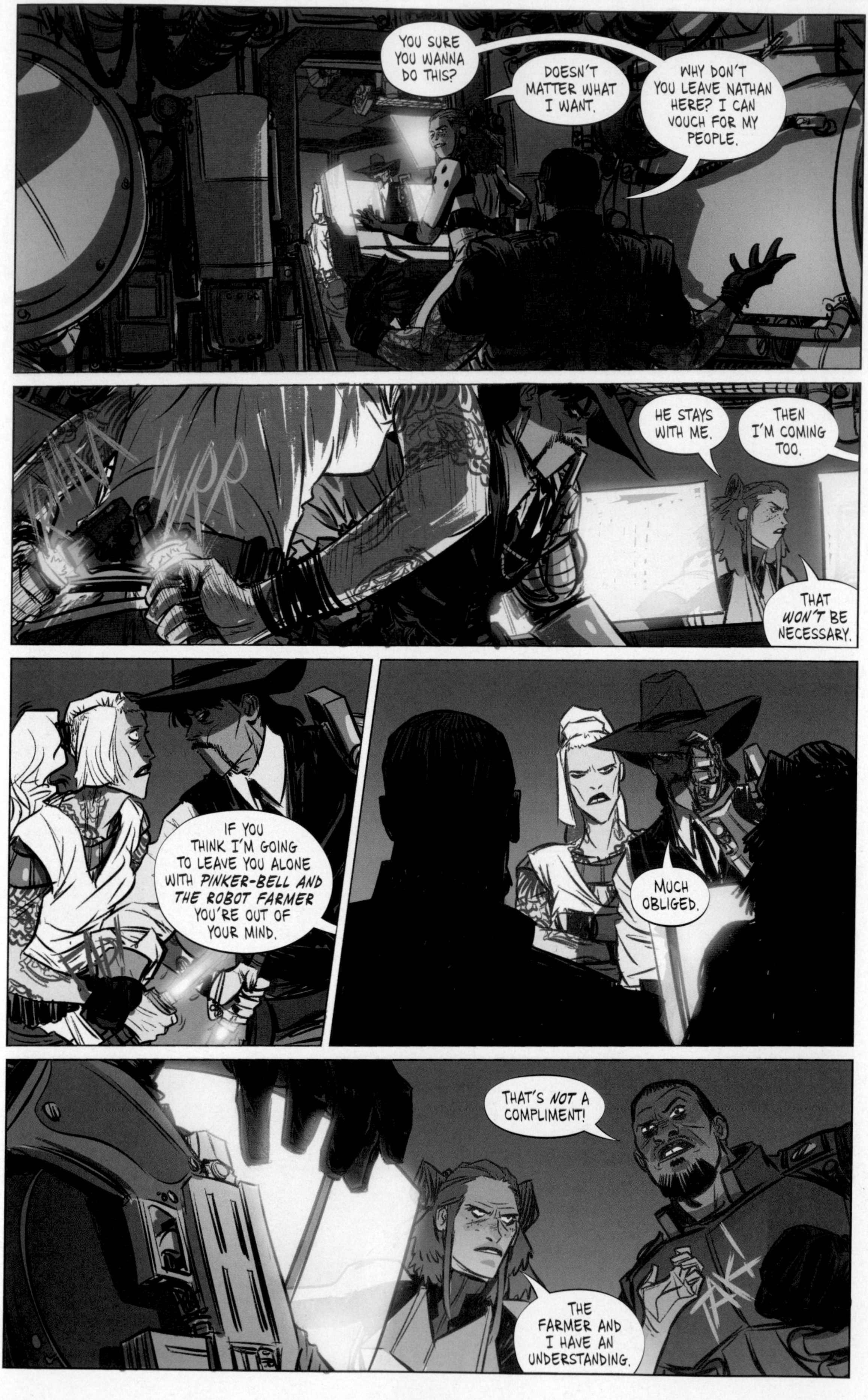
YOU SURE YOU WANNA DO THIS?
DOESN'T MATTER WHAT I WANT.
WHY DON'T YOU LEAVE NATHAN HERE? I CAN VOUCH FOR MY PEOPLE.
VWRR
HE STAYS WITH ME.
THEN I'M COMING TOO.
THAT *WON'T* BE NECESSARY.
IF YOU THINK I'M GOING TO LEAVE YOU ALONE WITH *PINKER-BELL AND THE ROBOT FARMER* YOU'RE OUT OF YOUR MIND.
MUCH OBLIGED.
THAT'S *NOT* A COMPLIMENT!
THE FARMER AND I HAVE AN UNDERSTANDING.
TAK

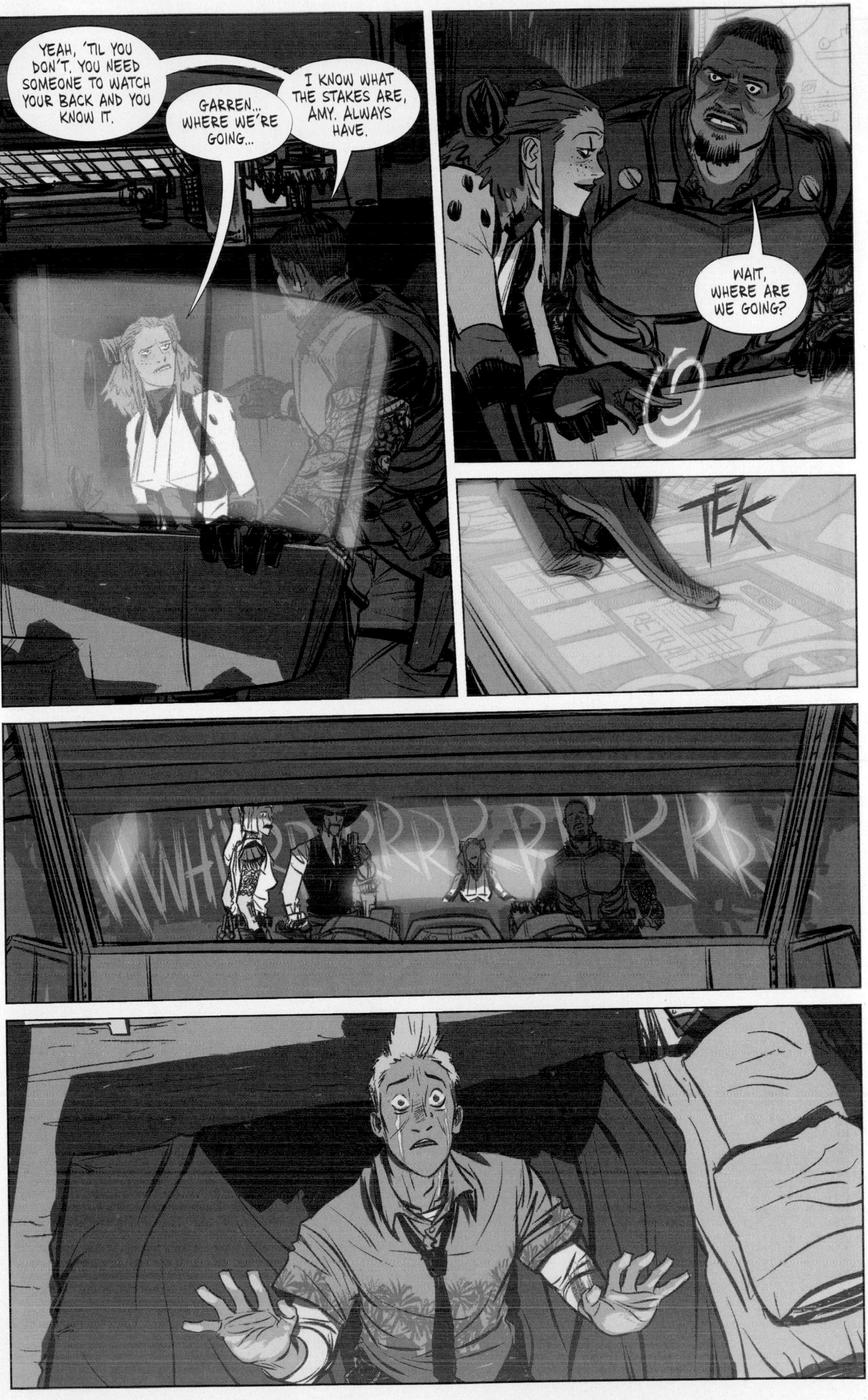
YEAH, 'TIL YOU DON'T. YOU NEED SOMEONE TO WATCH YOUR BACK AND YOU KNOW IT.
GARREN... WHERE WE'RE GOING...
I KNOW WHAT THE STAKES ARE, AMY. ALWAYS HAVE.
WAIT, WHERE ARE WE GOING?
TEK
WWHIRRRRRRRRRRRR

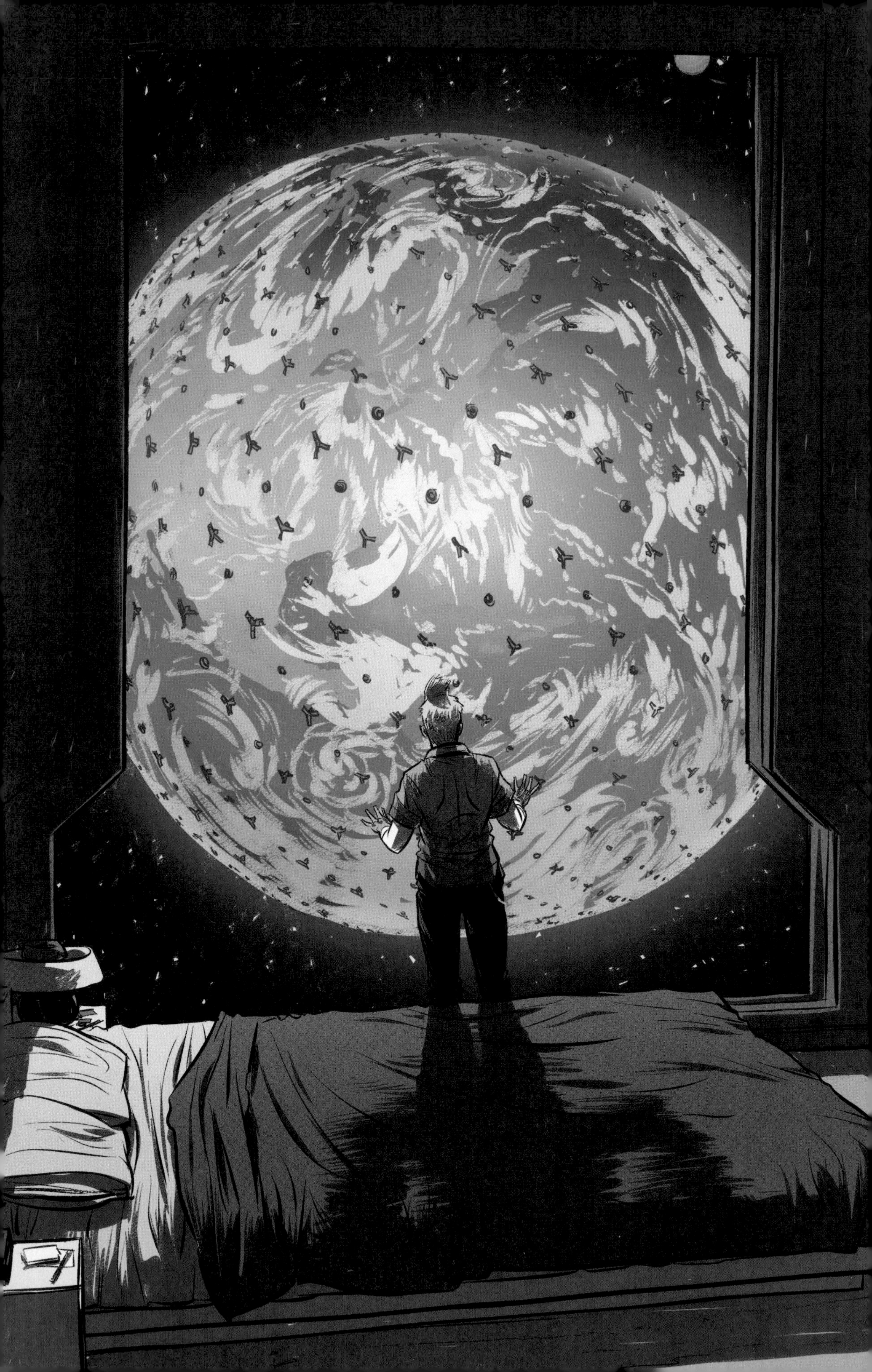

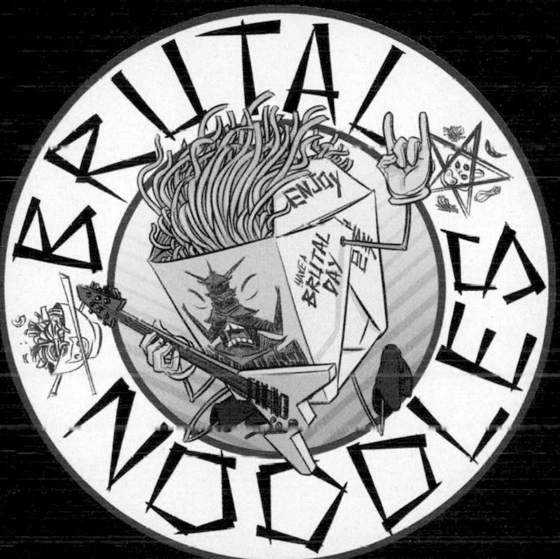
BRUTAL NOODLES
ENJOY
HAVE A BRUTAL DAY

The Weather Man.

Jody LeHeup
Nathan Fox
Dave Stewart

$3.99 USD
Second Printing

1

image

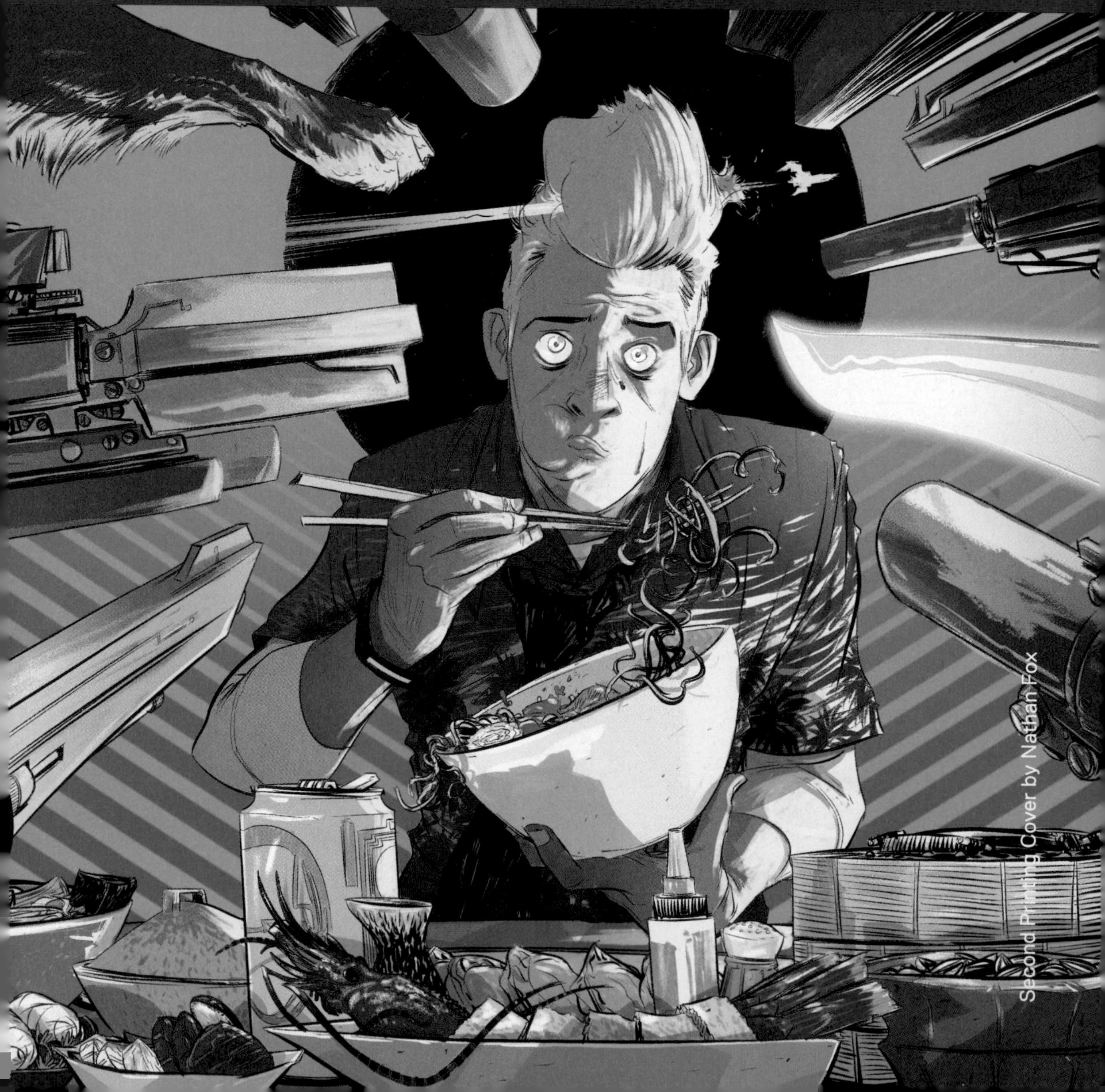
Second Printing Cover by Nathan Fox

The Weather Man.

Jody LeHeup
Nathan Fox
Dave Stewart

$3.99 USD

2

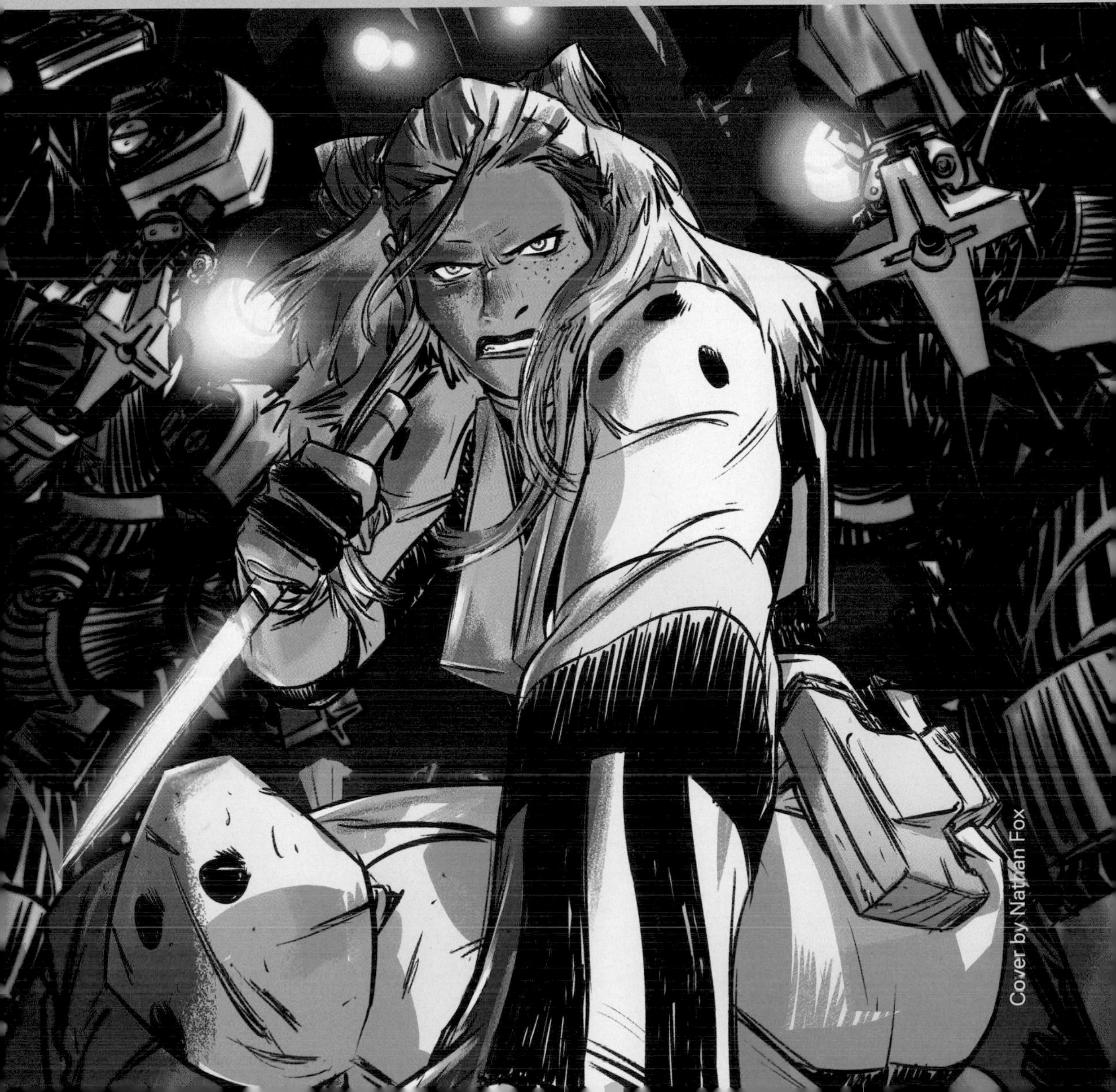
Cover by Nathan Fox

The Weather Man.

Jody LeHeup
Nathan Fox
Dave Stewart

$3.99 US

3

image

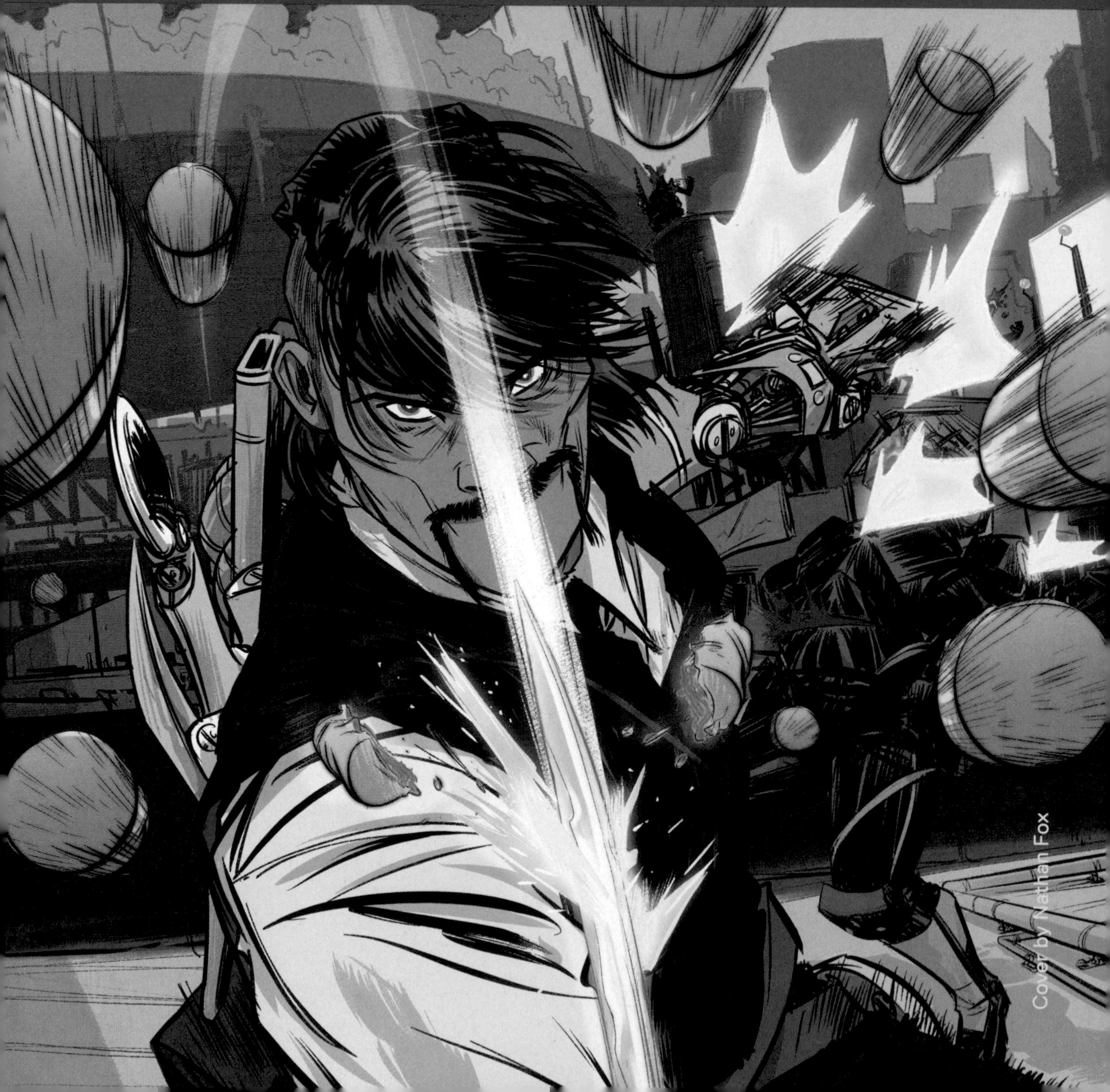
Cover by Nathan Fox

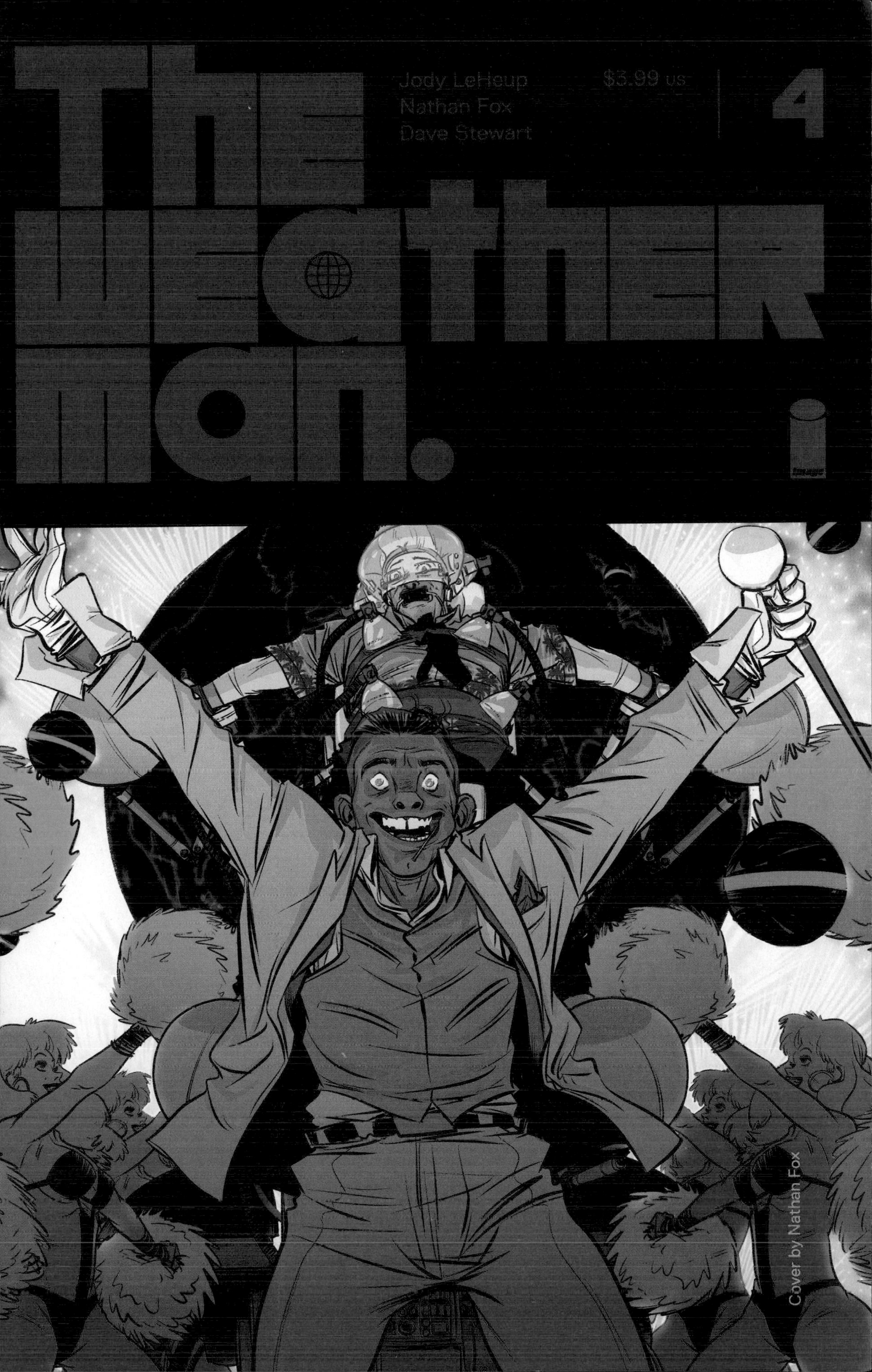
The Weather Man.
Jody LeHeup
Nathan Fox
Dave Stewart
$3.99 us
4
Cover by Nathan Fox

The Weather Man.

Jody LeHeup
Nathan Fox
Dave Stewart

$3.99 US | 5

image

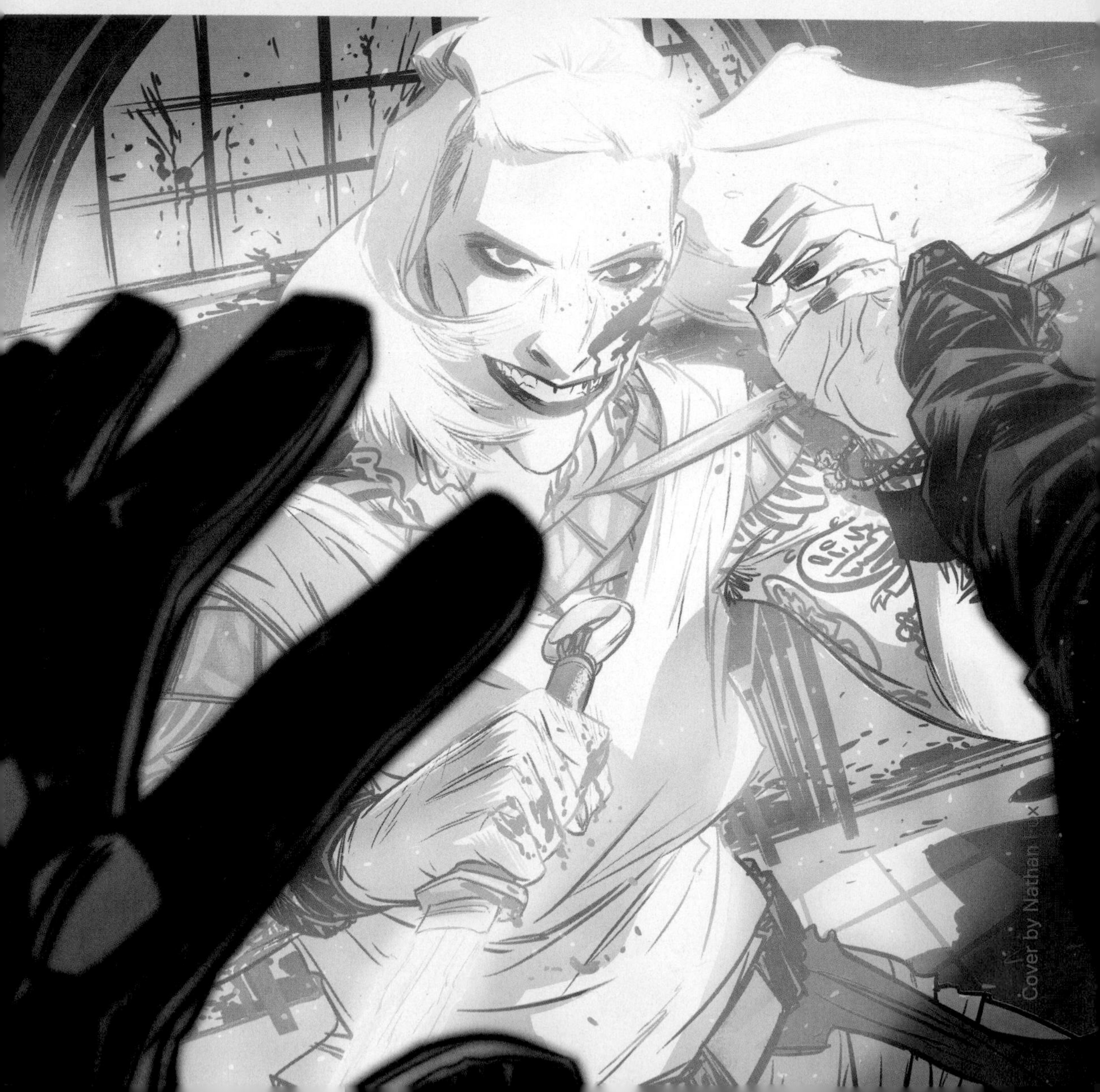
Cover by Nathan Fox

The Weather Man.

Jody LeHeup
Nathan Fox
Dave Stewart

$3.99 US

6

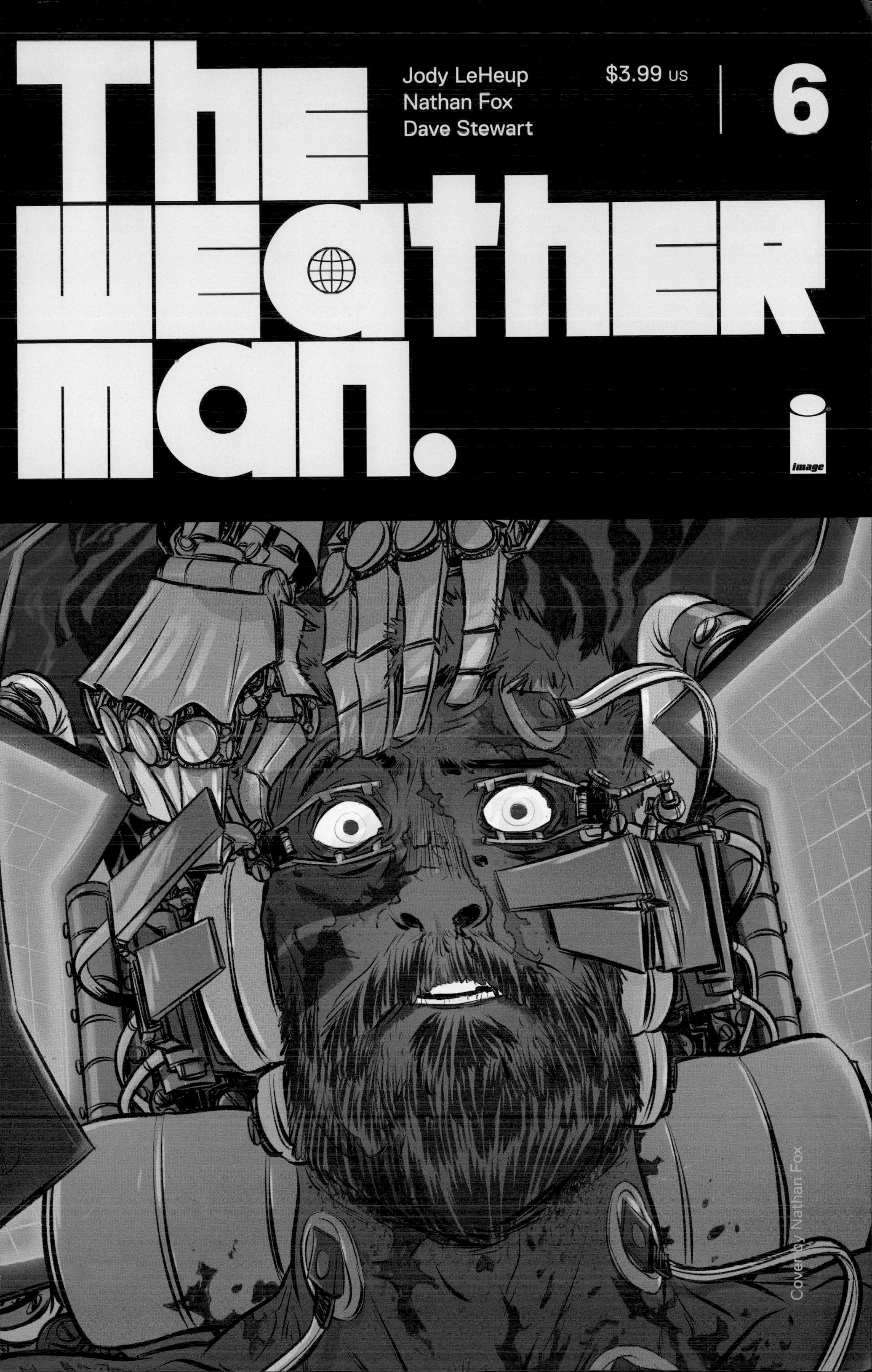
Cover by Nathan Fox

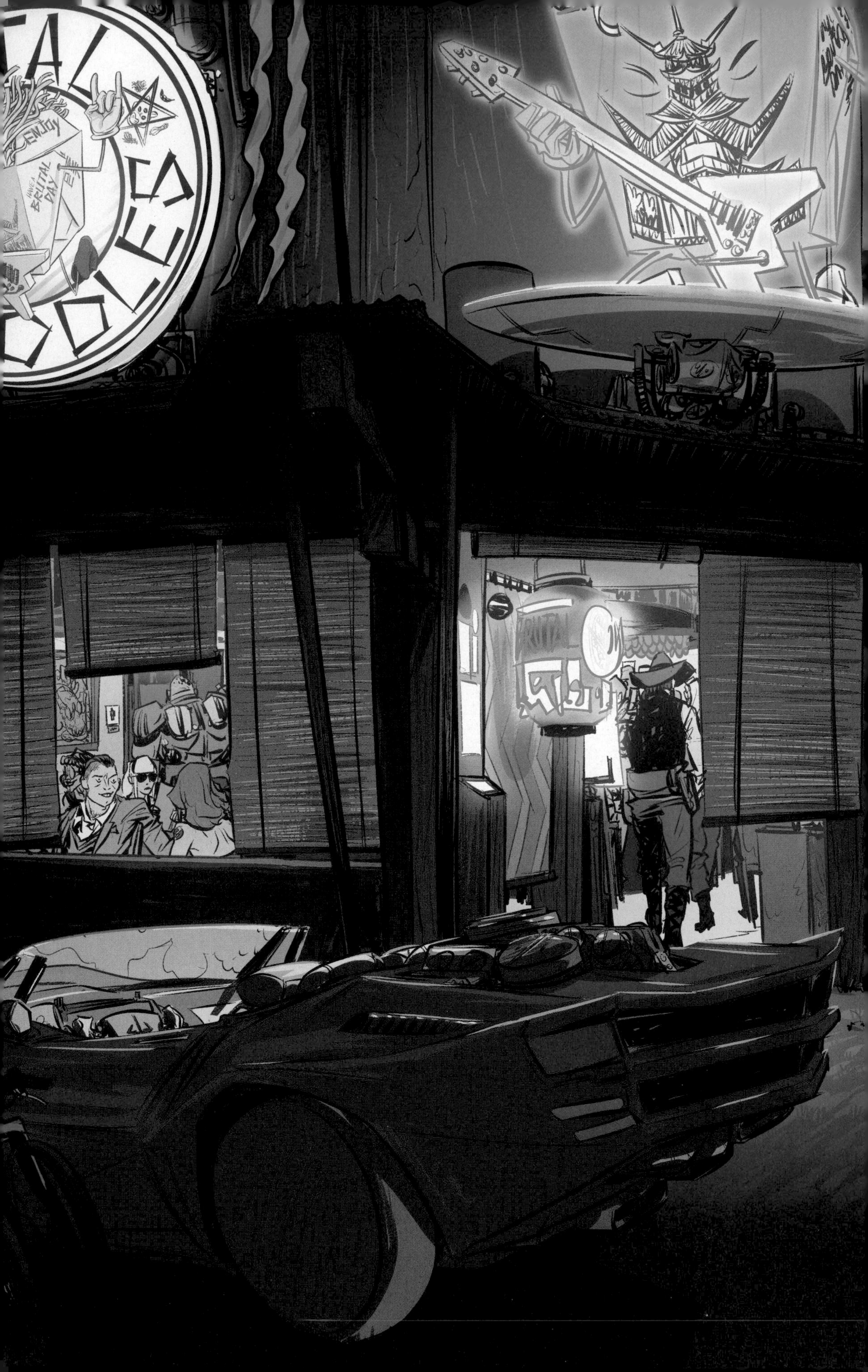
ENJOY
HAVE A BRUTAL DAY
BRUTAL

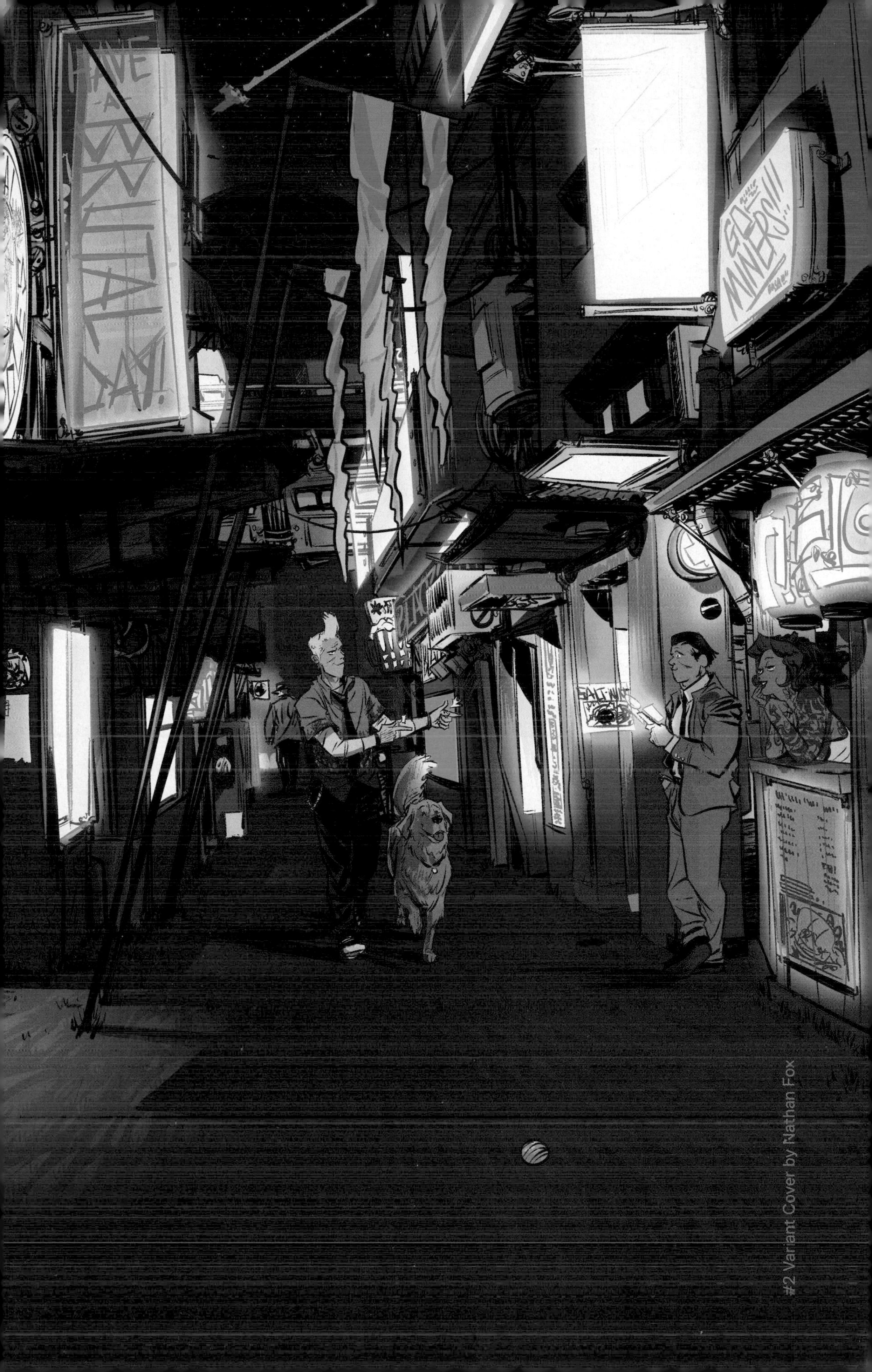
HAVE
-A-
BRUTAL
DAY!
GO
MINERS!!!

#2 Variant Cover by Nathan Fox

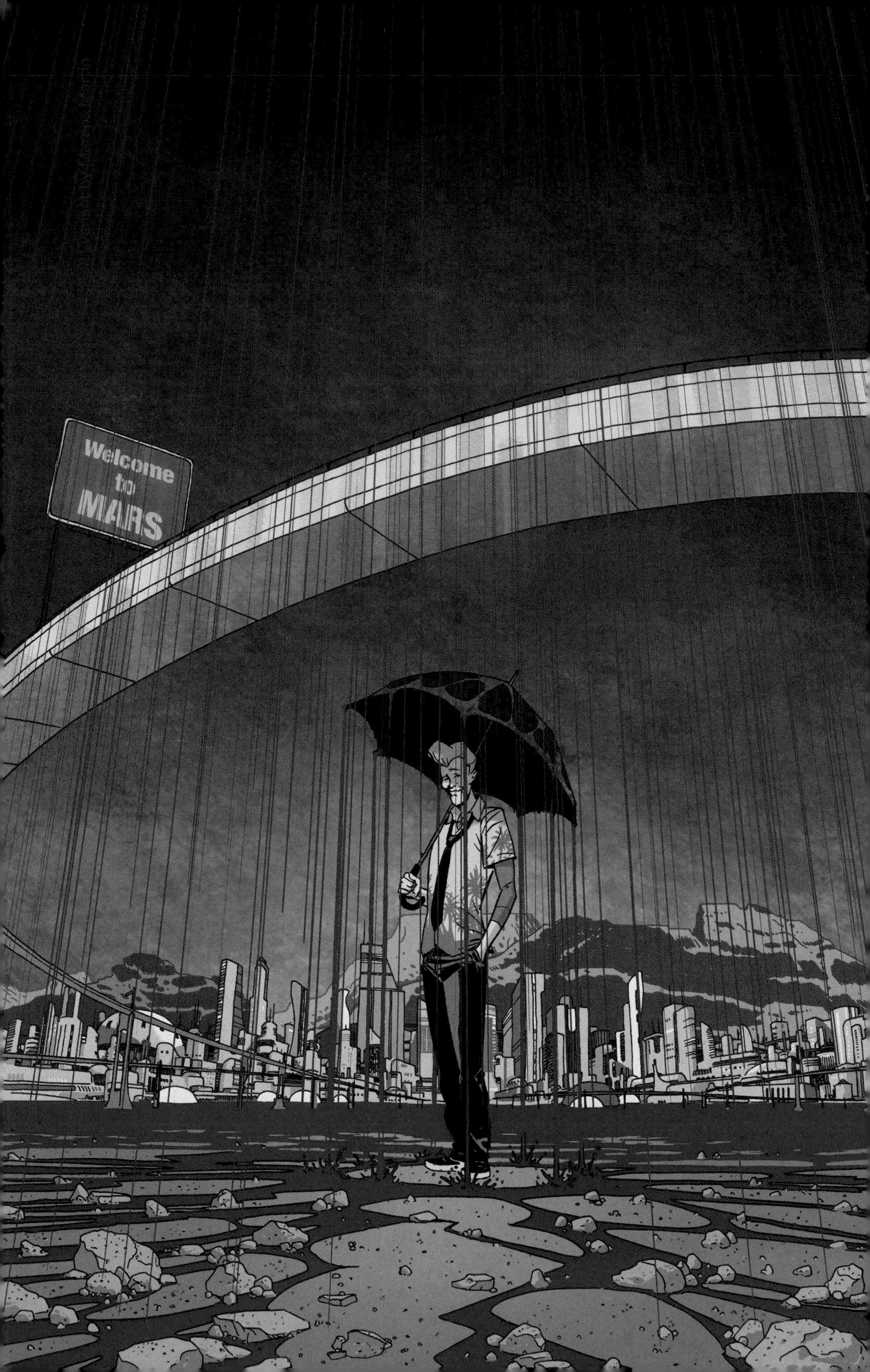
Welcome to MARS

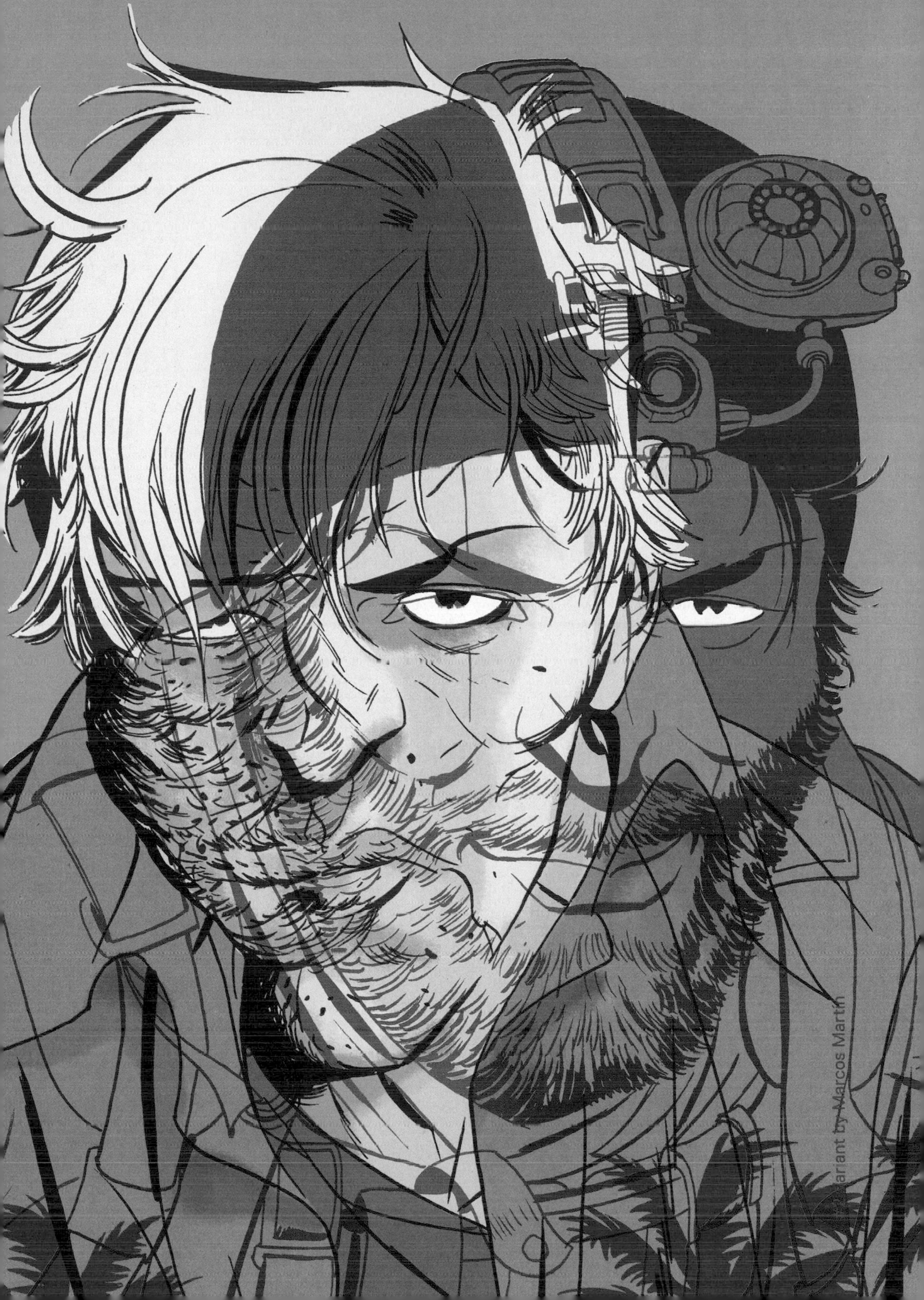
Variant by Marcos Martín

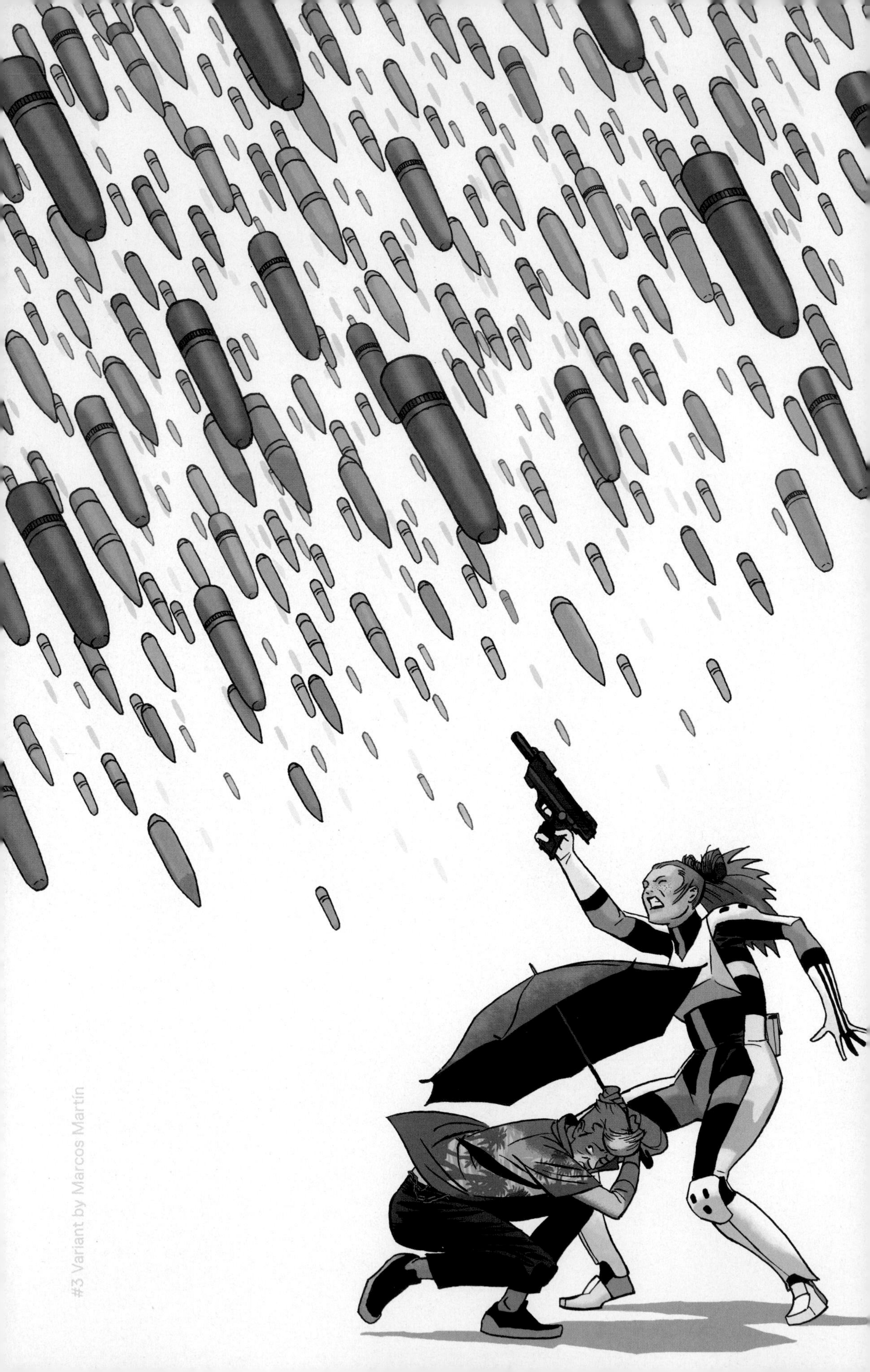

#3 Variant by Marcos Martín

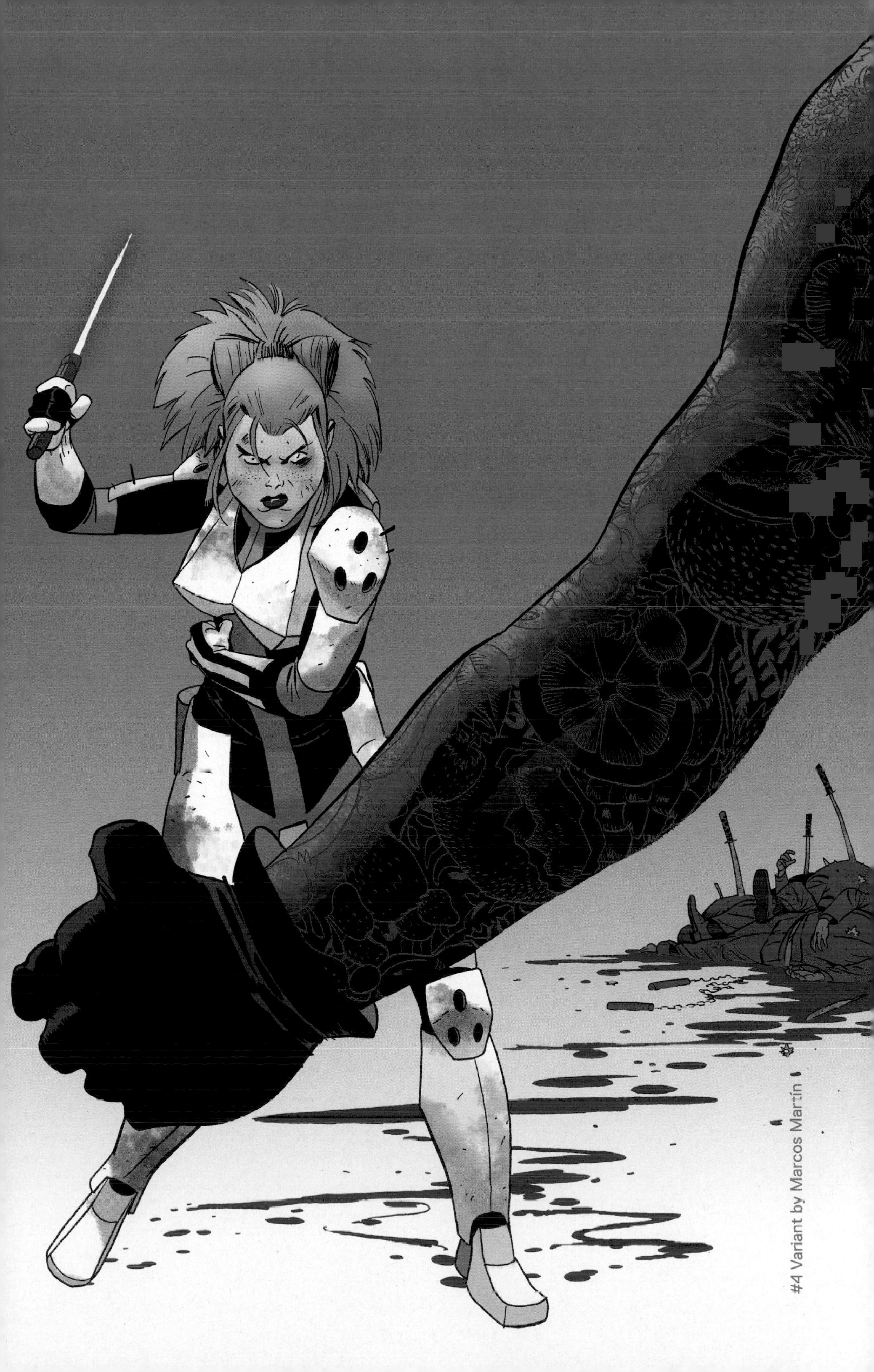

#4 Variant by Marcos Martín

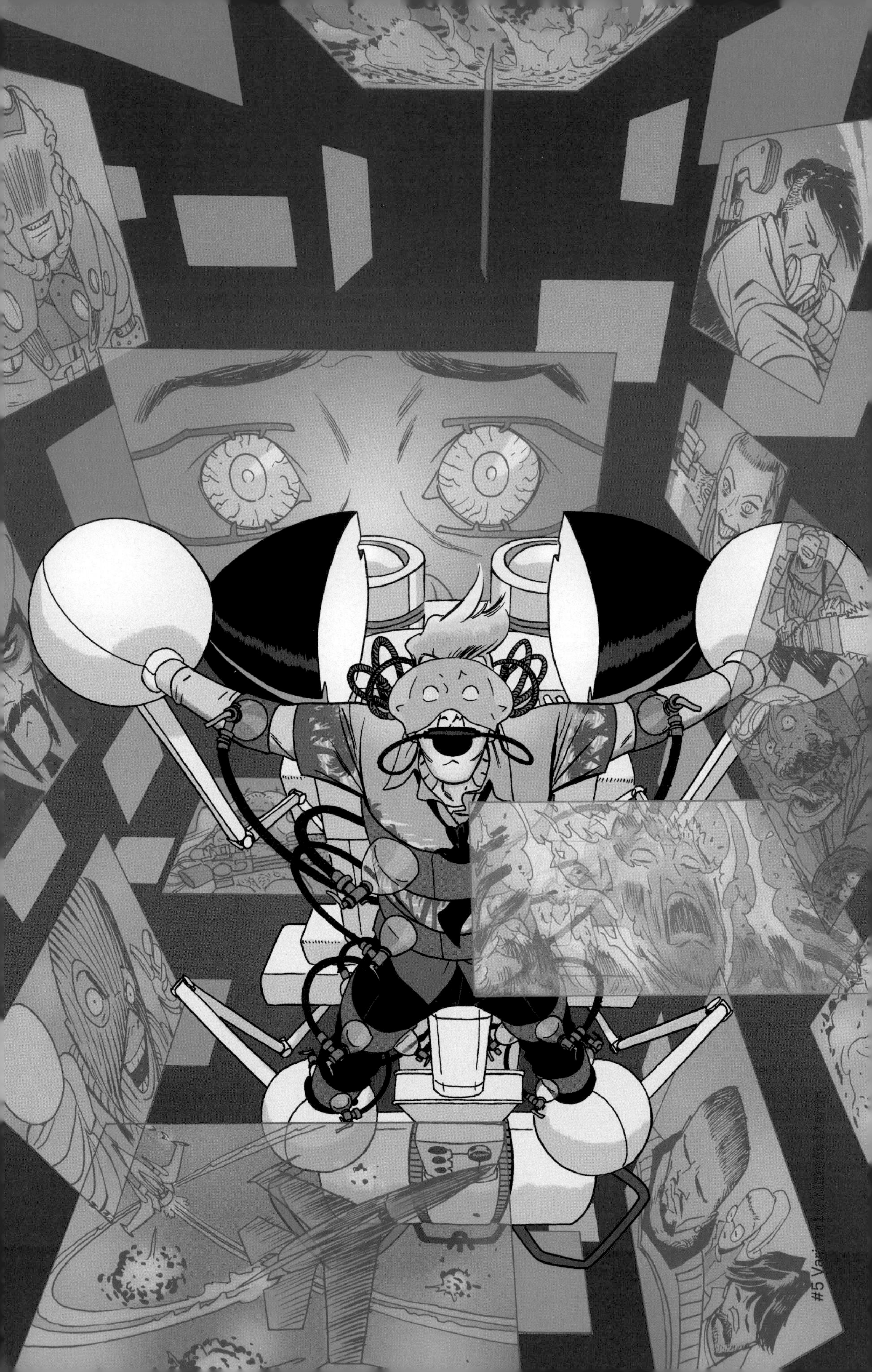

#5 Vari

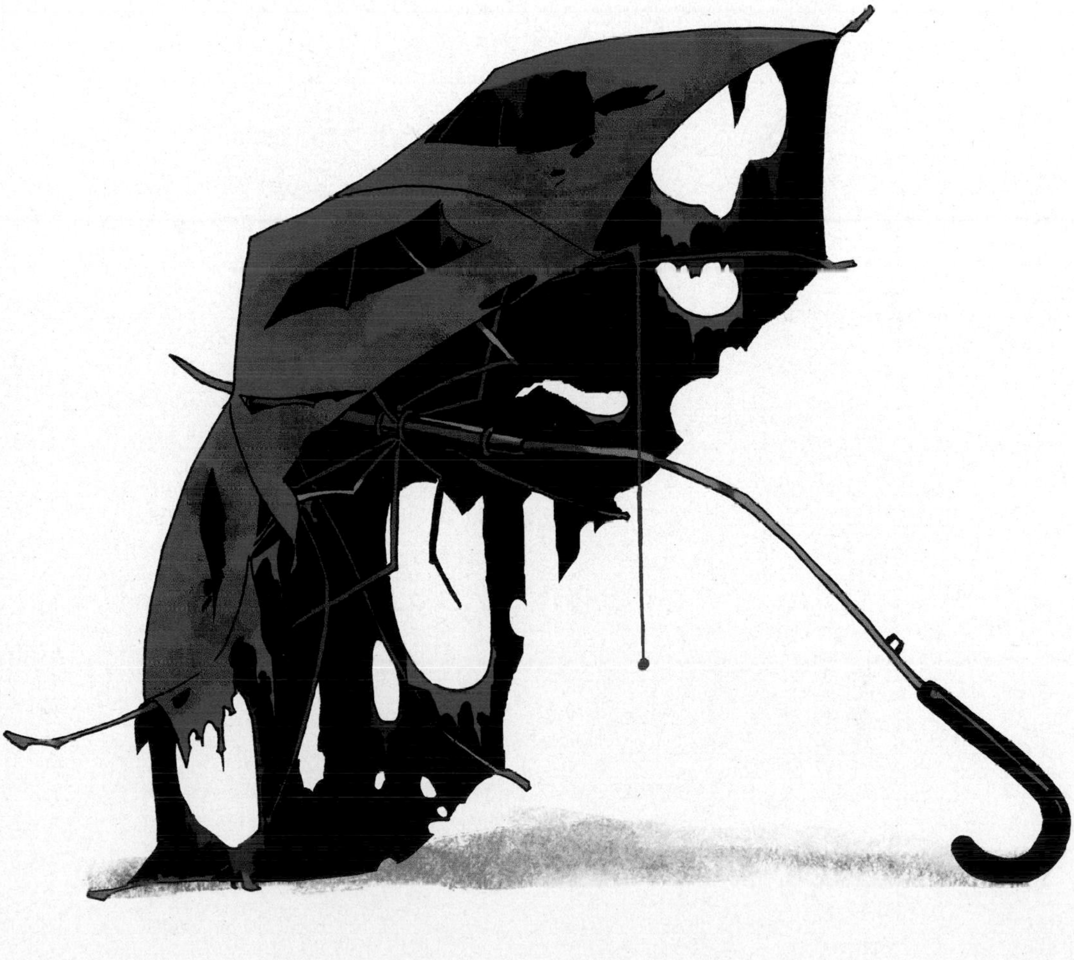

#6 Variant by Marcos Martín

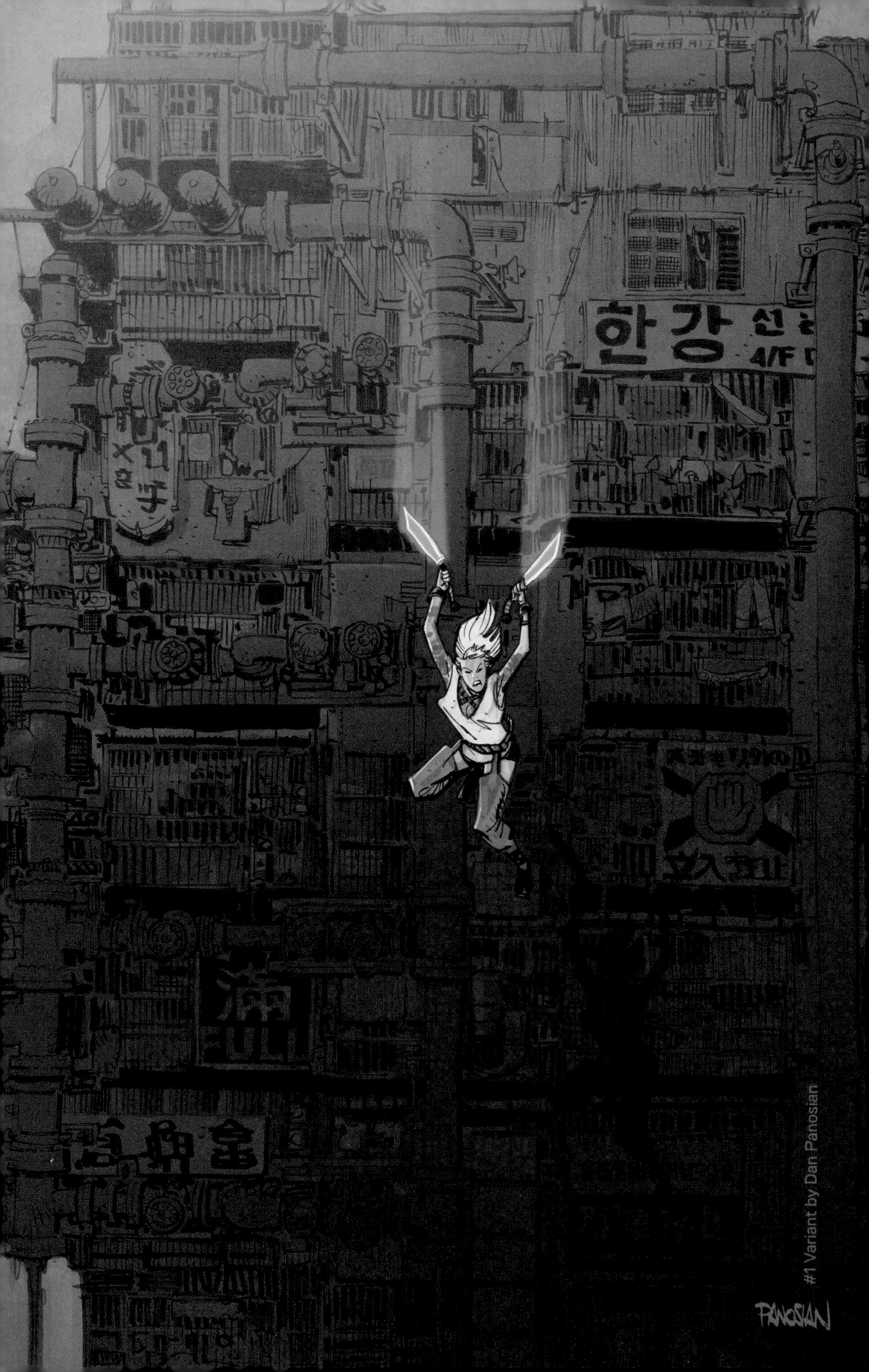
한강
4/F
PANOSIAN

#1 Variant by Dan Panosian

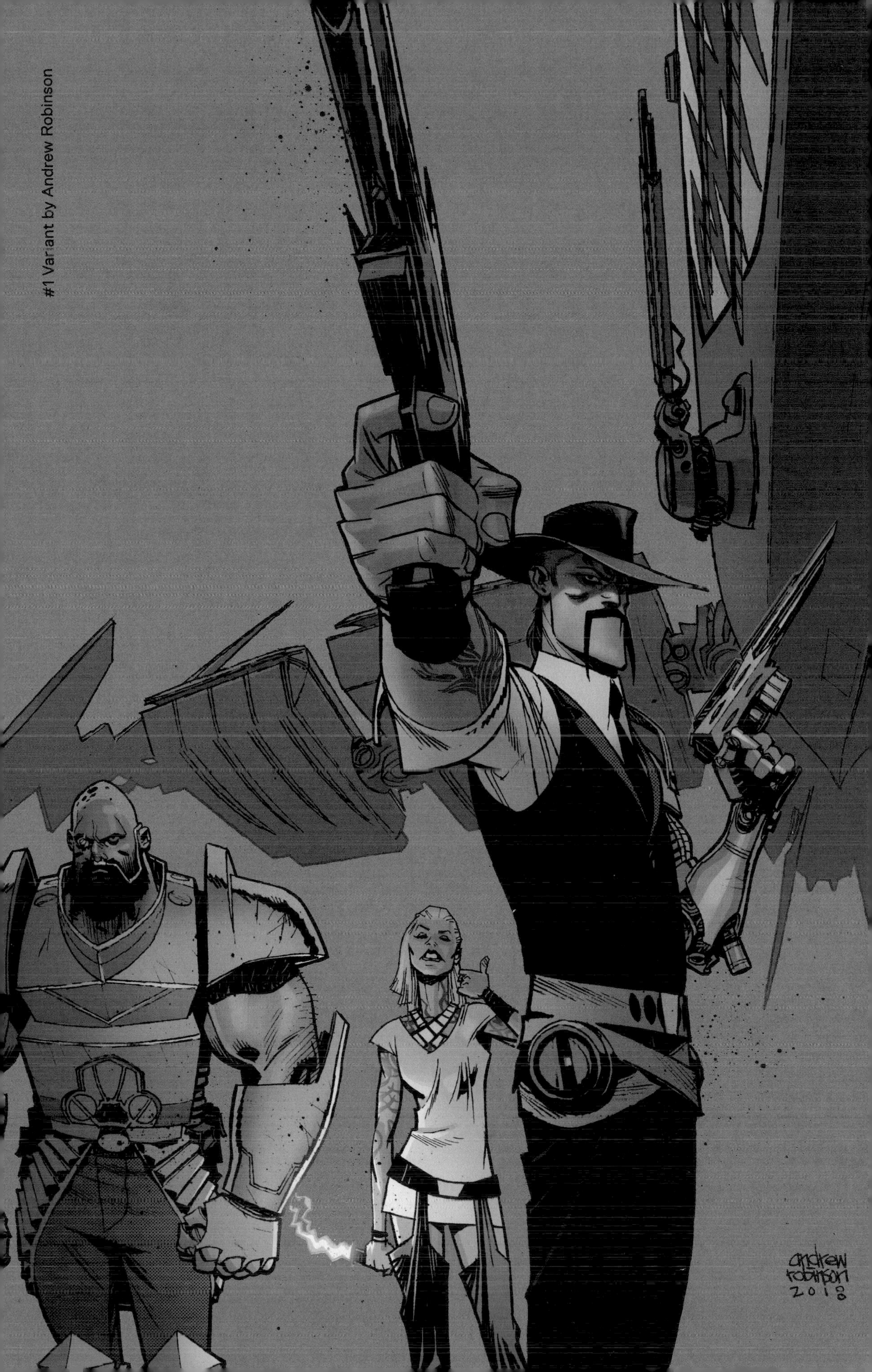
andrew robinson 2018

#1 Variant by Andrew Robinson

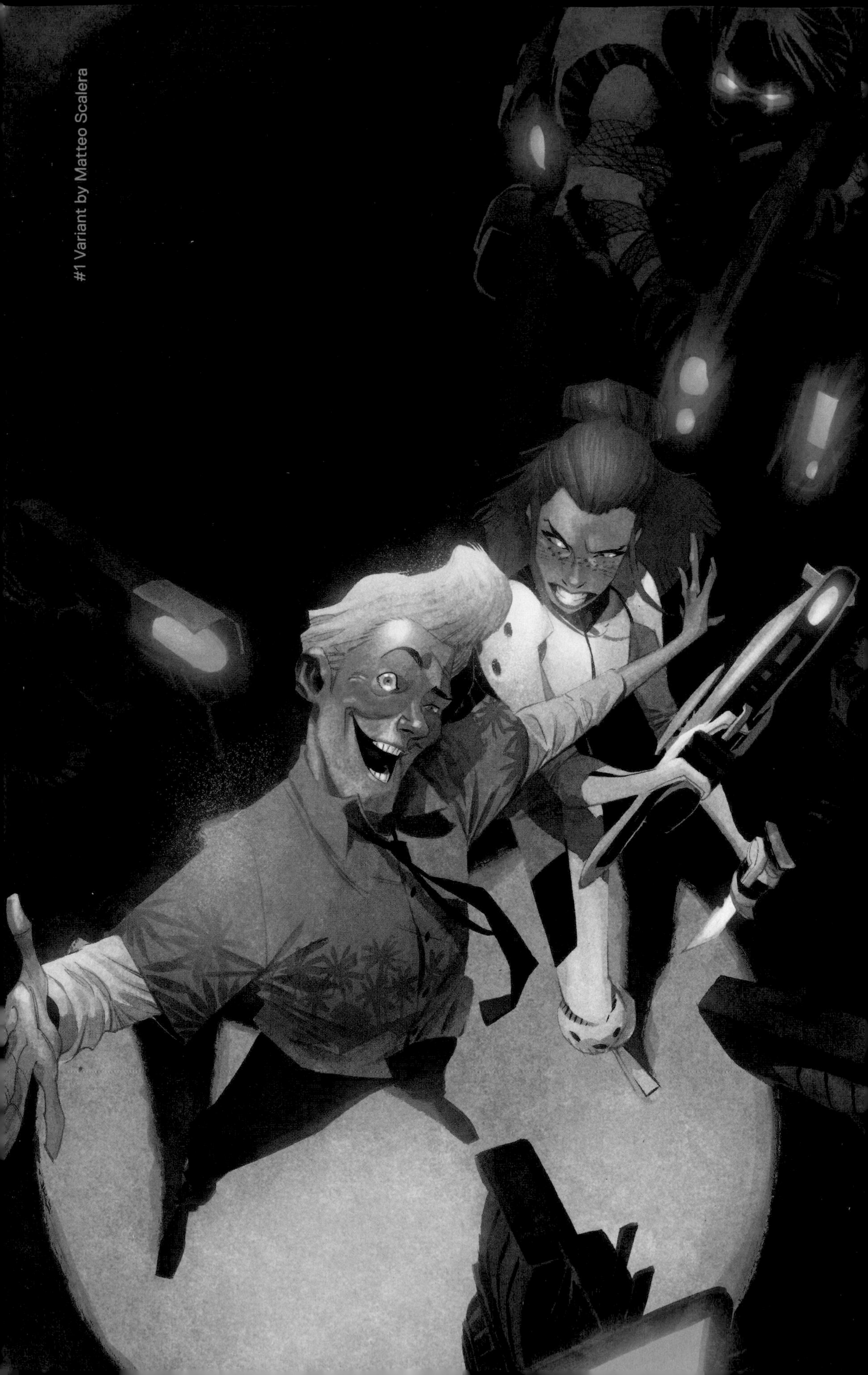

#1 Variant by Matteo Scalera

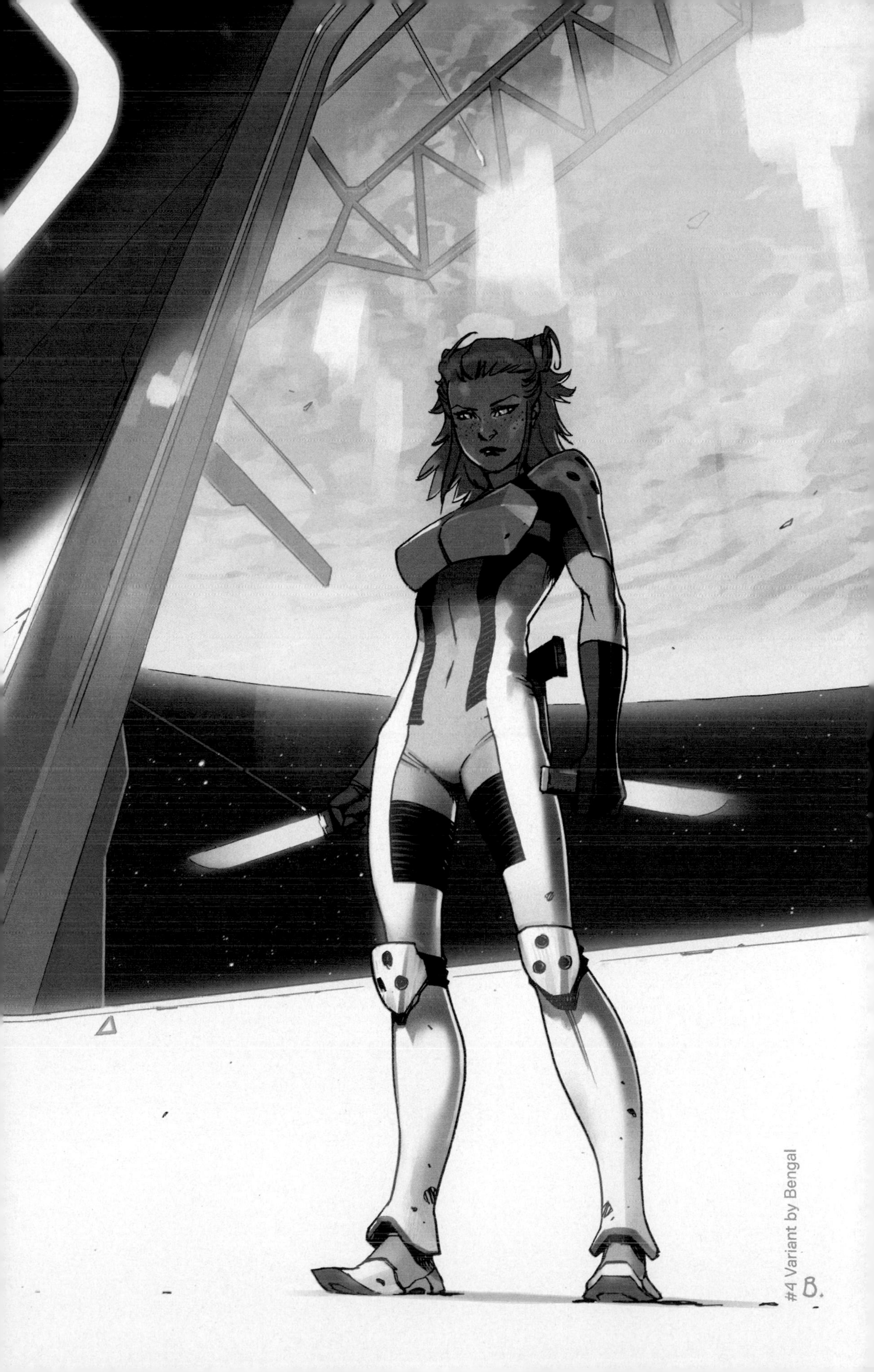

#4 Variant by Bengal

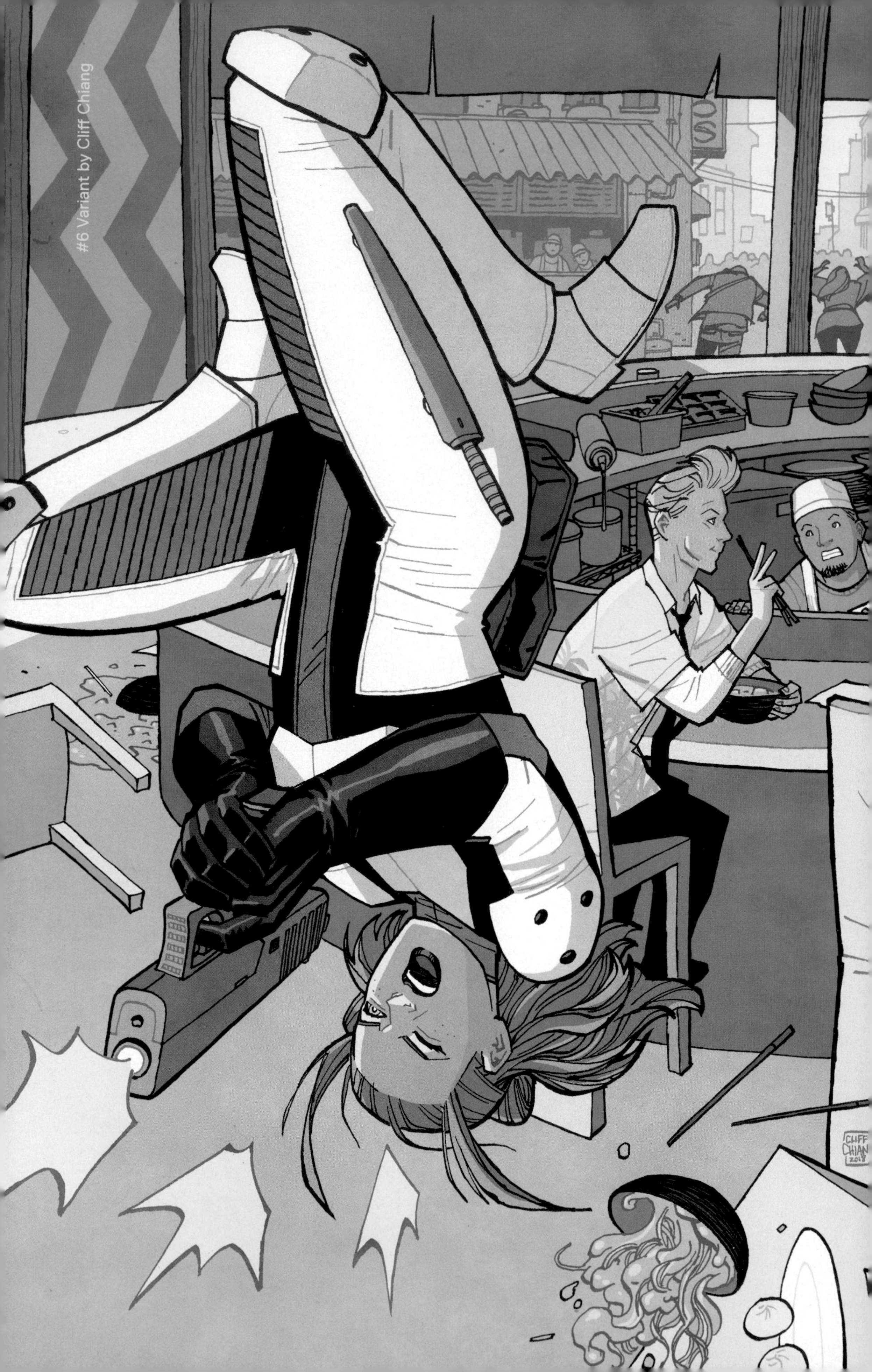
CLIFF CHIANG 2018

#6 Variant by Cliff Chiang

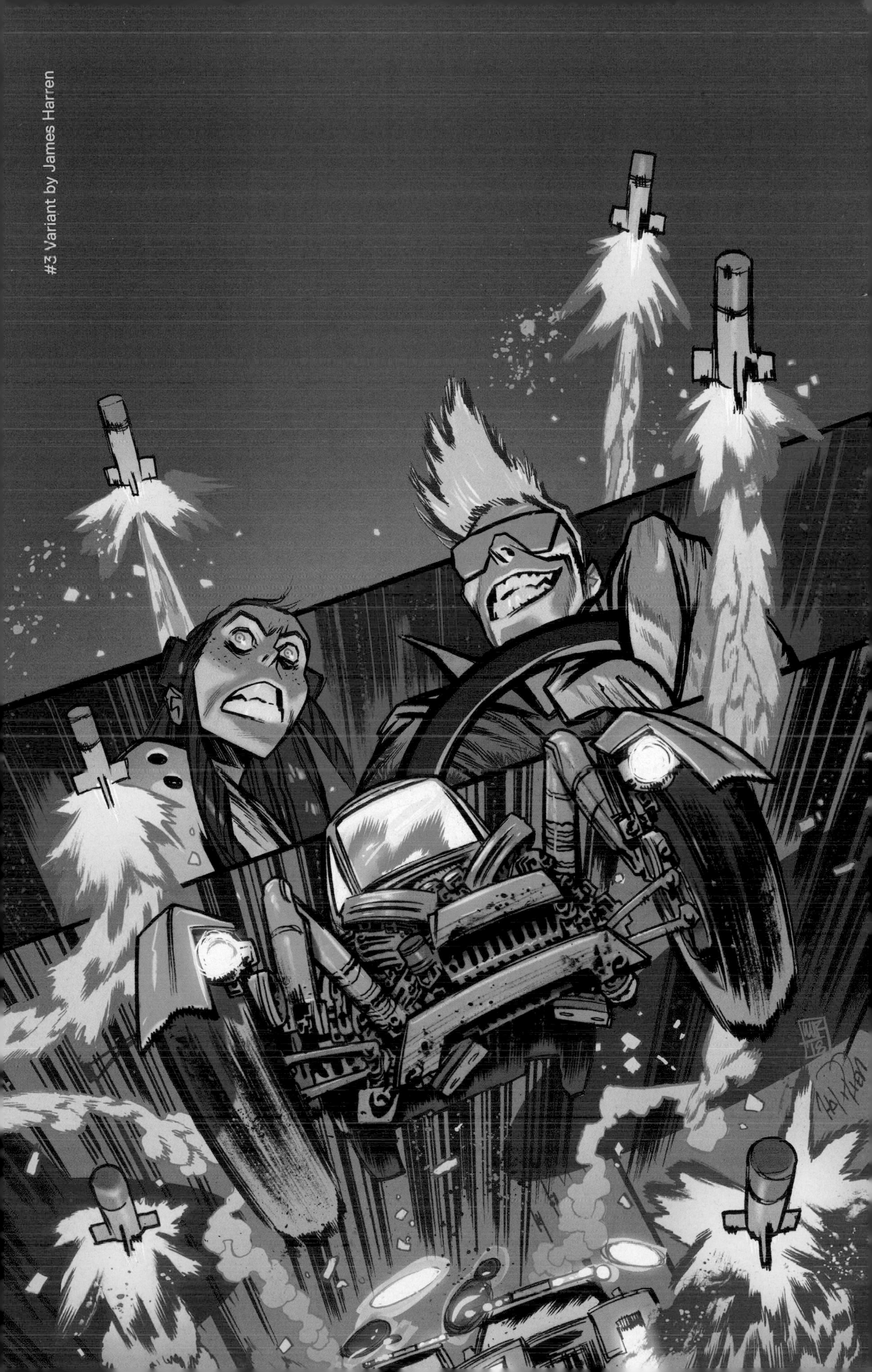

#3 Variant by James Harren

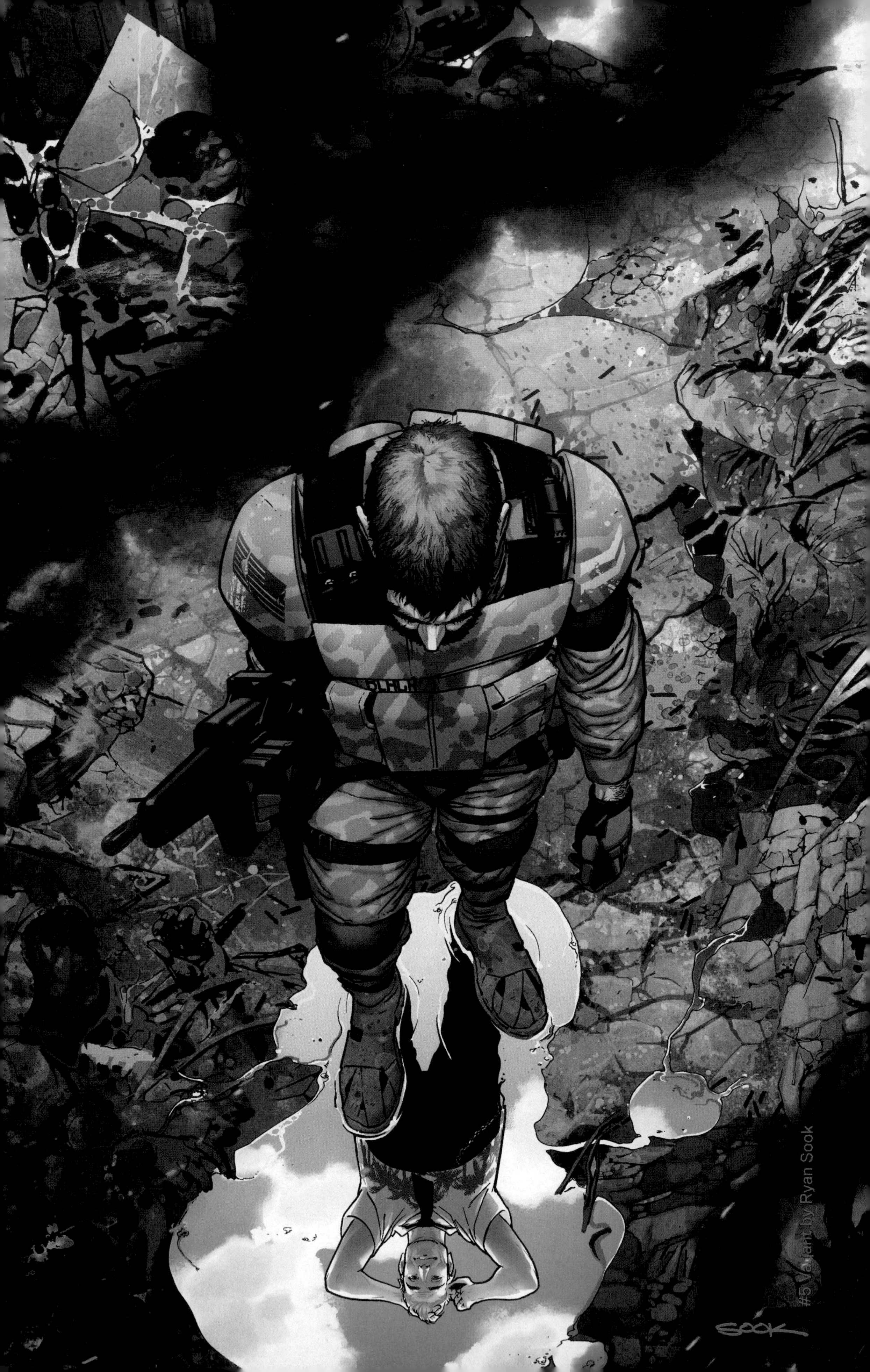
BLACK
SOOK

#5 Variant by Ryan Sook

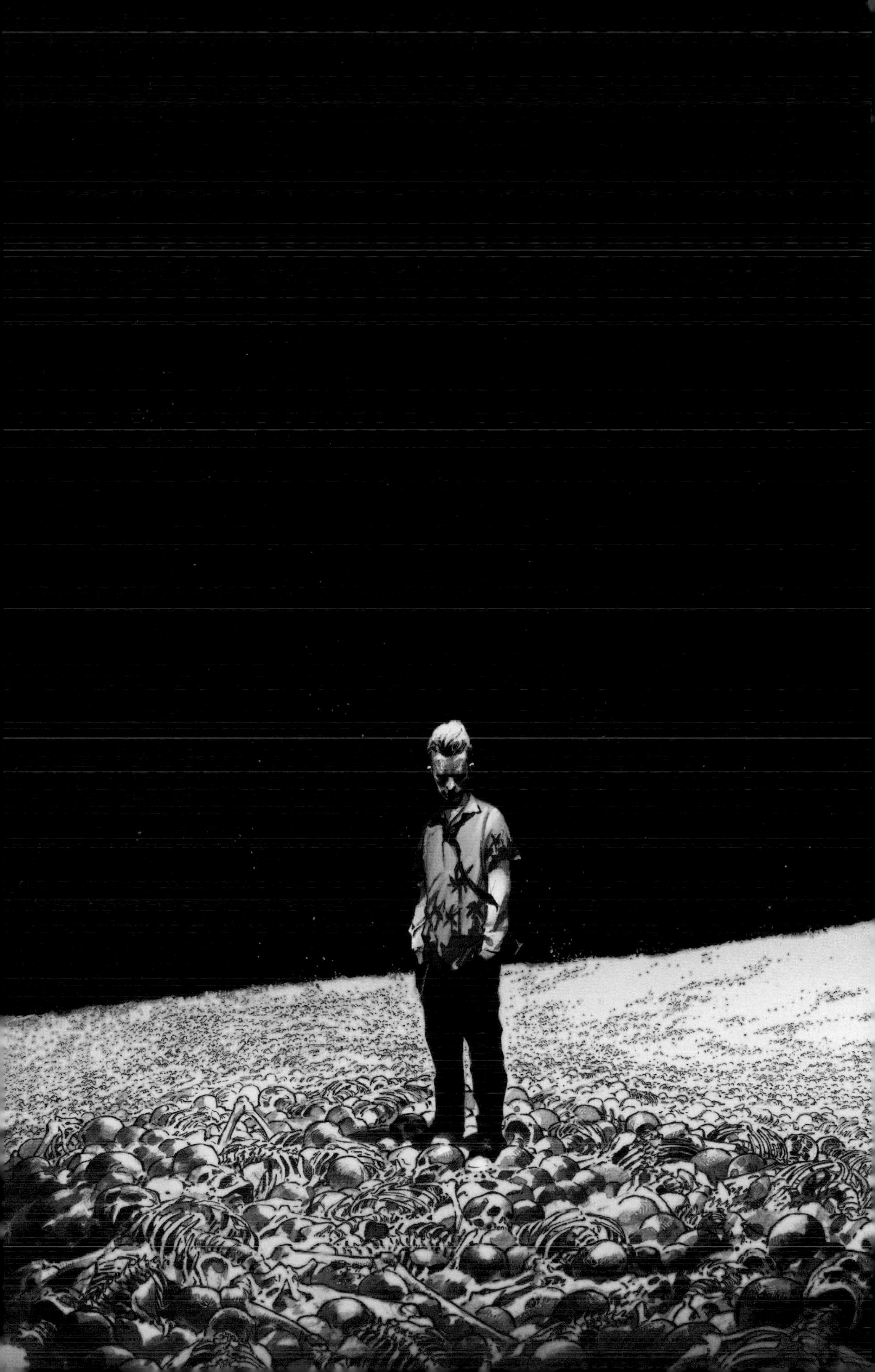

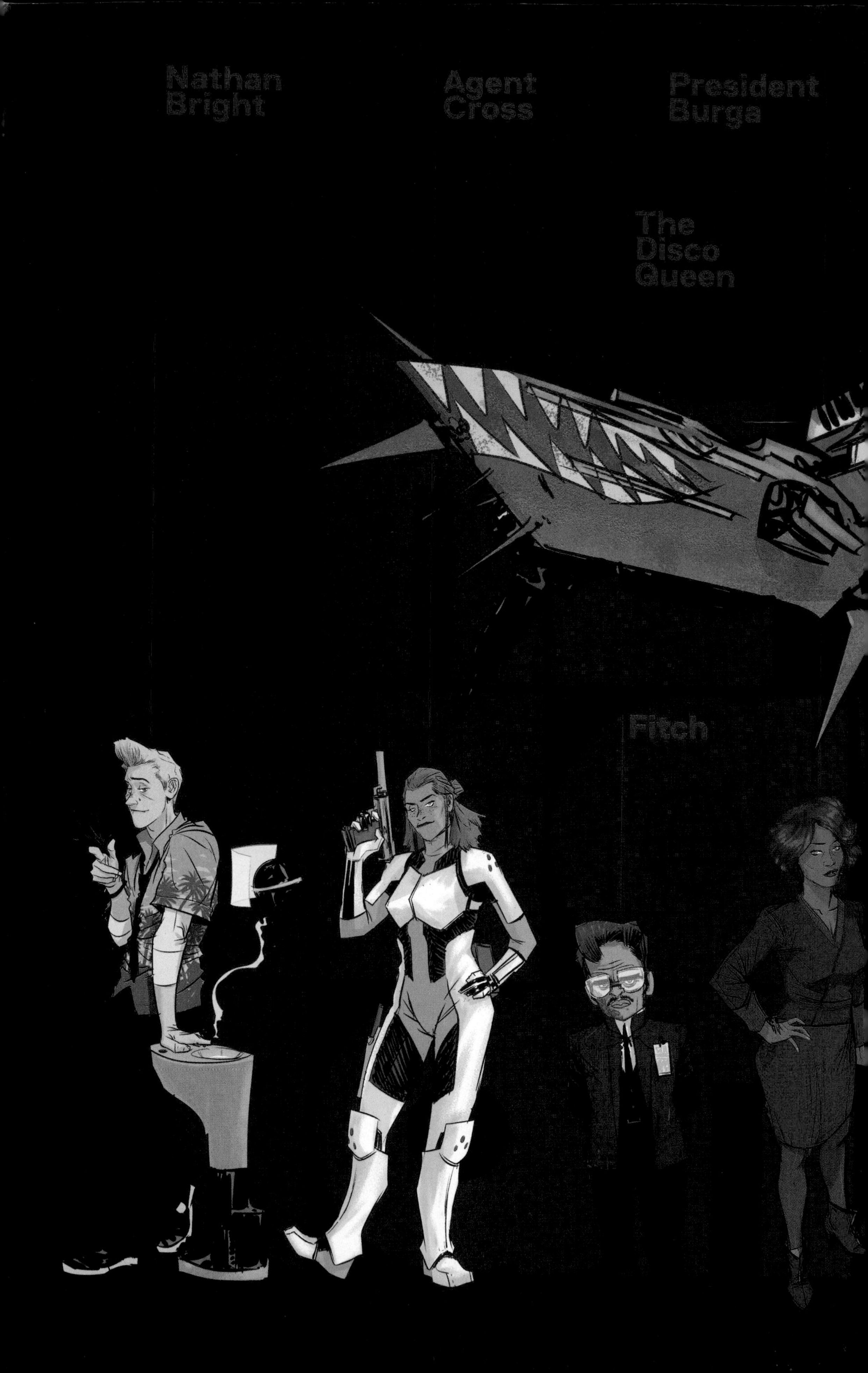

Nathan Bright
Agent Cross
President Burga
The Disco Queen
Fitch

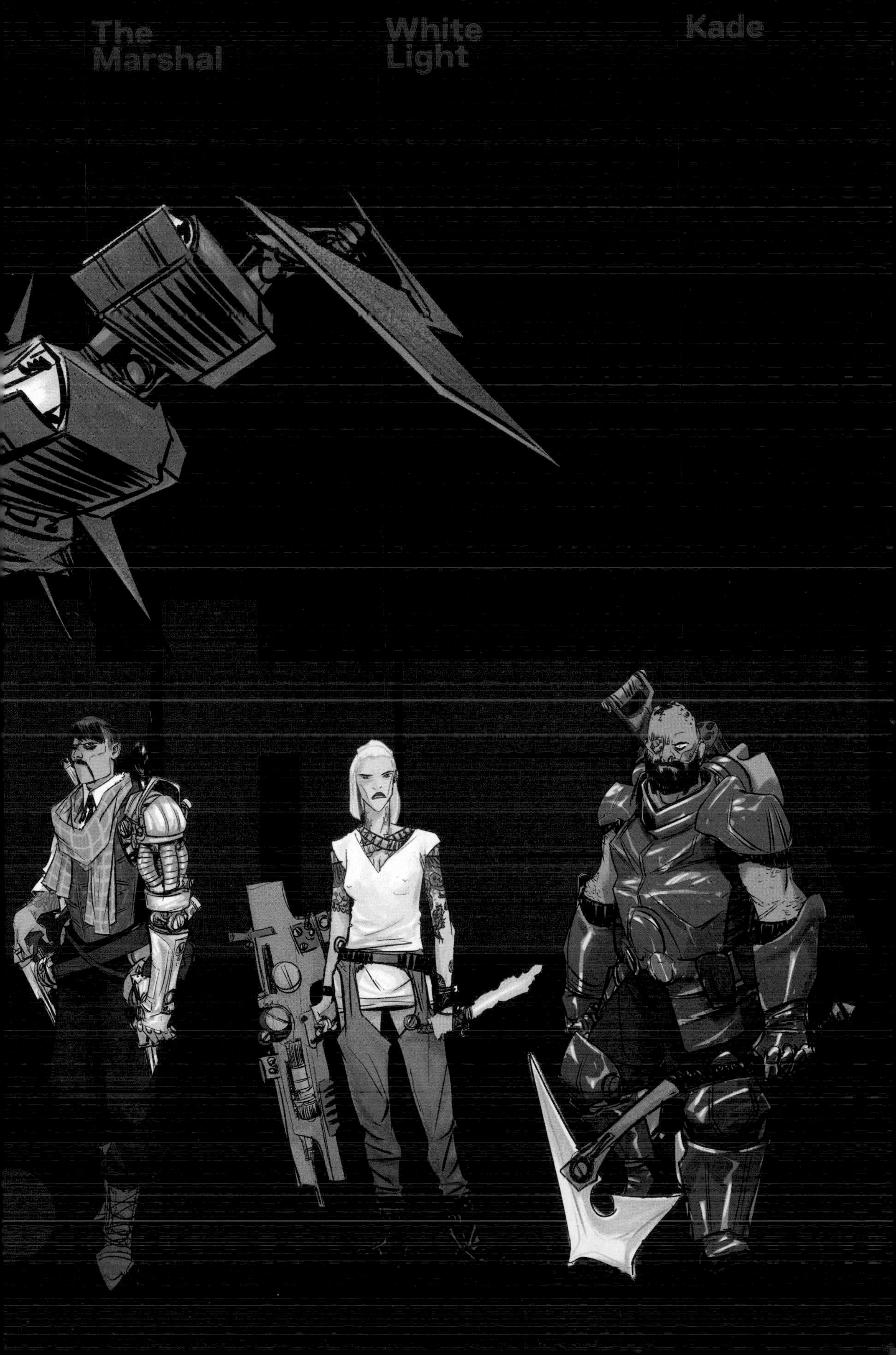
The Marshal
White Light
Kade

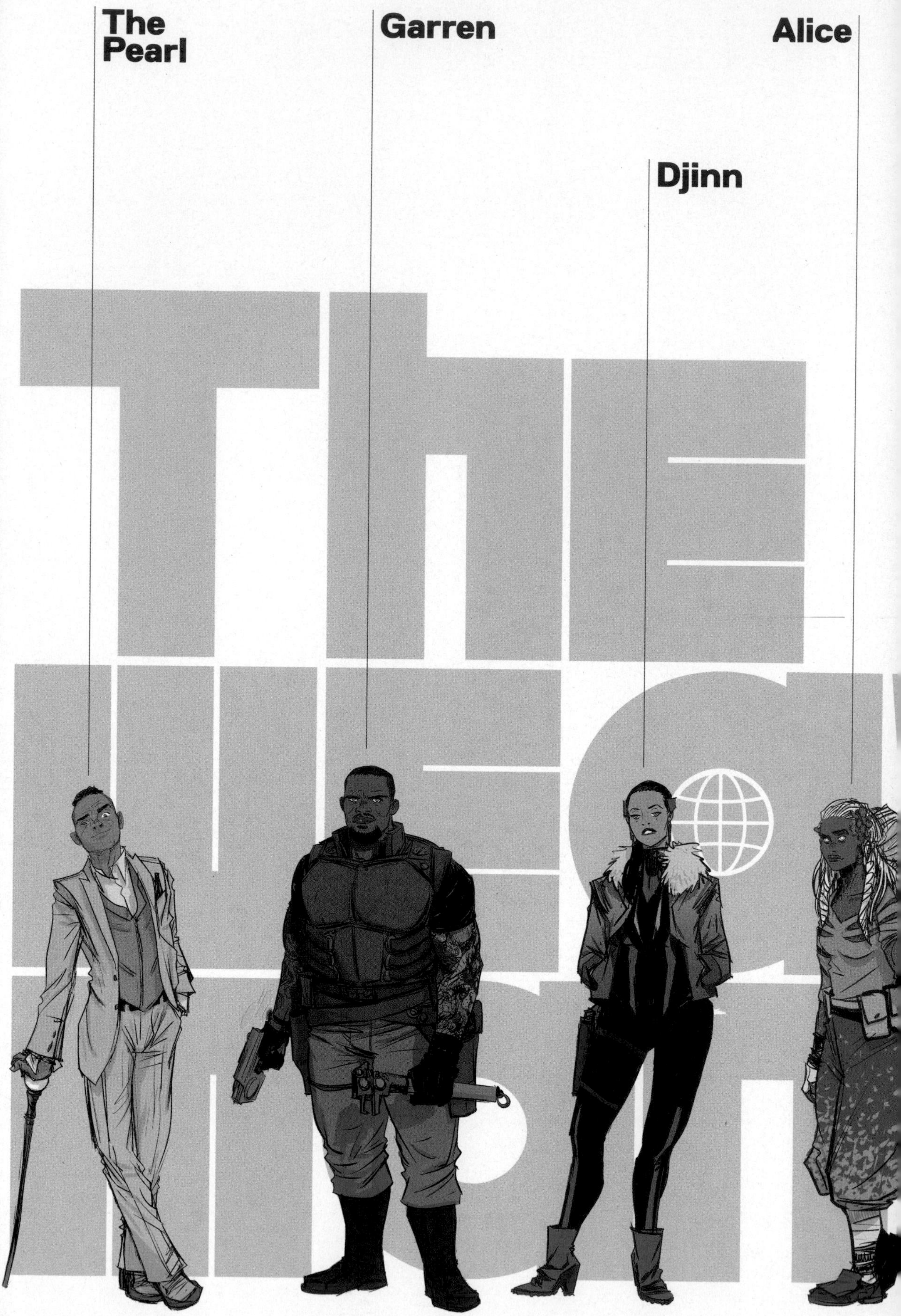
The Pearl
Garren
Alice
Djinn

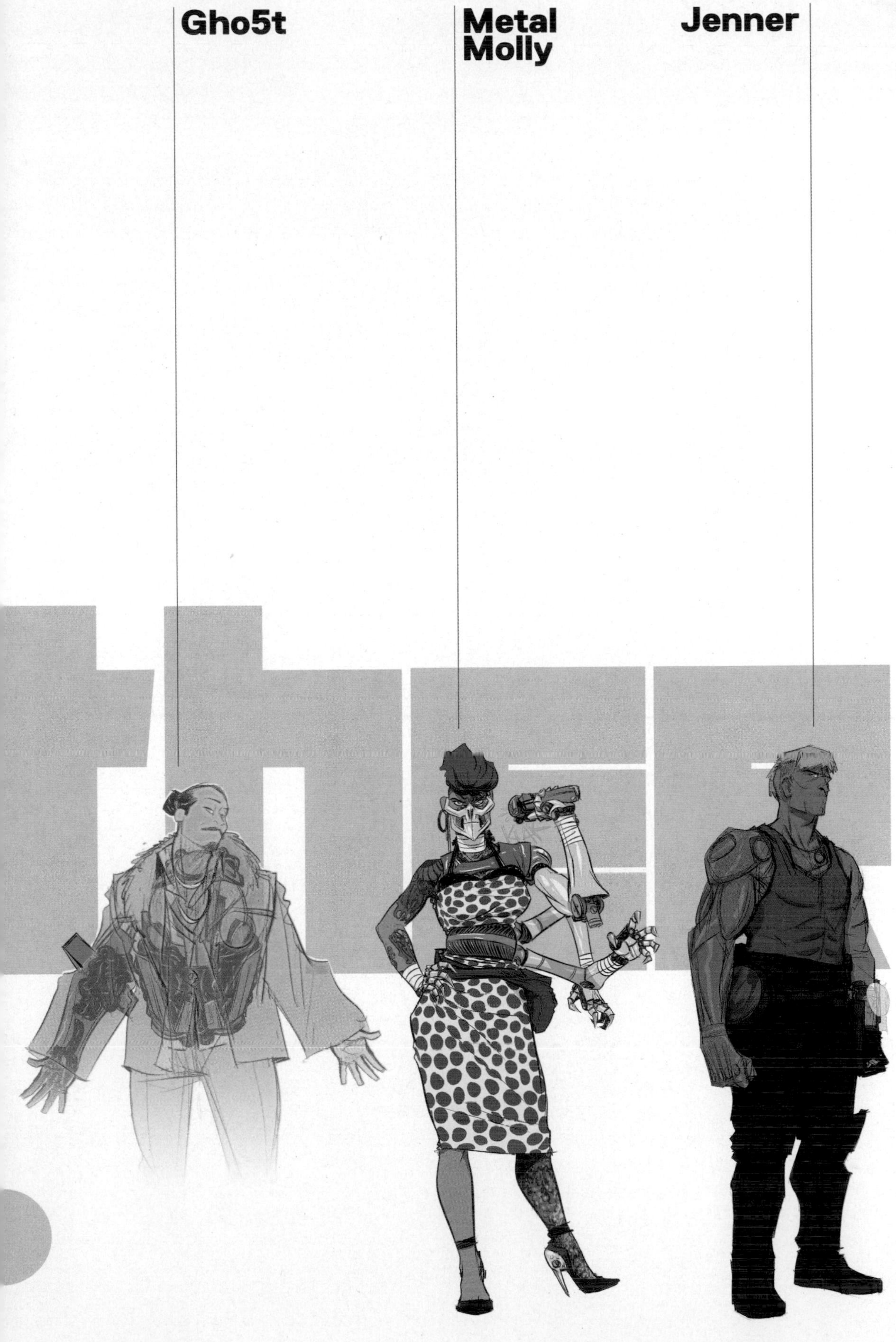
Gho5t
Metal Molly
Jenner

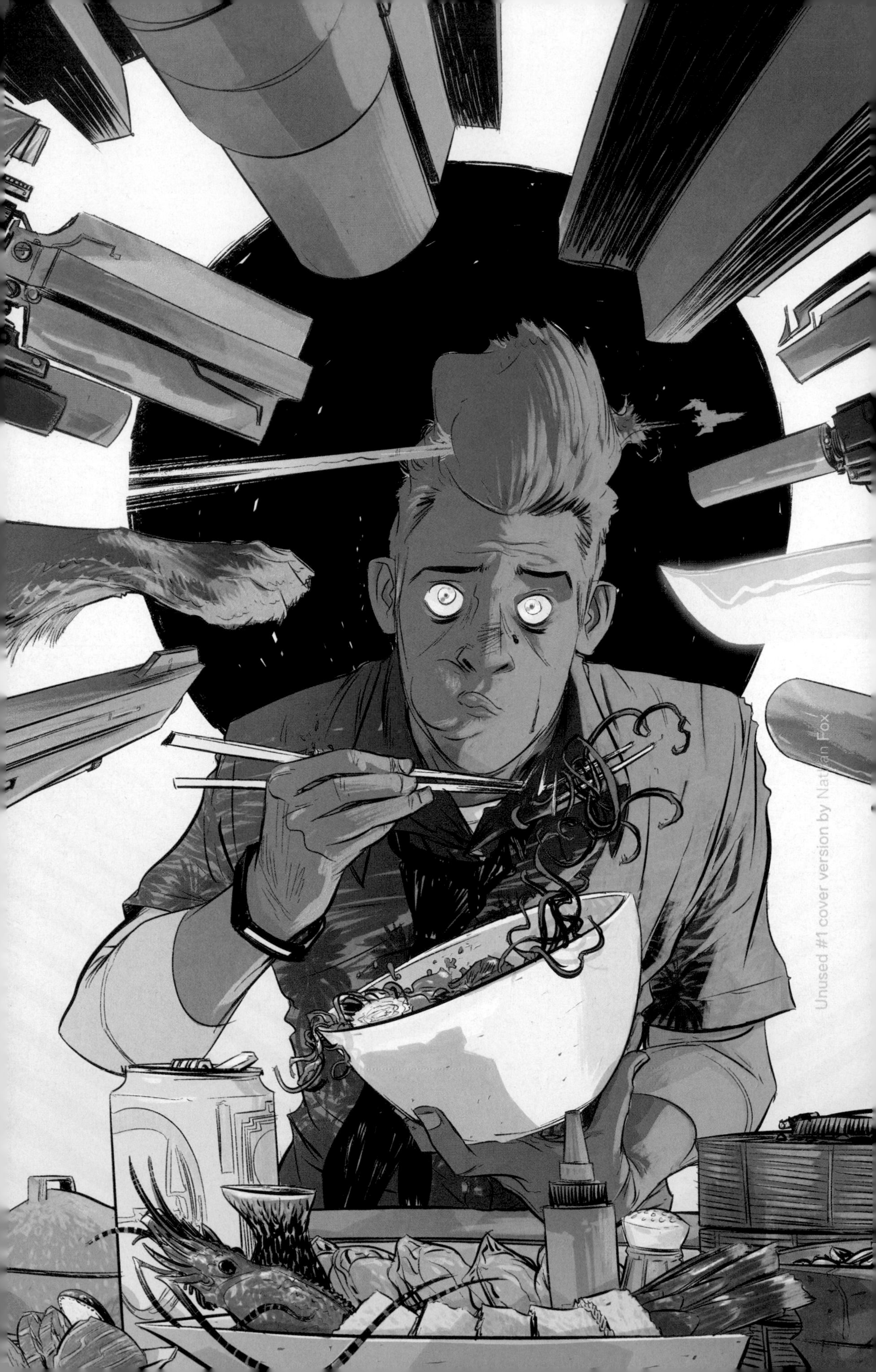

Unused #1 cover version by Nathan Fox

THE WEATHER MAN

ORIGINAL SYNTHWAVE SOUNDTRACK!

ONLY AT **SOUNDCLOUD.COM/ THEWEATHERMANSOUNDTRACK** FEATURING:

MAGIC SWORD

POWER GLOVE

MAKEUP AND VANITY SET

Betamaxx.

LAZER HAWK

LE MATOS

Jody LeHeup

is the writer and co-creator of the IMAGE COMICS series THE WEATHERMAN and the co-writer and co-creator of SHIRTLESS BEAR-FIGHTER!. A former editor, Jody edited many titles including UNCANNY X-FORCE, DEADPOOL and STRANGE TALES for MARVEL and QUANTUM AND WOODY for VALIANT. He lives in Queens, New York.

Nathan Fox

is the artist and co-creator of the IMAGE COMICS series THE WEATHERMAN, the artist of DARK REIGN: ZODIAC for MARVEL, and a contributing artist on DMZ from DC/VERTIGO and HAUNT, also from Image. He's the chair and founder of the MFA Visual Narrative program at the School of Visual Arts in New York and a prolific commercial illustrator with clients including Nickelodeon, the *NY Times*, Rockstar Games, Sony, *Esquire* and *Rolling Stone Magazine*, among others.

The Weatherman.

WILL RETURN IN VOLUME 2!

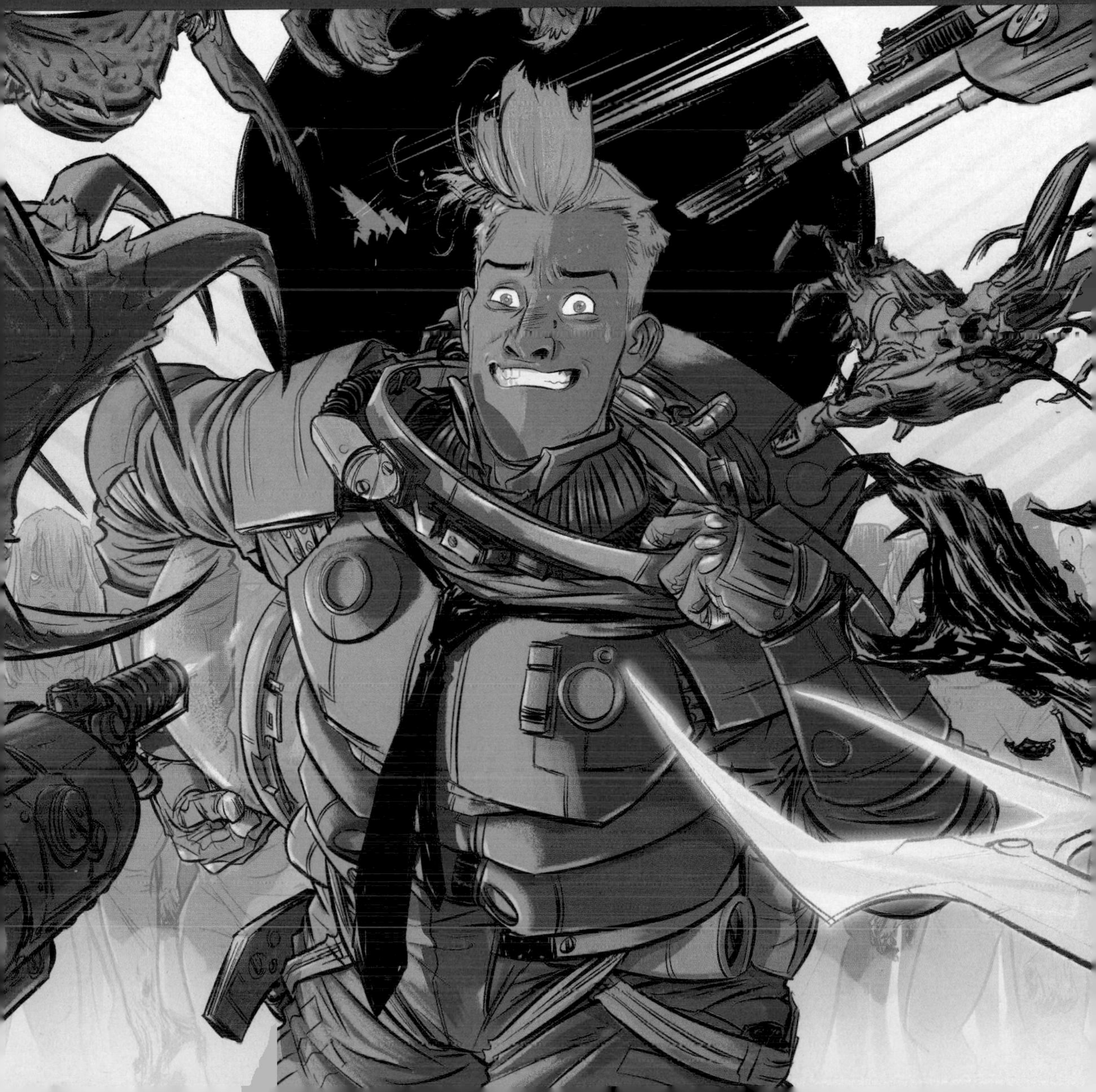

THE WEATHERMAN Volume 1. First printing. February 2019. Published by Image Comics, Inc. Office of publication: 2701 NW Vaughn St., Ste. 780, Portland, OR 97210. Copyright © 2019 Brutal Noodles, LLC. All rights reserved. Contains material originally published in single-magazine form as THE WEATHERMAN #1–6. "The Weatherman," the The Weatherman logos, and the likenesses of all characters herein are trademarks of Brutal Noodles, LLC, unless otherwise noted. "Image" and the Image Comics logos are registered trademarks of Image Comics, Inc. No part of this publication may be reproduced or transmitted, in any form or by any means (except for short excerpts for journalistic or review purposes), without the express written permission of Brutal Noodles, LLC, or Image Comics, Inc. All names, characters, entities, events, and places in this publication are entirely fictional. Any resemblance to actual persons (living or dead), entities, events, or places, without satiric intent, is coincidental. Printed in the USA. For information regarding the CPSIA on this printed material call: 203-595-3636. All inquiries: theweathermancomic@gmail.com. ISBN: 978-1-5343-0873-2.

IMAGE COMICS, INC. Robert Kirkman: Chief Operating Officer / Erik Larsen: Chief Financial Officer / Todd McFarlane: President / Marc Silvestri: Chief Executive Officer / Jim Valentino: Vice President // Eric Stephenson: Publisher — Chief Creative Officer / Corey Hart: Director of Sales / Jeff Boison: Director of Publishing Planning & Book Trade Sales / Chris Ross: Director of Digital Sales / Jeff Stang: Director of Specialty Sales / Kat Salazar: Director of PR & Marketing / Drew Gill: Art Director / Heather Doornink: Production Director / Nicole Lapalme: Controller

IMAGECOMICS.COM

All inquiries:
theweathermancomic@gmail.com

 WM_Comic